Destiny's Journey

The Maiden Voyage

By

Richard K. Thompson

authorHOUSE™
1663 Liberty Drive, Suite 200
Bloomington, Indiana 47403
(800) 839-8640
www.AuthorHouse.com

This book is a work of fiction. People, events, and situations in this story are purely fictional and any resemblance to actual persons, living or dead, is coincidental.

First published by AuthorHouse 09/14/04

ISBN: 1-4184-1984-2 (sc)
ISBN: 1-4184-1983-4 (dj)

Printed in the United States of America
Bloomington, Indiana

This book is printed on acid-free paper.

To those who inspired it's writing, especially my two best friends, Richard Burns and Jacklyn Dakovich, without whose help and understanding this book might never have been completed.

Table of Contents

Part 1 Saying Goodbye To Billy **1**

Chapter 1
Sad News 3

Chapter 2
Dinner Can Wait 23

Chapter 3
Flying High 37

Chapter 4
Visiting Yesterdays 61

Chapter 5
Goodbye Old Friend 75

Chapter 6
Thanks For The Memories 103

Chapter 7
Return To Paradise 139

Part 2 The Aftermath **159**

Chapter 8
Welcome Home 161

Chapter 9
Paving the Way 179

Chapter 10
Return To The Nest 197

Chapter 11
Trouble's Messenger 217

Chapter 12
Cocktails and Dinner 235

Chapter 13
When Old Friends Get Together 253

Chapter 14
Missing.. 269

Chapter 15
Prelude To Discovery.. 283

Chapter 16
Gone Fishing.. 297

Chapter 17
Chasing The Goose.. 311

Chapter 18
Redemption.. 329

Chapter 19
Journey's End... 357

Prologue

After years of gradually mounting marital problems, Neal Thomas finally found the courage to ask his wife for a divorce so they could each enjoy the remainder of their lives free from the deception, arguing and financial worries that had plagued their marriage for the past several years.

The divorce, unlike most, was amicable and spared both parties the sometimes-bitter aftermath that many of their friends had experienced. Confident that his future was financially secure, he pledged not to suffer through the ordeal of dividing up the family assets. Instead, he offered his wife the option of paying him a relatively small sum of money for his interest in their home, an amount she was only too willing to pay considering the value of everything he was leaving behind. Thus, with only his clothes and a few personal belongings he left the area to fulfill his destiny as a single person with a dream of success and a clear conscience

For several years following his divorce he spent most of that time contracting his engineering skills to companies that sent him to a host of different construction sites around the country and overseas. Although his income and benefits flourished, he missed his friends and the company of his three daughters so he decided to retire before time and money robbed him of his lifetime ambition to become a recognized artist.

Ironically, while looking unsuccessfully for a suitable place to call home, his former wife suggested that he visit a condominium complex on one of North County's most pristine beaches. He fell in love with its carefree atmosphere immediately and moved in that week. It was there that he met and became intimately involved with his neighbor, Paula Dillon.

Paula was an attractive younger woman who was also divorced and the mother of two grown children. Both son and daughter had recently graduated from college and had lived with her for a short period until they could afford to move out and begin lives of their own. Neal's three daughters, two of whom were married, had become well adjusted to their parent's divorce and treated them respectfully as individuals, rather than enemies.

It wasn't long into their relationship before Neal and Paula became aware that the time they were each spending in one another's apartment had become a source of amusement among their neighboring tenants. This situation, along with the expense of two separate rentals, prompted them to consider the practicality of finding a home they could share. With that purpose in mind a search was begun.

As it turned out, trying to locate a reasonably priced rental home in an area of their mutual liking was not an easy task. After several weeks of unsuccessful looking, dumb luck and a wrong turn brought them to an elderly man nailing a *For Rent* sign on a tree at the entrance to a heavily landscaped piece of property overlooking the beach. Excited by the prospect of being able to continue living so near the ocean, they turned into the driveway and asked the old man if they could tour the place.

"Sure," he replied. "I'll be with you in a minute."

Encouraged by the old man's friendly response, they continued along the driveway until the house came into full view. While waiting for the old man to catch up, they hastily scanned the property beyond the house. The back yard itself stretched nearly one hundred feet beyond the house to a bluff hosting a spectacular view of the ocean.

"Go on in. It's open," a voice encouraged them from behind. "Excuse the mess, I'm in the process of moving."

They turned in unison to see the old man approaching with a hammer hanging from his weathered hand and a toothy smile on his equally tanned and wrinkled face. Extending his hand to Neal, he introduced himself.

"My name is John Fahey. I'm the owner of the place."

Neal took his hand and replied," I'm Neal Thomas, and this is my lady friend, Paula Dillon. We're looking for a rental, and to tell you the truth, I hope we don't have to look any further. What a beautiful view."

Out of courtesy, they waited for Mr. Fahey to open the door for them and then followed him in. From there, he went to the kitchen and opened a door leading to the garage where a large dog had been barking since their arrival.

"Don't pay any attention to him," Mr. Fahey said, hushing his bark, "He's more curious than anything else. He'll settle down as soon as I feed him."

After spooning a can of dog food into a large plastic dish, he turned toward his curious guests and encouraged them to look the place over.

"I'll be out on the porch while you look around. Come and join me there when you're finished. Take your time, I'm in no hurry."

Eagerly, the excited couple retraced their steps to a stairway that lead to the second floor and walked up to investigate. At the west end of a short hallway they passed through a doorway opening into a large bedroom brightly illuminated by an oversized, plate glass window. The view, as they had witnessed from below, was spectacular.

Further inspection revealed a large private bathroom with a tiled, walk-in shower, and one large closet that spanned the entire length of one bedroom wall.

Returning to the hallway they passed another door that opened into a second bathroom, complete with built-in tub, shower and a large cabinet for towels and utility storage. Another door at the east end of the hallway opened into what must have been a spare bedroom. Neal's eyes lit up as he visually estimated its size. *What a great room for a studio,* he thought.

"I know what you're thinking," Paula remarked, "but believe me, there's a much better room for your studio downstairs. I noticed it when we came in."

After returning to the first floor they found Mr. Fahey relaxing in a chair on the back patio deck, smoking a cigarette while his dog stretched out on the floor beside him. As they approached, he began a melancholy dialogue:

"My doctor told me I should move to a drier climate. Seems my lungs aren't what they used to be. I have relatives in Phoenix that have been after me for years to move there. I suspect they made the offer so they could keep tabs on me. They meant well, I guess. The reason I haven't gone there before now is because I've lived here all my life. I'm sure you both can appreciate why I would be reluctant to leave."

After taking a final drag on an unfiltered cigarette that threatened to burn his fingers, he snubbed it out in a sand-filled coffee can resting on the deck beside him. As he continued to speak, his gaze remained fixed on whatever had captured his attention out on the ocean.

"This place is paid for, lock, stock and barrel," he began. "It's my grandson's inheritance, except he doesn't know it yet. I've decided to take my doctor's advice and accept the hospitality of my relatives as soon as I can find someone who's willing to take care of this property until my grandson finishes his education. Even after that, there's no guarantee he'd want to live here. He might very well choose to keep it as rental property for tax purposes, or sell the place. Anyway, that's the situation as it stands right now. There are no realtors involved and you're the first people I have talked to. That sign I just nailed up is the first and only one that has ever been posted here. I never thought things would work out this way."

"We both love the place, Mr. Fahey," Paula remarked, excitedly. "It's everything we were hoping to find, and more. How much rent are you asking?"

"In a minute," he answered, "but first, I'd like to ask you a question. Do you enjoy taking care of plants and flowers?"

"Mr. Fahey," Paula replied with strong resolve in her voice, "when I was married and had two small children to raise, I owned my own nursery and maintained it for several years following my divorce. Be rest assured that your years of hard work will be in safe keeping, that I can promise you. And, I'm sure my friend feels the same way."

"I expected as much," the old man said with a grin. "I liked you the first time I saw you, young lady. Kind of a second sense, you might say. Yes indeed, I believe you'd be damn good for this place. How does twelve hundred a month sound to you?"

They looked at each other in silent disbelief, which prompted Mr. Fahey to second-guess their surprise.

"No, I'm not crazy," he said, with a chuckle, "Real estate companies have been hounding me for years. You wouldn't believe what I've been offered for this property. Hell, I don't need the money. Lets just say I like you two and let it go at that. I consider myself to be a pretty good judge of character. First impressions have always served me well. You write me a check for eight hundred dollars as a gesture of good faith and I'll apply it toward your first month's rent when you move in. Fair enough?"

"That's more than generous," Paula replied. "Especially for this location. Will you give us an hour to bring you our deposit? I'm afraid we were totally unprepared for this turn of events."

"Take all the time you need," Fahey replied. " I suspect it will take at least thirty days to settle your business and move in. Call me at this number when you're ready and I'll give you a set of keys. We can finalize everything then."

The next thirty days were a nightmare of activity for the two of them, but the time passed quickly. And although they hadn't expected it, Fahey was more than generous with his help and patience. When the transaction was finally completed all three celebrated with a bottle of champagne Fahey had given them as a house warming present the day before he left for Phoenix.

Eight years and several grandchildren later, Neal and Paula were comfortably settled into mutually satisfying and rewarding lives. Neal retired several years later and spent most of his time creating works of art, fixing things that needed fixing and frequenting a local pub to drink a beer or two with those he had befriended.

Paula, on the other hand, continued her work in local government. For relaxation, she spent most of her time fulfilling her promise to look after Mr. Fahey's landscaping.

Their evenings, for the most part, were spent in front of the television, sipping their preferred libation and taking turns thinking up different ways to prepare the food they enjoyed. Occasionally, the opportunity to travel came along, taking them away from the sometimes-monotonous boredom of their routines. Life was good and uncomplicated until one Tuesday afternoon Neal received a phone call from his former wife advising him that a very dear friend of theirs had been killed in an accident. That news set off a chain of events so disruptive that their way of life, to which they both had become so accustomed, was changed forever.

Part 1
Saying Goodbye To Billy

Chapter 1

Sad News

After retirement, the names of weekdays began to take on less meaning for Neal Thomas than when he was fighting traffic on freeways trying to get to work on time. Life was hectic then and filled with personal as well as job-related commitments. Since his retirement, however, each day was becoming more or less a repeat of the previous one, except for those special days when the trash was picked up, or it was a holiday to celebrate something he no longer had much interest in. Tuesdays and Fridays, on the other hand, did offer some relief from the monotony of his daily routine in that on those days he could gather with a small group of male friends to drink, play Bumper Pool and test one another to see who could out-intellectualize the other. Despite some heated debate occasionally, it was all in good fun and understood between them that nothing they argued about was important enough to jeopardize the fraternal bond that had kept them friends for years.

Tuesday and Friday gatherings were held at the home of Ron Barns, Neal's best friend. His house was located North of San Diego in the coastal City of Del Mar. The house was old and small and had been purchased shortly after his divorce. Over the years he had managed to fix it up to suit what he referred to defensively as his "relaxed lifestyle." To most of Ron's friends, though, especially Neal Thomas, the word "relaxed" terribly misrepresented the reality of Ron's complete disregard for domestic order, and more appropriately resembled a lifestyle that had simply collapsed. None the less, he remained undaunted in the face of occasional fun-poking, and when someone was bold enough to make a comment on the un-kempt surroundings into which they had been invited, he simply replied: "Hey, this is the way I live. If that bothers you, don't let the door hit you in the ass on your way out!"

It was Ron's total disregard for traditional housekeeping practices that made his domicile the ideal place for weekly gatherings of the *Via Cortina Social Club* – as he and his cohorts jokingly referred to themselves. Once occasional guests became accustomed to everything being in complete disarray, they seemed to enjoy the novelty of its lack of ambiance and soon ignored the mess that was everywhere.

Sooner or later, depending on how many drinks one had consumed, those who were not particularly interested in shooting pool, or joining others in whatever topic was being discussed at the time, sought the fresh air of his front porch to enjoy a late afternoon sun setting over the lagoon nearby.

In keeping with the traditional scheme of things there were no prohibitions of any kind relating to individual behavior. Even though he had quit smoking himself some years ago, Ron was permissive with those who had not, and posted a sign over the bar that read: **"No Provisions Have Been Made For Non-smokers."**

Elsewhere in the house much of the available wall space was hidden behind a maze of newspaper clippings, snapshots and reproductions of artwork created by Neal. Because it was not unusual for wives and significant others to join the men on Friday afternoons, Ron made sure (sometimes) that the seat on his only toilet had been cleaned and sanitized. For the more finicky imbibers freshly washed glasses were available from the dishwasher. Most of the women, however, preferred to wash their own and were not hesitant to do so.

Tired from the eyestrain that painting generally left him with he took a quick glance at his watch and was pleased to see that it was three o'clock on another Tuesday afternoon. Time to quit for the day and join his friends.

Unlike most other Tuesdays, however, this one held an added bonus: a "Kitchen Pass." To friends who were familiar with the term, a Kitchen Pass meant that Paula would be an hour or two late getting home from work that day. That hour or two gave him some extra time to accompany his friends to Bully's, an infamous Del Mar watering hole that he had been frequenting for years. He was well known to bartenders, waitresses and a *pot pouri* of patrons who were referred to in jest as "The Frequent Fliers." To all, it was a convenient, safe and friendly home away from home. However, not many wives would have agreed with that characterization.

Anxious to be on his way he ceased work and began putting his studio in order, listening occasionally to the ending of one of his favorite television programs, one more reminder that his workday had officially ended. That accomplished, he stopped briefly in the kitchen to fill a flask with vodka before leaving for the afternoon, unaware that in a few hours a phone message from his former wife would turn the quiet order and contentment of his everyday life into chaos.

Typically, each mile he traveled south brought the salty smell of ocean air through his car windows, melting away the soreness that had settled in the back of his neck from too many hours of concentration. The breeze, mixed with the sound of Rachmaninov's Second Piano Concerto took him in reverie to the day he first arrived in California and witnessed the Pacific Ocean shimmering in the sun. He thought, as he had thought then: *this is truly paradise.*

As usual, Ron's pickup truck was in the driveway when he arrived. Entering the wide-open sliding glass doors on the front porch, he greeted him as he always had on this special day of the week, "Hello Mr. Barns, it's that time again."

"Good afternoon, Mr. Thomas," Ron replied enthusiastically. "Good to see you. Fix yourself a drink."

After their customary handshake he made his way to Ron's small kitchen where he made himself a drink and sat patiently watching television until the other three club members arrived. Ron, undisturbed by Neal's presence, continued playing solitaire; mouse in one hand, and a canning jar full of gin martinis in the other.

Soon after Ron turned off his computer for the day, Don Curtis arrived with a brown paper bag of non-alcoholic beer tucked under his arm. Don was a family man and, professionally, an extremely talented computer hardware analyst. He had not worked for a number of years because of a medical disability that forced him into early retirement. To make matters worse, he had recently been diagnosed with liver cancer that was not responding to conventional treatment, so he had given up alcohol altogether and chose to treat himself with health food alternatives. Thus far, they had provided him with a measure of comfort that conventional methods had not. To compensate for the booze he could no longer enjoy, he delighted in starting technical debates. This sometimes aggravated his fellow club members because of his preoccupation with what they thought were superfluous details. Their aggravation, however, was of little consequence. It was just Don's way of having a little fun by confusing the issues.

As he entered and greeted everyone ceremoniously the telephone rang. Since it was sitting right next to him, Neal picked it up. After a moment or two he hung up and announced that their friend and fellow club member, Johnny Holland, would not be attending that afternoon because his wife was weak and very tired from their recent, month-long vacation. He expressed his regrets, but felt his time would be better spent if he remained at home with her.

Johnny's cancellation came as no surprise. Phyllis Holland had been diagnosed with cancer some years ago, and had undergone many treatments that typically left her weak and nauseated. Like Don Curtis, she too stopped them. Fortunately for Polly, her husband was a very wealthy man, retired and in a position to give her whatever time she needed during those post-treatment periods. The decision to stop the chemotherapy was not an easy one for Phyllis, but weighed against the quality of life she was forced to endure because of it, she chose to live in dignity for as long as she could. Everyone, especially Don, understood.

Neal was on his way to the kitchen when he noticed another car pulling up behind Don's SUV. The style and color told him immediately that it was Joey Siegel, the last of the Tuesday afternoon pool shooters to arrive. Joey, like all members of the group, was retired. A bachelor, he lived in a condominium overlooking the racetrack and had the singular distinction of having been married several times. He was mild-mannered, good-natured and never hesitant to offer play strategy to whomever he drew as a partner whether he asked for it or not. They generally listened to him patiently and then proceeded to shoot as they had intended in the first place, much to Joey's disgruntlement. Typically, as the day progressed and more drinks were consumed, strategies became more vocally animated and patience dwindled. So, in an attempt to diplomatically neutralize the time consuming practice of debate over each shot, Neal suggested that each shooter be allowed to analyze his own shot without comment from his partner. After all, he reminded them, they were all grown men and capable of making their own decisions.

In the interest of speeding up the game they all agreed to abide by Neal's suggestion. Which, he admitted in silence, was presented with tongue-in-cheek sincerity, knowing full well that none of his friends could hold up under the pressure of maintaining silence for very long. The fun of it all for Neal was speculating on who would be the first partner to break down.

Much to Neal's surprise the silent partner rule lasted longer that he thought it would. Ironically, though, the first sign of weakening began to reveal itself in Ron Barns, whose pride in masterminding strategy was equaled only by his inability to keep quiet during any activity or situation where choices had to be made. Finally, when his partner, Don Curtis, was about to make a game-jeopardizing shot - which Neal felt he would never have chosen had he not had too much to drink - Ron interrupted the shot by shouting, "Goddamn it, Neal. This silent partner rule of yours sucks."

Both Don and Joey agreed unilaterally, glad that Ron had saved them the trouble of having to express themselves similarly.

Neal knew he had struck a nerve. Without offering any resistance to Ron's outspoken objection – realizing he had succeeded in pissing everyone off – he smiled quietly and remarked, "Hey! If you guys want to waste my kitchen pass and turn this game into a marathon event, please, be my guest."

"What the hell time is it?" Ron shouted, still a little irritated.

"My watch says six-thirty," Joey answered immediately. "Time for Bully's"

Ron agreed they had played well past their usual quitting time, so he suggested they finish the game and gather at Bully's where he would be pleased to buy the first round. All mutually agreed and set about finishing the game without any undue conversation.

Bully's was packed to the front door when Neal arrived. He was almost tempted to turn around and go home when the familiar face of a woman sitting at the bar changed his mind, so he waited patiently in line and finally entered.

Ron, Don and Joey had arrived separately and were seated at the small high bar motioning to him that they had a seat saved. The short distance to where his friends were gathered led him to within brushing distance of the woman he had recognized from the doorway. She was sitting with her back to him drinking a glass of wine and talking to a woman he did not recognize. As he passed behind her, he rested both hands gently on her shoulders and sang in a whisper through the soft blond hair covering her ears, "I've got a crush on you, sweetie pie….."

Recognizing the face imaged in the mirror across the bar in front of her, she closed her eyes and sang softly in response, "All the day and night time hear me cry."

Setting her glass down she turned slowly around to face Neal, then stood up. Placing her arms around his neck she kissed him quickly, full on the mouth. After their lips parted, she patted him playfully on his cheek and asked, "Neal Thomas, you dirty old man. Where in the hell have you been all this time?"

Neal laughed as his eyes glanced quickly over to the high bar to determine if his friends had witnessed the over zealous greeting he had just received. They had. It was obvious from the looks on their faces that he would have some explaining to do when he joined them.

"I'm retired now, Judy," he admitted. "I live up the coast in a condo I share with a lady friend I met several years after my divorce."

"Well, I'm happy you got out of that mess." She commented. "Believe it or not, I've thought about you now and then and wondered how you were getting along. I should have known you wouldn't stay uninvolved for very long. You look great. She must be taking very good care of you, lover boy. Is your friend with you tonight?"

He could sense she wanted him to chat for a while so before he became involved in a situation that he knew from experience might turn out to be more trouble than it was worth, he replied, "I'm with the guys tonight. They're sitting at the high bar holding a seat for me. I don't come by here very often any more, only when my significant other works late. Tonight happens to be one of those nights. I'm glad it worked out this way otherwise I wouldn't have had this opportunity to see you again. By the way, how is Russ?"

Judy reached around for her glass of wine and answered, matter-of-factly: "Well, thanks to you, Russ gave up that bimbo he said he couldn't live without and moved in with me right after that weekend you and I dated. I guess that means I owe you one."

"Believe me, the pleasure was all mine. What are friends for?"

She giggled, put her mouth close to his ear and whispered, "Half that pleasure was mine, you know."

Backing away quickly, she added, "Now, before both of us say something stupid, you better mosey on over to the high bar and join your buddies. They look like they're about ready to bust a gut. Give me a call sometime when it's convenient and we'll have a drink for old time's sake, okay?"

He nodded that he would, and as he bent down to kiss her cheek whispered, "I'd like that."

A cocktail was waiting for Neal when he arrived at the high bar, along with three eager faces that couldn't wait for him to reveal the identity of the lovely lady that had delayed him. He knew he had some explaining to do, but side stepped it with half an apology: "Sorry guys. I know what you're thinking, but that delightful woman is the personal property of a guy I played tennis with years ago. She's just a friend, and nothing more."

"Oh sure, and I was born yesterday, "Joey chided. "I guess that's why she tried to suck your face off. You better wipe that lipstick off your mouth. I don't think Paula would understand just how friendly some of your friends really are."

Just as Neal started to reach for his handkerchief, Joey grabbed his arm. "Not with yours, dummy. Here, use this bar napkin."

Both Ron and Don were having a hard time containing their laughter while Neal's face began to take on a rosy glow of embarrassment as he wiped away the lipstick and remarked, "I guess that would be a little incriminating, wouldn't it?"

"Isn't she Russ Chandler's significant other?" Ron asked. "I see the two of them in here together almost every Friday night."

"Yes she is," Neal replied. "They've been going together for as long as I've known them. I'm surprised Russ isn't here with her tonight, although they do have a history of getting pissed off with each other occasionally. That kiss she just gave me tasted like she might be out testing the waters for some companionship, but it sure isn't going to be me. I'm having a *roader,* and then I'm down the highway."

"Hell, you just got here you old fart," Don complained. "I thought you had a kitchen pass tonight. Or have you and your girl friend over there got something cooked up for later?"

Neal remained silent for a moment, then looked directly into Don's eyes and said, "Funny you should mention that, Donny boy. The thought entered my mind for a moment but I decided it would be unfair to deprive my buddies the pleasure of my company, especially after one of them was generous enough to buy me this drink." Turning toward Ron, he asked, "I assume you are my benefactor."

"My pleasure, Mr. Thomas. I don't think Don need be overly concerned with your plans for the rest of this evening. If he'll notice, Judy's significant other just came through the doorway, and I doubt if he's looking for the men's room."

"I'd say you rejoined us just in time," Don commented. "My apologies for misjudging your intentions. Even though I'm inclined to think there's a little more to your friendship with Miss Kissy Face than a man of your strong moral fiber would admit."

Neal finished his drink and sat the empty glass down on the bar, tapping it gently for a moment before turning to leave. "Me thinks you think too much, Donald." he remarked. "I'm outta here!"

"Oh, come on, Neal. I was only kidding," Don replied, almost apologetically. "Let me buy you a *roader*."

"I know you were," Neal responded with a grin. "If I thought you were serious I'd have to start worrying about you, and that would put your wife out of a job. But thanks anyway. I really am getting tired. I've had more than enough to drink for one day. Besides, I've got a hell of a lot further to drive than you guys. I'll see you all this Friday." Reluctantly, they all agreed that leaving was a wiser choice and wished him a safe journey home.

After he left Don signaled their waitress to bring another round of drinks. When she arrived he thrust a twenty-dollar bill at her and insisted, "This one's on me, guys."

Smiling seductively she took the bill, stuffed it casually in her bodice and wiggled her way back through the crowd, Joey's eyes tracking her body movements every step of the way. Before she returned, Joey looked over at Ron and asked in a hushed voice, "What's going on between Neal and Judy Bass? You've known him a whole lot longer than we have so don't give us a lot of bull about not knowing."

To all who knew him, it was never difficult to conclude when Ron Barns was getting drunk, because he had a peculiar way of moving his lips around while he spoke. Joey's question started the process. After a moment or two of mouth-twitching and thoughtful silence, Ron smiled at his amusingly attentive friends and replied with a slight slur: "I could tell you, but then I'd have to kill you both."

Resigned that he was not going to get any sensible answer out of him, Joey gave up his inquiry in favor of watching the body movements and partially exposed breasts of his favorite waitresses, and other women scattered around the restaurant. Content to do the same, Ron just sat there smiling, pleased that he had not given in to the temptation of revealing what his friend had confided in him. Though he was jealous of him at the time, he recalled, there was no reason to betray him now.

Once out of the restaurant parking lot, Neal drove the back streets until he was safely away from the center of town where the possibility of being stopped by police was more of a risk. Minutes later harm's way was merely a reflection in the rear-view mirror as he cruised North along Old Coast Highway, considerably more relaxed and thoughtful. Not much time had passed on his journey when the mixture of alcohol he had consumed that day and the radio's music lulled him into a state of melancholy in which he found himself remembering the kiss he had received from an old friend that night, and the bizarre circumstances that had led to their brief but intimate relationship many years ago:

****

There was a period of time following his divorce when Neal avoided becoming seriously involved with any of the women he dated on occasion. His job was demanding and often required traveling to distant places for several weeks at a time. When home, tennis became his leisure activity, mostly on weekends and one or two nights during the week. It was through tennis that he became acquainted with Russ Chandler, a nice guy, but a fiercely competitive player.

Russ was dating a woman by the name of Judy Bass who was a neighbor in his condominium complex. Although Judy had no interest in playing tennis, she was a very successful real estate broker, a job that demanded working odd hours, especially on weekends. When time permitted, she did manage to attend matches, but mostly to make sure Russ was not tempted into a mid-life crisis with another woman. During one of those rare occasions when she accompanied Russ, Neal and Judy met for the first time and were attracted to one another immediately. Because of her relationship with Russ, however, they each remained politely aloof. Then, quite unexpectedly one Friday afternoon at his office, he received a call from a woman who simply asked, "Can I buy you a drink after work?"

"That sounds like a damn good idea to me," he replied agreeably, "By the way, who is this?"

"It's Judy Bass, Silly. Who did you think it was?"

He sank down in his hi-back swivel chair and tried not to sound as surprised as his blood pressure was telling him he was, and remarked, "Oh, oh! Something tells me I've forgotten to do something I should have."

"No!" she replied, amused by his surprise. "I'd like to buy you a drink, if you don't have anything planned after work. I'm at Mille Fleurs in Rancho Santa Fe."

Looking quickly at his watch he told her he would meet her there in forty-five minutes.

Fifteen minutes after her call he left his office with one question on his mind: *Why would Judy Bass be calling out of a clear blue sky, just to buy me a drink?* He doubted that, especially at such an expensive restaurant. But her sudden interest intrigued him, so he put his curiosity on hold and drove excitedly away in search of the answer.

The back road to Rancho Santa Fe was a pleasant drive at any time of the year. Its winding two lanes were flanked on both sides with sprawling, multi-acre estates, golf courses and endless numbers of eucalyptus trees. Wild flowers and magnolia trees were in bloom, filling the air with the perfumed smell of late spring. The center of town was typically alive with people walking casually about. Some were window shopping and others sat in patio-dining areas slowly filling with a California mix of middle-aged women dressed in expensive tennis attire, and older ladies carefully shaded with round, broad-rimmed hats.

Occasionally, one or two celebrity residents could be seen entering the town's only liquor store. Luxury automobiles were parked everywhere, making the likelihood of finding an open space highly unlikely.

After circling the block a number of times he realized he was going to be late, but held hope that she was the kind of woman who could forgive some reasonable tardiness and allow him a little leeway. Frustrated and ready to look elsewhere, he pulled around the corner on his last attempt and noticed a long, black, chauffeur-driven limousine jockeying back and forth in front of the restaurant in an attempt to leave. Several maneuvers later the limousine made its awkward way out and slowly drove away, leaving behind the space he had been searching for.

Quickly making his way into the restaurant he was relieved to find her still waiting and comfortably seated in a small booth near the end of the bar sipping a large, half-empty glass of wine. Glancing at her watch she remarked with a note of sarcasm, "Are you on Mexican time today? I figured you were either tied up in traffic or looking for a parking place, so you're forgiven. Tell Gloria what you want to drink, she'll bring it."

He gave his order to the attractive young woman behind the bar and then slid into the booth beside his impatiently waiting date and said, "Sorry I'm late, I left right after you called but couldn't find a parking place until just a moment ago."

"Not to worry. I'm just glad you showed up. I was beginning to think you might have changed your mind."

"No way," he assured her. "My curiosity broke the speed limit all the way over here trying to figure out what was going on in that devious little brain of yours."

"Haven't you learned about exercises in futility yet," she asked? "Most men I know gave up trying to figure that one out right after their first date."

He shook his head in agreement and replied, "Yeah, I guess you're right. I should have had better sense."

Several drinks later when conversation had mellowed, she hesitated for a moment and then said, "The reason I've asked you here is because I want you to do me a personal favor. But, before I tell you what it is, I want your solemn oath that you will never reveal to anyone what is discussed between us today, or what may take place in the future as a result of our conversation. Deal?"

Having only had a light lunch, Neal was beginning to feel his drinks, but not to the point where he was incapable of making a rational decision. Besides, the whole *cloak and dagger* atmosphere of what was going on intrigued him, so he took Judy's hand in his and replied, "Deal. I hope you know that it wasn't necessary to set me up just to ask for my help."

She hesitated for a moment, looking off into space as if the words she wanted to speak were written there for her to read. Realizing they weren't, she took a deep breath and began to speak. "I recently discovered through a friend that Russ is having an affair with another woman. When I confronted him with the fact that I knew what was going on, he lied about it until I presented him with irrefutable evidence; pictures and statements from friends whose names I would prefer not to mention. Then, knowing he had been caught, he gave me some cockamamie, lame brain excuse about not being able to live without the two of us, because we both had special qualities that he didn't want to lose. I told him he was out of his tree if he thought I was going to accept sharing him with another woman, and if he didn't stop seeing her immediately, I was going to exercise the same privilege." Taking a moment to wash down the words that had dried her throat, she added, "And that, sweet man, is where you come in."

"Wait a minute," Neal gasped. "How the hell did I wind up in the middle of all this?"

Motioning to Gloria to bring another round she put her arm around his neck and whispered in his ear, "I have to go to the lady's room. When I come back I'll explain what I'd like you to do for me."

As soon as she was out of sight he walked to the men's room and splashed cold water on his face to hopefully re-sharpen his wits. While there, a thought crossed his mind that he might be getting himself mixed up in something that could come back to haunt him someday. He hoped she was going to ask him to do something that he felt comfortable with, rather than having to say no to such an attractive woman.

When he returned to their table fresh drinks were waiting, along with an equally fresh and contented Judy Bass. A soon as he was seated, she asked, "Feel better?"

"Considerably, thanks. Now, what's this favor you want from me?"

She gathered from the tone of his voice that the moment of truth was at hand, so she said quite candidly, "If Russ can fool around, so can I. And, if I'm going to fool around, I can't think of anyone I'd rather do it with than you. I'm having a party at my place one week from tomorrow. I'd like you to attend as my date. Russ won't be there so you don't have to be concerned about that. It is my intent to let him know that I don't plan to sit around on my butt waiting for him to throw me a bone every once in a while. After all, two can play that game. Are you interested?"

"Sure, why not! What are friends for? Hell, I thought for a minute you were going to ask me to help you do the old boy in."

"Don't give me any crazy ideas," Judy laughed. "Not that I haven't thought about it at times. But, I figure if he doesn't want me bad enough to give up that other broad, especially after he finds out I've been dating you, then good riddance. Then, I can get on with my life."

He took her hand in his almost as if he were talking to one of his daughters and said, "If the man has any brains under that bald head of his, he'll be back on his hands and knees. Not because of me, but because of you."

"Thanks, I'm grateful for your understanding. "Why is it you always seem to know the right thing to say?"

"Your welcome," he replied, "but tell me something, now that everything is out in the open. Why me? You must know a dozen guys who'd love to do what you're asking."

She studied him for a moment while she finished the last of her wine. "Yeah," she replied, "But I couldn't trust them."

Outside the restaurant a few minutes later she walked into his arms as he stood ready to leave and gave him a gentle hug and kiss, saying convincingly, "I'm really looking forward to next Saturday night with you, Neal. The party starts at six o'clock, but come early. I'll call you next Wednesday as a reminder."

The following week passed by quickly. As promised, she called that Wednesday to remind him of his commitment. Despite some apprehension about what Saturday evening would hold in store, he shrugged it off, convinced that the worst thing that could happen to him would be sitting at the piano for most of the evening and drinking too much. *So what's new,* he thought, reflecting on similar occasions in the past. *Been there, done that.*

At five-thirty sharp that Saturday afternoon, he arrived at Judy's ocean-view condominium. The late afternoon sun had just begun changing the horizon into a pallet of mixed blues, yellows and oranges. He could hear the doorbell inside announcing his arrival, and the soft sound of music playing in the background. Despite pledging not to let his nervousness show, he felt the palms of his hands becoming moist from gripping the flowers he had brought as a gift. Then the door opened, revealing a different Judy Bass than he had expected. She was elegantly dressed in a black, v-necked cocktail dress, and had completely made over her hair. She looked so different he almost forgot the greeting he had rehearsed. "Good evening madam," he managed to stammer, handing her the bouquet. "I'm your Rent-a-Guy escort for the evening. May I come in?"

Judy's reaction was just what he had hoped for. After recovering from the nonsense of his somewhat theatrical entrance, she wiped her teary eyes and pulled him inside with a friendly tug. "Damn you, Neal Thomas," she laughed. "I was all made up to make a serious impression on you. Now look what you've done. Go to the bar and make yourself a drink while I put these lovely flowers in water and freshen up a bit. You've ruined my eyes."

After cutting their stems and arranging the flowers carefully in a crystal vase, she placed the vase in the middle of her dining room table and then stood back for a moment to admire the bouquet. Satisfied with the ambiance his flowers had provided, she turned away and walked quickly to the spiral stairway leading to her loft bedroom. From the bar, he was able to observe every movement of her slender body as she ascended the stairs. The dress she wore draped to just above the knees, exposing her beautifully developed calves. Though not large, her breasts hid impressively under the v-neck of her dress, and moved in rhythm with every step, teasing his imagination.

From his vantage point at the bar he made a casual survey of her home, noting in particular how beautifully furnished it was and how everything was so tastefully color coordinated. What impressed him most was the ebony-black grand piano located near the fireplace. It came as no surprise that his talent at the keyboard may have been one of the reasons why Judy had invited him. That, he accepted with pride, suited him just fine. His presence there wasn't the first time he had been invited to a party for that reason. Even in college and at home during the holidays, he remembered, wherever a piano was available, so was he. As he sat there alone sipping his drink, he couldn't help thinking about how good it made him feel to be someone special. Someone who gave to others what only his kind of music could: a safe haven in which to enjoy one's innermost feelings.

When Judy returned, she asked him to un-cork a new bottle of champagne that had been chilling in the refrigerator for just the two of them. Using the puller she had handed him, he withdrew the cork slowly until it "popped." Nary a drop was wasted. Holding out her glass, she looked thoughtfully at him from behind the bar and said in praise: "It feels good to be in the company of a man who knows what he's doing, so let the games begin!"

For the next several minutes they talked reminiscently about each other's lives, their pasts, what was going on currently, and what they were looking forward to in the future. Soon, however, each of them began to struggle for bits and pieces of "happy talk" to keep their conversation light and alive. So, in keeping with his traditional reliance on humor to lighten up an awkward situation, he handed her his empty glass and remarked, "As long as you're back there why don't you see if you can find me a glass that doesn't have a whole in the bottom."

She took his glass and handed it back filled to the brim. "I hope you realize how much your coming here tonight means to me," she remarked. "I'm not in the habit of asking for help with my love life. But, as one wise old person so aptly put it some time ago, "desperate situations call for desperate measures, or something like that."

"I was under the impression you invited me here to entertain your friends. As far as I am concerned, that's all anyone has to know."

Coming out from behind the bar she draped her arms loosely around his neck. "Thanks," she said, and was about to kiss him when the doorbell rang. "Damn!" she cursed. "Talk about bad timing. This will have to wait until later."

During the next hour she gracefully greeted each of her guests with all the charm and poise she had exhibited throughout her professional and private life. She was equally generous in her praise of Neal whom she announced was a dear friend and had offered to entertain at the piano before dinner.

Of the twenty or more invited guests, Neal recognized only about half. Those he didn't know he assumed to be Judy's business associates. Unlike most of the parties he was used to attending, dress was not casual. Predictably, however, as the evening progressed, well-mannered behavior soon began to digress into loud laughter from small groups of men who had isolated themselves from their wives, or lady friends, to joust with one another in matters of politics, golf and dirty jokes, dispelling the notion that clothes make the man. It was during this noisy prelude to dinner that Judy made her way through the crowd and found Neal outside on the patio deck quietly enjoying his drink and gazing out over the ocean at what was left of a beautiful sunset. "It's time," she said." I hate to tear you away from this tranquility but the natives are restless. Won't you please play for a while?"

Accepting his fate he put his arm around her shoulder and escorted her back into the living room where she stood on the fireplace hearth and announced in a loud, pleading voice, "Quiet everybody! Please give me your attention. I have an announcement to make."

As he took his place at the piano and the room quieted, she thanked her guests for coming and announced, "My dear friend, Neal Thomas, is going to provide us with some music while you serve yourself in the dining room. So, please don't be bashful. There's plenty of food. Extra tables and chairs are available by the pool, so enjoy!"

Thirty minutes after he had started playing he realized he had made a tactical error in not eating something before leaving home. However, a swallow every now and then from the drink Judy made sure was never empty was all he needed to drown the sound of emptiness that gurgled periodically from his stomach. The more he drank, the less important food became, and the pleasure of hearing himself play so well became all the nourishment he needed to sustain the creative juices flowing through his fingers. So much so that he failed to notice the approach of a woman who had been standing nearby watching him. When the song he was playing came to an end she leaned over and asked, "Do you know, Body and Soul?"

Smiling as his eyes locked briefly on hers, he replied, " One of my favorites."

Through the shuttered service window separating the kitchen and dining room Judy was able to keep an eye on her guests while she began cleaning up after them. As she scraped plates and loaded the dishwasher, she caught a glimpse of one of her associates leaning over the piano, giving him a bird's eye view of her impressive cleavage. Were it not for her reputation as an aggressive flirt, she might have dismissed the scene as just another woman's infatuation with a musician. But, she knew how much he had been drinking and how typically defenseless he would be if she didn't intervene.

Motivated by the eminent threat, she quickened her effort to put her house in order and then circulated nonchalantly among her guests, some of which were already showing signs of leaving. When she approached the piano she could tell by his eyes that he was getting tired. So, without appearing invasive, she turned to her associate and remarked, politely, "Thanks for keeping an eye on him for me, Helen, but its time to feed the poor man. He hasn't had a bite to eat all evening."

When he finished his last song he put the key cover down, picked up his drink and thanked Helen for being so attentive. A little miffed at Judy's intrusion, she politely excused herself and left to join the few women who were still milling around trying to convince their escorts to call it a night.

Following her timely rescue, he snacked from the small plate of leftovers she had set aside for him while she closed the door behind the last of her guests, turned off the lights and joined him, grateful for the sudden quiet that had at last engulfed them.

While she sat pondering the evening's activity and talked as if he were listening, he began to realize that the longer he remained there the heavier his eyelids were becoming. So, like a little boy in school, he closed them for a moment and rested his head back against the wall, hoping for just enough shuteye to get him home.

When she finally turned her attention back to him and saw that his eyes were closed, she gently lifted the empty glass from his hand. Turning off the kitchen light she returned to where he sat quietly snoring and whispered softly in his ear, "Come on, little boy, it's time to go to bed."

Befuddled from having been suddenly awakened, he responded willingly and followed the gentle pull of her hand, assuming he was being navigated toward the downstairs bedroom. But, when she cautioned him about the stairs and guided his hand onto the metal banister, he realized he was being led upstairs. Like a dog on a leash, and too tired and sleepy to care where he was being led, he continued to follow until she had him seated on the edge of her canopied bed. After removing his clothes, she playfully ruffled his hair and pushed him gently over on his back, remarking, " I'll be back in a minute."

Under the pale glow of moonlight that was just beginning to show through the balcony doors he slid beneath the sheets. Overhead, a ceiling fan stirred the night air while soft, barely audible music came from somewhere in the room. As the light beam on the curtains continued to grow and the overhead fan began revitalizing his ability to think, it suddenly occurred to him that his hostess had been in the bathroom for considerably more than a few minutes. But, considering how the evening had turned out thus far, he thought, *Take all the time you need, honey. I'm not going anywhere.*

No sooner had he banished his craving for sleep than the bathroom door opened. There, standing in the pale amber glow of her night-light was her silhouette draped in a thigh-length negligee. At first he thought he was dreaming. But, as her shadow-like presence walked toward the bed, and he felt the mattress give way beneath her weight, the dream became reality and what was taking place became abundantly clear. Moments later the contour of her freshly bathed body closed the space between them as she whispered, almost comically, "I'm b-a-c-k."

Several weeks following her party he met regularly with her at Mille Fleurs as a prelude to the intimacy they had begun to expect from one another. That routine, however, ended abruptly one Friday when he revisited the restaurant, assuming she would be meeting him there.

Gloria greeted him with his customary drink and immediately informed him that she had received a telephone call from Judy earlier that afternoon asking her to give him a message when he arrived. "I don't quite understand all this, Mr. Thomas," she admitted, apologetically, "but Judy told me she couldn't contact you at your office earlier today, so she asked me to give you a message."

"Which is?" he asked, placing a twenty-dollar bill on the bar.

"She told me to tell you that the runaway sheep had returned to the flock, and to thank you for the loan of your crook." Looking somewhat puzzled she picked up the twenty and remarked, "I hope that makes some sense to you?"

"Yes, unfortunately, it does," he replied with an impish grin. "But don't you worry your pretty little head over it. When you see her again just tell her I was glad to be of service. The agency was grateful as hell for the business."

Somewhat bewildered, she shook her head and looked around the unusually empty lounge and said, "Ms. Bass mentioned to me not long ago that you play the piano very well. Since we're pretty much alone here for a little while, would you mind playing something for me? Drink's are on the house."

"Never could say no to a pretty woman, or a drink for that matter," he replied. "Are you sure it's all right with the manager?"

Gloria sat a drink down in front of him and winked, "This time of day, my friend, I am the manager."

As a general policy the beautiful grand piano in the lounge was always kept locked to pacify the restaurant's regular entertainer. Gloria, however, was custodian of the key, so she unlocked the key cover and began to ramble from one song to another, content with his dreamy-eyed audience of one.

Not long after he began playing, customers began to arrive and made comments about the new entertainer. Gloria explained that he was a friend and had agreed to play a few songs at her request. It wasn't until a women sitting alone at the bar sent a request for "Stardust" via a five-dollar bill that he knew it was time to leave. After finishing the request to enthusiastic applause, he locked the piano and returned to the bar. Handing her the key and the five-dollar bill he said it was time to leave. To the woman who had made the request he remarked, in passing, "Thanks, you have good taste in music."

On his way out, the restaurant's manager stopped Neal near the entrance and expressed his pleasure in hearing him play. "I hope you will come back again soon, Mr. Thomas. It's always a pleasure to listen to someone who plays so beautifully."

Heading west toward the coast, he glanced at the digital time display on his car radio and decided it was time to pay a visit to his friend, Ron Barns. Though disappointed that his brief and somewhat bizarre tryst with Judy Bass had ended, he took some consolation in the fact that he had established a beachhead at Mille Fleurs. Content with the memory of an unexpected pleasure that had interrupted the every day monotony of his uneventful life, he drove contentedly to his friend's house where he knew nothing had changed.

****

By the time he finally reached home that evening the memory of his brief affair with Judy Bass had faded like the sunset. Approaching their garage he noticed that Paula's car was not in its usual parking place, warning him that some strong language regarding the stupidity of some of her supervisors would be forthcoming. Resigned that all he could do to comfort her would be to listen patiently, he entered the house and activated the Jacuzzi, hoping that she too might find some relief in his pagan delight. Charged by that possibility he climbed the stairs, changed into a beach robe and returned to the kitchen. While he stood at counter fixing a drink the phone rang. For an instant his gut feeling told him to ignore it, but the possibility that it might be Paula changed his mind. The voice on the other end, however, was that of his former wife, Janet, who sounded as if she was having a difficult time trying to speak. "What's the matter?" asked, somewhat concerned. "Are you alright?"

For a moment there was just silence, followed by the sound of nose blowing. Then she continued, still sniffling: "Excuse me, Neal. I'm having a hard time handling some sad news I just received from our daughter, Karen."

That his only grandson had somehow been killed or injured in an accident scared him into asking, frantically: "What's happened, for God's sake. Is Bob alright?"

"No! No! It's not any of our family," she explained. "It's Billy Newman. He's been killed in a horrible boating accident. No one seems to know what happened, so don't ask for details. I'm just calling to let you know poor old Billy is dead."

Stunned by the tragic news, he sat down heavily into a nearby chair and asked, "How did Karen find out about this?"

"Billy's daughter, Cindy, called Karen today because she doesn't have either of our phone numbers. They have remained friends over the years and still keep in touch with one another, so she called Karen to tell her the sad news. I received the news from Karen just a little while ago. I still can't believe it."

"Have you tried calling Jennifer Newman?"

"Yes, but no one answered. I was going to call Henry and Polly Hughes, but it's too late back there. I'll try tomorrow."

He realized from the way she was slurring her words that questioning her any further would be useless. Emotionally upset himself he ended their conversation by suggesting, "Never mind, Janet. I'm going to get Cindy's telephone number from Karen and call her myself. That way nothing will get lost in the translation. Thanks for calling, and go to bed."

"I will," she promised, "but please call me when you find out how it happened." Hesitating briefly, she added in a sad, raspy voice, "Poor old Billy. He really got the dirty end of the stick this time."

"Yeah," was all he could manage to say before hanging up, deeply saddened.

It took a few minutes for him to recover from the tragic news of his old friend's death. A friend who, despite his own problems and heartache, had never failed to be there for him when he needed a break from the turmoil and frustration that periodically upset his own life. In many ways, he recalled, he and Billy were much alike.

Walking slowly to the Jacuzzi, he struggled to reconstruct the various possibilities that might have taken place at the time of Billy's accident. Nothing he could come up with made any sense. Billy was a qualified and skilled boat owner in every sense of the word, knowledgeable about courtesy on the water, safety and good boat maintenance. On the other hand, if he had been drinking anything could have happened.

Once in the hot swirling water he began to reminisce about the good old days when he and Billy were busy raising their children. The more he thought about his friend, the more he realized that the drink he held in his hand was partly to blame for most of the trouble they both had gotten themselves into over the years. It had also been the underlying reason for the untimely death of both his parents, and his only brother having to agonize his way through life with only one kidney. He laughed out loud, knowing in his heart that he too was a potential victim, but dismissed the addiction because it had not yet jeopardized his own health or his ability to function normally. How arrogant, he thought, that he would not take heed to such an ominous forecast, one that had already claimed so many. Raising his glass toward the starlit heavens in defiance, he toasted the demon its contents represented and called out, "Sorry, old buddy, I ain't ready yet!"

While he was preoccupied with trying to convince himself of his own infallibility a voice from inside the house alerted him to the fact that Paula had finally arrived home: "What the hell is all that yelling about out there?" she shouted.

Moments later she appeared fully clothed with glass in hand. Sitting down inside the Gazebo she submerged her feet in the water and asked, "What was all that yelling about a minute ago? She asked. "I thought you were talking to someone."

"I was," he replied, starting to slur his words. "I was talking to Billy Newman,"

She looked at him leery-eyed, suspecting all along that he had had too much to drink. "Is he hard of hearing?" she asked, sarcastically.

"No... he's dead."

During the few minutes that followed she listened sympathetically to his accounting of the phone call he had received earlier that evening. Somehow, griping about her mindless meeting with inept colleagues paled in comparison to the sad news her dear friend and companion had just received. Sipping her wine occasionally, she listened attentively to what he had to say, aware of the hurt he was trying so desperately to hide. Soon he became weary of it all and suggested that they get something to eat. She agreed. After shutting down the Jacuzzi, he put on his robe and followed her upstairs to change into something more comfortable. When they returned she insisted on making sandwiches and suggested that he watch television for a while rather than engage in conversation just for conversation's sake. He obeyed without a word and retired to his lounge chair. Half an hour later he was sound asleep, his head tilted awkwardly to one side and snoring.

Frustrated with everything that had taken place that day and unable to wake him, she put his sandwich in the refrigerator and ate alone watching "NYPD Blue." When the program ended she was still unable to wake him so she turned off the television and climbed the stairs to their bedroom where she collapsed wearily into bed. Lying there alone watching the moonlit clouds drift lazily past her window she sighed and wondered, *Where the hell do we go from here?*

Chapter 2

Dinner Can Wait

As it had every day for as long as she had been working, the radio alarm on her side of the bed sounded with irritating persistence. Consistent with his behavior on most of those mornings was the large groping hand with which Neal attempted to encircle her waist, a sure indication that he was, if nothing more, alive and well. She often wondered what manner of man she had welcomed into her life that woke up almost every morning wanting to fondle her. Occasionally, she reflected, the touch of his unusually soft hand stimulated the sensitive nerve ends of her sexuality, seducing them into a need for gratification. This morning, however, she resolved not to succumb. Before he could pursue his intentions any further she slid out of reach and stood up. "Not so fast, lover boy," she warned, "I've got one hell of a day ahead of me and you draining down my battery isn't going to improve my performance. Now, be a good little boy and go put the coffee on."

Safely inside their bathroom she removed her gown and stood naked behind the door as she peeked out and asked, "By the way, how do you feel this morning, Mr. Socialite?"

Wearily, he stretched his body and rolled over onto his back, groaning, "Like Mexican road kill." Staring at the ceiling for a moment before swinging his feet over onto the floor, he added in painful reflection: " But at least I'm alive, which is more than I can say for poor old Billy. What a hell of a way to go."

Following her shower she joined him in the kitchen. The coffee was much too strong but withheld any comment by asking instead, "Have you given any thought to attending the funeral?"

"I'd like to," he replied, "but I should talk to Cindy Newman first to find out when and where the service is being held. I'm sure Henry Hughes would volunteer to meet me at the airport. I'll know more after I talk to Cindy, then we can discuss air travel and other arrangements when you come home tonight."

When the time for her departure arrived, she gathered up the various work-related paraphernalia she brought home from work every night and walked to her car with Neal walking attentively at her side. Once kissed and finally on her way, he returned to his studio and set about looking into the particulars surrounding Billy Newman's death, an inquiry that would permanently alter the course of his own destiny from that day forward.

The first call he made was to Karen Stone, the oldest of his three daughters. Following a brief discussion regarding her conversation with Cindy Newman, she gave him her telephone number and praised her dad for making the effort to attend the funeral.

After taking time out to prepare a fresh pot of coffee, he returned to his studio and called to the number Karen had given him. By the fourth ring he was sure he was going to have to leave a message and began wording it in his mind when the receiver lifted. A sad and frail voice acknowledged, "This is Cindy."

For just an instant he regretted placing the call, however, realizing his silence might be misunderstood as indifference to the death of her father, he continued, "Cindy, this is Neal Thomas in San Diego. I just learned about your Dad's death from Karen and felt I should call to let you know how badly we all feel about the accident. I know it's painful for you, but can you tell me anything about how it happened?"

Hearing the voice of her father's best friend brought on a flood of tears. It took a moment or two for her to regain her composure, but she managed and replied, "The frustrating thing is, nobody really knows. There was an eyewitness, but he was too far away to give the authorities anything specific. According to him, dad's boat left the marina and headed in the direction of a waterfront bar where he used to hang out for an hour or two almost every day. I forget the name."

"I remember it well," he remarked. "It's called, Shep's Marina. Me and Billy used to hang out there on Sunday afternoons while Janet and your mother took you and Karen horseback riding."

"That's right. Well, the witness said dad's boat had only gone about a hundred yards when the engine stopped. When it wouldn't re-start, he opened the engine compartment hatch to see what the problem was. When he did, there was a tremendous explosion that blew off the entire back of the boat, sinking it immediately. They never did recover his body."

"But how did they know it was Billy's boat?"

"Easy," she replied. "The witness said he saw the words, *Ain't Misbehav'n,* painted on the transom when it left the marina. You should remember that name."

"Indeed I do," he affirmed, remembering how drunk he and Billy had gotten the day they painted it there. "Your Mom got so mad she had the whole transom repainted."

For the first time since answering the phone she laughed. It made him feel good to know that he had brought a little sunshine back into her life at a time when life seemed terribly gray and threatening. He cautioned himself about reminiscing too much for fear of bringing on more tears, so he asked, "Will there be a funeral?"

"No there won't" she replied. "Daddy specifically mentioned in his Will that he wanted to be cremated and his ashes sprinkled in the ocean out in front of our beach house. But, since there isn't a body to cremate, Mom's going to have a wake for him at Nick's Restaurant and invite all their friends and neighbors. Nick offered to close the place to the public for a few hours so family and friends could gather to pay their respects. Like he told Mom, Billy was sure going be missed."

During the few seconds of silence that followed he glanced up at the calendar and asked, "What day is the wake?"

"This coming Saturday starting at four p.m." she replied, hoping he was planning to attend.

"Pass the word, sweetheart. I'll be there. With any luck I can talk Henry Hughes into getting me a motel reservation somewhere near the airport this Friday. Tell your mother I'll be there, one way or the other."

Reluctantly, they said goodbye. She cried a little, more from the joy she felt in Neal's resolve to attend the wake than from the sadness she continued to be burdened with. His return to say one last goodbye to her father was a fitting tribute to a friendship that had bound their families together for many years, and weathered storms that at times had threatened to destroy them both. She couldn't wait to pass the good news on to her mother.

Teary-eyed, he hung up and reached for the address book that held Henry Hughes' business number and placed the call. Several rings later a woman answered and informed him that Mr. Hughes had left the office but was expected to return within the hour, and would have him return the call.

After some time had passed without contact he decided he had better make his own arrangements. Ironically, the phone rang. There was no mistaking the southern drawl that spoke from the other end: "Neal, baby, where in the hell have y'all been? I've been trying to get a hold of you for two days to tell you your buddy, Billy Newman, died. Seems he was in a boating accident a few days ago. I thought you'd want to break the news to Janet and the girls."

"I know, Henry," he replied. "My daughter, Karen, got a call from Cindy Newman about the accident. She told Karen what she knew, which wasn't much. Karen called her mother right away and then called me."

Pausing briefly to get some ice from the refrigerator he happened to notice that the message light on the answering machine was not illuminated. Irritated, he remarked, "Guess what. I just noticed that the damn answering machine was turned off. That's why you couldn't get in touch with me. Sorry about that?"

As he switched the phone over to his other hand to pick up his drink, Henry asked, "Are y'all making plans to come back for the wake? The local newspaper has it listed for this Saturday at Nick's. You remember Nick's, don't you?"

"How could I forget? That place got Billy and me into more trouble than I care to remember. I told Cindy to tell her mother I'd be there, one way or another. As for when I get there, that depends on what flight arrangements I can make. I'll also need someone to make a motel reservation for me somewhere close to the airport. I'll rent a car when I get there. Paula has to work, so I'll be traveling solo."

A delay in Henry's response, and some muffled words he couldn't understand, implied that a second party on the other end had interrupted him. Leaning back in his chair, he sipped his drink and patiently waited. Several moments passed before Henry and the background sound of female laughter, came back on line: "Excuse me, Neal," he apologized, "Polly has been standing here talking all kinds of trash about what we're going to do when you get here. The bottom line is, I'll pick you up at the airport. Polly insists that you stay with us, and no arguments. Just call when you have your flight schedule confirmed. Okay?"

He thanked his friend for the offer of hospitality and assured him that he would have the information for him by noon the next day. Curious about whether or not Henry and Polly had continued to socialize with the Newman's after he had moved to California, he asked, "Tell me something, Henry. Before Billy died, did you see their family often?"

"No, not often," he replied. "Our only connection was through Polly's cousin, Robby Sherman. He and Billy had known each other for years. Even before you and Janet were married and settled here. Several years after you moved to California, Billy and Jennifer got divorced. Billy took the big house in town and Jennifer moved to their beach house with the children. Cindy and Danny are both married now with families of their own. When Billy decided to retire, he sold the big house on the river and moved to a condo downtown near the marina where he kept his boat. Several years after that Robby Sherman passed away quite unexpectedly. It broke Billy's heart at the time, but like every other hurt in life, he got over it and spent a lot of time hanging around Shep's Marina. From that day on we saw very little of the Newman family. It almost seemed as if your moving to California marked the end of an era in all of our lives. I think that's why Polly and I are so excited about the prospect of you coming back for the wake. It will be like old times again. Do you still drink vodka? I want to make sure we have a bottle in the house when you get here."

"Yeah, I still drink the stuff." he admitted openly. "More than I'd tell a doctor, though. But I don't want you paying for my bad habit. I'll pick up a bottle on the way to your house. It's been a while since I've been in an ABC store."

"Bullhockey!" Henry blurted out. "It took Billy's death to get you back here after all these years. I'll be damned if I'm going to let a damn Yankee buy his own booze while he's a guest in my house. After all, there's still such a thing as southern hospitality. Besides, Polly says you could use a little spoiling."

Knowing it was futile to argue with him Neal gave in and replied, "Have it your way, Henry. I'll call you tomorrow."

After talking to several airlines for almost an hour he realized he wasn't getting anywhere. Frustrated, and becoming more irritated by the minute, he decided to call Paula, hoping that she could suggest some option he had not considered.

When they connected she could sense that he was fed up with the whole airline reservation system, so she seized the opportunity to diplomatically remind him, "First of all, you were too upset and drunk last night to ask Janet when the funeral was going to take place, so I called Karen this morning. She told me that the wake was planned for this coming Saturday afternoon."

"Yeah, I know," he interrupted. "I just got off the phone with Cindy Newman a little while ago. I haven't had much luck making reservations, though. Got any ideas?"

"I took the liberty of making a few inquiries on my own, my dear, and it paid off."

"Ah-hah!" he sighed with relief. "What's the good word?"

"Well, I called my friend Connie at Conway Travel and asked her to look into what was available if you left this Friday and returned the following Monday. She hasn't called me back, so why don't you call and ask her if she's had any luck. I'd do it myself, but I just don't have the time."

"By the way, how did you know that I had decided to go? I never mentioned it to you."

"How long have we been living together?" she replied. "We're both Capricorns. I knew you'd go because I would have if my best friend had just died. Now, call Connie and let me get back to work. We can talk about this tonight."

Several rings after placing the call a perky female voice came on line. "Good afternoon, Conway Travel," she greeted him. "This is Connie."

"Hello, Connie. This is Paula Dillon's friend, Neal Thomas. She tells me you've been trying to find me a round-trip ticket to Norfolk this weekend. Any luck?"

"As a matter of fact, yes," she replied. "Thanks to a scheduled rate change that goes into effect tomorrow, I can get you there and back for two hundred and sixty bucks. How does that sound?"

"You just played my favorite song. I'll be down tomorrow morning to pick up the tickets. Thanks so much for your help."

Relieved that his travel arrangements were no longer a matter of concern, he sat back and relaxed, surprised at how quickly the end of another day was approaching. Deciding it was too late to do much of anything, he opted to enjoy a naked soak in the Jacuzzi to relax away his trying day before Paula arrived. Possibly his nakedness in the swirling water might give rise to a similar response from her. With that thought in mind he hurried upstairs to change, congratulating himself along the way on what a clever lad he was.

He hadn't been in the water for more than a few minutes when his peripheral vision caught a glimpse of the blinking light he had installed to signal the approach of visitors. Assuming that the light had been activated by her approach, he laid back and waited. When she hadn't appeared within a reasonable length of time he left the water and walked quietly around to the kitchen window to ascertain why she hadn't come looking for him. To his surprise he found her sitting motionless at the kitchen table with a full glass of wine in her hand, looking blankly ahead. She presented the perfect picture of someone whom if approached might have responded, *"Leave me alone. I don't want to talk about it."*

Tip-toeing back to the gazebo, he dried off, put on his robe and entered the house. As he walked into the kitchen, he was reminded of an e-mail letter he had received from Ron Barns recently that quoted a few words from, *The Wisdom of Will Rogers*. It read: "*There are three kinds of men:*

The ones that learn by reading, and the ones who learn by observation. The rest have to pee on the electric fence to learn for themselves" – or words to that effect.

When he entered the kitchen to freshen his drink, she realized she had acted out of character by not greeting him when she first arrived. Feeling suddenly guilty about ignoring him, she broke silence. "Would you fix me one too, please," she asked. "I'm sorry I didn't greet you when I first came in. I thought if I didn't get some wine in me right away I'd say something stupid and spoil whatever kind of nice day you had had. I didn't want to do that."

"That's okay, I'll live. You might want to consider boiling some of that anger away in the Jacuzzi," he suggested. "It did wonders for me."

"I wouldn't be the kind of company you're looking for, Curly," she replied. "I'm afraid my job and that jackass I work for have drained me emotionally. What you see here is an apparition of someone you used to know. But, I will survive."

"Of course you will," he agreed sympathetically. "A couple more glasses of wine and you'll be chirping like a Magpie. Call your daughter. She loves hearing from you. In the meantime, I'll get dressed and fix dinner."

She smiled for the first time since arriving home. She didn't want to, but somehow the picture of him standing at the sink with wet, gray hair hanging down his forehead in ringlets presented an image of comic relief that somehow eased the feeling of anger and frustration she had brought home with her. Concluding that it was not an appropriate time to call her daughter, she changed the conversation to a more pressing issue and asked if he had made any headway with his airline reservations.

His response was enthusiastic, especially in light of what her friend, Connie, had come up with. Briefly summarizing his flight schedule for her, he turned to the content of his conversation with Henry Hughes, noting in particular his family's generous offer of hospitality.

Realizing she could no longer delay telling him she couldn't take him to the airport on Friday, she refilled her empty glass and explained the dilemma. "There's been a real screw up at the office today. Some valuable information has either been lost or intentionally deleted from our computers. Since my boss feels that I'm the only qualified person who can either find or recreate it, I'll have to work this Friday. That's why I was so upset when I came home this evening."

Appreciating her situation, he coaxed her up into his arms and held her close. "Not to worry, my little road-runner. There are more people who owe me a trip to the airport than Carters got pills. I'm sure I can embarrass one of them into taking me."

"But you don't have to. Your daughters have already volunteered."

"My daughters? How did they get involved in this?"

Knowing she had to appeal to the soft spot he held for his daughters, she kissed him tenderly and sat back down to explain. "When I called Karen this morning to find out when Billy's wake was to take place I mentioned that I was planning to ıake you to the airport if at all possible. You can imagine my surprise when she jumped right in and immediately volunteered."

Ruffling his tasseled hair he recalled the last time Karen had driven him anywhere. What a nightmare. She drove just like her mother – one foot'n the carburetor. However, since the opportunity to visit with any of his three daughters didn't happen very often, he welcomed the opportunity. "That was very generous of her," he remarked. "Should I notify the Highway Patrol?"

For the second time that evening she laughed and replied, "Be nice, now. And yes, it was generous. The drive will give you both a little one-on-one time together. So, enjoy it and don't be so critical. I'm sure her driving is not as bad as you make it out to be."

While he amused himself by preparing dinner, Paula excused herself and went upstairs to change into her favorite bathrobe, comfortably naked and, for the first time that day, pleasantly relaxed. She even considered the possibility that a dip in the Jacuzzi might feel good before going to bed. Anticipating that eventuality she brushed her hair, applied a fresh coat of lipstick and sprayed on a hint of perfume. Tying her robe securely around her waist she returned to the living room to find Neal clicking the remote in pursuit of something entertaining to watch during dinner. She being the more practical one went straight to the TV Guide. When his aimless clicking finally drained her patience, she interrupted and suggested: "Dear, your favorite John Wayne movie is on Channel Twenty-four."

Clicking immediately over to that Channel he watched the tall, lean figure of his hero struggling with saddlebags and a Winchester rifle as he walked slowly across a large expanse of parched and barren wasteland. "Only one man on the planet ever walked like that," he remarked, "and that's, 'The Duke'. Can you stand to watch *Stagecoach* again, honey?"

Knowing full well that she had very little choice in the matter, she replied, "Yes, dear. You watch. I'll read."

Less than thirty minutes into the movie, and well into the second half of his sandwich, he glanced over at Paula to find her eyes closed and her head drooped downward almost to her chest. He knew the day had been a tiresome one for her. And though he wanted her physically, he didn't have the heart to do anything but wake her gently and guide her upstairs to collapse into bed without a murmur.

When the alarm went off the next morning she quickly silenced it and patted him on the shoulder. Before he could roll over and pursue the playful ways she had become accustomed to, she threw her covers back over him and leaped out of bed. Laughing, she curled her finger and said. "Come on Mr. Coffee Man, time to rise and shine."

In a feeble attempt to grab her arm, he rolled toward her side of the bed and became tangled in the covers, exposing his naked bottom in the process. She smacked it playfully on her way to the bathroom and remarked, in a sultry voice, "Tonight, Curly."

Clumsily untangling himself, he rolled back over and came to a sitting position while watching the door close quickly behind her. In a voice he knew she could hear, he laughed and yelled, "Promises, promises! That's all I ever get are promises!"

After making sure his personal business was in order that same morning, he drove into town to complete final arrangements for his trip. Entering the Conway Travel office a tall blonde woman with Scandinavian features greeted him. "Hi, I'm Connie. May I help you?"

In high heels she was easily his height, and endowed with a large, well-harnessed bosom that displayed quite an eyeful of cleavage as they both sat down across the desk from one another. Before he could introduce himself she followed up with a comment that surprised him. "I can tell by the description Paula gave me that you must be Mr. Thomas. Please, sit down, and we'll finalize your reservation. May I see your credit card?"

After typing in the data she left her computer and entered a small room nearby, returning a few moments later with an electronic printout. After giving him a copy, she offered a friendly hand and remarked, sincerely: "Well, Mr. Thomas, that should do it. Sorry your trip isn't for a more pleasurable purpose. Let us help you when it is."

Tickets in hand, he left the travel office and returned home to pack his suitcase. It wasn't a lengthy process because he was content with re-wearing the same clothes during short trips. Thus, to avoid undue criticism for not preparing for every social eventuality, he packed the bare essentials, laid out the clothing he intended to wear the next day and sighed, "That's that!"

With little left to do for the remainder of the afternoon he decided to spend it with another old friend whom he was grateful was still very much alive and always glad to see him. Picking up the telephone he placed a call to his buddy, Ron Barns. When he answered, Neal greeted him enthusiastically and explained why he had called. "I'm leaving for Virginia tomorrow to attend a wake for my dear old friend, Billy Newman. Consequently, I won't be at our regular meeting tomorrow. But, if you're receiving today I'll stop by for a *bon voyage* drink."

His response was as it had always been, "I'll be here, my friend."

Traffic on the freeway that afternoon was not moving at its usual speed-up and slow-down mode, making the short trip to his house more relaxing than he was sure it would be the following day. The sun had been bright all day but was slowly disappearing behind a heavy marine layer that had begun blanketing the coast. Typically, it would soon move inland past the freeway causing motorists to turn on their headlights and slow down a bit, as did he.

Before long his freeway exit sign appeared in the misty distance ahead, prompting him to move into the shoulder lane. He was about half way down the exit ramp when the screeching sound of skidding tires followed by a loud crash echoed through the thickening fog on the freeway just above him. Hesitant to take his eyes off the road to see what had happened, he proceeded west along the lagoon road, grateful to be off the freeway. When he entered his house, Ron looked up and remarked, "If it stays this foggy overnight, you may not be going anywhere tomorrow."

"That crossed my mind driving along the lagoon," he replied. "It would be just my luck to have my flight delayed and screw up everything at the other end. Not to mention that if I had been ten seconds later getting here, I might be on my way to a hospital right now."

"What happened?"

Neal sat his bottle bag down next to the kitchen sink and replied, "I was about half way down the exit ramp when I heard a terrible crashing sound on the freeway behind me. Scared the hell out of me."

Showing little concern for the gravity of the situation his friend had just narrowly escaped, he looked over the rim of his glasses and suggested, "You'd better fix yourself a drink. There's not a thing you can do about all this."

"I agree" he replied, and proceeded to do just that.

Moments later he seated himself comfortably at the bar and began watching television until Ron looked up from his book, and remarked, "Don Curtis is scheduled to go into the hospital tomorrow. His doctor is recommending a series of tests to determine if they can surgically remove that tumor on his liver. He called earlier to let me know he wouldn't be at tomorrow's meeting either. He was not a happy camper."

"How's Mary taking all this?"

"I didn't ask" Ron replied. "What choice does she have? I know they've had problems throughout their marriage but this goes way beyond those kinds of problems. Knowing Mary, she'll do whatever has to be done, regardless of any personal animosities. She's just built that way?"

Reflecting briefly on his comment, he struggled to find some reasoning for the selection process that was slowly taking away their friends, seemingly at random; friends that were an integral part of both their lives. But, the process defied all reason. For those individuals with strong religious convictions and blind faith, God's will and its associated beliefs concerning the giving and taking of life would seem to suffice. He, however, thought differently. His personal reflections regarding the influence of religion on humanity, given its sometimes gruesome and controversial history, was more prone to favor his own interpretation, rather than those recorded in the *Old and New Testaments*, or in later, more modern interpretations such as James Redfield's, *The Celestine Prophesy*. Contrary to his Episcopalian upbringing, he was more inclined to treat religion as a cultural restraint; more like a psychological crime versus punishment or *Law and Order* mechanism. The fundamental purpose being to assure the propagation of world order and morality, both of which seemed to be currently out of control in its contemporary context. Simply stated, he had adopted the attitude that life and death were the direct result of a random selection process, programmed by the interaction of people under varying conditions in a biologically harsh environment over which very few had any positive control. Only members of the medical profession, he theorized, came close to having any real influence over the process, regardless of claims to the contrary that have been documented by religious theologians and historians over the centuries. Life and death, he accepted without question, was no more than a crapshoot - you win a few, you loose a few, you play every day.

While he stood staring blankly out over the misty lagoon he was suddenly distracted by Ron's excited voice from in front of the television. "Hey, Neal! Here's that accident you almost got mixed up in. Looks like an eighteen-wheeler jack-knifed across three lanes and has traffic backed up for miles. Man, what a mess!"

He walked from behind the bar just as a helicopter camera zoomed in on the accident scene. Police cars were everywhere, and a life-flight chopper had already landed. As he watched the flurry of activity taking place, his thoughts went anxiously to his trip to the airport the next day. Checking the time, he realized the accident was going to make northbound traffic worse than usual, so he quickly finished his drink, remarking to Ron as he prepared to leave, " See you next week. I'd better get my tail home while I still can."

"I would." he advised. "Have a safe trip."

There were no lights on in the house when he finally arrived home but Paula's car was where she always parked. Concerned that something was wrong he quickly turned off his headlights and came to a slow stop. Quietly, he walked in darkness to the dining room window and looked in. There on the table were two lighted candles and two of her hardly-ever-used crystal wine glasses. Place settings had been arranged with her favorite china dishes, and an ice bucket containing a corked bottle shrouded in white linen sat at one end.

Overcome with curiosity he quietly let himself into the dimly lit interior. On a hunch, he proceeded directly to the back patio door where he could see Paula's naked body illuminated by underwater lights of the Jacuzzi.

Not wanting to waste any more time speculating on what was excitingly obvious, he hurried upstairs, changed into his robe and returned to the kitchen. Seconds later, he walked nonchalantly to the Jacuzzi and removed his robe. Unable to contain his delight with the whole scenario, he laughed and asked: "Expecting someone?"

As she watched him slide gingerly into the hot bubbling water, she couldn't resist commenting, "Well, Curly, as a matter of fact, I was. Ever since your visitor light started blinking."

He shook his head, realizing that she had been aware of his presence since the moment he had entered their driveway. Reflecting on the irony of the situation, he remarked, "Isn't there a parable about a hunter who gets caught in his own trap?"

"A million of them, Sherlock," Paula laughed. "Are you getting hungry? I fixed some beef lasagna and a tossed salad."

Having only had a meager lunch he admitted he was. Then, sliding around to thank her for being so thoughtful, he suggested, "Lets cool off and finish our drinks. Then we'll eat and go to bed. Okay?"

"Sure. I'm cooked," she remarked. "You're not going to fall asleep on me again, are you? I've had enough of this, promises, promises, business."

"Not a chance, sweetheart. I'm up for the duration," he assured her.

Sitting on the patio deck their naked bodies soon dried from the night air drifting in off the ocean. Chilled by it, they put on their robes and walked inside holding hands in anticipation of enjoying a romantic dinner together. With a sense of physical longing still fresh in their minds they entered their dimly lit kitchen where a spontaneous wave of passion suddenly engulfed them both. Simultaneously, they turned and pulled their trembling bodies together in a crushing kiss, caressing and fondling each other until he broke away, took her by the hand and led her gently up the stairs. "Come on," he pleaded, "Dinner can wait."

Lying in bed with her body still pressed hard against his, she cupped his face in her hands and sighed, "What's the matter, big guy. Did yeah loose your appetite?"

Later, after exhausting him to sleep with what she could only diagnose as her pent up lust, she rose from the bed where he lay motionless, tiptoed out onto the small balcony off their bedroom and lit a cigarette. There, in the thickening fog, she let Mother Nature dry away the sweat she had generated in her enthusiasm to make her lover's eminent departure a memorable one. Finally dry and content, she returned to bed smiling about the uneaten lasagna that was still in the oven, a testimony to his unbridled passion that evening. "Yes," she finally whispered before dozing off, "dinner could wait."

The next morning was not at all what he had expected it to be. Paula had forgotten to turn on the wakeup alarm and was hurriedly taking a shower. He reluctantly threw back the sheet and proceeded to the kitchen to make coffee. Without it, he reflected, she could easily terrorize a terrorist.

The coffee on and perking, he returned to their bathroom where he replaced Paula in the shower, congratulating himself as he shaved on how smart he was to have packed for his trip the day before. By the time he finished she had returned from the kitchen with a large cup of coffee. As she primped in front of the mirror she could see his reflection toweling dry, and remarked, "That was sure a nice dinner we had last night, lover boy. Don't forget to put the lasagna in the frig,"

He laughed. "I did make a pig out of myself, didn't I?"

"In a manner of speaking," she admitted, openly, "Yes you did."

The hour that followed was a flurry of activity while they prepared to go their separate ways. There was little time for trivial conversation that under ordinary circumstances would have been an integral part of their morning routine. When all was in readiness, however, they did slow down long enough to express their feelings for one another. Before she made a positive move to leave, he encircled her waist with his arms and drew her close to him. "Hey, Toots, I need a hug. Won't see you for four days, "

As if he were a little boy going off to school, she kissed him. When they separated, she lingered long enough to pat his face and reply to his child-like expression: "I'm going to miss you, Curly. Have a safe trip, and call me this evening when you're settled."

Chapter 3

Flying High

In his rush to get Paula off to work, Neal hadn't paid much attention to the weather until he put his bag and briefcase next to the front door. Although there was still some fog covering the area, he could tell by its brightness that the sun would soon burn it away.

Walking through the house for one last check before his daughter arrived, a familiar, pizza-like odor coming from the kitchen attracted his attention. When he approached the oven his eyes caught sight of the temperature control knob still set on "Warm." Last night's untouched lasagna dinner was inside, blackened and completely dried up.

Amused by his discovery, he turned the oven off and sat the dish on a breadboard nearby so it could cool while he went to his studio, suddenly struck by an amusing idea. Returning to the kitchen with a note pad and black marker in hand, he chuckled and wrote, **Thanks for dinner**, and left it on the plate, imagining the look on Paula's face when she returned home that night. Pleased with his silly expression of humor he picked up his bags and walked outside, locking the door behind him.

He hadn't been there long when Karen's car arrived right on schedule. However, as she drove nearer it became obvious that there were two additional individuals in the car. As it came to a stop the passenger-side window lowered and revealed the smiling face of his second-born daughter, Susan. "Hi, Pops," she greeted him. "Guess who's in the back seat?"

Pleased to see her again, he kissed her through the window and reached to pick up his bags, but stopped when the rear door opened and his youngest daughter, Laura, appeared unexpectedly and announced, with comic formality, "Sunshine Limo at your service, Sir. May I take your bags?"

Struggling not to laugh, he entered the back seat and sat there with a broad smile on his face while Laura manhandled his bags into the trunk. "Nothing but the best for our Dad," she remarked after sliding in beside him. "Right, ladies?" They all agreed.

Soon after their departure, all three immediately began the endless exchange of chatter that he remembered being so synonymous with their childhood. Chatter, he had often verbalized, was genetically common to all women.

It wasn't until after Karen had driven onto the freeway that the chatter stopped long enough for him to ask, "Considering your distances from one another, how were you able to arrange this little get together. I certainly never expected anything like this."

Laura was the first to reply. "I called Karen last night to invite her and Derek over to dinner Saturday night. That's when I found out that you were going to Billy Newman's wake and she was taking you to the airport. That seemed like an ideal time to catch up on what my dad and sisters have been up to, so I called Susan to clue her in on what was going down. She immediately jumped on the bandwagon and said she wanted to go too. So, here we are every body. What's new"?

From that time until they reached the airport Neal and his fun-loving daughters shared conversations relating to their jobs, husbands, other people's husbands, wives and, in general, just about everything except their sex lives, which, according to his recollection as a child, everyone shied away from. Amusing, he thought, that he should now be sitting in a car with his grown-up daughters wondering if they ever gave a thought to the intimate side of his life. After all, he reasoned, they were all married and Karen was the mother of his only grandson. Living proof that Mommies and Daddies did more than just sleep in the bed they were rarely permitted access to as children.

Watching his departure gate gradually come into view he reached the conclusion that his daughters knew and remembered more about their parents' extra curricular activities than they would ever admit. He was reminded of the remark their mother used to make when she tried to coax information out of them, even when they swore they knew nothing: *"Everyone has something to hide, even if it's only a bit of dirty laundry."*

Despite his seldom-expressed notion that Karen had learned her driving skills from the legendary racecar driver, Barney Oldsfield, Neal was impressed that she had actually arrived at the airport ahead of schedule. As luck would have it, a hotel shuttle pulled away from his check-in station as they approached, opening up a large space in which Karen could easily park. While he hugged and kissed her goodbye, Susan and Laura quickly retrieved his bags and carried them to the check-in station. After a flurry of hugs and kisses there, the two sisters broke away and ran back to the car, laughing and pointing in various directions at what looked like the oddest collection of peculiarly dressed sizes and shapes they had ever seen.

With the windows down and their arms waving frantically, Karen maneuvered away from the curb and into the endless river of cars that continually circled the terminal entrance. An attractive, dark-haired woman who had been standing in front of him watching the farewell scene smiled and remarked: "That was quite a sendoff, are they your daughters?"

Surprised that anyone in line was paying any attention to him, he laughed and replied, "Yes, I'm proud to say, they are. And lucky I am that they got together and volunteered to drive me here. The other option, I'm certain, would not have been as pleasant."

Noting by the expression on her face that the woman's curiosity was begging for an additional comment, he added, "Nothing like being dumped unceremoniously at an airport by someone who, under ordinary circumstances, would not have been caught dead there without good reason."

"Yes, I understand perfectly," she remarked, "but then again, that someone might not have left their mark on you."

"Excuse me?"

After quickly rummaging around in her handbag she offered him a tissue. "If a woman is meeting you at the other end of your flight," she remarked, "she may be a little suspicious about how you came by that lipstick on your face."

Since he couldn't know exactly where his daughters had left their mark, the woman guided him through the removal process and tossed the stained tissue into a nearby trash container. As she started to turn away he thanked her for being so astute, asking: "Am I to assume that you've had some personal experience with this situation?"

The woman looked up at him out of the corner of her eye and smiled. "Not for a long, long time," she replied.

The baggage check-in line moved surprisingly fast that morning. Within minutes he was standing in front of its attendants while the woman who had given him the tissue walked leisurely toward the terminal entrance and disappeared into a swarm of people headed for the security gates.

There were already passengers in line when he arrived at his boarding gate, but it moved quickly. In a matter of minutes he presented his ticket to a very neatly dressed woman who was particularly friendly with passengers and appeared to be enjoying herself. After the usual courtesy greeting and security questioning, she turned to her computer and rapidly typed in the data, looking up at him occasionally and smiling. Impressed by her pleasantness, he asked, "What is it about your job that obviously amuses you? You seem to be having a lot of fun at it."

Handing him his ticket she hesitated a moment, as if reluctant to answer, and then replied: "Whenever I process passengers I can't help wondering what they do for a living, especially those who fly First Class. Like yourself, for example."

"Well, if knowing will keep you as happy as you appear to be, I'm a retired person and am returning to √irginia to bury an old friend of mine. Sorry, to disappoint you, my dear, but I'm not flying First Class."

"Not according to our computer, Mr. Thomas," she remarked. "According to our data, you were booked First Class from the 'get-go.' Someone paid for it, so enjoy yourself."

Puzzled, he thanked her and walked toward one of the large observation windows overlooking the tarmac where the B-757 jetliner in which he would soon be a passenger was being serviced. While he watched the baggage being loaded his thoughts went in search of an explanation for the change in his ticket. Maybe his daughters had contributed in some way, but discarded the idea because only Paula had access to that information. Then it dawned on him. She must have conspired with Connie at the travel agency to pay the difference. What a lady, he thought, grinning noticeably. What a wonderful lady.

After several minutes of watching airplanes land and take off, he checked the time and realized that he still had forty-five minutes before boarding would begin. Dismissing the thought that cautioned it was too early in the day to start drinking, he rationalized that it was five o'clock somewhere. With briefcase in hand and a contented look on his face, he walked like a man of purpose back to the '**Cocktails'** sign he had passed only minutes earlier.

As he approached the bar, he could tell at a glance that the place was packed with young men and women drinking beer or wine in casual attire, some carrying backpacks and wearing visor caps on backwards. What a strange group this younger generation is, he thought. Whatever message they were trying to convey was certainly wasted on him.

While he stood outside trying to convince himself that he really didn't need a drink bad enough to brave the crowd, a waving arm near the back of the room caught his eye. It was the woman who had given him the tissue. She was sitting at a small table with one seat empty except for what looked to be a small carry-on bag, which she promptly placed on the floor.

Deciding he had nothing to lose and still some time to kill, he ordered a Bloody Mary and squeezed his way back to where she sat sipping one also.

"Hello again," she said with a friendly smile. "I guess you're stuck with me. I seem to have the only empty chair in the place. Would you care to sit down?"

"Thank you. I was about to give it up until I saw you waving at me. I have a little time to kill before my flight leaves. And, to be quite honest, I really could use a drink. This is proving to be quite an interesting day."

Placing his drink on the table, he sat down and was about to explain what he meant when she interrupted. "I know. Before I left the departure gate I overhead your discussion with the attendant. How wonderful. Someone thinks very highly of you."

He laughed, remembering the incident and how annoyed the passengers behind him appeared to be getting. To mask his embarrassment he raised his glass in a toasting gesture and said, contentedly, "Cheers."

While he took an eager swallow and sat his glass back down he could sense that she was waiting for some explanation about who had changed his ticket. "The truth is," he confessed, "I have a pretty good idea who changed my ticket, but I won't be able to confirm my suspicion until I return from this trip. And, while we're at it, please excuse my bad manners for not introducing myself. My name's Neal Thomas."

"Mine's Sandy," she said, offering her hand. "Sandy Sterling."

He shook her hand firmly and offered to buy another round. She hesitated a moment but shook her head, no. "We'd better not. We're getting pretty close to boarding time. You don't want to miss your first class surprise, do you?"

He smiled. "Not for a lousy drink, I don't."

Once outside the bar he made an attempt to carry her bag but she hesitated to give it up until he remarked, "Chivalry isn't dead, you know. Its been trampled on a lot by this new generation, but its still alive for some of us. Besides, it isn't that heavy."

Thanking him for his gentlemanly gesture she walked silently by his side until they reached their departure gate. While waiting for the attendant to announce the boarding process he noticed her staring at him, occasionally, as if to encourage him to reopen a conversation so he asked, "Where's this flight taking you today?"

"I'm on my way to Philadelphia to talk with a client about a book," she replied. "Nothing exciting," she added. "Certainly not a vacation. How about you?"

Before he could answer, the gate attendant announced the early boarding order. When he didn't respond to the call for First Class, she nudged him and remarked, "Hello-o-o-o, they're calling us!"

Embarrassed, he showed his identification and proceeded into the boarding passageway. Behind him he heard Sandy giggling in a way that made him grin. The kind of silly grin a man wears when a woman reminds him that his fly is open.

"Why didn't you tell me you were flying First Class?" he asked, as they approached the forward boarding hatch.

"More fun this way," she replied. "It's not often I get a chance to help a First Class senior citizen."

Inside the jetliner they separated and settled into their respective seats, grateful to be ahead of the on-rush of passengers that were soon to follow. He thought of Paula and silently thanked her for sparing him the turmoil that was passing by in the narrow aisle leading to the Coach compartment. How considerate, he reflected, that she had arranged for this extra measure of comfort. Something, he admitted, he would never have given himself.

In her seat across the aisle, Sandy Sterling rested thoughtfully as she observed the gray-haired man across the aisle who had stirred up memories she thought were buried with her husband years ago. Tired and apprehensive about what waited for her in Philadelphia, she closed her eyes and listened to the whining sound of the massive jet engines that moved the huge aircraft slowly down the runway and came to a momentary stop.

Less than a minute later, the Captain's voice directed all flight attendants to take their seats as he turned onto the main runway. Pausing for only a moment, the two engines roared to full thrust, pressing everyone back against their seat while they sped down the runway and lifted off into the cloudless, mid-morning sky.

As the big jetliner continued its climbing turn over the shimmering Pacific Ocean, an attractive, dark-haired stewardess made her way about the cabin performing the service she had been trained to give. Though her nametag bore the name, "Vicki," she reminded him of Sela Ward, the beautiful actress and model he had admired from the first time he had seen her perform on TV commercials.

Paula had made jest of his adolescent infatuation with her at the time, reminding him one evening during her commercial, "It doesn't seem likely that she would have much time to waste on an old fool like you, as busy as she is."

He remembered agreeing with her at the time, but watching Vicki move so gracefully about the cabin brought another thought to mind. One that Billy Newman used to express on occasion: *"They can't lock me up for what I'm thinking!"*

Soon after the aircraft reached cruising altitude the Captain turned off the *Fasten Seatbelt* sign, which prompted the attendants to begin serving lunch. Watching Vicki move about the cabin brought back memories of an older woman he had been infatuated with when he was a young man, but couldn't remember her name. So true of many things he was failing to remember of late, and a grim reminder that there was no escaping the bitter reality of increasing forgetfulness. He shivered at the thought.

It wasn't until she spoke directly to him that he realized Vicki had been standing patiently in the aisle next to him trying to get his attention. "Welcome back," she joked. "I was afraid for a moment we had lost you."

"They're calling it a senior moment these days, my dear," he remarked, somewhat embarrassed. "I just call it wishful thinking. That way I don't get myself into a lot of irreversible trouble. May I call you Vicki?"

"That's my name, and yes you may," she replied. "Now, may I offer you something?" From the expression on his face she knew she had opened the door to a funfest. So, before he could reply, she rephrased the question, "May I bring you something to drink before lunch?"

His smile broadened. "You certainly may, young lady. I'll have a Bloody Mary. I'm afraid I was bitten by a dog last night, if you know what I mean?"

Still smiling and shaking her head, she turned away and walked back to her small service compartment thinking how refreshing it was to have at least one passenger who seemed to enjoy life by playing with it like little children do – just for the fun of it.

Until she returned he passed the time by watching the Arizona desert pass by some thirty thousand feet below. At that altitude, major highways and dirt roads appeared etched there as they wandered down shallow canyons and over thousands of acres of scrubland patched with barren dunes.

What an awesome lady *Mother Nature* was, he reflected, to have created this vast wasteland as a challenge for pioneering men and women to suffer crossing in search of the paradise he had left just an hour ago. Unconsciously, as he watched the ever-changing landscape pass below, his thoughts drifted back to the airport where he had met Sandy Sterling for the first time, and the humorous series of events that now put them across the aisle from one another. Curious, he turned in her direction to observe how she was spending her time and found her seat empty. Speculating that she had gone to the restroom, he returned to occasional ground watching and waited patiently for his drink to arrive.

After everyone else had been served, Vicki finally approached him. Carefully setting his drink down, she amused him by returning his humor. "I certainly hope this medicine helps that dog bite, Mr. Thomas. "I don't think we have a vet on board."

Pleased by her good humor he asked what was being served for lunch. Before she could answer Sandy returned to her seat and resumed reading, seemingly oblivious to others around her. It was at that precise moment that he decided to ask her to join him for lunch. Motioning Vicki to lean over so he couldn't be overheard, he whispered, "Would you please ask the lady across the aisle if she'd care to have lunch with me?"

"Why, you old rascal." she laughed. What's the matter, cat got your tongue?"

Amused by his out-of-character shyness, she stood up and approached Sandy. "Excuse me," she said, politely, "the gentleman across the aisle would like you to join him for lunch. May I accept his invitation for you?"

She looked up into Vicki's eager face and then over at Neal's hand motioning her to join him. Nodding her acceptance, she moved across the aisle and occupied the empty seat next to him. Curious about why they had taken off with an unoccupied seat, she asked Vicki if she knew why.

"The passenger never showed up," she explained. "Unfortunately, there were no standbys. It's rare, but it does happen every now and then. Apparently, this is your lucky day." Nodding toward Neal, she added, "Or maybe his."

As she turned to leave, she winked at him, as if to say: *I know what you're up to, you sly old fox.* He winked back.

Once she was beyond hearing distance Sandy turned toward him and confessed, "Had you asked me earlier I would have been happy to join you then. After all, we're not total strangers."

"Well, to tell the truth, the first time I looked in your direction you seemed to be preoccupied with a book. The second time you weren't there. I assumed you had gone to the lady's room and waited for you to return. I used our attendant as an intermediary to avoid the embarrassment of you turning me down. Which, I'm delighted to say, you didn't."

Observing the gray hair covering his tanned complexion and sparkling blue eyes more closely, she became suddenly conscious of the features that until that moment had gone un-noticed. Although the skin beneath his eyes was a little puffy, and wrinkled at the comers, the rest of his face was smooth and unscarred by the etching of time so common in men his age. His smile was pleasant and unforced. When he laughed his whole face smiled and made her glad that he had wanted to share her company. Sensing that she might be making him uneasy by examining him so closely, she looked away and asked, "Are you going to Washington for business, or pleasure?"

"Neither." he replied, reaching for the service button directly overhead. "One of my oldest and dearest friends died in a boating accident a few days ago. Considering how close our families were I thought the proper thing to do would be to attend his wake. I'm sure he'd have done the same for me."

The somber tone in which he had answered her question conveyed a message that she had opened up a fresh wound that only time could heal. In an attempt to regain the lightness of their former conversation she offered a suggestion: "When I was a little girl I can remember how emotionally upset I became when misfortune fell upon one of my friends, or a favorite relative passed away. My mother used to advise me not to dwell on sadness because it only made matters worse. Her cure was to associate the misfortune with something funny that had happened to them. Isn't there a humorous incident you can remember about your friend?"

Contemplating the wisdom of her suggestion he struggled to remember which one of the many situations Billy had gotten himself into would amuse her most. Vicki's arrival with his Bloody Mary, however, interrupted the process. When she stopped and replaced the glass on his tray with a full one he looked up grinning and asked, "Do you read minds too?"

"That's what I get paid for," she replied. "And by the way, you two, we'll be serving lunch in thirty minutes."

Amused by her light-hearted, devil-may-care attitude, Sandy turned toward him and remarked, "Don't you just love her? I wonder where she's from?"

His eyes were still following Vicki's hips up the aisle when Sandy's voice finally captured his attention, prompting him to reply in jest, "I don't have a clue, but I'd gladly follow her there."

She laughed, and remarked, "Well, based on what I remember seeing at the airport, and what I just witnessed a moment ago, I'd have to conclude that younger women are attracted to you. In a fatherly way, of course."

The subject matter of their conversation was beginning to moisten his forehead so he reached up and increased the airflow from his ventilation nozzle while he searched his memory for a humorous episode from Billy Newman's past.

Observing his reaction to the fatherly image she had characterized him with, she realized the sensitive nature of the subject and decided not to embarrass him further by pursuing it. Watching him fidget with his drink and turn away to look out the window told her all she wanted to know about the man who was beginning to exhibit some of the qualities she had adored in her late husband, qualities that represented a vulnerability that could be easily penetrated by any physically attractive woman whose life had become as lonely and frustrating as her own.

After her husband's sudden death, her personal adjustment to meet the professional demands of a large and successful publishing company became increasingly more difficult, and severely cut short the time that was needed to raise their only child. A daughter they had named Jessica.

At a time during her formative years, she remembered reading her the results of a study that supported the premise that girls inherited most of their intellectual capacity from their fathers, and emotional makeup from their mothers. According to that same article, further studies showed that much of the friction that develops between mothers and daughters, as the daughter continues to mature, emanated from the competition they engaged in to win the father's approval. As a general rule, fathers tended to become more affectionate toward daughters as they grew older. Mothers, on the other hand, instinctively began instilling safeguards to deal with hormonal changes that resulted in everything from zits to pregnancy.

Thinking back over those troubled years she couldn't help wondering if pregnancy might not have been the easier option when compared with the changes in her personality and lifestyle that resulted from her husband's untimely death. His sudden demise seemed to have opened a floodgate of bitterness and resentment against what Jessica had often times sarcastically referred to as, "*The Senior Establishment*."

Recalling her teen years, she remembered that Jessica's reaction to parental do's and don'ts had been limited to typical sullenness, escaping to her room for hours at a time and hanging out with friends instead of coming home for meals. As she grew older, however, her personality began to take on more of a rebellious and unpredictable nature. She frequently missed school and stayed away from home on weekends without letting anyone know where she was, or whom she was with. Then one day after she and Jessica had engaged in a heated conversation about her suspected drug related activity, she remembered coming home from work and finding Jessica's clothing strewn haphazardly around her bedroom. There was a note written with lipstick on her vanity mirror that read: "**So long, bitch**!"

For several months after Jessica's disappearance she recalled the hours spent trying to locate someone who could provide her with information regarding her whereabouts, but to no avail. Reluctantly, she finally called the morgue, hoping against her worst fears that no unidentified female body had been sent there. The answer was no.

In the months and years that followed, the grief and remorse that had saddened her heart for so long finally disappeared. Alone and bitter, she buried herself in the business her husband had left behind content in the knowledge that she was a very rich and powerful woman.

Aware that her brief interlude of emotionally painful reminiscing had turned her travel companion to watching the earth below, she interrupted his silence with a challenging remark: "Surely you must have done something with your friend that was amusingly out of the ordinary. Based on our brief acquaintance, I can't imagine there not being such an incident."

"There was," he replied, obviously amused. "One that will surely give us both a good laugh." And then he began:

****

"My former wife's maiden name was Janet Fletcher. She and Billy Newman were both from prominent families who had lived in the Tidewater Area for years and had dated each other in high school. It had always been Billy's intention to marry Janet, possibly after they had graduated from college. Billy told me years later that he had tried his damnedest to get Janet into bed with him, but she was just as determined that he wasn't, at least until after they were married. Well, as fate would have it, each of them went away to different colleges; Janet to the same one her mother and sister graduated from, and Billy went to Military School.

Two years later, Billy realized he wasn't cut out for a Military life, so he dropped out and went to work for his father, the hometown owner of a very successful furniture business. It was during that period of his swinging bachelor years that he met and began dating an attractive blonde by the name of Jennifer Connors. She worked as a secretary for a local law firm. Unbeknownst to Billy at the time, she had had her sights on him as soon as he returned home from school and manipulated an introduction through a mutual friend. Soon after they began dating Billy introduced her to his family without knowing that she had gained somewhat of a reputation in High School as being "fast," as we called it in my day. And so began the infamous seduction of Billy Newman."

****

Pausing for a moment, he reached for the overhead service button to order another round of drinks when she gently held back his hand and suggested, "Why don't we wait and have a nice glass of wine with lunch. These bloodies are beginning to get to me and I don't want to miss a word of this story. Okay?"

"Sure," he replied, eyebrows raised, "a glass of wine would be an excellent choice. How come you're so smart?"

"It doesn't take a mental giant to figure out that we're both going to be on our ear if we continue drinking these things," she replied with a snicker. "Now, tell me how Billy was seduced by that wicked girl, Jennifer. Sounds intriguing."

He rested his head back against the seat and continued:

****

"One day after playing golf, Billy and I stopped off at our favorite watering hole. After several drinks, he got a little silly and talkative about things he and Jennifer had done before they were married. In particular, he liked telling me about the time they went to a late afternoon picnic on a deserted beach with several other couples. They had been drinking for some time when Jennifer led Billy off behind some grassy dunes after the sun went down, stripped off both their bathing suits and led him out into the moonlit surf. Poor Billy. He told me that what she had done to him in and out of the water that night brought him to his knees in church one month later and ended his bachelor's life forever, or so he thought."

****

Shifting in his seat to get more comfortable he sighed and looked over at his captive audience. Her smiling almond eyes met his with all the eager anticipation of a young child being read a new and exciting storybook. Speaking in a whisper, he teased, "Now for the exciting part."

From the confines of her small service compartment, Vicki began loading luncheon trays into a mobile service cart while her thoughts drifted back and forth between what she was doing, and what she wanted to be doing. What she was doing, despite every effort she had put into making her job exciting, never blossomed into the flower of fantasy she had imagined it to be when she made her decision to become a Flight Attendant. Even though the opportunity to visit romantic places was part of the allure in the beginning, her heart longed for the quiet solitude of the beach community she had grown up in and the people who lived there. People like her passenger, Mr. Thomas, and his travel companion who were comfortable and fun to be with, laughing and enjoying themselves.

When the last tray was loaded, she turned and checked her appearance with the small mirror that was kept in the compartment's utility drawer. Satisfied, she smiled and whispered at her image, "Hang in there, girl. Tomorrow you'll be home."

Sandy's patience with Neal's intermittent interludes of distraction watching Vicki move about the cabin was wearing a little thin. Slightly amused by his boy-like infatuation with her, she raised her hand and waved it in front of his face, chanting, "Hell-o-o-o, earth calling."

He laughed self-consciously, apologized and continued his story:

****

"Several years and three daughters later I settled down one Sunday evening to watch television with Janet and the kids for an hour or two and then put them to bed. The rest of the evening consisted of the usual two or three drinks and then we called it a night. We were sound asleep when the phone rang sometime after midnight. I picked it up wondering who would be calling at that hour? Some out of state friend or relative came to mind. I couldn't have been more wrong. It was Billy. He was in a Virginia Beach police station and begged me to come and get him. I could tell he had been drinking, but before I could ask him what had happen, he cut me off and said he would explain everything when I got there.

By this time of course, Janet was fully awake and demanding that I tell whomever it was that I would call them in the morning. I promised Billy I'd be there as soon as I could get dressed, and hung up.

Janet, having gotten more irritated by now, asked me who had called, and what they wanted. When I told her it was Billy she just rolled over and muttered, Oh, for Lord's sake, what kind of trouble has he gotten himself into this time?

I told her what little I knew and started dressing, which only irritated her more. When I left the bedroom and started down the stairs, she yelled after me, How come he didn't call Jennifer?

Having been awakened from a sound sleep it took me a while to collect my thoughts, but as I drove off in the early morning darkness I thought about the question she had asked me, and asked myself the same thing."

****

Before he could continue, his story telling was interrupted once again. A male flight attendant from the coach section arrived to help Vicki serve lunch. When they arrived at the row where Neal and Sandy were seated, she looked at her assistant and winked as she remarked, "Doesn't Mr.

Thomas remind you a little bit of John Wayne? Except for the gray, of course."

The attendant looked at Neal, then back at Vicki, realizing she was trying to have a little fun with the passenger. Looking back at Neal and rolling his eyes upward, he said, "Don't pay any attention to her, Sir. She thinks I look like Jim Carry."

Both were amused by the bantering that was going on between Vicki and her assistant as they finally finished serving them and moved down the aisle.

Before they began to eat, Sandy raised her glass of wine to him and, mimicking 'The Duke', remarked, "Well, Neal, shall we get on with it."

He touched his glass carefully against hers and returned to his story, eating bits and pieces of his lunch every now and then while doing so:

****

"Fortunately, before Billy hung up that night, the officer on duty gave me a shortcut route that got me to the station quicker than the route I would normally have taken. When I entered the building, I saw Billy talking to an officer who was applying a large Band-Aid to a bruise on Billy's forehead. When he asked Billy how he was holding up, he assured the officer that he was fine. After nervously signing some release forms, he looked over at me with his bloodshot eyes and whispered, Let's get the hell out of here.

When we left the station I assumed we would return home on the same route I had taken to get there, but he had something else in mind. A few miles down the road he directed me through a couple of turns that put us on a street headed in the opposite direction. Confused, I looked over at him and asked, Billy, where the hell are you taking us? This isn't the way home.

He fingered the Band-Aid on his forehead, wincing a little from the soreness, but never losing focus on the road ahead. Moments later the reflection from another car's head lights on the opposite side of the road came into view causing him to cry out, There, Neal! Up ahead on the left!

I slowed immediately and peered in that direction. As we approached my headlights illuminated the other car. It appeared to be in a shallow ditch, so I drove by and made a u-turn. There was no mistaking its identity. Holy crap! I moaned, that looks like Jennifer's car!

While I sat there with my motor running, he jumped out and made a half-assed survey of the vehicle to determine how badly it was damaged and then quickly returned.

Old buddy, I'm in deep yogurt, he sighed. Take me home. I need a drink.

During the trip back to house he explained that Jennifer and their two children had left town to visit her sister in Atlanta for a few days. Because she refused to ride anywhere in his pickup truck, especially with their children, she insisted they all drive to the airport in her car. After bidding them fond *adieu,* he decided to spend the rest of the day relaxing in the sun at their beach house, have a few drinks and then go home.

As soon as he mentioned the beach house what followed became painfully clear. Looking over at my droopy-eyed friend trying to light a cigarette with a lighter that refused to cooperate, I asked, quite sure of the answer, That car back there was Jennifer's, wasn't it? His nod confirmed that it was."

****

Vicki and her assistant had just finished picking up luncheon trays when Neal excused himself to go to the men's room. During his absence, Sandy reflected on the day's events, wondering what was in store for her travel companion when he arrived at his final destination. After so many years of being gone, would he find his friends as he remembered them, probably not. But she hoped the changes would not be too disappointing. Reflecting on her own past, she thought about the wisdom in some prophetic saying she had heard so many years ago: *Anticipation is the greater part of realization.* How true, she admitted. It was all about disappointment, and she had had enough of that thus far in her life.

Following him to his seat on his return from the men's room, Vicki waited for him to be seated before asking both of them if they wanted more wine. Neal snickered, and replied, "Well, I just got rid of some. I guess I've got room for a little more. How about you, Sandy?"

"You're a bad influence on me, Neal Thomas," she replied before nodding her consent. "What have I got to lose at this altitude?"

Vicki laughed and went for the refill bottle, envious of the good time the couple seemed to be having, but content in the knowledge that in a few hours she too would be enjoying the same frivolity.

After she left, he turned to Sandy and whispered, "I'm glad you said yes. I hate to drink alone, especially in the presence of such a good listener."

"Then get on with it, Pilgrim." She replied in a low, throaty voice.

****

"Well, after Billy confided in me that it was his wife's car in that ditch, he looked over at me with that goofy look he always had on his face and confessed, Neal, I had sex last night with my neighbor's wife, and I'm in love, man. So help me God!

I was so shocked I almost ran off the road. When I recovered, he had finally managed to light his cigarette. Comically, he just sat there exhaling bluish-white smoke like exhaust from a car's tailpipe on a cold winter's morning. I was so pissed at him for dragging me out in the middle of the night I could have kicked him out of the car. But after thinking it over, I actually started feeling happy for him. He and Jennifer were not what you would consider happy with one another, if you get my meaning."

****

From the corner of her eye Sandy noticed Vicki returning with a towel-wrapped wine bottle. Feeling just a bit embarrassed by his unexpected dissertation on Billy's sex life, she placed her finger over his lips like a little boy being hushed by his mother, and whispered, "S-h-h-h, hold that thought. Here comes our wine."

Vicki filled their glasses to the brim and winked as she left, encouraging them to give her a buzz when they wanted a refill.

Carefully sipping her generous over-fill, she encouraged him to continue, remarking, "Yes, I did get you're meaning, but I'll reserve judgment until I hear the end of this amusing escapade. You two must have been quite a pair."

Making note of the time, he reflected on where he had been in his story, aware that they would soon begin their slow descent into Dulles Airport. Not wanting to ask her where he had left off, he began with a generality that got him back on track:

****

"Had that been the only time Billy told me he was in love I might have been surprised. But the truth of the matter was he fell in love with every good-looking woman he ever met. And some not so good looking, depending on how well they had bed him down. So, I simply listened to him relive the previous day and reminded him of the mess he was going to wind up in when his wife found out what had happened to her car. As I remember it, this is what he told me happened that day:

After dropping his family off at the airport, he started to go directly to their beach house but stopped along the way to have a drink at the community's only watering hole. It was there that he ran into the very attractive wife of one of his neighbors who had stopped to order some take-out food. Her name was Trisha Wells. She noticed Billy sitting at the bar by himself and came over to share some conversation with him while she waited.

What Billy didn't know at the time was that Trisha's husband was already having an affair, but had only been told about it recently by a sympathetic, well-meaning friend. News of the affair turned her into a notorious party animal. Word got around that she was making up for lost time and getting even with the bastard she had married.

From this information, and what I had gathered on my own from some of Billy's friends, I knew my little, unsuspecting friend was no match for Trisha Wells, and so did she."

****

Reluctantly, Neal turned to his eager companion and confessed that all his talking had made him thirsty, and would she join him for another glass of champagne.

Sandy replied she would, but only if he promised to finish his story before they landed. Reaching for the service button he apologized for being so long-winded and assured her that they would not part company with an unfinished story.

Moments later, Vicki came down the aisle with her bottle again and was about to fill his glass when a sudden jolt of turbulence buffeted the jetliner and caused her to lurch over the seats. With surprising reflex, Neal threw out his arm and grabbed the seat in front of him, creating a barrier that Vicki grabbed with her free arm.

"Thanks," she gasped, after regaining her balance, "We've got to stop meeting like this."

Chuckling at her quick humor the two held out their glasses. She had just filled Sandy's glass when another series of smaller jolts hit the jetliner prompting her to remark, in jest, "Wear it in good health."

After she left, they clicked their glasses together while he smiled and sheepishly asked "H-m-m-m, where was I?"

"Billy was at the town's only bar when his lovely neighbor came in," she replied.

****

"Ah, yes. Well, Billy said his brain turned to oatmeal when Trisha approached him sitting alone at the bar. He invited her to join him and asked if she would like a drink while she waited. She accepted, of course, and slid up onto the stool next to his.

One drink led to another, and so on. Billy said he could tell by the lengthening shadows outside that darkness was not far away. What to do, he asked himself; pay the bar bill and leave, or spend the night at his place and go home the next morning? Good sense did not prevail.

It was Trisha who made the move by insisting that Billy follow her home for one last drink and a bite to eat. The trap had been sprung and Billy knew it. Like a little puppy on a leash he followed her home with but one question on his mind: Where the hell was her husband, Sonny?

Fortunately, their houses were only separated by a short stretch of beach, making it possible for him to park at his place and walk to hers. He admitted being a little uneasy with what he was doing, but couldn't erase the mental image of her body seductively hidden under her shawl as he drove the short distance to his beach house.

Trisha, in the meantime, had parked her car in the garage to hide it from sight, sensing that Billy would walk the beach route rather than run the risk of being seen. Only a few minutes passed before she heard Billy's soft knock on the door. Before he could ask the question that had been on his mind every step of the way, she took both his arms and placed them around her small waist. Holding his face in her hands, she kissed him full on the mouth with such uninhibited passion that he said he could feel her whole body tremble."

****

He paused for a moment to wash away the dryness in his throat while his eyes focused briefly on a large formation of clouds into which his story telling would soon be flying. He wondered with amusement at the possibility of Billy's spirit hiding somewhere out there warning him against continuing with his story. What a silly notion, he thought, and turned to continue.

He was met by Sandy's two big brown eyes smiling at him over the rim of a half-empty glass that hid her freshly painted lips as they whispered, "Welcome back. Have a nice trip?"

For the first time since meeting her, he looked closely at the attractive, well-poised woman who had been sitting next to him for most of their trip. Not many, he admitted, would be as attentive and amused by a stranger telling a story about the demise of a friend. He hadn't paid much attention to it before, but there was a pleasant softness about her, even in the voice that had just politely reminded him of the story he had yet to finish, so he continued:

****

"After her passionate welcome she assured Billy that her husband was out of town and wouldn't be returning for several days. Relax, she told him, touching his face softly with her hand, Let's go upstairs and have a drink. Billy followed, thinking he had died and gone to heaven.

It was sometime after midnight when he and Trisha separated from what had been one of the most memorable evenings he had ever experienced. After the initial exhaustion wore off he attempted to go for round two, but Trisha advised against it. Her concern was that one more would knock them both out and forfeit Billy's departure in the darkness that still lingered outside.

Respectful of her wise assessment of the situation, he dressed while she remained naked on the bed, bathed in the moonlight that sparkled on droplets of sweat trickling down between her small but beautifully rounded breasts.

Seeing her lying there, he confessed, tugged at him as if he were being seduced by the Sirens of Greek Mythology who lured sailors onto their island with irresistible chanting, keeping them there forever. His infatuation, however, was not fatal. The spell had been broken.

Walking back to his car in the first light of dawn had a sobering affect on my tired little buddy. It wasn't until he woke up in a ditch behind the wheel of his wife's car that the cold sweat of reality broke out on his forehead. Rather than stay there until someone came along, which wasn't very likely at that hour in the morning, he started walking, hoping to locate a call box somewhere along the way. He hadn't been walking very long when a police night cruiser picked him up and took him to the nearest station."

****

"What happened to the car? Surely the police would have been curious about why your friend was walking alone on a deserted road at that time of the morning."

He smiled, amused by what normally would have been a logical question under those circumstances, then continued:

****

"He told the officer he had met a woman at a party the previous evening who offered to drive him home because she thought he had had too much to drink. Somewhere along the way he got the impression that she was coming on to him, so he made a playful pass at her.

Contrary to what he thought she was doing, the woman got mad and slammed on the brakes, grabbed a gun she had hidden under the seat, and told him to get out.

Instinctively, he threw open the door and leaped into some thick bushes along the shoulder of the road where he hit his head on a rock. The officer bought the story."

****

Before he could continue she covered her mouth as tears of laughter rolled down her flushed cheeks. Barely able to contain herself, she apologized for interrupting and encouraged him to, "Please continue."

Surprised and energized by how much enjoyment she was getting out of listening to his comically dramatic accounting of Billy's escapades, he became more articulate and proceeded eagerly toward the much-anticipated conclusion of his, *Ode To Billy*.

****

"By the time we arrived at Billy's home that morning the sun was coming up. No sooner had we entered the house than he went straight to the bar and opened two cans of beer. As I sat enjoying the cold taste of it I couldn't help but wonder how my worried little friend was going to get out of the hole he had dug for himself. However, I could tell by the typical way he paced up and down behind the bar that a plan was in the making. To my surprise he turned on the television to watch the last round of a championship golf tournament that was ending that day, seemingly oblivious to my presence.

Mid-morning was full upon us when the emotional impact from the situation Billy had gotten me into finally made its presence known. Racked with guilt, I thought I had better call home to let my family know that Billy and I were at his house and out of harms way.

After several rings, my oldest daughter, Karen, answered. With diplomacy way beyond her years she cautioned that her mother was very upset with me for having been gone all night. Then, as if that concern had suddenly vanished, she told me that she and her horse were jumping in competition that afternoon, hopefully for a prize ribbon.

I responded with fatherly excitement and then asked to speak with her mother, only to be interrupted by my other two daughters arguing over who was going to ask me about Mr. Newman being in jail all night.

Before I could explain, Janet got on the phone and demanded that I explain where the hell I had been all night. To say the least, she was not a happy camper so I made the explanation brief and promised to be there when she and the girls returned home from the horse show. The dial tone that followed made it perfectly clear that our conversation was over.

After I hung up Billy came over and apologized for putting me in the doghouse. I'm sorry about all this he told me, halfheartedly. I know she's pissed at you, but the next time I see her I'm going to tell her how you saved my life.

That didn't help much, but at least I knew I had until five o'clock that evening to get the mess he was in resolved. The family mess, I'm afraid, took a little longer."

****

His expression brought the point home that remembering the situation his friend had gotten him into was not a joking matter because it had forced him to choose between conflicting loyalties; his friendship with Billy, and a genuine desire to share in his family's activities.

"It would appear that you had gotten yourself between that proverbial rock and a hard place," she commented, "I'm not sure what I would have done in that situation. But that's of little consequence. What about the car?"

Struggling for a moment in an attempt to condense the many events of that crazy Sunday into a brief ending, he looked briefly out the window at the thickening clouds, and then continued:

****

"After his half-assed apology for the family mess he had gotten me into, he picked up the phone and dialed a number he had been looking for in the phone book while I was talking to Janet. Moments later he connected with his neighbor, Nelson Rozelli, who I recognized immediately as the owner of a local Ford dealership. Billy told him the whole story of how he had wrecked Jennifer's car and asked him if he could recommend a good used car he could pick up that day.

He listened quietly for a couple of minutes, shaking his head up and down and occasionally winking at me. A few minutes later, smiling and looking quite satisfied with himself, he hung up and told me Rozelli was going to call back in ten minutes. He thought he had something Billy would be interested in.

While we waited he opened two more cans of beer and came from behind the bar to join me, relieved that a solution to his problem appeared to be at hand.

As we sat there sipping our beer, I finally asked him what Rozelli had told him, specifically.

He looked back at me with that silly, *what, me worry,* look on his grinning face and said Rozelli had a late model, repossessed Thunderbird that had just came in the day before. It belonged to some single sailor who was being shipped overseas for a couple of years and didn't want the expense of it, so he told Rozelli to come and get it.

The little high from the two beers we had consumed, coupled with the good news we were anticipating from Rozelli, relaxed him and prompted more talk about his previous night's soirée.

I just listened as I had so many times before knowing that time, distance and opportunity would eventually take the romantic wind out of his sails, and once again leave him becalmed on that all too familiar sea of flighty infatuation. Then, as he said he would, Rozelli called.

Only a few seconds later he hung up, beaming from head to toe. Come on, old buddy, he said grinning from ear to ear, we're getting momma a new set of wheels.

When we arrived at Rozelli's dealership showroom, Billy introduced himself to a salesman and asked to see the manager. After a brief explanation about why we were there, he led us to the manager's office. The manager was a serious looking person who shook our hands politely and asked us to be seated. After looking at us as if we were suspects in a felony carjacking, he remarked, Mr. Rozelli called me an hour ago and explained your situation, Mr. Newman. I have already dispatched one of our trucks to the location where you ditched your car and had it brought here to be credited to your purchase as a down payment."

As I sat there watching him fill in the paper work I thought, you little twit. If this situation had happened to me I'd be under the jail by now. The next thing I knew we were being escorted out into the garage to pick up the car."

****

"Oh, look!" Sandy interrupted, nodding toward the window.

He turned toward the window just in time to see the runway lights of Dulles Airport as the pilot dipped his wing into the downward turn of his approach. Less than a minute later the wheels touched down and the two large jet engines roared into reverse thrust, slowing the jetliner to taxi speed. As they turned toward the terminal building, she looked anxiously at him and asked the question she had wanted to ask before the plane came to rest and all hell broke loose. "How did Billy's wife react when she returned from Atlanta and found Billy waiting for her in a used Thunderbird?"

He shook his head and laughed. "Contrary to what I think you already suspect, she was surprised and somewhat pleased with him for recognizing that her car had needed replacing for some time. That is, until she received her first payment due notice and became painfully aware that Billy had registered the car in her name, both with the bank and the DMV. She was pissed!"

Her hands rose up again to cover the laughter his story's ending had brought, gasping with surprise, "Oh, my God! I would have killed him."

He too struggled to contain his own amusement as the jetliner came to a complete stop at the terminal. Immediately, the aisle filled with passengers removing their carry-on luggage from overhead compartments. As she stood to remove hers, she looked down and told him that she would be waiting just inside the terminal should they become separated. "I have something I want to give you," she added before slowly moving toward the exit.

He nodded his understanding and moved into the aisle not far behind. When he reached the exit, Vicki held out her hand in a friendly gesture and said, "It's been a pleasure meeting you, Mr. Thomas. I'll look forward to the next time."

"Me too, " he replied, releasing the warm softness of her hand. "The pleasure was all mine."

When he entered the terminal building Sandy was standing there waving at him. "How much time do you have," she inquired.

"An hour."

"Good. I'd like to buy you a drink before we go our separate ways to express my appreciation for making my flight so enjoyable. They're generally pretty dull."

"I'd be honored," he replied, "It's not often I receive such an attractive offer."

There was a lounge conveniently located nearby where comfortable seating and bar service were available. After ordering a glass of wine she reached in her handbag and brought out an initialed business card holder. Handing one to him, she explained the reason: "As the owner of a publishing company I read constantly. Much of what I read isn't worth the pulp it's written on. The plus side is, it has taught me to recognize the difference between mediocrity and real talent, the kind that writes memorable works, and some who have the potential to become commercial best sellers. This may come as somewhat of a surprise to you, but I believe you have that talent. Have you ever done serious writing?"

"I did a lot of technical writing before I retired," he replied as the waitress appeared with their order. "Procedures that described how to build and use large mechanical equipment that I had helped design. Some were very complex. But, to answer your question, never a novel, though I've always wanted to. I really enjoy writing."

His answer was just what she was waiting to hear. After giving the waitress a fifty-dollar bill, she raised her glass to gesture a toast and looked at him very seriously, "You have a gift, Mr. Thomas. I became aware of it listening to you describe the antics of your friend, Billy. You paint wonderful word pictures and should consider writing more seriously. You have my card. Please get in touch with me if you ever decide to write your novel. Send me a copy before you make any effort to get it published? I promise a frank and unbiased appraisal."

He looked across the table at her eager face and thought: What the hell have I got to lose? "Sure, and thank you," he replied. "I'd welcome your comments."

As they chatted about book-related subjects the waitress returned with Sandy's change and left with a sizeable tip, he observed.

Placing the bills in her wallet, she unsnapped a single photo holder and exposed a photograph of a young girl who looked to be in her late teens. "This is my only child," she said with a touch of melancholy. "She ran away from home after her father died. I haven't seen her since, and probably never will. Not that it matters, but I would like you to know that I was once a mother."

With empty glasses staring up at them, she glanced at her watch with noticeable regret and reminded him, "The bewitching hour is here, my friend. We really should leave."

Standing in the concourse outside the lounge, he offered his hand to the lovely lady for whom he was developing a special fondness. While he struggled to phrase a meaningful goodbye that didn't imply finality, she placed her hand behind his neck and kissed him tenderly on the cheek. "I don't know why I felt compelled to do that," she said, feeling just a little embarrassed. "Maybe it's because I was afraid you wouldn't."

As he would have with any one of his daughters, he took her into his arms with a gentle, friendly hug, and smiled affectionately. "Thank you, my dear. You've just made an old man's day."

Lingering a moment to implant the memory of his tanned and friendly face in the archives of her mind, she turned away without uttering a word and walked into the river of people traveling to wherever they were going, seemingly anxious to get there.

With the smell of her perfume still lingering on his face, there was little left for him to do but sit in the departure area for his next flight and speculate on what was waiting for him at the other end.

Chapter 4

Visiting Yesterdays

Neal's commuter flight to Norfolk departed on schedule. After reaching cruising altitude the attendant informed passengers that only non-alcoholic beverages would be served due to the flight's short duration. By any standard, she wasn't Vicki Daniels, but blonde and pleasant.

After asking for a diet cola, he opened his briefcase and took out a small, airline-sized bottle of vodka and placed it in the seat pocket in front of him, a practice he had adopted when drinking on airplanes had ceased to be affordable.

While the attendant was preoccupied serving other passengers, he spiked his cola, much like his father had done back in the days of prohibition. He felt a little guilty doing it, but the temptation was much stronger than the guilt and did seem to amuse the woman sitting across the aisle. After an exchange of smiles, he turned his attention to the cloud formations that would soon disappear in darkness and thought about when he had first seen them from the air:

****

It had been a hot, humid day in the middle of July when Neal and his father arrived at a one-hanger airport not far from town. He was ten years old at the time. Scattered clouds hung in the air bringing some relief from the summer heat with them as they floated slowly over the fields and meadows encircling the airport.

The excitement of watching other people taking off and landing was a thrill in itself, but when he heard the loudspeaker announce his father's name his heart skipped a beat. Both his sneakers felt as if they were stuck to the ground. Aware that his son might be experiencing some pre-flight jitters, he took Neal by the hand and walked him quickly over to the airplane where the pilot helped them climb into the forward cockpit and then climbed into the one behind them. Looking excitedly up at his father he said, “Gee, dad, I never thought I’d be taking a ride in one of my models. This plane is just like the one hanging over my bed.”

Following a brief check of the cockpit instruments the pilot eased the throttle forward, carrying his two, wind-blown passengers down the bumpy runway and like a bird lifted them gently up into the deep blue sky that hung above them like a big umbrella.

The flight only lasted thirty minutes, but the memory of watching the control stick and rudder pedals moving in the cockpit, while the pilot executed a series of slow, banking turns, remained with him as vividly as the day he had experienced them.

****

He was still remembering that day when the stewardess took his empty glass and told him to buckle-up. The downward angle of the aircraft and decreasing whine of the jet engines gave notice that he would soon be landing at his final destination. Fastening his seatbelt he watched the Chesapeake Bay glistening in the late afternoon sun as the pilot fully extended the flaps and lowered the landing gear. Minutes later they were on the ground taxiing toward the terminal where he looked forward to greeting his old friend, Henry Hughes, again.

Once inside the terminal, he proceeded directly to the baggage claim area where he stood anxiously waiting for his suitcase to arrive. Looking around occasionally to determine if Henry was there trying to find him, he noticed a young man with a mustache holding a sign above his head that read: **Hello Mr. Thomas.**

Waving frantically, he managed to attract his attention. When he approached there was a familiarity about his face that he couldn’t associate with a name. The mystery ended when the man smiled and offered his hand. “Hi, Mr. Thomas,” he greeted him, enthusiastically. “Remember me? I’m Dan Hughes.”

Neal shook his head and laughed, embarrassed by not having recognized him. “My God, Dan, how long has it been? Where’s your dad?”

Releasing his hand, he replied nervously, “I’ll explain later, Mr. T. Meet me out front after you get your bag. I’m illegally parked out there.”

The urgency in his voice was reason enough for Neal to encourage him to go back to his car and wait there.

It wasn't long after Dan had hurried out of the building that he saw the familiar multi-colored ribbon Paula had encouraged him to tie on his suitcase handle. Good old Paula, he thought, always looking out for him in so many little ways.

When he exited the terminal building, Dan was nowhere in sight. Guessing that a traffic cop had made him move, he waited patiently at the curb and became reacquainted with the heat and humidity he had grown unaccustomed to since relocating to California. His only consolation was in the knowledge that in a few days he would be returning to the cool ocean breezes of Southern California, his paradise. As he wiped the sweat from his brow, he spotted an arm waving from a black limousine moving slowly in his direction. It was Dan.

They had no sooner driven onto the Toll Road a few minutes later when Dan mentioned there was a cooler in the back seat with a bottle of Vodka and Tonic mix in it. "Compliments of mom and dad," he remarked. "They wanted you to feel right at home, so help yourself. I'm your designated driver tonight."

By then, the air-conditioning had cooled them down to the comfort level he was used to and the offer of a cold drink sounded very appealing, even in light of what he had already consumed that day. "Your parents know me too well," he chuckled and helped himself.

Comfortably resting back against the Cadillac's plush seat, he turned his attention to Dan and asked, "Tell me what you've been up to all these years, Dan. Based on this snazzy car you're driving, I'd say you've done pretty well for yourself."

He could see the reflection of Dan's smile in the rear view mirror as he replied, "Well, for starters, this car belongs to dad's business. I guess if you consider material things as a measure of success, he's done very well for himself. He asked me to come and get you because he was in the middle of a very important meeting involving a large parcel of land his company wants to develop into a shopping center. He's been working on this transaction for almost a year now, and from what he tells me, which isn't much, it's almost ready to close.

As for me, my parents tried their best to get me educated, but after flunking out of several schools in the process they gave up and turned me loose to determine my own fate.

I couldn't stand the thought of being cooped up in an office so I got a job with mom's cousin, Robby Sherman. He, as you probably remember, was a small-time sewer contractor and a good friend of Billy Newman. Robby had a son who was my age. We hung around together and worked side-by-side digging sewer pipe trenches for a few years. But as time passed, I got bored with the job and decided I wanted to be a pilot. So, I started taking flying lessons. Almost all the money I made back in those days was spent on those lessons. Everyone thought I would probably end up killing myself. As it turned out, getting my pilots license was the smartest thing I ever did. When friends and daddy's business associates learned that I was licensed, they began hiring me to fly them on short business trips and vacations all over the place. It didn't take long before I was able to buy a twin-engine Beechcraft."

Listening to Dan recall his fascination with flying when he was a young reminded him of a time during his younger days when he rode his bicycle to revisit the small airport where his father had treated him to his first airplane ride:

****

He had been walking around in the small, sheet metal hanger building looking into the cockpits of several small airplanes when a man wearing sunglasses and a flying jacket approached him. "You come out here quite often, don't cha boy? I seem to remember you hanging around here before."

With youthful embarrassment he admitted he had, and started to leave when the man placed his hand on his shoulder and asked him to stay. "I have to log in some flying hours today. How would you like to take a short hop out over the lake with me?"

He couldn't believe his ears, but was quick to reply, "Yes sir!"

It was a beautiful day with only a few scattered clouds drifting lazily across the sky. The lake shimmered in the distance as the two lifted off the ground and flew the small Piper Cub out over the water. What made the flight such a memorable one was what followed, an experience he would never forget.

The pilot had instructed him to put his hand gently around the control stick and his feet on the rudder pedals so he could get a feel for how they controlled the airplane. Several minutes later the pilot took his hands off the controls and gripped the cabin braces over the instrument panel, hollering back over his shoulder, "Okay, young man, its all yours. Just don't make any quick movements, and keep your nose level with the horizon. This plane will fly itself if you let it. Now, take us home."

After the initial nervousness of actually flying the airplane began to subside, he finally relaxed and began his return to the airport with only minor help from the pilot. Minutes before they arrived, however, the pilot took control and landed. Grateful for the chance of a lifetime, he thanked the pilot and headed home, anxious to share his wonderful day with family and friends.

****

Abruptly, the sound of Dan's voice ended Neal's flashback as he continued narrating his accounting of what he had been doing during the years following his ascension into manhood. "When you and your family still lived here I thought there was a fair possibility that Karen and I would get together. However, those hopes were dashed against the rocks when we both went off to different schools. I never saw much of her after that. Besides, I was pretty sure she knew I was doing drugs and hanging around with people she didn't approve of, so I got on with my life. Looking back, I'm glad everything worked out the way it did. She sure as hell would never have accepted the lifestyle I chose."

It took a moment or two for him to recognize the implication in Dan's last remark. Out of curiosity, he asked the obvious question: "Where did she ever get the idea that you were involved with drugs?"

Dan thought briefly about how far into that subject he wanted to venture, considering it was really none of Neal's business. He concluded, on the other hand, that Neal deserved an honest answer, so he explained:

"Most of your generation never had to deal with the type of social pressures mine did. In your day drugs were something doctors gave people when they got sick. My generation, however, found out in a hurry that there were other kinds of pain, depending on how your parents and friends treated you. How well you did in school, for instance. Or, how willing you were to fight in a useless, politically motivated war in some God-forsaken jungle half way around the world. Lord knows I was never a student, and too small to be any kind of an athlete. And, a reject as far as the military was concerned. Yeah, I smoked a little pot and snuffed a little coke back then, because that's what most of my peer group did. But, that's another story. I'll tell you about it sometime."

Never realizing that the sandy-haired, blue-eyed son of one of his closest friends had grown up with so much anger and resentment, he laughed half-heartedly and replied, "I'll look forward to that, Dan. My life pales by comparison. By the way, how's your Sister?"

He paused for a minute while he lit a cigarette and then replied, "She'll be at the party tonight. You can ask her yourself."

"What party?"

"As soon as you called Daddy and told him you were coming to Billy's wake, he called a bunch of your old buddies and invited them to the house tonight. So, drink up Mr. T, he laughed. "Your evening is just getting started."

The thought of walking into a house full of drunks prompted him to take Dan's advice.

Midway through the process Dan turned and requested that he mix him one too. "There's a pint of Bourbon and some Ginger Ale in the cooler," he remarked. "Might just as well join you now that we're out here in the boonies and almost home. I suspect we'll have a lot of catching up to do."

Neal obliged him and made note of the familiar landmarks passing by that signaled they were nearing the Hughes' estate. It was a beautiful place, conveniently located on an inlet that provided boat access to Chesapeake Bay. More than enough justification for having invested in the large, twin-engine cabin cruiser they kept docked behind their house. Every winter, he recalled, they packed up and boated down the inland waterway to Florida where they lived until early spring. He had always envied Henry that option, and wished at times that his income could have afforded his own family the same luxury. But, in keeping with his general philosophy on that sort of thing, that just wasn't meant to be.

As he continued to think back on the good times he had shared with his friends, Dan broke the silence. "While you're here, I'd like to take you out on the bay in my boat for a few hours, if you have the time. How about Sunday? You did say you were leaving on Monday, didn't you?"

"Yes, Monday's the day. However, let's wait until we know what your Mom and Dad are going to do after the wake. We can decide then. I really would enjoy going out on your boat, though. Reminds me of the good old days. Thanks for inviting me."

There was no mistaking the Hughes estate. The entrance, which consisted of two brick columns joined together at the top by iron latticework bearing the family name, was gated. The two-story colonial home in which he had partied so many times in the past lay nestled among a number of large trees scattered around the water's edge that sheltered an evening of events that he would not soon forget.

Approaching the front door they were greeted by sounds of revelry coming from within. One sound in particular brought a smile to his face when he heard his old friend, Jimmy Mullins, hamming it up on the piano. This, he thought, was going to be one hell of an evening.

Dan retrieved his bag and briefcase from the limo and handed them to him, suggesting, "You go ahead. I have to check my boat before I start partying. Tell Mom and Dad I'll join them in a little while."

"Sure," he replied. "Take your time. I don't think this party's going to end any time soon."

Prepared to face the horde alone, he walked to the large screened-in porch looking out over the water behind the house. Taking a deep breath he trudged up the steps and entered. Though there was plenty of activity going on, Henry was the first to notice him and yelled, "Hey, everybody! That damned Yankee is finally here!"

He knew most of the people who came to greet him. The others he assumed to be special friends of Henry and Polly, or 'the usuals,' as Henry often referred to them. One in particular was a tall, attractive woman who appeared to be in her fifties, and alone. Though his tumultuous arrival had not permitted much more than a polite introduction at that time, he vowed to seek her out when the novelty of his return had quieted down.

On one convenient occasion during the early part of the evening, he took Polly aside to inquire who the woman was. She told him her name was Sally Porter, a recently divorced friend who had no interest in pursuing a serious relationship with anyone. Her presence at the party, as Polly further explained, was her way of getting her back into the swing of things. As she turned to rejoin her guests, she smiled at him in a devilish way and remarked, "She's in the room next to yours."

He noticed that for the entire time he and Polly had been talking that Sally had made no attempt to replenish her drink. Sensing that she might feel embarrassed to do so, he crossed the room and asked if he could bring her one.

Exhibiting obvious relief she smiled and replied, "Out of all these people wouldn't you think someone would recognize a damsel in distress? Yes, thank you. I'll have a scotch and water." Handing him her glass she added, "Now, your name I know, Sir Galahad, mine's, Sally."

On his way to the bar he had to pass the piano where Jimmy Mullins was still playing. When he saw Neal he pleaded with him to take over for a while so he could use the bathroom and get a drink.

"In a minute," he put him off, holding up two empty glasses. "I'm on a similar mission. Take a break. You look like you could use one."

Jimmy quit playing immediately and followed Neal into the large, paneled family room where Henry's black bartender was preparing drinks. Recognizing Neal, immediately, he held out his hand and said, "You've been gone a long time, Mr. T. What can I fix you?"

"Vodka tonic and a Scotch and water, Jason," he replied. "Good to see you again."

While the grinning old black man set about mixing his drinks, Jimmy asked Neal if he knew anything about the circumstances surrounding

Billy Newman's death. Neal told him that all he knew was what Billy's daughter, Cindy, had told him.

Pursuing the subject further, Jimmy shielded his mouth and whispered, "Sometime before this shindig is over, you and me should have a little talk, privately. There's something I think you ought to know."

About that time, Jason handed Neal the two he had ordered, along with one for Jimmy. As an expression of thanks for remembering his nickname, Neal slipped him a generous tip and turned to leave, when Jimmy nudged him and asked, "What do you think about that character?"

Neal turned in the direction he had nodded and saw Dan Hughes enter the room, approach the bar and order a drink. "What do you mean by, that character," he asked, somewhat taken aback by his inference. " That's Henry's son, Dan. He picked me up at the airport a little while ago."

"I know who he is. Just be careful what you say in front of him," he remarked with a scowl furrowing his forehead. "I'll explain later."

Hesitant to engage in further conversation with Dan at that particular moment, he picked up his two drinks, looked over at him and half-whispered, "Sally Porter's waiting on the porch for this drink. Poor thing. She probably thinks I've run off with someone. I'll see you later."

He had no way of knowing at that moment that Dan had too much on his mind to bother about what was going on between he and Sally Porter. As he turned to leave, Dan waved him off with a forced smile and thrust his empty glass at the bartender. "Jason!" he barked, "hit me again."

Out on the porch, Sally sat patiently waiting for Neal's return and looked pleasantly relieved when he appeared in the doorway. He apologized for being gone so long, but explained about being detained by Jimmy Mullins. "I promised to spell him at the piano for a little while, so I'm afraid I'm going to leave you again. Do you mind?"

She looked up at him for a moment and then replied, "Not in the least. Thanks for bringing me my drink first, though. I was beginning to think you had disappeared."

The Hughes' piano was a full grand, but modified electronically to provide instrumental sounds and rhythms that Jimmy had not used because his real talent was the guitar. Admittedly, he was only a mediocre, self-taught pianist and unfamiliar with its electronics. He truly was a ham, but a good one.

The reaction around the room when Neal began playing was immediate. People stopped talking. Even those who were eating stopped to enjoy the beautiful sounds he was creating. As he continued to play his eyes wandered briefly to the large French doors opening onto the back porch where Sally stood against one of the casings, motionless and smiling. Then, Henry came up behind her, whispered something in her ear and walked casually away.

Sometime later, when he had already decided to turn the piano back over to Jimmy, Sally approached with Henry's message: "Some of your friends are getting ready to leave," she whispered. "Come say goodbye."

Throughout the ensuing hour guests said their goodbyes with mixed sobriety, leaving only a few of the predictable die-hards to prolong the evening until unceremoniously being asked to leave. One of those die-hards was Jimmy Mullins. He had remained, as he had mentioned to Neal earlier, to discuss Billy Newman's accident. After seeking out the privacy of Henry's pier and lighting a cigarette, he looked at Neal leaning up against one of the pilings and expressed himself in all sincerity. "I couldn't say anything about this inside," he muttered, "but as sure as I am standing here talking to you, Billy's death was no accident."

Suddenly, the light and frivolous mood of the evening took on a more somber note. "I think you'd better explain yourself, Jimmy," he challenged immediately. "That's a pretty serious statement."

"I know I'm drunk, but so help me God, Billy was set up. I've had a boat at the marina for years, and I've made a lot of friends on the water, including some who work for the Harbor Police. The scuttlebutt around here is that Billy's boat was rigged to explode when the engine compartment hatch was lifted."

Neal looked out over the moonlit water and questioned the validity of the scuttlebutt he had referred to. "How the hell would anyone know that?' he asked. "I understand from his daughter that the whole stern of the boat was blown to smithereens, and the rest of it sank immediately, according to an eyewitness. How could anyone prove such a theory?"

"I know all that," he continued. "Only one other person knows what the police know, and that's a friend of mine who works for the salvage company that picked up the pieces. He's the guy who actually pulled up what was left of Billy's boat, including the engine."

"And?"

"He's the one who discovered a piece of steel wire attached to the carburetor air intake valve, and a mangled piece of what he said looked like a small timing device attached to the other end. Investigators think the engine was rigged to shut down sometime after Billy left the dock. That would have forced him to open the booby-trapped hatch to see what was wrong. Wham! Goodbye Billy."

Neal watched him flick what was left of his cigarette into the water and down the rest of his drink before asking, "Where's the investigation going from here, and who's in charge?"

"Damn if I know," he slurred in reply, "though rumor has it the DEA has been snooping around here recently." Looking at his watch and yawning, he sat his empty glass down on the piling behind Neal and said, almost incoherently, "See you tomorrow, sport. Jane's gonna to bust my ass when I get home. Some things never change… do they?"

As he turned to leave, Neal threw the rest of his drink in the water and asked, "Who in the world would have had any reason to kill Billy Newman? I don't remember him ever having any enemies, least of all one who would kill him. Of all the people I can think of, Jennifer had more reason than anyone, but you and I both know she'd never do anything like that. I just can't believe someone hated Billy enough to kill him."

Jimmy stopped after only a few steps and replied, "Or had him killed. You've been gone a long time, Neal. Lot's of things have happened since you left, and a lot of people have changed. I don't try to understand it. Remember what "The Shadow" said on radio years ago? *Who knows what evil lurks in the hearts of men?* Shit happens, old buddy. See yeah tomorrow."

For the next few minutes Neal remained on the dock watching him stagger up the hill and disappear in the darkness. The next sound he heard was a car engine starting and the crackling of gravel beneath its tires.

It was well after midnight when he walked up the same path Mullins had taken. The warm, humid air and short climb had dampened his shirt so he proceeded straight to the family room where the lights were still on. A nightcap was in order he was convinced, although the taste in his mouth and a threatening headache advised against it.

Entering the house he observed that all the guests, including the bartender, had left. Henry and Polly must surely have already gone to bed, leaving Dan, and Sally Porter sitting alone at the bar still drinking and quietly talking.

As he approached, Dan turned to face him. "You seemed to have made quite an impression on Ms. Porter with your piano playing, Mr. T. You sure haven't lost your touch. I can still remember mom and dad dragging me along to parties at the Newman's beach house, staying up late and listening to you play that portable keyboard of yours. Man, you oldies sure knew how to party."

Though he was in no position to judge anyone at that hour, he could tell Dan was beginning to feel his drinks. Sally, on the other hand, seemed to be holding up pretty well, although her eyelids appeared to droop a little at times. Too tired to respond with anything that sounded intellectually profound, he replied, "Well, Dan, when a person does something over and over again, they ought to get pretty good at it."

Not having said much since he had joined them, she interjected an observation: "Some people, that is."

Both men smiled respectfully at her dryly-put comment. Neal, however, perceived a pinch of sour grapes in her remark and wondered why. It may have been fallout from her recent divorce, he speculated, or the company she was keeping. Regardless, it was also becoming noticeable that her eyes were beginning to stay closed longer between blinks. So, to end the evening, he sat his empty glass down on the bar in a gesture of finality and said, "I don't know about you two, but I'm going to bed. See you in the morning."

A glimpse at her drooping eyes reminded him that he hadn't been told which of the two upstairs guest rooms he was to sleep in, not knowing that Polly had already made the decision for them and had their luggage placed in the two adjoining rooms.

"Yours is the one with the door left open," she explained, "I guess that was her way of preventing you from wandering into mine."

As he walked toward the stairs, he became amused by her comment and the consequences of making such a mistake. Based on what little he knew about Ms. Porter, he concluded that, if nothing else, she did have a good sense of humor. Climbing the stairs he overheard Dan tell her goodnight and explain that he would be spending the night on his boat and would see her in the morning before she left.

Seemingly reluctant to follow the lead of her two departed companions, she remained at the bar until she had had emptied her glass. With little to be gained by having another, she turned out the lights and climbed the winding stairway to her bedroom.

It was a hot and sticky evening, but bearable due to the ceiling fan above her bed. Turning out the lights, she slipped into a lightweight, knee length gown and was about to crawl onto the bed when a noise on the balcony outside her screen door attracted her attention. Curious, she tiptoed over to the door and stood there briefly trying to determine who, or what, was out there. It was a man wearing only boxer shorts and a tee shirt. Obviously, it was her neighbor. Being careful not to startle him, she gently opened the screen door and stepped out onto the balcony, whispering, "What are you doing out here?"

Raising his finger to his lips in a gesture to be quiet, he motioned for her to join him. In response to her question, he whispered, "There's another boat along side Dan's that wasn't there earlier. I'm just trying to figure out what Dan's doing at this hour in the morning." When he saw how little she was wearing, he couldn't help remarking, "I might ask you the same question?"

Her response was, "I heard you moving around out here and thought you might like some company. Don't be embarrassed. You're not the first man I've seen in his underwear. What's going on down there?"

To avoid becoming further distracted by her almost transparent gown, he turned around and pointed in the direction of Dan's boat. "When I was down on the dock with Jimmy Mullins earlier, Dan's was the only boat there. Now, there are two. I heard the engine noise of the other boat when it arrived and mistakenly thought it was Dan leaving. To answer your question, that's why I'm out here."

"Maybe they're friends of Dan's and are getting an early start to go fishing. They could be loading supplies."

"Not today," he argued, "Dan's supposed to be at Billy Newman's wake this afternoon."

"Well, I really don't care what they're doing," she sighed, "I'm going to bed. Are you coming?"

His tired and bloodshot eyes looked over at her standing in the open doorway, and blinked. "What did you say?" he stammered.

With both arms folded under her breasts to create a seductive cleavage, she couldn't help but be amused by the expression on his face. "Shall I call for an interpreter?" she answered, amused by his reply. "I thought I made myself perfectly clear."

Standing and leaning back against the railing as he wiped the perspiration from his forehead, he looked at her smiling at him in the shadows and asked, "Now what would you want with an old fool like me? I'm probably twenty years older than you are, been up since six o'clock drinking all day, and my body clock is three hours behind yours. Unless you belong to a cult that practices raising the dead, all you're going to do is embarrass me. And, I don't think that was your intent."

Slowly, while he stood nervously in the moonlight waiting for her to respond, he watched the corner of her mouth curl up into a smile, and then chuckle. "If you think I'm in any better shape than you are my presumptuous friend, I'm flattered. But that's not what I meant. What I meant to say was, don't you think we ought to get some sleep?"

Her response surprised and embarrassed him. Feeling small enough to fall through the crack in the floorboards he was standing on, he hung his head and stammered, "Please forgive me. I had no right to talk to you that way. California seems to have cast a bad influence on my Yankee upbringing."

"Not from my point of view it hasn't," she replied. "As a matter of fact, I had considered that possibility earlier, but Dan's presence made it awkward. Besides, the sun will be coming up in an hour or two and we'll both be going our separate ways. What a pity."

Despite a screaming voice that advised him to pick up his marbles and go to bed, the admission that she had actually entertained the thought of seducing him awakened an unexpected surge of energy that prompted him to ask: "Are you still interested?"

Walking over the short distance that separated them, she placed his large, sweating hands around her waist and exposed herself. "I'm not a kid any more you damn Yankee, full of movie-like fantasies. I'd be satisfied with a hug and a pat on the butt, if that's all there is. You're really not that old. You just think you are. Give it your best shot, big guy, fly me to the moon!"

Too far down the road to resist her openness, he leaned forward and kissed her on the lips and asked, "Your place or mine?"

Chapter 5

Goodbye Old Friend

When Neal finally woke up that morning he was alone and somewhat vague about what had transpired over the past few hours. A quick glance around the room, however, reassured him that Sally had not yet left the estate. The gown she had worn lay neatly folded in her open suitcase at the foot of the bed. How clever she had been to provide him with the opportunity to return to his room un-noticed while she distracted the attention of those who were already up and about. Grateful for her thoughtfulness he rolled across her side of the bed where the smell of her still lingered and walked gingerly back to his room.

There was something therapeutic about a shave and showering, he thought, toweling his body dry in the large bathroom connecting their rooms. Dressing later, his recollection of the previous evening began to improve somewhat. Second only to her spirited affection, the incident that began reshaping itself most vividly was Jimmy Mullin's theory about how Billy Newman had died. Last but not least was the mysterious activity that had gone on between Dan's boat and the unidentified latecomer. Events he felt were somehow related, but as yet, did not involve him.

Dressed only in shorts, a sport shirt and sandals, he combed his hair, patted on some aftershave and headed downstairs toward the smells that were wreaking havoc with his stomach.

When he entered the kitchen, Polly was standing at the stove frying bacon and tending to a deep fat fryer full of corn fritters.

Henry sat at one end of the kitchen table talking loudly over the phone while Sally sat at the other end chatting with Polly. When Neal entered she turned her eyes toward him and said, "Welcome back to the land of the living, party boy. Did you sleep well?"

Neither Polly nor Henry saw the wink she gave him that prompted his reply. "I must come here more often. The room service is excellent."

During a break in his phone conversation, Henry welcomed him silently with a friendly hand gesture and continued talking intermittently, as he left the kitchen and went into the family room, closing the door behind him.

Hearing the door close, Polly turned away from her cooking long enough to comment, sarcastically, "One of these days I'm going to divorce that man for alienation of affection. I think he's in love with that damn cell phone." Pausing to flip the bacon, she added, "If I ever catch him kissing that thing, he's outta here!"

Neal and Sally looked at one another simultaneously trying desperately not to laugh, but when Polly did, they joined her until tears came to their eyes.

Inside the family room Henry had just concluded his conversation when he heard loud laughter coming from the kitchen. Curious, he returned to find them all still laughing and wiping their eyes. "Okay, you guys, what in the hell is so damn funny?" he asked, starting to laugh himself.

Neal was the first to recover. "Polly thinks you're having an affair with your cell phone, Henry."

"Ho-ho-ho," he responded, taking Polly's remark in stride. "That cell phone's making me a lot of money, honey, so don't knock it. Now, lets get serious. Neal, why don't you make all of us one of those Bloody Marys you're so famous for. That'll get this day started on the right foot. I'm sure Billy would second the motion were he here, God rest his soul."

Neal was only too happy to accommodate the suggestion and started for the family room. At the same time, Sally stood up and said, "While he's doing that, I'm going upstairs and pack my suitcase. I'd like to get an early start home right after breakfast." Hesitating for a moment, she asked, "By the way, has anyone seen Dan this morning? He said he would be here to say goodbye."

"He's probably still asleep on his boat," Henry replied, "Let me go check on him."

When he reached the dock Dan's boat was no longer there. Surprised and a little angry, he returned to the family room and approached Neal. "His boat's gone! Did you hear him leave?"

Neal's thoughts flashed back immediately to the scene he had witnessed the previous evening. For a moment he hesitated saying anything about the mystery boat, but felt Henry should be made aware of the incident in case it should repeat itself in the future. Handing Henry his Bloody Mary, he asked, "Does Dan go fishing early in the morning very often?"

"Not to my knowledge," he replied, "If and when he does go, he usually flies his plane to Nags Head and goes out on his friend's boat. He figures it's cheaper that way."

A moment later he commented, rather dryly, "He calls it fishing. I call it, cigarettes, whiskey and wild, wild women. I can't complain, though. Last year he was our top salesman. Sold almost a million dollars worth of property. That's pretty remarkable for a kid who flunked out of every school we put him in, wouldn't you say?"

"Yes, I would," he agreed. "I only dreamed about that kind of money when I was his age."

As they started toward the kitchen, he stopped Henry for a moment and described what he had seen taking place on Dan's boat just after midnight. When he finished, he questioned him on the incident, "Now both boats are gone. Does that occur very often? Or, were you even aware that it happens?"

Henry looked very concerned. Before entering the kitchen he prompted him not to mention anything about what he had witnessed to the women. "I want to confront Dan about this first."

Neal agreed.

When they entered breakfast was already on the table. The women, as one might expect, were busily helping themselves, chatting and, for the most part, ignoring the men.

He and Henry had only been seated for a few minutes when the phone rang. Henry excused himself and went back into the family room again to answer the call, suspecting that it might be Dan with some lame excuse for why he wasn't here. Meanwhile, Neal filled his plate and avoided mentioning anything about Dan's whereabouts. After all, Dan's affairs were none of his business.

"Did Henry ever get that lazy-ass son of ours out of bed?" she asked, obviously irritated. "Sally will be leaving soon."

"I don't know," he lied. "I was fixing the drinks and didn't pay much attention to what Henry was doing. You'll have to ask him."

Several minutes later Henry returned. Judging from the expression on his face, the phone call had upset him. Keeping his focus on the plate he was preparing, to control his anger, he calmly announced, "That was our son calling to tell us he would not be joining us this morning. Apparently, one of his friends ran his boat onto a shoal and called him to come and pull him off. At least, that's the story he told me."

Over the top of her glasses Polly looked back at him and said, angrily, “Baloney! He just didn’t want to get stuck with driving us to the wake so he’d be free to do his own thing when it was over. It doesn’t take a mental giant to figure that out.”

“Well, whatever,” he said, visibly upset. “He promised to meet us at the restaurant, and expressed his disappointment for not being here to say goodbye to Sally. As usual, he passed the buck to me.”

She accepted the news graciously, and for everyone’s sake acted as though the news was of only minor consequence.

From that moment on everyone concentrated on breakfast. Conversation purposely avoided any reference to Dan, or his whereabouts, and refocused more importantly on Sally’s departure. When she was ready to leave, they gathered in the front hallway. In an effort to discourage Henry and Polly from following them, Neal stepped forward immediately and picked up her bag, offering to escort her to her car. The gesture was obviously made to give them a few minutes alone, so Henry and Polly hugged her goodbye and stood in the doorway waving as the two walked slowly across the yard to her car.

Before getting in she rose up on her toes, kissed him affectionately and whispered, “Thanks for being such a good sport last night, Sir Galahad. I shall remember you always. You’re a nice man, and I hope I have the opportunity to tell your lady friend that someday. Goodbye and good luck. I’ve got a feeling you’re going to need it.”

As her car drove away in the hot, early afternoon sun, he spoke quietly after her, “I’ll never see you again, my funny Valentine, but you will be remembered.”

Returning to the house, he joined his host and hostess in the kitchen where they were discussing a plan Dan had suggested to his father when he talked with him earlier. The plan, as Henry explained it, was suggested to accommodate Dan’s invitation to take Neal out on the bay the following day and to provide him with a ride to the airport on Monday.

Since Henry and Polly had originally intended to return home immediately following the wake, Dan suggested that Neal spend Saturday and Sunday nights on his boat. After all, he pointed out, the marina was much closer to the airport than their home, and would allow Neal more time with Billy’s family, instead of wasting it on the highway driving back and forth from their estate.

“There really isn’t that much for you to do here” Henry admitted, “but there is at the beach. Besides, I’m sure Jennifer and her friends would enjoy spending more time with you after coming all this way. Unaccustomed as I am to praising him, I think Dan’s plan makes good sense.”

"And he doesn't make very much sense that often," Polly added. "I think you'll probably have more fun with him than with us old fogies. Go ahead and enjoy yourself while you're here. Who knows when you'll get back this way again?"

"Well, if it's okay with both of you, it's okay with me," he conceded. "I guess it does make sense. I'll change my clothes and pack my bag. Call Dan to let him know he's going to have company. I just hope he knows what he's letting himself in for."

Polly looked at him with her eyebrows raised and chuckled, "It just may be the other way around, my friend. Please be careful."

In no time at all, he had returned downstairs and noticed an old grandfather clock standing majestically in the entry hall with its hands pointing toward two-thirty. When he inquired about it, Henry told him the clock had been in his family for generations. "I shudder to think what will happen when my two kids start fighting over it," he sighed.

Recalling how long it had taken to reach the beach when he used to travel there with his own family, he estimated Henry would want to leave around three o'clock. Leaving his bag and briefcase near the front door, he proceeded to the family room to kill the remaining time. With slightly nervous hands he mixed a vodka tonic and sat alone at the bar attempting to sort out the unanswered questions surrounding what had happened on the dock last night, including what Dan had told his father over the phone that morning.

First of all, he was sure Dan didn't know that he and Sally were both witnesses to the mysterious boat arrival the previous evening and the questionable activity that took place between the two boats. Secondly, why would Dan make up a story just to get out of driving his parents to the wake, unless there was another reason why he had to get there early? Finally, what connection did this have with Jimmy Mullins' questionable theory concerning Billy's death? Unfortunately, there were too many unanswered questions to establish a connection without more information. Maybe, he hoped, more would come to light after he talked further with Dan, Jimmy and possibly others.

By the same time he finished his drink, Henry and Polly reappeared and suggested that they leave so they could enjoy their long overdue opportunity to see the Newman family again without being hurried. Thoughtfully, he remarked, "Seems as though the only time we get to see our old friends anymore is when one of them dies."

Soon after they were in the limousine and on their way, he recalled how every one in the Hughes family enjoyed conversation of any kind, except for Polly. She listened well, but only spoke when what she heard sounded like a bunch of nonsense.

Henry, Dan and their daughter, Mary Ellen, on the other hand, would talk to a rock, as Polly put it. So, most of the conversation during their occasional trips to the beach was between the three of them. Curious why their daughter hadn't made an appearance at last night's party, he asked Henry what had happened. "Mary Ellen phoned yesterday just before you and Dan arrived from the airport," he explained. "She told us that the gear shift linkage under for her van was loose, so she had to stay home until the mechanic came to fix it, temporarily. Unfortunately, he was late getting there. And by the time he got it working again, it was too late to bother. She expected to see you sometime over the weekend, not knowing that plans had changed this morning, and that you would be spending the next two days at the beach with Dan."

"I called her this morning," Polly interrupted. "She told me the mechanic who fixed her chair lift yesterday strongly encouraged her to bring the van to his shop today so he could fix it permanently, rather than run the risk of causing more damage or possibly serious injury. That's why she couldn't make it over to say goodbye. That, she left up to me."

"I feel badly about coming all this way without seeing her," he apologized, "I only talked with her briefly before leaving San Diego."

"Not to worry," Henry assured him, "I'll make sure she knows that you asked about her. That will make her happy."

For the next several miles everyone seemed preoccupied with the scenery and gray clouds forming over the ocean until Neal broke the silence. "For that matter, I've had very little time to discuss in any detail what Dan's been up to all these years, except what he mentioned about being a licensed pilot. I know he works for you now, but what about all those in-between years?"

"You tell him, Henry," she remarked, keeping her eyes focused on the clouds in the distance. "I'm tired of those memories."

The tone of her voice was indication enough for him to realize that he had asked the wrong question. Henry, on the other hand, seemed eager to explain her remark and began a explanation that lasted all the way to the beach. "I doubt that you were even aware of the situation, but when Dan was a teenager he had a crush on your oldest daughter, Karen. Though they didn't attend the same school together, she found out that he was hanging around with a rowdy bunch of kids who were into smoking marijuana. Pot, as they called it then. That, of course, ended whatever chance Dan thought he might have had with Karen, because she wasn't interested in anyone who fooled around with the stuff. For having that much sense, you can give credit to Janet and her mother."

"I guess there were a lot of things I didn't have a clue about back in those days, considering everything that was going on in my life at the time. Open-eyed blindness, I guess you'd call it."

"We fully expected Dan to wind up in a rehab center one day, but for some strange reason he suddenly developed a serious interest in flying. The way he explained it to me years later was that a friend had offered to take him up to teach him how the controls operated, so Dan took him up on it, just for kicks. When he came back down to earth he was hooked. Getting his pilot's license was all he could think of and gave him the incentive to clean up his act. It literally saved his life."

"And just in time, according to his doctor," Polly added. "He was one messed up kid."

"Is he still flying?" Neal asked, amazed by the drama that was unfolding.

"For a time he was content to fly for hire, but that soon bored him. One weekend after returning from a party at the beach he told us about a man he had met from Florida who offered him a job flying supplies to small resort hotels in the Bahamas Islands. After that, we only saw him once or twice a year. Long enough to let us know how well he was doing and how many celebrities he had met. We finally thought the day had arrived when we could stop worrying about him."

"Unfortunately, we were sadly mistaken," Polly remarked.

Based on familiar landmarks that were passing by occasionally, he recognized that they were rapidly approaching their final destination and felt compelled to pursue the meaning behind Polly's last remark.

"What do you mean, sadly mistaken," he asked, "Don't leave me out there hanging on a limb."

Polly laughed. "We don't have enough time to go into details," she replied. "You'll be with him this evening and all day tomorrow, so ask him then. I'm sure he'll be more than willing to answer your questions."

The beach community where Jennifer Newman lived had only one restaurant called Nick's. The restaurant, and a small grocery store next door were the only source of food, drink and entertainment for the entire community. Its location boasted an unobstructed view of the ocean and a never-to-be-built-on public beach. Nick struggled to make end's meet, initially, because the community was so remote. Ironically, its remoteness was what began attracting more and more residents and eventually turned it into a gold mine. It was fitting then, that the owner should offer to host

Billy's wake by restricting access to the general public for a few hours so the Newman family and their guests could honor his passing privately.

Jennifer's beach house was located on the community's ocean road about a mile south of Nick's. Only a short driving distance away was the marina that provided docking facilities for property owners and visitors. Dan, as Henry explained, maintained a slip there for his boat. The same boat where he had suggested to his father that Neal spend the next two nights, a wise and practical plan at the time.

When Henry's shiny black limousine stopped in front of the restaurant, a uniformed security guard signaled him to lower his window and asked to see his invitation. After checking its authenticity he smiled and looked past Henry into the back seat. "You would be Mr. Neal Thomas?" he asked.

"That is correct, officer. Do you want to see my driver's license?"

"No, that won't be necessary," he replied, refocusing on Henry. "That roped off area in front of the restaurant was reserved for you, Mr. Hughes. Pull right in."

Before entering the restaurant, Neal's eyes made a quick survey of the oceanfront across the street and the sunlit thunderheads that sat ominously on the horizon. Turning to Polly, he remarked, "Jennifer never does anything half-assed, does she? I hope it doesn't rain on her parade."

As the three of them entered the bar area they were greeted by a nicely dressed young man in his early forties whom Neal recognized immediately as Billy's son, Carl. After greeting them all, he turned to Neal and invited him into a friendly hug that caused Carl to tear-up. Remembering him to be a sensitive child, he held him for a moment, patting his shoulder and encouraging him to, "Let it out, kid. Let it out."

When the two men finally separated, Carl pulled out his handkerchief and said, sheepishly, "Thanks, Mr. T. I knew I'd lose it. Mom's waiting for y'all in the dining room."

Suggesting that Henry and Polly take the lead, he followed and reminisced about a time when the Newman and Thomas children played together on the beach in front of their house, happy and carefree as little puppies.

When Jennifer saw her son approaching with three familiar faces following close behind, she smiled and rose to greet them. With outstretched arms, she embraced both Henry and Polly, and then turned toward Neal. As she came into his arms the years they each had spent raising their separate families seemed to vanish. She was still the blue-eyed blonde that had seduced his best friend and bore him two beautiful children. There were no tears. Except for some noticeable weight loss, she looked exactly like he had pictured her before they arrived.

Following her mother's lead, Cindy Newman also greeted him with a friendly embrace and suggested enthusiastically, "You must find time to tell me all about Karen and your family before you leave, Mr. T. I'm dying to hear all about what y'all have been doing way out there in California."

"Deal!" he promised, seating himself next to her mother at the family table while Henry and Polly did the same. All of the remaining tables in the room were filled and alive with spirited conversation. Unofficially, he assumed, the wake had begun.

Almost immediately, a waitress who Jennifer introduced as Sue came to the table to take orders. It was a lengthy process but she managed to complete the task in good humor, having served Jennifer and her friends and family for years. Being the mother of several children herself helped matters considerably.

Moments after she left, Jennifer stood and tapped her glass with a spoon several times to get everyone's attention. Then, after all but a few had quieted down, she addressed the gathering. "First of all, we're here to honor Billy's passing, not to cry in our beer. It would upset Billy if he knew we were wasting good booze. As specified in his will, he wanted everyone to eat, drink and have a good time on him, just as you would at any Irish wake. Even though, as you all well know, he wasn't Irish."

She paused for a moment to let the laughter subside, and then continued: "As I'm sure you all are aware, Billy and I had our problems. But, who hasn't? Water down the toilet. We loved each other as best we knew how, given our differences. So, I'm not going to stand here and make excuses for either of us. What's done is done, and that's that. Now, let's have a good time for his sake, God rest his ornery soul."

Only seconds after she sat down, Carl remarked, "Gee, mom, you could have at least waited until we got our drinks!"

"Sorry about that, son," she replied, and then laughed. "You sounded just like your father."

Sue's arrival was welcome relief from the sobriety Neal had pledged to maintain until after he had met and paid his respects to Jennifer and her family. That promise had now been fulfilled. It was time to honor his old buddy's last wishes.

In keeping with that same thought, Jennifer waited until everyone had been served before raising her glass in a sweeping gesture and crying out loudly, "To Billy!"

Contrary to what he had expected, there seemed to be a deliberate attempt to downplay formality, to the extent that most guests were dressed casually in beach attire. Puzzled, he turned toward Jennifer and said,

"If I had known the wake was going to be this informal, I'd have worn shorts."

"You should have," she replied, "I told everybody to wear whatever they were comfortable in. Billy would have wanted it that way. After all, this is the beach, and this is what beach people wear. Billy would have a fit if he knew his old buddy had come to say goodbye in a coat and tie. Besides, it's hot!"

He made no attempt to argue the point. Everything she had said made sense, so he removed his blazer and necktie to help reduce the droplets of sweat that were already starting trickling down his back.

"Now you look like the Neal Thomas I used to know," she remarked, "Not some damn funeral director."

As he settled back in his chair to observe the sea of faces that had gathered there, he noticed Dan Hughes approaching with an attractive woman at his side. It wasn't until they were directly in front of him that her features caused his heart to skip a beat.

"This used-to-be girlfriend of mine claims she knows you, Mr. T," he remarked, as if doubting her claim. "Care to comment on that?"

Ignoring Dan, he got up, walked around to where the couple stood and confronted her. "Vicki! What in the world are you doing here?" he asked in surprise.

Dan's mouth fell open and his eyes bulged as the answer to his question became embarrassingly obvious. Unable to contain herself any further, she laughed and replied in a liquor-flavored, western drawl, "Well pilgrim, I live here. What's your excuse?"

Unaware that Vicki was the daughter of Jennifer's friend and neighbor, Trisha Daniels, he took her by the arm and escorted her over to Jennifer and attempted to introduce her. Jennifer, however, interrupted his good intentions by explaining, with some amusement, "Neal, "I've know this woman since she was a little girl. She's Sam and Trisha Daniel's daughter. Your girls used to play with her when you and Janet came down on weekends." She paused a moment to embrace and welcome Vicki, and then turned back to remind him, sarcastically, "You wouldn't remember her as a child, my dear friend, because most of the time you and Billy were off drinking someplace, probably up here. You guys didn't know what time it was, let alone who the kids were."

Immediately after Jennifer returned to her chair, Vicki sat down to chat with Cindy, ignoring Dan completely.

Dan, somewhat peeved by her indifference, sat next to his parents who seemed to be engaged in serious conversation.

Jennifer couldn't have cared less about what was going on around her until Neal said he was going to the bar to get another drink. "Wait a minute," she said, "I'll go with you."

Seeing her enter the bar empty handed was signal enough for the bartender to begin mixing her drink and he had it ready when she arrived.

"Might as well give Mr. Thomas a double vodka tonic while you're at it, Freddie. He's the gentleman who came all the way from California to say goodbye to Billy. I'd say that deserves something special, wouldn't you?"

"Yes m'am," he replied. "Be my pleasure."

As soon as Freddie handed Neal his drink, Jennifer took him by the arm and led him to the outdoor patio deck where they sat facing away from the growing noise inside. That's when she asked, "What was all that arguing going on between Dan and his parents? Sounded like he was being raked over the coals."

"I'm not quite sure. It could be related to something I saw late last night just before I went to bed."

"Which was…?"

"Jimmy Mullins was the last one to leave the party last night, but before he did we met outside on Henry's dock briefly for a little talk. He told me pretty convincingly that Billy's death was no accident. Are you aware that an investigation is underway to prove he was murdered?"

Jennifer's calmness in the face of what he had just told her convinced him that what Jimmie Mullins had revealed to him was not all together his imagination working overtime. Before he could apologize for bringing up the matter, she turned her eyes toward the rapidly approaching storm out over the ocean and said, "I know all about what Jimmy thinks he has exclusive information on. He has a big mouth, and it's going to bite him on the ass one of these days. Before that storm chases us indoors, go get us two more drinks and I'll tell you a little story about your best pal, Billy."

Purposely avoiding anyone who might interfere with his prompt return, he entered the bar and stopped one of the waitresses, giving her the order. "We'll be out on the patio deck," he explained. "Bring them there."

The five-dollar bill he stuck down her blouse brought a smile immediately. "Thank you, sir! You certainly do know how to get a girl's attention."

Returning to the deck he moved a chair closer to Jennifer, whose attention was still focused on the gray wall of rain that threatened to arrive in only a matter of minutes. "Drinks will be here in a jiffy," he assured her, "Now, what's this story you want to tell me?"

"After Billy and I divorced, he lived in town and I moved down here because it was nearer my job. After he retired, he sold the town house and moved into a condo near the marina. With nothing better to do, and no hobbies except his art collection, he began a routine of boating to a place called Shep's, a waterfront bar not too far away where he knew everyone. And, probably had a thing going with one of the waitresses."

"That's a given," he joked. "Didn't he always?"

"One day Pete Boggs, Shep's manager, asked Billy if he would mind bringing him a few hard to get supplies that a friend would deliver to his boat once a week. Of course, big-hearted Billy agreed. For services rendered, Boggs gave him all of his drinks on the house."

"Billy bankrupted him, right?"

She laughed and was about to continue when their waitress arrived. When Jennifer attempted to tip her she explained that the nice man sitting beside her had already taken care of that.

Jennifer shook her head, told the girl to bend over and shoved a few dollars down her bodice and remarked, "I can see why."

When the buxom young women left and was no longer a source of distraction, she continued. "Several weeks ago Billy received an official notice that he was being called to testify in a court hearing about his relationship with Pete Boggs. Apparently, Boggs was suspected of being involved in the distribution of drugs throughout the area. Private boats like Billy's were suspected of being used for that purpose. As a result, some of the local boat owners were being called in for questioning."

"No offense Jennifer, but Billy wasn't smart enough to traffic drugs. He couldn't find his butt with a working party, let alone smuggle drugs."

"You're assuming the dumb-ass knew what he was doing."

"Boggs set him up, didn't he?"

"Bullseye! Now you know everything big mouth Mullins knows, except what I'm going to add to your plate."

Leaning close to him, she whispered, "Call it a gut feeling, but I'll bet you my house against your plane ticket home that Dan Hughes is somehow mixed up in all this. I hope I'm wrong."

Hesitant to mention what he had witnessed the previous evening, he shook his head and slumped back to think about the advisability of spending the next two nights on Dan's boat. The threat of loosing the opportunity to confront him about what Jimmy Mullins and Jennifer both suspected, and an explanation for the statement his mother had left him with just before they arrived earlier that day, only reinforced his resolve. Rather than turn the afternoon into a snipe hunt, he remained silent, giving the impression that he was seriously considering her bet.

Because of his prolonged silence, she became concerned that she might have hurt his feelings, given his close relationship with the Hughes family. To put him at ease again, she reached over and patted his hand. "Not your problem, my dear Mr. T," she assured him. "What will be, will be, regardless of you and me. So let's forget about Dan and get on with our day."

About that time Henry and Polly approached from inside. They appeared to be miffed about something, or someone. Out of courtesy, Neal stood to offer Polly his chair but she preferred to stand while Henry explained that they had decided to leave early because of the approaching storm. From the look on his face, and the emotionless tone of his voice, Neal suspected that something else had happened to encourage their early departure, however, he made no attempt to change their mind.

After expressing his regrets and embracing Jennifer, briefly, Henry turned toward Neal, shook his hand and said, almost as if he were preoccupied with some other thought, "It's always a pleasure to see you, Neal. Next time I hope you'll bring Paula and stay with us again. Please give our fondest regards to Janet and the girls. We really do miss y'all."

When she knew her husband had finished, Polly stepped forward to embrace Jennifer and whispered something that no one else could hear. As they started toward the door, Henry stopped abruptly and turned toward Neal. "I have instructed Dan to spare no expense in making sure you're well taken care for the next two days, and to get you to the airport on time."

"I appreciate that, my friend. I'll be in touch."

After the couple passed through the restaurant on their way out, Neal threw his warm, iceless drink over the railing and suggested that they rejoin the party inside, but she just sat there staring up at him.

"Something wrong?" he inquired.

"You waited all this time to tell me you weren't going back with them," she answered, obviously upset with him.

She had always been a feisty little spitfire. He could tell by the look in her eyes that she hadn't changed much. Before she could utter another word, he described what had taken place that morning. The explanation seemed to pacify her a bit, especially the part where Henry had convinced him that he would have a much better time at the beach than with them.

"That's true," she said, smugly. "They truly did do you a favor."

Inside the restaurant the young waitress that had first served them noticed they were empty handed, so she had the bartender make two fresh drinks and delivered them outside. As she approached, Neal glanced at his watch. It was almost six o'clock.

"You're very observant, young lady," he remarked. "You just saved me from getting my butt chewed out."

Unable to resist the window of opportunity he had just left open, Jennifer waited until he was about to tip her and cautioned, "I wouldn't be too sure about that if I were you, lover boy."

Embarrassed that she had arrived in the middle of something personal, the young girl excused herself and started to leave, however, not before Neal playfully stuffed another five dollar bill where he had before, and joked, "Will you still love me when the well runs dry?"

Laughing at his silly question, she humored him and replied, "You bet, lover boy!"

Reminded of how much she had always enjoyed his verbal playfulness with children, and women of all ages, for that matter, she thought how satisfying it was to know there was still someone from her troubled past who had not changed with time. What a splendid testimony to their friendship for him to have come from so distant a place to say goodbye to his best friend. She wondered if Billy would have done as much if the situation had been reversed. She doubted it, but then again, what did it matter.

Of significantly more importance was the task of trying to discourage him from becoming further involved with Dan Hughes. A step in that direction, she decided, was to distract him with what her dear friend and neighbor, Graham Stone, had cooked up for Billy's grand sendoff at seven o'clock. Observing that he was still visually preoccupied with the busty young waitress who had just flattered him with her attention, she asked, "You remember Graham Stone, don't you?"

"Sure do," he replied, "As a matter of fact, I had a brief chat with him in the men's room earlier and he told me not to leave before seven. He told me you had put him in charge of Billy's grand finale."

"That's right," she replied. "Right about now Nick is going to make an announcement instructing everybody to come out here to watch the event. Hopefully, before that storm hits."

Even as she spoke, people began migrating outside. Some found chairs, some stood anxiously by railings and some wandered across the street to watch from the beach.

Next to the railing where they had moved to take advantage of an unobstructed view, he placed a comforting hand on her shoulder and recalled a weekend many years ago when he and his wife had come to the beach to attend a party hosted by Graham and Maggie Stone.

The Stones' had no children. For that reason, a lot of time was spent collecting nautical memorabilia and other oddities. One of those odd pieces was an old barber's chair that he placed behind a hand-built, western-style bar that included a full-size mirror, bottle shelves, ceiling fans, brass rails and highly polished spittoons. When they entertained at home, Graham took particular delight in sitting in his barber's chair, mixing drinks and smoking cigars, to everyone's annoyance. A career Navy man, he had retired with the rank of Master Chief, having served most of those years at sea. He was a fun loving rascal who had no equal other than Billy Newman. They were the best of friends.

As he had explained to Neal earlier, it was his plan to hide in the dunes with an old WWII, muzzle-loading mortar, and fire a series of three parachute flares out over the ocean at precisely seven o'clock. According to Neal's watch, that hour had just about arrived.

The threat of rain and growing winds were having a disturbing affect on some beach observers who began to show signs of seeking shelter when a loud "thump" captured their attention. Seconds later, two more "thumps" were heard. One by one, three successive bursts of brilliant light appeared high in the sky high and floated down until they extinguished themselves in the water some distance from the beach.

Back on the restaurant deck, Neal raised his glass skyward. In a raspy voice choked with emotion he murmured, "Goodbye, old friend!"

A few spectators cheered, some whistled, the rest watched silently until the last parachute hit the water.

Self-conscious that he might see her watery eyes, Jennifer dabbed them dry with a tissue and turned her back to the ocean. The nasal sound of her voice, however, told him she had actually shed tears for the man she had probably never really loved. "Let's get the hell inside before we get our butts wet," she uttered, turning and hurrying through the door. "It's all over but the hangover."

Sitting next to her at the bar moments later he watched the first droplets of rain splatter and trickle down the windows. Amused by what he was thinking, he shared it with her. "I think Billy just spit in our eye."

Outside, people were scurrying in every direction, gathering up children and belongings, trying to get to their cars before the full force of the storm inundated the parking lot with wet sand and mud.

Jennifer had excused herself and gone to the rest room when her son and daughter came to say goodbye. They talked thoughtfully of old times and current activities as they waited patiently with Neal, explaining that they had each hired babysitters rather than go through the hassle of dragging along all that would have been necessary to spend the night. When their mother finally returned, there were no ceremonies, only quick hugs and kisses mixed with emotion and some tearful words. "I love you, mom." They sobbed in unison. "Tell everybody, Hi, Mr. T."

Though she begged them to spend the night, they left as they had arrived; two different people living two entirely different lives.

With the wake over and a thunderstorm in progress, it was unlikely that Saturday night at Nick's would entertain any more people than were already there. Jennifer, despite the emotional trauma of the day, seemed content to sit at the bar with Neal and wait for the rain to let up.

Surveying the room for familiar faces, he noticed Vicki Daniels and her mother sitting alone in a corner drinking and talking loudly.

Dan Hughes, he observed with little surprise, was talking to the young waitress Neal had flirted with earlier. Their conversation, however, was cut short when his cell phone rang and he excused himself to seek the privacy of the sheltered entranceway outside.

"I hope that young waitress Dan was talking to has more brains than he does," he remarked, "or I'm going to be out of a place to sleep tonight."

"She doesn't need any brains," she replied, nonchalantly, "Her boy friend will be showing up here soon to drive her home. He's in the Navy."

While ordering their last drink of the evening, she asked the bartender to figure out what her bill was for the day, explaining she would come by and pay it the next day. While she waited, she turned toward Neal and asked, "You're not seriously thinking of spending two nights on Dan's boat, are you?"

While mulling over how to answer her loaded question, he was momentarily distracted by Dan's return and his hurried walk to the booth where Vicki and her mother were seated. Following a heated discussion that could be heard all over the room, he left in a huff, yelling back, angrily, "That suits me just fine!"

Surprised and curious about what the outburst was all about, he refocused his attention on Jennifer and asked, "Now, what was that all about?"

"Damn if I know," she replied. "One thing's for sure, though, Vickie isn't going to be spending the night with him. Are you sure you want to spend the next two nights on that boat with him. He'd drive me crazy."

Recognizing that she had definitely put him on the spot, he replied, "I'd rather not, but I did accept his invitation earlier today before I learned how complicated the whole idea is turning out to be. I'd feel badly just not showing up. I don't know where he went just now, but if he doesn't come back, I won't be able to find his boat anyway. Besides, don't they have a coded lock on the marina gate? I couldn't get in there even if I wanted to."

Choosing her words carefully so as not to give away the alternative suggestion she was prepared to offer, she assured him the gate code was not a problem. To solve the dilemma, she suggested that he ask Vicki if she thought Dan would be returning. Accepting that as good advice, he invited her to join him and walked over to the booth.

When they approached, Vicki exhibited none of the pleasing joviality that he was attracted to on his recent flight to Washington. Disappointed, he phrased his question as diplomatically as he could, considering the situation. "Excuse me for interrupting, ladies. I noticed Dan left the restaurant a few minutes ago, apparently upset about something. Can you tell me if he's coming back? I'm supposed to be spending the next two nights on his boat."

Lowering her scowling eyes, she replied, "How the hell would I know? Ask the waitress he was talking to when he received a call on his cell phone a few minutes ago. Maybe she knows. All I can tell you is, he was in a very crappy mood when he came back after that call. Someone must have really pissed him off, as you may have witnessed. That, and his reaction to seeing me here unexpectedly this afternoon hasn't made him someone I'd care to spend the night with, on or off a boat. I probably should have told him my vacation stated today. But that's water over the dam, I guess."

Pausing to take a rather lengthy swallow from the glass she was nervously playing with, she said, slurring her words a little, "That's the trouble with taking men for granted. They very rarely can be. Knowing Dan, I'll bet he's already got some bimbo on his boat, if that's where he is."

Outside, rain was still falling steadily. Glow from the few streetlights located up and down the beach road lit up raindrops as if they were snowflakes falling on a winter's night, lending an aura of cinematic drama to what was taking place.

Bothered by the dismal picture Vickie had just verbally painted, Jennifer foresaw only two eventualities in store for the mother and daughter duo that she and Neal had unwittingly approached for what seemed to be the answer to a simple question. One was fairly obvious; Trisha seemed dedicated to finding male companionship for the rest of the evening. Vicki, on the other hand, seemed compelled to do doing something she would more than likely regret having done the next morning.

As any concerned mother would have tried to do for a daughter in Vickie's state of drunkenness, Jennifer asked if she had driven her car to the restaurant.

Before she could answer, Trisha interrupted and informed Jennifer that they had driven there together and were perfectly capable of taking care of one another.

Possibly because the last swallow of her drink turned out to be the straw that broke the camel's back, Vicki turned toward Jennifer and asked if she would take her home, admitting openly that she was afraid she might get sick.

Jennifer, relieved that she had asked for her help, put her arm around her supportively and slid her out of the booth. With Neal's help they managed to get her on her feet. While he guided her slowly toward the front door, Jennifer hesitated a moment and threw some words of anger back at her mother. "Just be glad we give a damn, Trisha! One of these days you're going to get yourself in a heap of trouble. I just hope that beautiful daughter of yours isn't with you when you do."

Catching up with him, she pushed the door open so she could help him support Vicki's weight for the few steps it took to reach Jennifer's car. Coincidentally, it was parked next to the empty space where Henry's limo had been parked earlier that day. Noticing it suddenly sent a chill through his body when he realized that Henry had driven off with his bag and briefcase.

"Damn!" he cursed, maneuvering Vicki's wet and near limp body into the back seat. "What the hell am I going to do now?"

Returning to the restaurant wet and disgruntled, he told Jennifer what had happened and went immediately into the bar to drown his anxiety. Realizing how demoralized he was, she went immediately into the dining room and returned carrying his bag and briefcase. Setting them down beside the bar stool he was sitting on, she asked, "Does your Mother know you're out, little boy?" Watching the silly grin he couldn't prevent, she laughed and said, "Polly brought them into the dining room when Henry decided to leave early. That's what she whispered to me when they came out on the patio to say goodbye."

Visibly relieved, he pushed away the rest of his drink, deciding he had had more than enough for one day. With his baggage in hand, he started toward the door feeling a little embarrassed. "Thanks, love, I owe yeah one," he remarked. "Now we can get Vicki home. Then you can drop me off at the marina. Hopefully, Dan will be there by himself."

Holding the door open for him, she glanced back over her shoulder at the booth where they had left Trisha. She was still there, but not alone.

Jimmy Mullins had already occupied the space where Vicki had been sitting. *There's two characters deserving of one another*, she thought. *Talk about an accident looking for someplace to happen!* .

With Jennifer behind the wheel, he took a quick look in the back seat to check on Vicki. To his surprise she was still awake, staring droopy-eyed at the raindrops splashing against the window and softly humming a song he couldn't make out.

"How do you feel, kiddo," he asked, with fatherly concern. "Think you'll make it?"

Slurring her woods a bit, she replied, "You betcha, Pilgrim. Gosh that rain felt good on my face. Makes me feel like getting naked and walking the beach."

"Just don't do it tonight, will you please," he pleaded, "I've had enough excitement for one day."

Only minutes after leaving the restaurant, Jennifer turned into the Daniels' driveway and waited while he escorted Vicki safely to the front door.

Without the front door light on, and still quite tipsy, she fingered unsuccessfully through her purse in search of the house key. Finally out of patience, he took her purse back to the car and asked Jennifer to find it.

She was somewhat amused by his reluctance to go rummaging around in a woman's purse, and halfway laughed at him when she took it. Obviously, she concluded, it would probably be on the same ring with her car keys, which she found tangled up in a small garment of some kind. Placing the ringed keys in his hand, she cautioned against leaving before Vicki was safely inside with the lights on.

Returning to the front door, he tried the various keys until he finally found the right one. During the process, Vicki remained propped against the house quietly vocalizing *Singing In The Rain,* off-key, and still slurring her words. With the door now opened wide, he guided her carefully inside and searched in vain for a light switch panel. Vicki, however, knew exactly where it was. While he fumbled around in the dark she slipped out of his grasp and flipped the porch light on, allowing just enough light through the open door to see one another. As he attempted to reach for the inside light switch she sidestepped in front of him, put her arms around his neck and whispered, "Aren't you going to kiss me goodnight?"

From her vantage point in the car, Jennifer could clearly see the front porch lights come on, and some moments later, several others. While she waited for him to return, she debated whether or not to mention the risk he was taking by spending the next two nights on Dan Hughes' boat. By the same token, she concluded, he had already been exposed to enough of

Dan's unpredictable behavior to figure that out for himself. Or, had she possibly been subconsciously building a case against Dan because she wanted Neal to herself? She felt a little flushed considering that possibility when he suddenly appeared in the doorway and hurried to the car in the weakening rain.

Backing out of the driveway, she hesitated for a moment to consider the wisdom of what she was about to say, and then gave in. "Maybe it's none of my business," she remarked, "but if you have any qualms about staying overnight on Dan's boat, you're more than welcome to spend them at my place. Frankly, I'd feel more at ease with you there."

"Funny you should offer," he replied. "I actually thought about asking if you'd mind, but I couldn't figure out what to tell Dan. After all, I am his guest, supposedly."

"Some host!" she remarked. "He suddenly goes off to who knows where leaving you and Vicki without any explanation, and still hasn't come back. Does that sound like the way you'd treat a guest? I don't think so."

"Well, you're driving," he replied, seemingly unconcerned. "Hell! I'll tell him you kidnapped me."

She saw her opportunity and seized it. "Look at it this way," she began, eager to pursue her plan, "Dan's not but so dumb. He knows that his mom and dad would consider it a thoughtful gesture if they knew I had asked you to be my guest. Hell, Dan couldn't care less. Besides, I'm inclined to go along with Vicki on this one. I'll bet the reason he got mad at her this afternoon was because he had made other plans, not knowing that she was going to show up down here. He knew I'd take you in and figured you'd much rather spend the night at my house than in a cramped bunk on his boat. How am I doing?"

Try as he may, he couldn't find anything wrong with Jennifer's logic. It surprised him a little that unknowingly he was being manipulated by his friends. "I suppose you're right," he conceded. "Now what?"

"I'm going to take you to the marina so you can tell him you're spending the next two nights at my place. The name of his boat is *Foxy Lady.* He always ties up stern in, so you shouldn't have any trouble finding it. There's a slip rental listing under a light just inside the gate. Check it to make sure what slip he's in. I'll wait for you outside the gate."

Grateful that the rain had almost stopped, he got out of her car and walked toward the marina checking the time as he neared the gate. It was almost nine-thirty.

"Damn!" he sighed, feeling tired and frustrated. "Isn't this frigging day ever going to end?"

Lack of sleep, too much booze, and the bizarre lifestyle of his friends was slowly taking it's toll. Opening the weather box at the entrance gate, he punched in the code numbers Jennifer had given him. It opened.

The marina's only office was closed for the evening when he entered. Except for the light illuminating the slip listing, and a few overhead ones located along the dock for security reasons, the place was ominously dark. Studying the small map that located the boats by name and slip number, he walked down the dock in the direction of Dan's boat.

All of the boats were apparently unoccupied that evening, except for the one where Dan's slip number was posted. Anxious to get the evening over with he headed in that direction, ever careful not to make any noise in case he had a female guest. When he got close enough to read the words *Foxy Lady* on the transom, the sound of two angry voices reached his ears, neither of which was a woman's. One was Dan's.

In surprising contrast to the shack-up Vickie had suspected would be there, a man of Spanish decent was sitting across the table from Dan arguing with him in broken English. Even though the porthole was open, he still couldn't hear what they were arguing about so he moved unnoticed into the darkness along side the boat and nearer to the porthole. After several moments of silence between the two men, the Hispanic spoke, only this time he was a little less aggressive.

"The bottom line here is, two packets of cocaine are missing from that shipment you delivered to Boggs this morning, Dan. I want to know what happened to them. If you know where they are, and turn them over to me, all of this goes away. If my people find out you took them, and lied to me, you'll be swimming with the fish along with your friend Mr. Newman. Do I make myself perfectly clear?"

His intense preoccupation with what was taking place inside Dan's boat was suddenly interrupted by the sound of an approaching car. For the first time since his arrival on the East Coast, he wished he were back in California watching television with Paula. He hoped the new arrival would be just another owner coming down to check his boat, but he was wrong.

When the gate opened a woman carrying what appeared to be a beach bag entered. She was dressed casually in shorts and a knotted blouse. As she turned in the direction of Dan's slip, he knew he had placed himself between the proverbial rock and a hard place. Making it appear as if he himself had just arrived, he moved out of the shadows onto the walkway and yelled, "Hey, Dan, It's Neal. Can I come aboard?"

Inside the boat both Dan and the Hispanic man stopped talking immediately, surprised by the unexpected presence of another person. Grateful that Neal had arrived when he did, Dan yelled back, enthusiastically, "Yeah, old buddy. Come on aboard, I have someone here I want you to meet."

Based on the conversation he had just overheard, and the as yet unknown woman approaching, it suddenly became unmistakingly clear why Dan had left Vicki so abruptly that afternoon. One reason was in the cabin with Dan. The other was just about to arrive.

Observing the woman's body movements as she approached convinced him that she was more than capable of climbing aboard without assistance but he waited for her anyway, more out of an inbred respect for the rules of chivalry than her helplessness. However, she surprised him by grabbing his hand as she jumped gracefully onto the after deck.

At the same time, Dan and a Spanish looking man came up from the cabin below and into the steering lounge where Dan introduced him as Miguel Ramirez, owner and manager of a chain of Mexican restaurants throughout the Tidewater Area.

The newly arrived, fourth party, whose more than ample breasts were threatening to burst from her blouse at any moment, introduced herself as, Donna Sanders, a friend of Dan's from Virginia Beach.

An awkward silence followed that gave Neal the opportunity to excuse himself, explaining that Ms. Newman was waiting for him in the parking lot. Turning toward Dan, he purposely avoided any mention of having been invited to sleep on the boat that night and remarked, before leaving, "Sorry for the interruption, Dan. I'll call you in the morning about our cruise on the bay."

Smiling, he turned to Donna and shook her hand, expressing his pleasure in meeting her. Then, reflecting on the conversation he had over heard only moments before, he turned toward Mr. Ramirez, bowed slightly without offering his hand and said, "Buenos noches, Senior Ramirez."

While he hesitated purposely on the dock, Dan came out of the steering lounge and hurried over to the transom, motioning for him to come closer. When he squatted to listen, Dan whispered, "Thanks for coming by, Mr. T. You got me out of a tight spot by showing up when you did. I'll explain all this tomorrow."

"All I want to hear from you tomorrow is the truth, Dan," he replied, seriously. "Just the truth."

"You will," he assured him. "I can talk more freely out on the bay. Try to be here by ten o'clock tomorrow morning." Pausing a second, he asked, "You wouldn't mind if I brought Donna along, would you? She's kind of fun to have around."

Wondering in the back of his mind whether or not Jennifer was still waiting for him, he rolled his eyes up and replied, "I'll just bet she is. Sure, bring her along. I could use a good laugh."

He had barely turned away when he remembered what he had intended to bring to Dan's attention regarding Vicki's reaction to how abruptly he had left her after the wake that afternoon.

"Hey Dan," he called back. "Maybe it's none of my business, but I think it would be a good idea if you cleared the air with Vicki whenever you can. She was expecting to see a little more of you this weekend. She's on vacation, in case you didn't know."

Rather than responding verbally, Dan raised his arm and gave him a smiling thumbs up and returned to the cabin wondering why Vicki hadn't called or written about her vacation. "Women!" he cursed. "Can't live with'em, can't live without'em."

While Neal walked quickly toward the gate, Jennifer sat nervously alone wondering what could be taking him so long. She had seen the young woman arrive and knew instinctively that she was more Dan's type, than Neal's. She was almost running out of patience when his silhouette appeared at the marina gate. Relieved that nothing had happened to him, she started the engine. While she waited, another man followed not too far behind Neal and left in a car that appeared to have been waiting for him. Turning on her headlights she was able to take a quick look at the license plate. It read: **MIGUEL**.

Once Neal was inside her car and they were on their way back to the beach house, he apologized for the delay and told her about his unexpected encounter with Miguel Ramirez, followed by the arrival of a girl named Donna. He did not explain, however, what he had overheard, or that Donna would be going on the cruise with them the next day. As far as he was concerned, those two topics would be better discussed after the cruise, when he had the benefit of hearing more about Dan's relationship with both of them.

As Jennifer turned into her driveway he suddenly laughed, remembering what both she and Vickie had accused Dan of earlier that evening. "You and Vicki were right about the shack-up," he remarked. "Not bad."

Walking into the Newman beach house after almost thirty-five years was like turning back time to a period when his arms would have been full of children's toys, beach bags and a liquor case packed with vodka. Not much had changed. A few new pieces of furniture had replaced the old, and some of Billy's painting collection had been rearranged. For the most part, however, the inside was very much the way he remembered it.

Setting his two pieces of luggage off to one side, he hung his damp jacket on the back of a chair and made himself comfortable at the kitchen counter while she sat a bucket fille . with ice and a bottle of vodka on the counter in front of him. Reaching into one of the overhead cabinets, she brought out two glasses and remarked, wearily, "Why don't you fix us a nightcap while I get comfortable. I think a little quiet togetherness is deserving before we call it a night, don't you?"

Walking toward her bedroom she heard him reply, "I sure do. By the way, which bedroom do you want me to use tonight. I'd like to get comfortable too."

"Either one. They're both empty."

In less than five minutes he had changed into a pair of shorts, a T-shirt and beach sandals, comfortable and relaxed for the first time that day. He was in the kitchen mixing their drinks when she returned with her hair attractively brushed out and her lips freshened with lipstick.

Typical of most women, she rarely went barefoot, preferring raised heels to give the appearance of being taller. Tonight was no exception. Whether she had selected it for his benefit, or for its cool, loose comfort, he felt a flush come over him trying not to stare at what her body was doing underneath the floor length gown she wore. On a thinner woman, the gown might have hung without contour. On her, however, it accented the full roundness of her breasts and buttocks, none of which bore any evidence of being contained by underclothes. The most distracting aspect of her attire was the undulation of her breasts as she moved busily about the kitchen, seemingly unaware, or concerned, about the affect she was having on him.

Having known for years that his moods could be easily influenced by the type of music he enjoyed, she moved casually to the CD player in the living room and selected what she knew would create the type of relaxing atmosphere they were both looking for: *Piano Masterpieces.*

Setting the volume to a level that was not distracting, she returned to the counter where he sat looking silently at the darkness outside and stood across from him.

"You think of everything, don't you?" he commented in a pleasing, complimentary voice. "Certainly beats the hell out of Dan's boat. Thanks for talking me out of that."

From the first time since she had seen him enter Nick's that afternoon she silently admitted that everything she had said or done that day was predicated on her intention to seduce him. Why? She didn't know, other than the fact that at one period in her life he had been the husband of her best and probably only true friend. For whatever reason, her jealous attraction to him had never quite gone away. Even at that moment the desire to have him was still alive and active. It was as if going to bed with him represented something she couldn't stand to deny herself, as was true of so many other passions she had had in her life. But, reluctant to cross that point of no return, she held back her desire to make an aggressive move, and asked, "What's on your mind?"

"If I thought it was what I hoped would be on yours, I'd tell you," he replied. "Being turned down would really ruin my day."

She relaxed in the clever humor of his reply and moved to the other side of the counter, smiling as she slid between his parted knees. It was obvious to her now that he too was laboring under the same hesitancy that had controlled her only a moment ago. Satisfied that they now stood uninhibited on the little piece of common ground that kept them apart, she brought her mouth close to his and asked, "What took you so long?"

The intense passion and reckless abandon that followed their embrace lasted only a few seconds. A loud, repetitive knocking at the front door, and a woman's voice hollering, "Jennifer, Jennifer!" frightened them apart.

Startled by the untimely intruder, she told him to remain at the counter while she went to confront whomever it was that continued to knock so frantically.

Opening the door only to the limit of its chain lock, she saw Trisha Daniels standing in the half-light from her living room window, her hair and clothing in complete disarray. Releasing the lock, she opened the door and stepped out onto the front porch where she gathered her into her arms and asked with genuine concern, "Trisha, are you hurt?"

Realizing that she could be injured and might need medical help, she led her inside, relocked the door and sat her down at the kitchen table. Once again she inquired, "What the hell happened to you? Are you hurt?"

Burying her head in her hands and sobbing, she asked Jennifer to get her a drink. Moments later, she wiped her eyes dry with the tattered dress she barely had on and tried to explain what had happened. "I'm sure you saw Jimmy Mullins come over to my booth when you left Nick's this evening. He told me he was alone, so I invited him to sit down. That's when he hit on me. As you know, I was feeling no pain, and neither was he. He bought me a drink and asked why was he paying for drinks when he had plenty of booze in his motor home. So, thinking that made good sense, we left and went there."

With her eyes half closed from crying, she hesitated a moment while she ruffled her messed up hair and then asked, "What the hell does a person have to do around here to get a drink?"

"Finish your story, Trisha, then I'll take you home," she replied. "You can have all you want there, but not here. By the way, how did you get here?"

"Hold your horses, will ya," she stammered. "Now, where the hell was I? Oh yeah, in the motor home. Well, we had a couple of drinks standing around this little bar he's so damn proud of. I guess he made it himself, or so he told me. Then he starts kissing me all over and begging me to lie down on the couch with him. When I said no, the jerk pulls out his penis and wants me to get him off right there, so I threw my drink in his face and ran back into the restaurant. I waited there until I was sure he had gone, and then drove home. I must have dozed off, because when I woke up I was stuck in the sand about a block from here. So, I started walking. When I passed your place I saw the lights on and came up, hoping I could use your phone to call Vicki. Sorry about the bad timing."

Disappointed that what was beginning to look like a very promising evening had been abruptly ended, Neal interrupted before Jennifer could volunteer, and said, "There's no need to disturb Vicki. She's not in any better shape than you are. I'll take you home."

Looking at Jennifer, he winked and suggested, "Why don't you finish making those sandwiches, while I make sure she gets home alright. It's only down the road a bit. We'll eat when I get back."

Jennifer went along with his plan and retrieved her keys from an ornamental holder hanging near the kitchen light switch. Tossing them to him, she winked back and asked, "Mustard or mayonnaise?"

While he drove Trisha the short distance to her house, he made conversation with by telling her how he had met her daughter, and how much fun it was to have flown with her. The trauma of her recent run-in with Jimmy Mullins, however, was still fresh in her mind, making it difficult for her to concentrate on much else. It was only after he had escorted her to the door that she finally spoke to him. "The scary thing about this stupid incident is, if I had had a weapon with me at the time," she confessed, "I believe I would have used it. I never gave him any cause to think that I was in the least bit interested in having sex with him. Is he some kind of a nut?"

Ignoring her drunken question, he responded critically to Jimmy's inexcusable behavior until he reached her front door and rang the bell, grateful that Vicki was there to let them in.

The house lights were still on, so he knew she was somewhere inside. He was about to ring again when the door opened and exposed a droopy-eyed Vicki wrapped in a beach robe looking as if she had been wakened from the dead.

Realizing that the late-caller was Neal holding her mother up in the doorway, she hid her amusement by covering her mouth and mumbling, "You sure get around, Pilgrim."

"Skip the humor, young lady," he replied, weary from the whole ordeal. "Help me find a place to put her down, preferably in her bed."

"Been there, done that," she snickered, while leading them down the hallway to her bedroom.

Once they had her straightened out on the bed, Vicki turned out the light and accompanied him back to the front door where she held him up for a minute and asked, "If and when I get another flight to San Diego, would you let me buy you a drink for being so nice to mom and me? I promise to be a good girl."

"You were never a bad girl," he replied, diplomatically. "Only mischievous. And, the answer is yes."

When he arrived back at Jennifer's, all the lights were out. Guessing that she had grown weary of waiting and had gone to bed, he climbed the stairs and stood for a moment watching remnant storm clouds periodically expose an almost full moon. The night air was still warm and heavy with moisture, but cool compared to the heat he had endured all day. Tired and getting sleepier by the minute, he removed his shirt and let the balmy ocean breeze play on his skin until a weary voice from inside the sliding screen doors to Jennifer's bedroom interrupted his solitude.

"Sorry, old man," she apologized, "I'm too tired for any more company. Your sandwich is in the refrigerator. Sleep well, I'll see you in the morning."

Chuckling quietly, he let the pathetic urgency that had spurred his hurried return die like the futility it represented and went to bed, ever grateful for her wisdom.

Chapter 6

Thanks For The Memories

Traces of the previous day's storm were still lingering in the sky overhead when Sunday's dawn began to brighten the bedroom where he lay dozing in the self-inflicted hangover he had inherited trying to act like a kid again. Wondering what time it was, he reached for his watch on the lamp table beside him and observed through poorly focused eyes that it was eight-thirty, plenty of time to prepare for his day on the bay.

For the next few minutes he rested listlessly reviewing the previous day's activities. Especially, the near fatal embarrassment he might have experienced were it not for the mature judgment exercised by his charming and sometimes provocative hostess. He and Jennifer had always had unspoken feelings for one another, he acknowledged, which both came to realize were more competitive than emotional, lacking the characteristic feelings of remorse and regret so typical of physical encounters indulged in by their friends. How much more fun, they had often discussed, to treat sex as a very pleasant form of exercise that could be washed away with no more trouble than a refreshing shower. Again, he bowed to her wisdom.

Sounds drifting down the hallway from the kitchen jarred him back to the day that lay ahead and into a much-needed shower. Moments later in the dining room, he was surprised to learn that she had been up and about for some time preparing them both a welcomed breakfast and a full pot of coffee. At first, the conversation between them was humorous and nonsensical, but in the advent of his forthcoming day, it took on a more serious note as time gradually passed and pressured them to leave for the marina. "There are a lot of unanswered questions regarding Billy's death." she remarked while clearing the table. "Whoever was responsible won't think twice about killing again, especially if they have reason to believe that someone knows too much."

He assured her he would watch his back and not volunteer any information, or take any unnecessary chances no matter where they went that day. He also told her he would call from the boat when they were nearing the marina so she could prepare to go to Nick's with him for dinner that night, if she was comfortable being in his company.

"Let's talk about that when you get back," she suggested. "I know you feel obligated to do something, and that's very kind of you, but let's wait and see how the day goes. A lot can happen between now and the time you return. Now, let's start by getting you to the marina on time."

They were almost to the marina gate when he looked over and told her, "I just want you to know how much I appreciate everything you've done to accommodate me since I've been here. After all these years, I was afraid even you might have changed. Just between you and me, I'm glad you haven't."

As she watched him walk to the marina, she thought, *what a sweet and naïve fool you are, my friend. If only you knew how much I really have changed.*

Making his way to the pier, he noticed the lingering wind from yesterday's storm still kicking up choppy water, even though the storm itself had passed. The gentle rocking of tied-up boats reminded him of the only time he could ever remember being seasick. Ironically, it had happened when he lived in the area.

****

He had been to a party until well past midnight and hadn't actually made it to bed until around three o'clock that morning. Even though he had never been that much interested in fishing, he had accepted an invitation to join Dan's father, and other friends, to go deep-sea fishing in the Gulf Stream off the North Carolina Coast. In addition to a two- hour car ride to reach the departure landing, the fishing expedition was a two-hour ride both ways.

He lasted about an hour going out when the sandwich he had eaten at the landing's snack shop decided it wanted out. From that moment on he spent the entire trip rushing back and forth from a sleeping position in the cabin, to hurling overboard.

An hour from docking on the return trip, he felt well enough to drink a beer and keep it down, and vowed never to go deep sea fishing again. A promise he broke many times in the years to come.

****

It was with that rather unpleasant memory that he approached Dan's slip, walked out on the dock and let his presence be known. Dan's smiling friend, Donna, came from inside the cabin to greet him on the dock. Although his boarding had not been all that graceful, he had managed not to fall in the water or break a leg. Grinning like a kid who had finally accomplished something of consequence, he gave her a hug, commenting in jest, "Thank you, young lady. I never refuse a helping hand, especially such a pretty one."

Following his somewhat awkward arrival, Dan emerged from the steering lounge where he had been talking on his cell phone. He greeted Neal with more enthusiasm than he had seen him express since meeting him at the airport. Donna, he thought, seemed to be responsible for his improved change in attitude and implied as much when he shook his hand. "This young lady seems to have taken some of the barnacles off your hull, Dan. It's good to see you smile for a change."

Looking at Donna, who sat seductively nearby in one of the deck chairs, he winked and added, "If you're not having any fun, you're doing something wrong. Isn't that right, girl?"

She grinned and winked back. "That's what my Daddy always told me, Mr. T."

"Okay, you two," Dan chimed in, "Let's get this show on the road."

Turning to climb up onto the weather bridge, he shouted back at Donna, "Cast off the mooring lines as soon as I get both engines started. Mr. T, you get yourself a beer and relax. Everything's in the cooler."

One at a time he started both engines, revving them periodically to determine that they were running smoothly while Neal sat leisurely on the transom watching Donna turn loose the two lines, then quickly jump back onboard. The instant her feet hit the deck Dan eased forward on the throttles, moving the boat gently out of the slip. Once clear of the controlled speed area, he advanced them to three quarter speed and headed for calmer waters where he intended to convince Neal that he had had nothing to do with Billy Newman's fatal accident.

Listening to the sound of the boat's bottom slapping against rough water, and the salt spray wetting his face every so often, brought back the memory of a time during his childhood when Neal's parents took on the added expense of sending him to summer day-camp at a yacht club located on one of Lake Ontario's many inlets.

****

To get there and return involved a daily bus ride that started in front of the city library where he and his grammar school friends met every day for two weeks to make the trip.

The bus rides were memorable, in themselves, but the thrill of learning to sail both *Dingy* and *Lightening* class sailboats was, at his young age, an adventure beyond description.

In addition to learning how to sail, there were other activities for both boys and girls that included aquatic sports, hide and seek in an abandoned stone quarry, and a host of other competitive events. The one incident remembered with total recall, however, was when he and all his male friends got into trouble with the camp counselor for peeking into the girl's dressing room. The boys were all taking turns and laughing, until one of the girls noticed an eye peeking through a knothole in the wall separating the two adjoining rooms. Shocked and embarrassed, she let out a blood-curdling scream that put a quick end to the sightseeing adventure quickly.

Immediately, the hole was boarded over and the boys thoroughly reprimanded for their inexcusable behavior. That day's trip back to the library was memorable for two reasons, he recalled; the first was because the girls were so embarrassed they wouldn't speak to the boys for the entire trip home. The second was because it was the first time he had ever seen the private body parts of so many young girls all at one time. And, it would be his last.

****

The smile of silly reminiscence was still on his face when Dan's voice yelled from the bridge, "Hey, Mr. T, how about grabbing a couple of beers and coming up here with me. I could use some company."

His sudden request for companionship made Neal aware that his reminiscing had sidetracked him from enjoying the scenery, and discussing the sensitive subject of Billy's demise that Dan had promised to clarify. With two cold beers in one hand and no knowledge of what Donna was up to, he climbed to the weather bridge and joined him.

The first sight that greeted him was Donna's half-naked body lying face down on a beach towel spread out on top of the forward cabin. The bottom half of her thong bathing suit was barely visible, and her top was untied, exposing the bulge of her flattened breasts.

"Ain't she something?" Dan remarked, amused by the expression on Neal's face. "Can't say as I'd blame you for what you're thinking, Mr. T. I'm thinking the same thing."

Neal shook his head and replied, "I'll leave that to you young bucks, Danny boy. For an old man, that's a heart attack looking for some place to happen."

After the fantasy faded, Dan looked at him and asked, "Last night you overheard part of my conversation with that butthead, Miguel Ramirez, didn't you?"

While he remained silent trying to phrase a diplomatic reply, Dan continued. "A couple of months ago I had a hidden motion detector installed on the walkway to my slip. When the detector beam is interrupted, it activates a small red light in my cabin that tells me someone is approaching. It blinks for a few seconds and then stops. Last night the light began blinking when Miguel was questioning me about two missing packages of cocaine that he accused me of taking. The sound of your voice so soon after the light stopped blinking made it clear that you had come out onto the dock to make sure I wasn't with a woman before making your presence known. Wasn't it then that you overheard his threat through the open porthole?"

Even behind sunglasses, Neal's eyes were squinting from the sun's reflection off the water, masking his surprise. Realizing that Dan was a good deal more intelligent and observant than he had given him credit for, he simply replied, "Pretty accurate."

Accepting the fact that Dan had skillfully opened discussion on the inquisition he had come there to conduct, he replied, "Why don't you start at the beginning and explain what this involvement with Ramirez is all about? Including what your mother and dad meant when they told me they were sadly mistaken when they thought you had put the drug business behind you. What did they mean?"

Watching Donna retie her bikini top and roll over on her back, Dan knew he had to travel back to a point in time when he lived in Key West, Florida with his wife and young daughter for Neal to make any sense out of what he was about to tell him. It was there that a stranger offered him a job to do the only thing he loved more than his family; fly an airplane. "Take the wheel for a minute Mr. T," he asked, standing and moving toward the bridge ladder, "I've got to use the head and get a couple of cold beers if I'm going to tell you my whole life's story."

Halfway down the ladder, he looked back at Neal and said, "Oh, by the way, don't worry about lunch. Donna brought a picnic basket full of food and wine for us to enjoy after we get where we're going. Be right back."

Caught up in the drama of finally getting some meaningful insight about what Jennifer had suspected all along, he moved behind the wheel and followed the compass heading Dan had given him.

The sun was high now, and hot. The bridge's canvas cover, along with a strong breeze, brought some measure of relief to his tired body, as he reminisced again about his younger days at the tiller of a sailboat. That and watching Donna, as if she were one of those naked young girls he had peeked at through a knothole, so many, many years ago.

When Dan returned, he insisted that Neal stay at the wheel and enjoy himself. Giving him a new compass heading, he explained that it would take them to the place he wanted him to see. Then, after settling back with his fresh can of beer, he continued. "The period in my life my mother was referring to began in Florida. I was married and had a twin-engine plane at the time that held six people. I made a decent living flying short charters back and forth between several resorts in the Bahama Islands. On one of those trips I was grounded for two days due to bad weather. I did a lot of bar hopping at various resort hotels and became acquainted with some very wealthy people, both residents and some from all over the U.S. and Mexico. Some, I might add, were very well known Hollywood celebrities and musicians. Well, when you've got that much money, it follows that sooner or later drugs are going to come into play. Having messed with the stuff on and off during the time I was flunking in and out of various colleges, I came to the conclusion that it made much more sense to sell the stuff than to buy it. I made sure the right people were made aware of my willingness to join the program, and then sat back and waited."

After pausing to wet his whistle, he started to resume his story when Neal interrupted. "Hold that thought, Danny boy," he said, standing up and heading for the ladder. "Now it's my turn."

When he climbed down from the bridge, Dan replaced him at the wheel. Changing course slightly, he sighted on a landmark that would guide the boat to a hidden inlet where what he wanted to show Neal lay hidden in the thick, swamp-like tree moss not visible from shoreline.

Returning to the bridge, Neal noticed that Dan had changed course and Donna was no longer lying on the forward deck. Speculating that she must have entered the cabin through the roof hatch, he returned to his seat and encouraged Dan to resume his story.

"It wasn't long after I had made the decision to seek my fortune by transporting narcotics to the mainland that I was approached by an agent of the island's most notorious drug lord, Carlo Puzzi. The agent told me Carlo wanted to talk with me and advised that it would not be in my best interest to decline the invitation. The fact that I had been approached at all was proof in itself that my reputation as a good pilot had preceded me, so I bit the bullet and made arrangements to meet with him.

For whatever reason, we hit it off right from the start. Needless to say, I easily succumbed to the luxury of his home, and a lifestyle he soon began sharing with me. It was like being in a movie, Mr. T. I think the real reason he liked me was because I was an American, a better trained pilot, and more dependable than his native islanders. Carlo used me often to fly him to heavily guarded sites at various locations in the islands and South America where drugs were being grown, harvested and processed. All of this flying, of course, resulted in my spending less and less time with my wife and young daughter. To compensate them for being gone all the time, I bought them a new house, a new car and arranged with the bank to give her a platinum credit card. The novelty of all I had done to please them, however, soon wore off and the problem, once again, boiled down to her unhappiness with long separations and the constant worry over how I was making my living . She worried that she would kiss me goodbye one day and never see me again, so she asked for a divorce, and I gave it to her. We parted friends, and she promised to be there for me, if and when I ever decided to quit the cartel. Well, as you might have already guessed, that's easier said than done. Especially, when you realize you're up to your ass in alligators and no way to drain the swamp."

"Tell me something, Dan," he asked, "What did your mother mean by saying she was sadly mistaken when she thought you had finally cleaned up your act?"

Just then, Donna came out of the cabin below, grabbed a can of beer from the cooler and joined them on the bridge, unaware of what they had been talking about. Her presence there, for obvious reasons, meant that any further conversation about Dan's nefarious past would have to be put on hold, at least for the time being. Ignoring his question, he changed the subject and remarked, "I'll fill you in on that later, Mr. T. Right now I want you to focus on where we're going so you won't forget how we got here. Who knows, you may have to come back here someday."

Convinced that Donna probably didn't know any more about Dan's past than he did, he turned his attention to the shoreline and wondered, why would I come back here?

About fifty yards ahead, what had been difficult to distinguish a few minutes earlier, was now gradually coming into focus. The entrance to an inlet began revealing itself through a dense growth of overhanging trees, so thick with moss that they diffused the sunlight into beams that shined through the foliage like flashlights on the water's surface. To Neal, the scene was strikingly reminiscent of old *Tarzan* movies where crocodile infested waters wandered through vine-covered jungles, and primitive natives and dangerous animals lurked in the shadows. How absolutely fascinating, he thought, to be boating in such an unlikely place, and to be experiencing the same sense of foreboding that the explorer, Stanley, must have experienced during his search for Doctor Livingston.

Donna was equally impressed and curious. In the few short months she had known Dan, this was the first time he had asked her out on his boat. As they ventured deeper into the diminishing sunlight, her curiosity began to change to anxiety, prompting her to ask, nervously, "Dan, where in hell are you taking us?"

"You'll see in a few minutes," he replied, exhibiting more and more excitement. "You're going to love this place."

Not at all sure that his statement was a realistic appraisal of how she would react to whatever they were approaching, she sought reassurance by moving closer to Neal and asking him if he knew where they were going.

Neal's blank look and shrugging shoulders assured her that he didn't, so she sat quietly drinking from what now had become a very warm beer. Moments later, as they rounded a bend off the starboard side of the boat, the object of Dan's excitement appeared in the sun- splattered shadows up ahead. Unlike Tarzan's elevated tree house, what came into view was a boat landing stretching the full length of a pitched roof, single story shanty not much bigger than a double-car garage.

Neal was awestruck immediately by its uncanny resemblance to his Grampa John's house and laughed out loud at the story-book-like scene that was unfolding. The entire wooden structure was supported over the water on treated pilings. They ha‿ been sunk into the soft, marsh-like bottom of the lagoon on which it rested, hidden from the world for who knows how many years.

Skillfully maneuvering his boat alongside the dock, he asked Donna to secure both mooring lines to the wooden cleats that sat bolted to the dock like those one might expect to see in old pirate movies. Once the engines were shut down and the boat was secured, he retrieved her picnic basket from the cabin and grabbed a bottle of wine out of the ice compartment. Handing them to Neal, he jumped onto the dock, reached up under the roof overhang and lifted a door key from a hook hiding in the darkness there. Upon entering, the thought that struck them all, simultaneously, was to open every window as soon as possible so fresh air could purge away the musty smell of the swamp-like environment. That done, the men relaxed while Donna went immediately to unpacking food and preparing the only table in the place for their mid-day lunch.

With her busily preoccupied with domestic activity, Dan and Neal sat in a pair of old worn out sofa chairs drinking wine while he explained how he had come to discover the hideaway:

****

"This place belonged to an eccentric old commercial fisherman by the name of Shark Hadley. His only contact with the real world was limited to the trips he'd have to make to the mainland to sell his catch at the local market. Everyone treated him as somewhat of a character because of the outlandish stories he'd tell whenever he was drinking, which, according to the locals, was most of the time. Then one day, Shark lost his boat during a hurricane that had caused millions of dollars worth of damage up and down the East Coast. Without a boat, he was forced to work in one of the local fish markets to make a living, and rented a room at a local boarding house where he lived in misery, cursing the storm that had ruined his life.

One Sunday afternoon after returning from The Bahamas to join Dad's real estate business, me and a few of my friends, who were partying on my boat at the time, decided to stop at Shep's Marina where many of the local fisherman hung out. It was on that day that I met Shark for the first time, drunk and telling his story about how Hurricane Becky had taken his boat, and ruined his life. A story everyone there had heard at least a dozen or more times.

Of those who were in the bar at the time, some were either laughing at Shark, or completely ignoring him. As for me, I was fascinated by the old man's story and listened with more interest than anyone had ever shown him before. When he finally finished his story, I offered to buy him a drink, which he gladly accepted. During our brief conversation, I made a serious offer to help the poor old man get another boat so he could return to the reclusive life he longed for. I told him I'd return the next day to discuss the matter, if he'd promise to be sober when I got there."

****

Interrupting to suggest that he continue his story at the table, Donna announced that she was ready to serve lunch. The aroma of what lay waiting for them was all the coaxing they needed.

No one was more surprised and grateful than Neal when he saw the food she had brought along in her basket. The light breakfast Jennifer had fixed that morning hadn't stayed with him very long, so the fried chicken, potato salad and baked beans that were spread out before him came as a welcome surprise. Wine that had been chilled on Dan's boat frosted the glasses as soon as it was poured. Eager lips took the first sip after clicking a toast to celebrate the great day they were having.

While they ate, Dan continued his story between mouthfuls, concentrating on brevity because their departure depended upon leaving the inlet before the outgoing tide made it too shallow to travel. Neal's curiosity, however, was not to be denied by the tide, as he kept the story alive by asking, "Did Shark show up sober?"

"Damn if he didn't!" he replied, "Truthfully though, I never believed he would. I had heard about the old man for years, but had never met him before. If I hadn't been drinking that day, I probably wouldn't have offered to help, but the poor old bastard just got to me. So. I offered to loan him the money to get another boat, not realizing at the time that he owned this place and needed a boat, not only to fish, but to get back and forth to the market. You can imagine my surprise when he signed the property over to me as collateral and willed it to me if he should pass away before the debt was paid."

Dan hesitated a minute in thoughtful reflection, and then continued:

"Poor old Shark. He died one day while at sea. The Coast Guard finally found him drifting around with an empty gas tank after folks got concerned and reported him missing. They brought his body in and took his boat to the marina. An autopsy concluded that he had been dead for several days. I'll say one thing for the old geezer he never missed a payment. I finally sold the boat because I already had one at the time. Looking back, I never would have known that this place ever existed if he hadn't marked it on a map, along with directions on how to locate the inlet. Every time I'd see him, usually in his cups, he'd tell me he was going to show me where he lived some day, but never did."

"What prompted you to go looking for this place? It's not some place you could find easily. And, I doubt if it could be seen from the air."

"That's right," Dan agreed. "I never dreamed that crazy old man owned anything worthwhile, let alone a hideaway like this. When he died, I just kissed the whole matter off as a bad investment. That is, until I got curious one day and decided to investigate the area he had circled on my map one day at Shep's. It took me two tries, but I finally found the landmark he told me to look for. I should have known he'd do something bizarre to help him find his way home."

By this time even Donna was eager to hear his story through to the end, and encouraged him to continue.

"On the second trip out I paid more attention to the tide, figuring high tide was the only time I could get in close enough to see any kind of a landmark on the shoreline. Sure enough, as I approached the coordinates he had circled, I could see a white, vertical cylinder sticking up out of some bushes pretty close to the edge of the water. I beached my boat, and discovered to my surprise, that he had dug a deep hole close enough to the water to allow it to seep in. The hole was lined with a fairly large diameter piece of perforated plastic pipe for reinforcement. It stuck up above the ground about three feet. Inside the pipe, a smaller, taller shaft of solid Styrofoam floated up and down with the tide. That was his dipstick, so to speak. He could always tell when there was enough water in the inlet to accommodate his boat. Pretty clever, huh?"

Neal agreed that the marker design had been quite ingenious, but still wasn't sure where his story was going, so he asked, "The house, Dan. What about this place?"

While Donna cleared the table and tidied up before their departure, Dan lit a cigarette, split what was left of the wine with Neal, and continued. "Since the high tide wasn't due to ebb for several hours, I followed the inlet until it led me here, just like today. It goes without saying that I was more than just a little surprised with what I found. And after having come that far, I wasn't going to leave before finding out what was inside this hidden treasure."

"Hidden treasure? What in the world did you expect to find in this dump?"

"Be patient, Mr. T," Dan cautioned. "Hear me out."

"My patience is not what's worrying me, Dan. But the tide is!"

"We have plenty of time," he reassured him, and then continued: "First of all, I had to figure out how to get in the place. Without knowing where the door key was I had to break in through a window, confident that I could repair it whenever I returned. The likelihood of someone stumbling onto its location was so remote I never gave it another thought. Bad weather was the only real concern I had, so I boarded it up. I searched the place from top to bottom, hoping to find something that would make my decision to return there someday worthwhile. It wasn't until I sat down and searched through the drawers of that old desk over there that I found his *Last Will and Testament*, naming me sole heir to the place and everything in it. Can you beat that?"

Thinking about all the people and events that he had been exposed to over the past two days, and the present situation that was becoming more and more complex by the hour, Neal was too preoccupied to adequately respond to Dan's somewhat questionable good fortune, except to comment, "If I were you, my friend, and knew what you know, I'd write a book."

"Hell!" he replied, laughing at the concept, "I'd have a hard time writing a letter, let alone a book. But that's an interesting thought. Very interesting."

Donna was in the process of taking her picnic basket and a plastic bag of trash to the boat when he turned toward Neal and whispered, "Come over here, away from the door. I want to show you something."

Wondering what new surprise he was going to come up with, Neal walked back to the table and watched him get a fairly large metal toolbox from the room's only closet and place it on the table in front of him. After removing the rusted lock, he looked over at Neal's puzzled expression and began to explain what it was doing there. "This box holds a moisture-proof bag containing my personal diary and enough pictures, documentation and microfilm to expose almost all of the drug activity in this area," he revealed. " It incriminates not only political figures, but individuals in government, local politics and the entertainment industry. It's a time bomb of damning evidence. I have accumulated it over the years for the purpose of getting even with those bastards that I used to do business with, if they ever decided to do me in. It's the only insurance I have against that eventuality. Should anything happen to me, however, I'll need someone I can trust to notify the DEA of its existence, and show them where it is. That's why I brought you out here today, Mr. T. As far as the world knows, you're just an old friend who came here from California to attend Billy Newman's wake, and I took you for a boat ride. Simple as that."

"What about Donna?"

"She's harmless, just along for the ride."

It had been a long time since Neal had experienced the uncomfortable feeling of becoming involved in a potentially life-threatening situation, and he struggled with what his response should be.

Recognizing the difficulty he was having trying to deal with the unexpected responsibility that had suddenly been dumped on his friend, he attempted to ease his mind by further explaining what he was asking him to do. "I'm sure that what I've just revealed to you has come as quite a shock, but I have to tell someone. Someone I can trust, especially after hearing the threat Ramirez made last night."

"Why don't you just go to the police? Surely they could provide you with protection."

"They don't protect criminals, Mr. T, They lock them up. And I am a criminal, you know."

"I don't understand. What crime have you committed?"

"None, unless I get caught." He replied, almost humorously. That's why I need your help."

"Please explain yourself, Dan. I have no idea what you're talking about, and we're pressing the clock on getting out of here."

Looking at his watch, he agreed and continued. "I've known and admired you ever since I can remember, and so did Billy Newman. I'm also convinced Jennifer thinks I had something to do with the explosion on Billy's boat, but as God is my witness, I didn't. I've got a damn good idea who did, though, but I have no proof. What's in this toolbox is all I have. To turn it over to the police would incriminate me too. As long I keep it, I have some leverage with those who may be planning my demise because they think I've double-crossed them."

"Why? Does it have anything to do with what went on at your parent's house early yesterday morning?"

He didn't know quite how to respond to that question because he needed more time to determine just how much Neal had seen. Putting him off for the time being, he admitted to why he had brought him to his hideaway and the story behind it. "First of all, I need your solemn promise that you will come back here to get this toolbox and turn it over to the police if something should happen to me. I won't have to be worried about the consequences of having this information if I'm under a mound of dirt somewhere. You're the only person who knows what I know. Who then is better qualified to champion my salvation? As for what you saw the other evening, I'll explain it all after we get the hell out of here. Now, will you help me?"

"I'll do what I can," he replied, not sure that it was the right answer. "I just don't want to get myself helplessly compromised in all this mess. I'm too old and tired to start worrying about who's around the next corner."

"Not to worry. If anything should happen to me, just promise you'll help the authorities find this place and show them where the toolbox is. Here's the other key to it, just in case."

He knew, instinctively, that he had made a mistake by accepting the key, but out of respect for Dan's parents, and an unexpected rush of excitement at the thought of being involved in a real live adventure, he replied, awkwardly, "I promise," never dreaming where that promise would eventually take him.

While Dan locked and put the toolbox back in its hiding place, Neal closed and locked all the windows. Assured that everything was secure, the two men left the hideaway, locked the door behind them and placed the key in its hiding place up under the overhang. To assist Dan while he started the engines, Neal remained dockside until Dan looked down from the bridge and yelled, "Turn'em loose, and climb aboard, Mr. T! We're outta here!"

Once under way, Neal got two cans of beer from the cooler and started up the bridge ladder when Dan yelled down, “Stow the suds, Mr. T! How about fixing us a couple of real drinks for the ride home.”

He nodded his approval and put the beers back, thinking, *I guess it must be cocktail time.*

By the time Neal had visited the head, mixed two drinks and returned to the bridge, Dan had brought the boat almost to the mouth of the inlet where he slowed to a crawl to point out where Shark Hadley’s marker was located. “I know you weren’t paying that much attention to it when we came in here, but if you look over there at that clump of bushes you’ll see the white Styrofoam cylinder I was telling you about.”

He sighted down Dan’s arm and removed his sunglasses for a clearer view. Sure enough, the marker was visible with its cylinder floating inside the pipe like the head of a tubeworm he remembered seeing when he used to scuba dive off Baja, California years ago. “Well I’ll be damned,” he remarked with surprise, scratching the top of his head, “I thought you were putting me on.”

“Most people would,” he remarked, “but old Shark was a hell of lot smarter than most people gave him credit for. You’d be surprised how much property that old shanty is sitting on. Picture a nice bay-view community, and a marina with a restaurant where some cool dude like yourself tickles the ivories for wealthy, lounge lizard widows to throw their money at. Sound like a plan?”

“For you, maybe. I’m afraid it’s a little too late in life for me to be acting your age. Besides, my plate’s a little full right now.”

By the time the marker had faded from view, Dan had the throttles set on three-quarter speed and the bow headed back to the marina. With the course set and smooth water ahead, he asked Neal to take the wheel for awhile so he could use the head and check on Donna.

Neal accepted willingly, glad for the opportunity to be alone on the bridge for a few minutes to think back over what he had seen and heard that day, while the refreshing wind cooled his hot and sweating body.

What bothered him most was Dan’s reluctance to go into much detail regarding his so-called planned exit from the local cartel. Also, there were his suspicions that a plan was being considered to do him in, as he had phrased it earlier. One could also question, if he were doing so well in his father’s real estate business, why would he still be associated with a man like Miguel Ramirez? Why hadn’t he made any effort to reunite with his wife and daughter? What had happened between the then and now to prompt his Mother to make such a remark about his failure to get his life straightened out? From Neal's point of view, there was still a major piece of Dan's past missing from the puzzle he represented. Without it, he felt as though he would never be comfortable living up to Dan's request, even though he as much as promised he would.

As he starred at the Eastern horizon, the marina's silhouette began to take on more recognizable features, reminding him that he should ask Dan to call Jennifer to let her know that they would be arriving within the hour. By then, he hoped, maybe that missing piece of the puzzle would fall into place.

Donna was with him when he emerged from the cabin, freshly made up and rested from her nap. They went to the cooler together to freshen the empty glasses he had taken with him and to get her a cold beer, patting her gently on the backside as he did so.

While she remained on the afterdeck wistfully looking back over the foamy wake at gulls diving for scraps of food she was tossing them, Dan returned to the bridge and asked Neal to continue at the wheel. A few minutes later Neal took what he suspected would be his last opportunity to quiz him about one of the questions that had been on his mind, and asked, "What about it, Dan. What did your mother mean when she confided in me that she and your father were sadly mistaken about where your future was taking you?"

A slow, grimacing smile began to show on his face as his eyes remained fixed on the gradually approaching marina. "I was wondering when you were going to get around to that again, Mr. T," he replied, "You're a persistent old cuss."

"Yeah, I guess so, but if I'm going to commit to the help you've asked for, I want to know the whole story, not just part of it."

Dan remained silent for a moment, and then replied, in a more friendly tone of voice, "Fair enough, Mr. T. I guess I owe you that much. Nobody I know can fly with only one wing."

Lying back against his seat cushion with his eyes squinting at the approaching marina, he began unfolding the history of his infamous past.

****

"Back during the days when I worked for Carlo Puzzi, I flew a plane that belonged to him. It was a twin-engine aircraft, similar to my own, but had been modified to provide a hidden storage compartment where packages of drugs could be stored. The compartment was on the underside of the plane behind the passenger cabin. It had doors on the underside of the fuselage that opened like bomb bay doors did on World War II bombers. They could be opened, or closed, by a hidden switch in the cockpit. Each box containing drugs was rigged with an electronic signaling device, similar to a commercial airliner's cockpit recorder, so it could be located no matter where it was dropped. The intent of all this was to allow the pilot to fly over an unpopulated water site, like a reservoir, and drop the boxes for recovery by boats equipped with electronic signal detection equipment. The pilot could also jettison the payload if he were being pursued and forced to land. Well, that happened to me once on a flight from Puerto Rico to the Bahamas, and I hope will satisfy your curiosity about my Mother's off-the-wall remark to you yesterday."

Neal hesitated a moment and then remarked, smugly, "As Frazier would say, "I'm listening."

"Unfortunately, I crash-landed the airplane I was flying at that time on a lonely beach in Cuba. That incident, and its aftermath, contradicted my parent's belief that I had given up my evil ways and had turned my life around. When they were inadvertently dragged into the mess that followed, and had to pay a bundle to get me out of it, you can understand why mom referred to being sadly mistaken in her belief that her only son was going to, straightened up and fly right, as the song goes."

Handing Neal his empty glass, he suggested, "Why don't I take over while you get us one more drink before we get to the marina. That's just enough time to finish telling you, the whole story, as you put it."

After they exchanged places, he looked back at Dan silhouetted against the deep blue sky as he prepared to go below, and wondered for a moment if his life had turned out differently might he and Karen have developed a more serious relationship. Grateful that they hadn't, he contented himself with the splendor that was passing all around him and climbed down the ladder, knowing that their time together was fast coming to an end.

When he reached the cooler, Donna was sitting comfortably nearby, seemingly content to be alone with her own thoughts, which prompted him to apologize for their indifference to her being left by herself.

"That's okay, Mr. T," she remarked, "Dan told me this morning that you two had things to discuss today, so don't worry about me. I'm happy just being here. I don't need to be entertained."

Reassured that she was enjoying herself, he returned to the bridge. After checking the time, he estimated their arrival at the marina to be less than a half an hour. For that reason, he asked Dan to call Jennifer. When she answered, he thought her voice sounded a little agitated so he came right to the point. "We're only about thirty minutes away from the marina. Can you come and get me?"

"Sure," she replied, "I just hope you two characters had a good time. It's been one hell of an interesting day here. Right now I need a drink, but I'll wait until you get here. I hate to drink alone. See you in a thirty minutes."

"Everything alright?" Dan asked, replacing his cell phone in its holder. "You look a little pinched."

"I guess so," he replied, "Go ahead and finish your story. I'll deal with Jennifer later."

"There's a hell of a lot more to this story than I may have time to tell," he remarked as Neal handed him his drink. "So, I'm just going to give you the highlights. Hopefully, before this drink is gone."

****

"I was on my way to deliver a cargo of drugs to one of those tiny islands in the Bahamas when a squall came up all of a sudden just north of Haiti and blew me into Cuban air space. I was picked up on their radar almost immediately and told to land, or be forced down by their already airborne fighter planes.

When I left Puerto Rico I had enough fuel to make the Bahamas, but not enough to play grab-ass with Cuban jet fighters that far off course, so I dove down and skimmed the water hoping to elude them. The winds were so strong it took all of my concentration just to fly the damn airplane, let alone navigate. Luckily, a hole in the clouds opened up briefly and I saw the shoreline of what I hoped was Haiti, so I brought the plane down for a closer look, safe for the time being from the jets whose speed at that altitude gave me somewhat of an advantage.

I wasn't below the clouds but a few seconds when I spotted a stretch of beach about a quarter of a mile long on the edge of what appeared to be nothing but jungle. With my options running out, my first reaction was to dump the drugs. I didn't need them weighing me down no matter what I was going to do, so I turned in over the trees several hundred yards from the beach and dumped the entire load. Continuing on, I completed a long, slow turn until I was once again lined up with the beach and attempted to land. I made two passes to inspect for debris and then bit the bullet and landed. Unsuccessfully, I might add."

****

When Dan stopped talking, Neal was so emotionally caught up in his story he wasn't about to say or do anything that would distract him from hearing the ending. Even his empty glass didn't seem to matter until Dan rattled his cup and asked for a refill.

Instead of going for them himself, he yelled below and asked Donna if she would mind doing the honors. She responded willingly.

While she busied herself mixing their drinks, Dan stared steadily ahead at the rapidly approaching marina and continued:

****

"Unfortunately, I estimated the beach to be much firmer than it was that day. I was in a normal landing mode when the two main wheels touched down on the wet sand. When I set the nose wheel down, however, it hit a shallow water pocket and collapsed immediately. Of course the nose dropped and hit the sand, which finally buildup enough resistance to stop me.

During the process, I was knocked unconscious for what must have been several hours. When I finally regained consciousness I was surrounded by a group of men in camouflage uniforms with weapons in their hands. I spoke English to them, but all they did was speak Spanish to each other, and made gestures that made it obvious they didn't understand.

Moments later, one of them who had remained inconspicuously in the background, came forward and spoke to me in perfect English, the soldier was a woman. She asked me who I was, and where I had come from. I was so surprised to be confronted by an attractive woman in the middle of God knows where, I remained speechless for a few minutes trying to collect my thoughts. My head ached like hell, and I had pissed my pants somewhere along the way, which left a large wet spot on my trousers that seemed to be amusing the men for some reason.

The woman paid little attention to the others. She just tossed a blanket over my lower body and cleaned the blood from my forehead with water from a canteen. Realizing that I had a potential ally, at least for the time being, I explained what had happened. I did not, however, mention anything about drugs or where I had dropped them. I figured, the less she knew the better off I'd be."

****

Neal's patience was about to get the best of him when Donna came half way up the bridge ladder and handed him the two drinks she had prepared. He thanked her and watched with fascination as she returned to the afterdeck, still content to watch the seagulls hovering above the boat's churning wake.

It was Dan's laughter that broke his momentary fascination. "Be careful what you wish for Mr. T," he cautioned with a grin. "She's a handful."

"I'll bet. Now, tell me more about that female soldier."

****

"Several days passed by before my head stopped hurting, but I had made some progress in convincing the woman that I was just an American pilot who had flown off course and crashed his airplane.

She, on the other hand, made me understand just how serious my situation was, having accidentally fallen into one of the revolution's guerilla camps herself. She offered no encouragement or speculation about what was going to happen to me, other than to say I was being held captive until the leader of the group returned to interrogate me. When that would be she didn't say.

As a civilian captive, however, she saw to it that I was fed and allowed to take care of my personal needs, but made sure I was guarded at all times, either by herself or by one of the other rebels. I gathered from the respect they showed her that she had rank. Or, was in some way accountable only to the group's leader.

The longer I stayed there, the more determined I became to find out what strange set of circumstances had caused this lovely young woman, whose name I still did not know, to end up in Cuba as a rebel. During the few friendly conversations I felt she had contrived to make me feel less threatened, I learned that she was a runaway, native Californian from San Diego. That's all the history she volunteered, however, my gut feeling told me there was a lot more to it than that.

I had been a captive for over a week, and had become very fond of my captor, when something totally unexpected occurred. She came to me around mid-afternoon that day when I was normally allowed to go for a swim. She told me to shave, bathe, and put on a pair of fatigues she gave me, explaining that arrangements had been made for me to leave the island by boat that night.

I was stunned. When I asked for an explanation, all she said was that I had been bought and paid for. And to count my blessings for being fortunate enough to leave before her commanding officer returned. He, she emphasized, might not be so congenial.

Later that evening, she and two other rebels accompanied me to the beach where I had originally crash-landed. To my surprise, the disabled plane was nowhere in sight. She explained that it had been partially dismantled and moved into the jungle where it was being repaired. Amused, she remarked that if I could fly it in there, she could fly it out.

It was a beautiful night, as I recall; full moon and stars all over the place. To pass the time, we chatted about a variety of things, including the reason she had chosen the kind of life she was living, and her growing desire to return to her own country.

Her answers to personal questions were vague and defensive. She did, however, express some remorse over the grief she must have caused her mother when she ran away from home. Dropping the subject quite suddenly, as if she were reluctant to discuss it any further, she broke a precedent and told me what had happened to bring about my release. She did so because her two companions couldn't speak any English, and because it was to her advantage to get me back where I came from, safe, and as soon as possible."

****

Unconcerned about Neal's growing frustration, He purposely delayed reaching the end of his story to heighten its drama. That is, until Neal reached over and grabbed him playfully by the arm and said, in jest, "If you don't finish this story before we get to the marina, I'm going to toss your ass overboard."

Dan laughed, not sure that what he was about to reveal would make any sense to someone whose only exposure to the world of drugs came from a doctor's prescription, but he continued anyway:

****

"I'm sure you're familiar with the time-worn clichés, *When in Rome, do as the Romans* do, and *Survival of the fittest,* et cetera. Well, the same philosophy applies to the drug underworld too, only more so. To survive you do as you are told, when you are told, and then forget about it. This, according to those rules, makes a man - or woman - healthy, wealthy and, more importantly, a hell of a lot wiser. Screw up, and you, swim with the fish, as The Godfather so aptly put it.

Confident that she would probably never see me again, my benefactor confessed that the name her troops gave her was Jess, as in Jessica. Her last name was Sterling. She further revealed that sources available to her had traced my passport, driver's license and aircraft identification number back to my boss, Carlo Puzzi, a high ranking member of the Mexican Mafia, headquartered in Puerto Rico. Evidently, from what little she was willing to tell me, some of the money that supported her commanding officer's band of rebels came from the drugs Carlo was selling throughout the Caribbean and the United States. As she explained, Carlo had a vested interest in supporting the military overthrow of Cuba's Communist Government because it would establish an additional base from which drugs could be shipped from Columbia directly into the United States, via Cuba.

Soon after telling me all of this, she admitted that shortly after my first week of captivity her rebels had stumbled onto the boxes of drugs I had dumped over the jungle. Putting two and two together, along with the information she had learned from her own research using my credentials, she contacted Carlo. He advised her to sell the drugs and send half the money to him and use the other half to finance their mutual interests.

****

"This is the damnedest story I've ever heard!" Neal blurted out, apologizing for interrupting again. "Talk about your small world."

Dan looked puzzled at his outburst and asked, "What small world are you referring to, Mr. T. It only has one size."

"Never mind with the humor, smart-ass. Finish your story and I'll explain later."

Running his fingers through his wind-blown hair, he continued:

****

"Within the hour a boat bigger than this one came out of the darkness and lowered a small one that headed toward the beach where we stood waiting in the moonlight. When it was only a stone's throw away, she shook my hand and left something in it. I didn't look at it at the time because it was too dark, so I put it in my pocket to examine later. Then, she hugged my neck and asked as we separated, if I would contact her mother in La Jolla whenever I got back to the States to let her know that she was alive and well. I promised I would.

Returning my passport and wallet, she thanked me for unwittingly providing her with an incentive to escape a life she had grown tired of. I've never seen her since, but I still have that outdated California Driver's License she gave me, if I can find it."

****

With the marina only a few hundred yards away, he pulled back on the throttles and slowed the boat to half speed for the final leg of their daylong journey. To put some finality to his story, he kept his eyes focused on the entrance to his slip and concluded his revealing tale of adventure.

****

"When I finally got back to Puerto Rico, you can imagine the reception I received. Carlo's boys met me at the airport in San Juan and escorted me directly to his estate. To say the least, he was not a happy camper, but because my disappearance and the loss of his plane had been caused by a freak storm, he gave me a thousand dollars and told me to get back to Florida as quickly as I could, warning that the authorities were aware of my return.

I had a mind to go straight to the private field where I kept my plane and fly the hell out of there, but I had personal things at my apartment that I couldn't afford to leave behind. Foolishly, I ignored Carlo's advice and went there to get them.

Just like in the movies, my apartment had been searched and put under surveillance. The authorities had been looking for me ever since I disappeared on radar, and failed to arrive at my scheduled destination. They assumed that I had gone down over the ocean.

I was taken into custody immediately, stripped of my money and passport and advised that my airplane had been impounded. I spent twelve days in their pigsty of a jail, accused of everything from running drugs to flying without a license. The Chief of Police was a horse's ass, but smart enough to know I was worth ten thousand American dollars to someone. After informing me what my release was going to cost, he let me make the necessary phone calls to collect it."

****

"I'm beginning to understand what your mother meant," Neal remarked, watching the, *Reduce Speed*, warning sign come into view. "What happened next?"

****

"My dad bankrolled the bribe with his own cash, and paid the travel expenses for a friend of his to fly down and make sure I got the hell out of there all right. The only positive thing that came out of the whole mess was letting me keep my wallet and passport. As you might have already guessed, the thousand dollars Carlo Puzzi had given me was gone.

If I live to be a hundred years old, I'll never forget the grin on the face of that Police Chief when I paid him off. His goodbye will ring in my ears forever: "Don't ever come back!"

****

Despite his misdirected youth and questionable maturity, he admired Dan for his skillful handling of his *Foxy Lady*. It was as if he were competing in a sports event that challenged one's ability to maneuver a large boat. He throttled the engines ever so slowly, swinging the stern around gracefully into position so the propellers could be reversed at just the right moment to back the boat gently into her slip. As he watched with envy, Donna jumped up on the dock to secure both mooring lines, while he sat silently watching the two unlikely mates and rethought everything he had seen and heard that day.

The one thing he was most curious about was the information Jessica - the renegade jungle warrior - had written on the outdated driver's license she had given Dan just before he left the island. Somehow, he was convinced, that information had some peculiar significance. When the docking maneuver was over, and the mooring lines were in place, he took Dan aside and asked: "Do you think you can find that driver's license Jessica gave you when you left Cuba? I'm certain she is the daughter of someone I met just recently."

"You're kidding," Dan replied, mildly surprised by his unexpected inquiry. "How could you possibly know her?"

"Know of her," he corrected. "If I'm not mistaken, I think she's the runaway daughter of a woman who sat next to me on my flight to Washington two days ago. The same woman who your rebel friend asked you to contact in San Diego."

While wracking his brain for some clue as to what he might have done with the license, Jennifer Newman came walking down the dock and stood at the stern of his boat, looking tired and irritated. "I hope you two had a good time," she said, sarcastically. "I wish now I had gone along with you. And you, Neal Thomas, have got a lot of explaining to do. We definitely need to have a little talk."

Surprised by her inference that something unpleasant had happened while they were away he waved and replied, "Thanks for coming to get me. I'll be with you in a minute."

Turning to Dan with his hand outstretched, he thanked him, enthusiastically, and remarked, "I had an incredibly enlightening day, my friend. One I won't forget any time soon. I'd be honored if you and Donna would join Jennifer and me for dinner later on. My treat."

Dan accepted the invitation with a promise to look for Jessica's driver's license as soon as he got his boat cleaned up. "I know it's here someplace, Mr. T," he assured him "Probably in among the many other pieces of junk memorabilia I've got stashed in my personal lock-up box."

When they left, Dan hosed down his boat, got rid of the bag of trash they brought back with them and then began rummaging through a lock-up box he kept under one of the cabin's window seats in the forward sleeping compartment. He was in the process of unlocking it when his eyes caught a glimpse of Donna's bare legs protruding from beneath the top sheet of his unmade bed. Puzzled by why she had gone to bed so early, he sat the box down and peeked under the sheet to determine if she was really asleep, or had just hidden there when Jennifer arrived. To his utter surprise and delight, he found her naked and tantalizing him with her two, well-rounded breasts as she smiled, seductively, from the shadows. Checking the time, he told her, "We've got two hours before we have to be at Nick's. Neal has invited us to be his guests for dinner. Is that okay with you?"

While he removed his clothes and snuggled into the warm softness of her encircling arms, she looked up into the incredibly blue eyes that had attracted her to him from the very first moment they met, she whispered, "Sorry, lover boy, I have something important to take care of tonight and have to be home by nine o'clock. Tell Mr.T I will take a rain check."

Jennifer had just backed out of the marina parking lot when Neal asked, "What did you mean back there when you said I had a lot of explaining to do?"

"Well, for starters," she began, "some nice looking young man showed up at my house this morning shortly after I dropped you off and asked if I knew where you were. I had never seen the man before so I was intentionally evasive. That is, until he showed me his badge. Turns out he's an agent for the Federal Drug Enforcement Agency (DEA). To put me at ease, he explained that you and he had been neighbors some years ago when you were a contractor working at a local nuclear power plant. Does any of this ring a bell?"

His slightly sunburned face gradually took on the grinning smile of a man who had just met an old friend in an airport halfway around the world. A man he was convinced, at the time, he would never see again. What a crazy coincidence, he thought, that after all those years without any communication, other than a Christmas card, Dusty Lewis, a young kid fresh out of college, would show up on Jennifer's doorstep looking for him.

The only explanation he could come up with was his recollection of having met Dusty's sister and parents when they had visited him during Neal's last week on the job before returning to California.

Dusty's sister, a pretty little tart who ran around braless most of the time, lived in Virginia Beach. He recalled her having invited him to give her a call if his travels took him that way when he began his vacationing trip back to the West Coast.

Over drinks one evening before they parted company, he remembered telling Dusty about his friendship with the Newman family, who also lived not too far from Virginia Beach. Even this limited information, he concluded, wasn't enough to track him to Jennifer's place, even for a government agent. Curious to learn more, he encouraged her to elaborate more about the conversation she had with his almost forgotten friend of so many years ago.

"He must be a pretty good agent," she continued, "because he called your ex-wife, Janet, who forwarded him on to Paula. She's the one who told him that you were staying here with the Hughes'. He called them and talked to Henry shortly after they arrived home from the wake yesterday. It was Henry who put the finger on me, and gave him directions on how to get here. You can imagine my surprise when he appeared on my doorstep and told me who he was. Once I learned about the connection between you two, I relaxed and invited him to come back later in the day for cocktails. He thanked me, but said he had a dinner date with his sister in Virginia Beach and had to leave. Before he left, however, he asked me to tell you that he was being transferred to San Diego soon, and would contact you after he was settled there. So, consider yourself told."

Even though Dusty had credentials and a badge to verify his identity, a seed of doubt still remained in her mind that there was more to the unexpected arrival of Neal's friend than was immediately apparent. Still a little frustrated and suspicious, she growled, "Okay, Neal, would you please tell me what the hell is going on here? Did your friend show up here just to renew an old acquaintance, or is there something you're not telling me?" "

He laughed in an effort to inject a little levity into the situation, knowing full well that Dusty Lewis' sudden and unannounced arrival was nothing more than pure coincidence. "No, I'm not holding back anything from you, " he replied, in all sincerity. "I swear, Mr. Lewis is just an old friend who hasn't got a clue about what happened to Billy."

Recognizing beyond any reasonable doubt that repeating what Dan had revealed to him that day might place her in jeopardy of becoming involved in something much bigger and more dangerous than either of them could imagine, he made light of the situation, suggesting that they relax and begin their last evening together with a cocktail. He promised with all the sincerity he could muster to prove to her that there wasn't any conspiracy going on.

His strategy worked. Her face relaxed into a soft smile as she cuddled up on one of the two leather sofas that provided her living room with a spectacular, panoramic view of the ocean. The stage was set. With a cocktail in each hand, he returned to the living room and handed her one.

Looking briefly out over the ocean, he seated himself on the sofa across from her and took a moment to gather his thoughts.

Feeling a little guilty for suggesting that he was hiding something, she took advantage of his hesitation to offer her own brand of levity, hoping it would normalize their relationship again.

"This better be good, my friend," she said, looking over the top of her glass, "Otherwise, you're going to be dining alone tonight."

Relaxed and comfortable for the first time that day, he began to explain the peculiar set of events that even he admitted would have confused him had their positions been reversed.

"First of all, that CEA Agent that showed up here today was a salesman fresh out of college when I first met him. He lived in the apartment above me in a swinging singles community called Brentwood. For a man my age, I never had so much fun in all my life than I did with Dusty and those crazy young people I worked with."

"I'll bet," she snickered.

"I worked twelve hours a day, six days a week for the entire six months I was there. Saturday nights and Sundays were the only days I had to relax and have a little fun, which, for the most part, they arranged. No matter what they did, or where they went, I was always included. Because we all worked the same hours, our socializing was pretty well limited to Sunday picnics. I hurt a lot on Mondays, but considering the money I was making for doing virtually nothing, I could easily afford the pain."

"That's not pain, that's a hangover!" she remarked, smiling over the top of her glass. "It's a wonder you didn't kill yourself. Sorry, please go on."

"I probably would have," he admitted. "But, for reasons I won't get into now, the contract ended and wasn't renewed. I can't say I was disappointed, though, because honestly, I was all pooped out."

"What, from doing nothing for six months?" she joked. "I could stand a little of that. The next thing you're going to tell, I'm sure, is you never had time for the ladies. Right?"

"That's right," he agreed, "except for the last weekend I was there. The guys set me up with a dinner date. A pretty little hairdresser I had admired from a distance but never put a move on because, after all, I was considerably older than her."

"No fool like an old fool," she remarked, amused by what she knew he coming. "What happened next?"

"I made the mistake of revealing my infatuation with her to Dusty Lewis one evening when I was in my cups. Surprised by what I had admitted, he and some of his cronies convinced the woman that I was just a harmless old man who had lots of bucks and would show her a good time. No strings attached. According to Dusty, it took some coaxing, but she finally gave in. I knew it would be awkward for her, so I joked a lot, drank too much and danced to most of her generation's music, just as if I knew what the hell I was doing. That, and the laughter, made the rest of the evening a lot of fun for both of us. But, then again, that's another story."

Jennifer couldn't resist the temptation to express her curiosity about where his story was suppose to take her, so she remarked, "I haven't a clue where you're going with all this, but if it's going where I think its going, I'm having another drink. Are you ready?"

"Sure, why not?" he replied, as she passed by on her way to the kitchen.

While waiting for her to return, he turned his attention to the ocean swells running in never ending monotony toward their demise on the beach. Deciding against further elaboration on that final night out with his contrived date, he let it dangle like a participle, and epilogued it with a clarification. "Suffice it to say that Dusty, and all my working buddies, were more like children to me at the time. I was "Pops" to everyone. The guy they all came to for sympathy when a heart got broken, or someone needed to get something off their chest. Having been recently divorced, their respect and friendship gave me a whole new perspective on where I thought my future was going, and what measure of success I might still achieve. In fact, they made me feel like a young man again; vital, needed, and, if you will, sexy. I shall remember my six months with those beautiful young people as long as I live. Some more so than others, I must admit, but, as I mentioned before, those are different stories."

"I'll bet they are," she commented upon her return. "Now I suppose you're going to tell me that you spent all that time without having intimate relations with any of those beautiful young ladies."

To admit that he had enjoyed such a relationship would have betrayed the trust and respect he had for the young woman with whom he had had an unplanned tryst. To avoid admitting the affair, he replied, "As I said before, dear lady, that's another story."

"I'm glad you didn't admit that you had," she remarked, almost as if she were giving him some measure of praise for maintaining his confidentiality. "I think it's much more fun to wonder whether you did, or didn't. Do you want to hear what I think?"

"Nope, I already know what you think."

Realizing that the conversation was beginning to stray from its intended purpose, he reorganized his thoughts and focused on what Dan had told him that afternoon, determined to try and absolve him from having any direct link to Billy's death.

"I learned a lot today. More than I could have imagined," he began. "Enough to have come to the conclusion that Dan Hughes had nothing to do with Billy's death."

He realized immediately that his conclusion had a certain note of absolution in it, so he added, "Please understand, I'm not condoning his past involvement with drugs, but he told me today that that period in his life was over. To prove that he meant it, he took me into his confidence by telling me that he has information tying some of your local dignitaries and politicians directly to the drug cartel operating in this area. Against my better judgment, I agreed to notify Federal authorities where the information could be found in the event that something should happen to him. Whether or not that was a wise decision is of little consequence now. However, the possibility still exists that I might have to return here someday. I would hope that I could rely on your help, if such an eventuality should occur."

With more than he had originally intended to tell her now out in the open, he waited anxiously for her to respond, knowing full well that her reply could be filled with some resentment. To his surprise, however, her reaction was to the contrary. "I doubt very much if you realize the seriousness of the responsibility you have taken on," she replied. "And, I doubt your lady friend, Paula, would go along with such a commitment, were she here. Be that as it may, I am still very much interested in knowing what Dan told you in order to gain your confidence. Can you at least share that with me?"

Relieved that she had expressed no resentment, he rose and stood by the window to watch the ocean fading into the evening's approaching darkness. "Trust me. I saw and heard enough today to convince me that Dan had nothing to gain by involving himself in Billy's accident. He feels badly that you suspect him of being a part of it, especially in light of your family's relationship with his."

The words were barely out of his mouth when their conversation was interrupted by a knock on the screen door, followed by a man's voice that asked, "Anybody home?"

There was no mistaking who the voice belonged to, so Neal replied, "Come on in, Dan, we've been expecting you."

Once inside, he turned toward Jennifer and shook her hand. "Good evening Mrs. Newman," he addressed her, politely. "I hope you don't mind my barging in like this. My friend, Donna, dropped me off on her way home and asked if I would convey her regrets for not being able to join us for dinner tonight. Apparently, she has some unfinished business to take care of tonight and couldn't stay for dinner."

"I understand perfectly" she replied, "As a matter of fact, I have obligations tomorrow myself that insist on a good night's sleep. So, if it's all the same to you two, I think I'll pass on dinner and turn in early."

Addressing Neal, she suggested that he could tell her all about today's adventures tomorrow on the way to the airport. "Take my car," she insisted. "I'll leave the door unlocked."

The two men looked at one another, each wondering whether Dan's arrival without Donna had prompted Jennifer's decision not to join them. After several well-meaning attempts to coax her into changing her mind, he shrugged his shoulders, accepted her car keys and promised not to be late.

"Don't rush your dinner on my account. I just don't want to be a third wheel. Enjoy yourselves and be careful."

Experiencing some disappointment, Neal expressed his thanks and led Dan down the porch stairs to her car. Moments later, they arrived at Nick's, eager to enjoy a good dinner and celebrate Neal's last night at the beach. As they left the car and walked toward the restaurant, Dan lit a cigarette and said, "I'm sorry about Donna bugging out on us. She really did have to leave for home. I still don't know what was so important that it couldn't wait for her to have something to eat."

"Maybe it's just as well. You and I need to talk about a few things privately before I head back home tomorrow."

Inside the restaurant, only a few tables and booths were occupied. Of those, most were locals relaxing in the quiet aftermath of a hectic weekend highlighted by Billy Newman's wake.

Unlike the previous day's activities, the place was relatively quiet so they proceeded to the dining room and occupied a table by a window facing the ocean. Moments later, a waitress approached and took their cocktail order. After she left, Dan pulled something out of his shirt pocket and flipped it on the table in front of Neal.

"That's what Jessica gave me," he remarked. "I finally found it in my personal junk box on the boat. Exactly where I put it when I finally got back to the States. It's been there ever since. How's that for dumb-ass luck?"

Eager to confirm his earlier suspicion, Neal picked up the wallet-size card and examined the woman's face and name that were pictured there. As Dan had told him earlier that day, the old, outdated driver's license had belonged to Jessica Sterling.

"You can have it, Mr. T," he said. "Who knows, maybe it will help you locate her mother."

Neal fingered the card carefully while his eyes memorized the features of the woman pictured there. Turning it over, he saw the name, ***Sandy Sterling,*** written there in ink, followed by the word, ***Mom.*** "I think I already have," he sighed with contentment. It was all he could do to contain his excitement when the waitress arrived with their cocktails.

"You guys need a little time before ordering," she asked, obviously bored from another long day there.

"Yeah," Neal replied. "Come back when these are empty. We'll order then."

After she left, he put the driver's license in his wallet and thanked Dan. Still excited, he took a more than generous swallow from his cocktail and diverted Dan's attention away from watching the waitress and explained why he was so glad to get the old license. "The woman you left on that beach in Cuba is the daughter of the same Sandy Sterling that sat next to me on my flight from San Diego. She didn't talk much about her family on the plane, but did mention that her husband owned a publishing company, and had died of cancer quite suddenly. Evidently, his untimely death had quite a devastating effect on their teenage daughter, who, she suspected, had gotten involved with drugs as a result. As I remember our brief conversation on the subject, Ms. Sterling seemed intentionally vague about her daughter, though she mentioned that she no longer lived at home.

Before Dan could react, their waitress arrived with fresh drinks and menus.

"You two guys look pretty intense," she remarked. "Give me a high sign when you're ready to order. I'll keep a weather eye on your drinks."

"Yes, that would be fine, and thank you," Dan replied, eyeballing her departure again.

As she turned and walked away, very much aware of the attention her backside was getting, she looked back with a coquettish smile and said, "Your welcome. Take all the time you need, boys, and enjoy the view."

The two men were looking at each other and shaking their heads in amusement when Dan brought the conversation back to where it had ended.

"If what you are suggesting is true, you could sure do me one hell of a favor by contacting Mrs. Sterling when you get back and telling her about this bizarre coincidence. News like this coming from me, a total stranger, could be terribly suspect. You at least know the woman. Doesn't it make better sense for you to contact her, rather than me stirring up the pot with a phone call?"

What reminiscently came to mind almost immediately was presidential candidate Ross Perot's comic reference to "that giant sucking sound," when he realized how much further he was becoming involved in Dan's personal life. But, contrary to his better judgment, he agreed without considering the possibility of consequences. As he had responded to other requests throughout his life, saying no was a difficult thing to do.

They had only enjoyed a few swallows of their second drink when Neal's eyes caught a glimpse of two men entering the restaurant, one of whom he recognized. Trying not to alarm Dan, he leaned across the table and whispered, "Don't look now, but isn't that the guy you introduced me to on your boat last night?"

Dan recognized the reference and turned his head just far enough to confirm whom Neal had recognized. Assuring him that there was no cause for concern he stood up and left for the doorway. "Order us a couple more drinks while I find out why he's here, will you. I'll be back in a couple of minutes."

As he walked away from their table, Neal raised his hand and motioned for their waitress to come to the table. When she arrived he gave her back the two menus she had left earlier and said, "Bring us two more drinks and the seafood combination for two. And by the way," he added, handing her his credit card, "my friend's money doesn't spend here tonight. Everything goes on this. Understood?"

"Loud and clear, Commander," she replied, "You're the boss."

Watching her walk away using the same body movements that had intrigued Dan earlier, prompted him to appreciate how well she handled herself. He wondered for a moment what it would be like to dance with someone who moved with such grace and precision, someone other than Paula, who he had been attracted to so many years ago for the very same reason. Interesting, he thought, how a few drinks could stimulate the comparison. His smile broadened at the fantasy his mind was imaging. "Time to go home," he murmured, quietly. "Back to paradise."

Soon after she left the scene, Dan returned to their table looking troubled. He hurriedly drank what was left of his drink, and spoke to him in a hushed voice that he recognized as being genuine concern. "I'm sorry to leave you here alone, Mr. T, but I don't have much of a choice. Ramirez and his henchman, Pete Boggs, have something they insist on discussing with me before they leave here tonight. I decided to take them back to my boat and get this thing over with. At least that way you can enjoy a quiet dinner."

"I'll survive, Dan. Go do what needs to be done. If you're not back in an hour, I'm going back to Jennifer's and hit the sack. Call me in a few days and bring me up to speed on what's going on."

"Thanks Mr. T," he replied, grateful that his friend was perceptive enough to recognize that he needed to go. "I'll be in touch."

Shortly after Dan's departure, he considered canceling their dinner order in favor of returning to Jennifer's to call and find out if Paula was still planning to meet him at the airport the next day. The growling in his empty stomach, however, changed his mind. He was hungry.

While he sat there waiting for the waitress to return, a woman entered the restaurant and sat alone at the bar. He didn't have to look twice to recognize that it was Vicki Daniels?

He was just on the verge of attempting to attract her attention when the waitress approached with his order. The expression on her face registered some surprise, as she inquired, "What happened to your buddy?"

"He's been called away on urgent business, and won't be returning. But I do have an alternate plan."

"And what would that be?" she asked, eyeing him suspiciously.

"I'm a friend of that attractive brunette sitting alone at the bar. Would you do me a favor and ask her if she'd care to join me for dinner?"

"Sure," she replied, expressing visible relief that she wasn't the alternate plan.

When approached with his invitation, Vicki's head turned quickly in his direction. A broad smile brightened her face as she picked up her glass and sauntered into the dining room to accept his invitation.

"All alone?" she asked, "Where's Jennifer?"

"Gone to bed," he replied, as if disinterested, "Did you pass Dan on the way in? He was with two other men?"

"No I didn't, although I do remember seeing three men get into a stretch limo as I drove up. They seemed in a hurry."

For the next half an hour, he described his adventure on Dan's boat that day, laughing and eating occasionally from the seafood platter. There was an awkward moment of silence, however, when they each struggled for something meaningful to say. Hoping he could clear up any misunderstanding that she might be harboring about Dan's failure to get in touch with her, he spoke on his behalf. "Dan told me today that he was unaware that you were going to be home this weekend, and would have planned to spend more time with you, had he known. But, some character by the name of Ramirez complicated matters by showing up, unexpectedly. Otherwise, I'm sure he would have invited you to join us on his boat today."

"I know," she sighed. "It was my fault for not contacting him before Mr. Newman's wake. But, that's the story of my life; an hour late and a dollar short "

Lifting her glass and clinking it against his, she said, quite matter-of-factly, "Oh well, what's done is done. No use dwelling on it. Let's have another drink and call it a day."

Rising, he excused himself to go to the men's room. When he returned their glasses had been filled, the table cleared and his bill was in a folder on the table.

"That was quick," he remarked.

She smiled. "Part of my friendly service. Remember, I do this for a living."

"How could I forget," he said smile, "That was quite an airline adventure for an old settled down grandfather like me. I'm not used to being catered to by two beautiful women."

She sat her glass down and looked over at him, scowling a little. "I wish you'd stop referring to yourself as old. Hell, I know men who are in their forties who act older than you are. In fact, you've got more sex appeal and vitality than most of the men I know. And they're half your age, so lets not go there any more, okay?"

"By all means," he replied, patting her affectionately on the hand. "And thanks for those kind words, I am flattered. Now, tell me what you know about this fellow, Ramirez."

"He, it's rumored, is the king pin of all drug activity in this area, and the principle reason why Dan and I ended our relationship a few years ago."

"How so?"

"I was afraid I would wake up some morning and read in the paper that his body had been found in a landfill somewhere. I wanted no part of that kind of life, even though I loved Dan at the time. He has told me several times since then that he is no longer involved, but if you saw him here tonight with Ramirez, you can bet your last dollar he's still involved."

"I suspected as much. After what I saw and heard today, I'm convinced he's in some kind of serious trouble with Ramirez, and too scared to tell anyone."

"I wouldn't be the least bit surprised," she admitted, "but even if I wanted to help him, I wouldn't know what to do."

"Do nothing," he advised her, "Just take this business card and call me if you see or hear anything that might shed some light on his involvement with Ramirez, or anyone else for that matter. Will you do that for me?"

"Yes, I will," she replied. "Now, I've got to get out of here. It's late and mom will be worried."

Respecting her for using good judgment, he credit carded his dinner tab and asked her on their way out if he could give her a ride home.

"Thanks," she replied, "but I have mom's car. I'll be just fine."

"Okay," he conceded, "At least let me escort you to your car. I'll sleep better knowing you're safely on your way."

Approaching her car, she thanked him for rescuing her from a lonely, boring evening and promised to keep him informed should anything develop involving Dan and Ramirez.

"Don't be surprised if you get a call from me the next time I'm in San Diego," she said in leaving, "Dinner's on me."

Standing alone in the parking lot watching her car fade out of sight, he experienced a sense of relief knowing the evening was almost over. Pulling into Jennifer's driveway he observed that all of the lights were out, except the one she had left on for him. Tired, and a little bit under the influence, he climbed the stairs and found the door unlocked, as she had promised.

After getting the cell phone from his briefcase, he returned quietly to the porch, rested in a lounge chair and dialed home. Expecting the answering machine to kick in after the forth ring, he began putting together a message in the event she didn't answer. Half way through hearing his recorded voice tell him that no one was home, a cheery voice broke in and said, "Hello, Curly. I've been waiting for your call."

"Am I getting that predictable?" he asked.

"About the same way you seem to know it's my daughter calling whenever the phone rings on a Sunday morning at precisely nine o'clock," she replied. "Ellen left a few minutes ago with sweet little Sarah sound asleep in the car seat. They visited over the weekend to keep me company while Daddy Mike was out of town on business. We had a fun time. How was your trip?"

"It's too complicated to explain over the phone," he replied. "Let me tell you all about it in the Jacuzzi when I get home tomorrow. Don't forget, my plane gets into San Diego at five-thirty tomorrow afternoon. Are you still picking me up?"

"I'll be there at six o'clock, darling," she answered, "My boss told me to leave whenever I wanted to. And, by the way, I have some things to tell you in the Jacuzzi, so get a good night's sleep. I've missed you."

He had hardly silenced his phone when a breath of ocean air flowed gently across his face, bringing with it a caress his eyelids could no longer resist. He let them close content to fall asleep outside under the millions of stars that twinkled in the darkness overhead.

Chapter 7

Return To Paradise

The screeching sound of seagulls circling above the wet sand in concert with the dawn of a new day awakened Neal to the sober reality that in a few hours he would be on a jetliner returning to a life style that would seem dull by comparison to the one he had been living for the past three days. The taste in his mouth and the stubble on his unshaven face were bold reminders of that reality. For the first time since leaving San Diego, he longed to return.

It wasn't that he hadn't enjoyed the unexpected and sometimes bizarre events that had occurred, or the boost they had given to his sexuality, but the thought of having to perform them on a continuing basis was more than his tired body could endure. Recalling the fantasies he had indulged in prior to leaving San Diego gave more meaning to the time worn cliché he had been cautioned by Paula not to forget: "Be careful what you wish for. You might just get it."

It was Monday. Knowing Jennifer would be anxious to get an early start to the airport, he picked up his shaving gear and treated himself to a badly needed shower. Almost immediately the cool wetness provided welcome relief from the gradually rising humidity he was still not accustomed to. It was with some reluctance that he finally turned off the water, patted himself dry and began to shave. Moments later, he heard a knock at the door and Jennifer's voice making him aware that she was awake and about to make coffee.

"I hope you're not a big breakfast person," she remarked. "I'm afraid all I have are sweet rolls and mixed fruit. How does that sound?"

"Perfect," he replied. " I'll be with you as soon as I get some clothes on."

"Take your time," she insisted. I'm not going to work today, so you might just as well pack your bag while you're at it."

It wasn't long before the aroma of freshly brewed coffee found its way down the hallway and into his bedroom. The smell reminded him of the ritual he performed every morning for Paula, whose lust for coffee was exceeded only by her need for wine when she returned home from work each evening. He smiled thinking how much they were alike in that respect. Not having several drinks before dinner was something he rarely denied himself, unless he was going to see a doctor the next day, or through some act of forgetfulness had failed to replenish his Vodka. Such forgetfulness, however, was a rarity. With those thoughts in mind, and his bags in hand, he headed for the kitchen, reassured that he was ready for his return to paradise and all that waited for him there.

When he entered the kitchen, he found her comfortably dressed in shorts and a lightweight tank top that hung loosely from her shoulders, doing little to hide the predominance of her breasts. As always, she moved about with little concern for how their partial exposure might affect her friend of many years, and could have cared less.

Watching her move casually about the kitchen, however, did stir up memories of a few Sunday mornings when he and his former wife, Janet, took their three daughters to visit the beach house in which he now sat reminiscing.

****

Hangovers were expected on those occasions, and were dealt with accordingly. Usually that meant that Billy had gotten into his cups the night before and had invited everyone he met to come to his house on Sunday to neutralize the intensity of Jennifer's caustic criticism for having made a fool out of himself; an act that all too often had cut him off from her affection. Be that as it may, it was all in good fun, though consistently predictable.

Of course, the children thought this was great fun, because it gave them an hour or two of almost unrestricted supervision, which rarely amounted to much more than playing on the beach by themselves, sunbathing on the front porch, or drinking more soda than their parents would normally have allowed them to drink. As much fun as it was, though, the down side was driving home late in the afternoon after drinking all day, and having to go to work the next day. Invariably, there would be an argument along the way over something silly. Fortunately, the children were almost always asleep.

****

While waiting patiently by the microwave for their sweet rolls to warm, she observed that Neal had become unusually quiet. Hoping he wasn't finding it awkward to be alone with her because of the passionate embrace they had shared the previous evening, she faced him and said, "Not to worry, old friend, you'll be back in your paradise by mid-afternoon and all this will be nothing but a memory. Any regrets?"

"Not really," he admitted. "It's been a most unusual experience, one I won't soon forget. I was just remembering all the Monday hangovers I used to have whenever you and Billy invited my family down here for the day. I really miss those times."

"Me too," she responded, laughing a little. "You two and your crazy goings-on really got to me on a number of occasions. But, reflecting on it now, I realize it was just plain jealousy on my part. I guess I just plain envied you guys. By the way, speaking of hangovers, do you have one this morning? It wouldn't surprise me if you did. You had quite a lot to drink yesterday."

"Well, let's put it this way, I've had better days, but I'll survive."

"Dan Hughes has that affect on people, and I'd be remise if I didn't warn you about getting too cozy with him, or his friends," she commented. "I don't know why he picked you to confide in. I wouldn't trust him any further than I could throw him. Talk about bad news."

While they enjoyed their breakfast together, he was reminded of Dan's sudden departure the previous evening and thought he should mention it to her. "Last night while Dan and I were having drinks before dinner, two men showed up. One of them was a Latino by the name of Miguel Ramirez, whom I had met yesterday after you took me to spend the night on Dan's boat. The other guy was Caucasian, big and mean looking. Dan told me his name. It sounded like Bugs, Bags, or something like that."

"Boggs," Jennifer corrected, "Pete Boggs. He manages Shep's Marina, the place where Billy used to do his drinking. Both he and Ramirez are rumored to be heavily involved in distributing drugs in this area. That's why I think that Dan was in some way involved in Billy's death. Something stinks, but I just can't put my finger on it."

After considering her opinion for a moment, he felt compelled to express his own. "You know, until last night I was willing to give Dan the benefit of the doubt, as far as his innocence is concerned, but now I'm not so sure. Something unusual happened after midnight on the evening I stayed at the Hughes' home that seems to be tied in with all of this."

"In what way?" she asked, surprised at what he had implied.

"Well, it was late, past midnight. Everyone had gone to bed. I couldn't sleep because of the humidity so I went out onto the balcony off my bedroom for a breath of air, such as it was. A few minutes later a boat with its running lights turned off pulled up along side Dan's boat and unloaded what looked to be small bundles of something. I couldn't make out what they were. As soon as the transfer was complete, the boat backed away and disappeared in the darkness. At the time I couldn't figure out what was going on, until I overheard a conversation between Dan and Ramirez on Dan's boat shortly after you dropped me off at the marina last night. He said Dan's delivery to Boggs that morning was two packages short, and he wanted an explanation. Dan didn't have one, so Ramirez gave him twenty-four hours to account for it. Or, as he phrased it, Dan might end up feeding the fish with Mr. Newman."

She remained silent for a moment watching him struggle to make some sense out of what he had seen and heard over the past few days. "Do you want to share a bon voyage drink with me before we leave for the airport?" she asked. "I think we both could use one."

"You're starting to scare me now," he answered, as his face changed from a serious scowl to a broad grin. "I was about to ask you the same thing."

Feeling somewhat more at ease, she began the process, while he took the opportunity to thank her for all she had done to make his visit a pleasant one, considering the circumstances. "Thanks for putting up with me for the past few days, kiddo. I know this whole mess has been pretty hard on you and your family. I hate to be a fly in the ointment, but somehow I have the feeling I'm going to be coming back. Call it whatever you will; intuition, premonition, or whatever, but I know just as sure as I'm sitting here, this is not the last time you're going to see me."

Handing him his drink, she clinked her glass against his and remarked, "Not that I wouldn't be glad to see you, but should you return, I hope it will be for reasons other than someone's death. I've had enough of that in my life."

"Me too. I've certainly had my share."

For the next few minutes they laughed about happier times when the subject of death was too far in the future to waste time thinking about it. Soon, however, the laughter ended, and the clock on the wall signaled it was time to leave. Toasting one another once again for good measure, they drained their glasses, content to pretend that all was well.

Not too far away, and not too happy about how his day was going, Dan Hughes was making preparations to leave the marina for his parent's home. Unlike Neal and Jennifer, however, his thoughts were more concentrated on his previous night's conversation with Miguel Ramirez and Pete Boggs. For the first time in his relationship with those two men, he was beginning to feel uneasy and threatened, especially since they had implied that he was somehow involved in the disappearance of two packets of cocaine, which he knew nothing about. As he gathered up the trash and empty beer cans that had accumulated over the weekend, he thought about how stupid he had been for not counting them. All he could conclude was, just like Billy Newman, he had been set up.

It took about an hour to make the boat ready for departure, during which time he searched every conceivable nook and cranny on his boat to make sure the missing packets were not on board. By the time he was ready to leave there was no doubt in his mind that someone who wanted him out of the way had set him up. But why, he thought? He hadn't done anything to give anyone a reason to suspect him of trying to branch out on his own. What he had done, though, was suggest to Ramirez several days earlier that he wanted out of the business, which he realized may have set him up for a pressure play to reconsider that decision.

It wasn't long after he had cast off the boat's mooring lines and climbed to the bridge to start the engines that he noticed something protruding from under the seat cushion behind the steering wheel. Pulling it clear, he discovered the navigational chart he had used the previous day to take Neal to his hideaway. The circled dot that Shark Hadley had drawn on the map to mark the inlet stood out like a sore thumb. Carefully maneuvering his boat from the slip and out into open water, he realized he should have made sure Neal had the map before leaving the boat. Without it, he feared, he would never be able to find his way back to the inlet where the chronicles of his past were hidden. It was too late to catch him before he left the marina, so he put the map in his back pocket, satisfied that mailing it was the safest and most practical alternative.

While he crossed the bay on his way home, perplexed and concerned about his future, Neal and Jennifer were arriving at Norfolk Airport where they parked briefly at Neal's check-in area. Pulling the trunk release, she detained him for a moment. "Thanks for coming all this way to pay your respects to my family," she remarked. "I know that wherever Billy is right now he's looking down at us and smiling. You were the only real friend he ever had."

For the first time since knowing her he became surprisingly aware of a rarely exhibited tenderness in her that caught him off guard and choked off the words he was about to speak. In an attempt to ease his embarrassment, she kidded him as he left the car, "Like you, my gut feeling is telling me you'll be back."

Smiling, he blew her a kiss and replied, "Then don't change the sheets!"

Minutes later, following a routine security check, he proceeded directly to his departure gate and checked in. His watch indicated that he had about forty-five minutes before boarding so he walked to the nearest cocktail bar and ordered a beer, content just to sit there watching a group of college kids laughing and teasing one another while they waited to board their flight. The scene was reminiscent of a similar gathering he was part of many years ago when he played college football.

****

One of his buddies had decided he wanted to make up a Rugby team to compete in a tournament being held in Bermuda during Spring Break. Because his friend was the only member of the rogue team who knew anything about the game, he acted as a playing coach. The rest of the players, a mix of running backs and linemen, learned the rules and strategy quite easily in only a few practice sessions. When Spring Break finally arrived, off they flew to Bermuda, full of life, enthusiasm and as happy as if they had good sense, a rare commodity at that time in their lives.

Ironically, as it turned out, he and his friends won the tournament, however, not without one embarrassing moment in the final game when Neal ripped the crotch out of his shorts during a scrum. The action had taken place close to the edge of the playing field, directly in front of a bleacher full of spectators. Fortunately, he was wearing a traditional jockstrap, which shielded his private parts from being displayed publicly, but not from the laughter. Even his teammates howled at his predicament. They did, however, finally come to his rescue by rushing in an extra pair of shorts from an opposing team member that were, to say the least, too big. Ignoring the spectator uproar, a tight circle was quickly formed around him and the exchange was made, much to the delight of everyone there.

****

After finishing his beer and walking casually back toward the departure gate, he smiled and thought about the beautiful young college girl he met and fell in love with in Bermuda during that crazy, drunken, fun-filled vacation so many years ago. By now, he guessed, she had probably already gotten married and had a bunch of kids just like everyone else. One thing was for sure, though, she was the Bermuda he would never forget.

Only a few minutes elapsed at the gate before the attendant announced that boarding could begin. Anxious to get on board and relax, he hurried down the stairway onto the tarmac where the small commuter jet sat loading passengers and baggage.

At the top of the boarding stairs stood a cute little flight attendant eagerly welcoming passengers and joking back and forth with the pilots. Since he was one of the first passengers on board, he picked a single seat just forward of the wing, buckled in and browsed half-heartedly through a magazine. Minutes later the forward hatch closed, giving notice that his flight was about to get under way.

By the time the pilot was cleared for takeoff, the early morning sun and humidity had rendered the ventilation system virtually ineffective. Some passengers in business suits and jackets began to wiggle and squirm with discomfort as they played with the overhead airflow nozzles and began removing whatever clothing they could. In what seemed to be an unusually long period of time, a voice from the cockpit announced that they were finally ready for takeoff.

Once in the air, it didn't take long for the ventilation system to restore a level of comfort that made the flight more enjoyable. The attendant, whose name he had noticed was Beverly, went out of her way to chat with each passenger as she took beverage orders. When she approached him, his eyes were focused on the landscape below, so she touched him gently on the shoulder and asked, "Would you care for something to drink, sir?"

His eyes turned slowly from the window and refocused on the smiling face looking down at him and said, for the fun of it, "Got anything for a three day hangover?"

With an accent he hadn't heard since he was in Georgia, she bent a little closer to him and whispered, "We definitely have a cure for that malady. How about a nice Bloody Mary? That ought to fix you right up."

"You're on," he replied. "Just what the doctor ordered."

For whatever reason, he was the last passenger to be served, and seemed to be the only person who had ordered an alcoholic beverage. Maybe, he thought, they were not normally available on such short flights, and he should apologize for possibly putting her in an awkward position, so he reached up and pushed the service light.

With only thirty minutes before they landed in Washington, she struggled in her cramped little service cubical to make a special drink for the only person on the plane who wanted booze. She saw his seat light come on and thought about his three-day hangover, while smiling at the coincidence of her having one too. It had been a wonderful weekend for her, but she knew all to well where the old, gray-haired passenger was coming from, and she empathized with him.

Mixing the vodka with some Worcestershire Sauce, lemon juice, "Red Hot" and a little horseradish in a large coffee cup, she walked down the aisle to his seat, still smiling. "I don't do this for everyone," she said, seriously, "but you remind me so much of my father, I just had to do something special. He would have ordered booze too, and said to hell with what time it was. I hope you like it."

Even if he didn't, it would have been difficult to tell that to someone as friendly and accommodating as she was. But it was delicious, and he said so. "I don't know what you've got in here, young lady, but you sure know what you're doing."

"Thanks, my ex-husband liked them too."

Viewing the countryside below made the time pass quickly. Coincidentally, when he finished the last of his drink, the metropolitan area around Washington came into view as the pilot began his final approach into Dulles.

Listening to the landing flaps extend and the wheels lower, he regretted not having called his younger brother, Joel, to suggest that they meet at the airport for a brief reunion. Thinking it over, though, he decided it would be too much of a hassle for him on a weekday, given Beltway traffic and the time of day, so he dismissed the idea as bad timing.

Moments later, the perky young attendant made her final check of the cabin before touchdown, stopping briefly by his seat to get her cup. "Feeling better?" she asked.

"Who wouldn't," he replied, "I just hope I didn't put you on the spot by asking for booze."

"Not in the least," she assured him, "I guess that's the one trait you have that reminds me so much of my father. More than just your blue eyes and gray hair, that is. He doesn't care what time of the day it is. If he wants a drink, he has one. He's so funny sometimes. I just love him to death. Do you have any children?"

Maybe it was the Bloody Mary, but all of a sudden he felt relaxed and mellow. Talking to the young flight attendant seemed almost like conversing with one of his own girls. "Three daughters," he replied, grinning a little. "The oldest is married and gave me my only grandchild, a boy. The middle one is single, but lives with a real nice, hard working guy who takes good care of her. The youngest reminds me a little of you, cute and perky, always on the go and very caring. Are you married?"

"Was," she answered, puckering her lower lip a little as if to imply a sense of regret. "Why is it you never get to see the other side of the person you fall in love with until after the wedding?"

From the change in expression on her face, he almost wished he hadn't asked the question. Hoping to divert her from an obviously unpleasant memory, he tried a little humor. "Honey, it's like looking at the moon. No one ever gets to see the dark side."

The landing was soft and well executed, unlike some he had experienced. Moments later the terminal building came into view as the plane taxied to a gentle stop beside the deplaning stairs that awaited their arrival.

As soon as the cabin door opened, passengers in the forward seats filled the aisle to retrieve their luggage, thus causing a madhouse of activity while those in the rear stood impatiently waiting for them to deplane – all but Neal.

Since he had an hour and a half to catch his connecting flight, he amused himself by watching the process, content not to be a part of it. Only after the last remaining passenger had reached the cabin door did he stand and walk to the exit hatch where the two pilots and Beverly stood laughing and joking with one another. As he approached, he pre-empted his departure with a compliment to the pilot on how skillfully he had landed, and then turned toward Beverly and thanked her for being so attentive to a tired, but contented, old man.

She smiled and remarked, rather cleverly, "Well, one thing's for sure, every time I look at the moon I'll know who the man in the moon really is."

"Thanks, young lady, you've made my day."

Entering the terminal, he focused his attention on how he was going to kill some time, but before he could decide, an all too familiar voice called out to him, "Hey, Bro, What's happening?"

Turning in that direction, he was greeted by the smiling face of his brother approaching with outstretched arms. Following their surprise reunion, Joel suggested that they get a bite to eat in one of the concourse eateries near Neal's departure gate. Once seated inside, they passed the time eating burgers with beer and talking about family-related topics, and trivia in general. Joel explained that he had tried to call him at home the previous Saturday and learned about his whereabouts from Paula. It was she, he went on to explain, that had given him Neal's return flight information so he could surprise him when he arrived at Dulles.

"Funny you should mention that," he remarked, self consciously "I felt a little guilty for not calling you last night to see if you could meet me here today, but gave it up as a bad idea because it was a workday."

"Well, not to worry, brother dear," he replied, "I have a doctor's appointment, so I took the whole day off. I was due for a three day weekend, anyway."

"Anything serious?"

"Oh no," he chuckled, "It's standard procedure in my department when someone gets promoted to the next level of their incompetence. What with my medical history, they want to make sure they're not promoting a problem."

"Nicely put. Congratulations, I'm proud of you, Bro. "

A few moments of silence passed between the two brothers as they concentrated on finishing their lunches. Then, quite unexpectedly, Joel asked a question that caught him off guard. "Don't you think it was kind of odd the way Billy Newman died? Paula told me he blew himself up on his boat. A guy who had been around boats all his life? I don't think so. Something doesn't smell quite right. Did you learn anything more while you were there?"

Knowing that his brother was not only a highly intelligent individual but also very experienced in criminal investigative procedures, he replied, "I learned from Dan Hughes shortly after I arrived in Virginia that local authorities had found some evidence to support your suspicion. Jennifer Newman told me that she suspected the same thing, but had no evidence that would hold up in court. Everything I know I've learned from Dan, who I understand is on everyone's shit list as far as his credibility is concerned. But, I'm not so sure. From what I've seen and heard so far, I think Dan is a key figure in the whole affair. Not for what he's done, but for what he knows. Billy, unfortunately, got caught in the crossfire."

Joel thought a moment before giving his older brother advice, especially on matters relating to old loyalties that were very special to him, so cleverly, he came in the back door. "I remember when mom and I used to visit you in Virginia when the girls were teenagers. As a matter of friendly courtesy, the Hughes and Newman families were always invited for cocktails and dinner whenever we came to town. The grown ups, traditionally, drank too much. Dinner, of course, was always late, and the children were pretty much left by themselves in front of the television, or playing in one of the upstairs bedrooms. Whether you knew it or not, it was during those visits that I found out from Karen that Dan Hughes was very much into smoking pot. So, for whatever it means to you now, be very much aware that he has gotten himself involved in drug-related activity that you don't want any part of."

What his brother had just revealed provided little enlightenment for him, especially after having just spent three days being told the same thing. Rather than reveal what he had promised Dan, he avoided any response by looking at his watch. Grateful that it didn't allow time for further discussion on the subject, he replied, diplomatically, "Yeah, I know, but it's time to go, Bro. Thanks for taking the time to come and visit with me for a little while. I don't feel quite so guilty now for not calling you, maybe next time. I have a strange feeling that I'll be back before too long."

As they shook hands, Joel added, "Always a pleasure, brother mine. I'll make sure your nieces know their Uncle Neal sends his love. They sure think you're the cat's meow. You and all that hair I wish I had."

He laughed, and watched his brother walk down the concourse until he could no longer see the top of his balding head. Grateful for the opportunity to reunite with him again, even if for only a short time, he turned and walked slowly toward the departure gate, concerned that his return home would probably result in more than what he had bargained for at the onset. Oh well, he thought, that's what life is all about in the fast lane.

Passengers had already begun entering the aircraft when he arrived at the gate. He took his place in line, and in minutes was once again stepping through the boarding hatch of another airplane. An attractive brunette flight attendant directed him to his seat in the First Class section. However, to reach it, he had to excuse himself to a woman seated on the aisle who was nervously flipping through pages of a flight magazine. She smiled and stood up to allow him to pass, seemingly disinterested in who her co-traveler was.

Content in the knowledge that in a few hours he would be home where he belonged, and probably never should have left in the first place, he rested back against the comfortable padding of his seat and entertained himself by watching activities taking place outside on the tarmac. How could he possibly have known that the lady sitting next to him would soon be responsible for redirecting the course of his life in a way he could never have imagined?

Climbing to cruising altitude was smooth, and proceeded with its usual ritual of preparing drinks and taking orders for lunch. The curtain separating first class from the coach section had been drawn, providing an ambiance of exclusivity and personalized attention that gave him a once-in-a- lifetime feeling of being someone special, thanks to Paula's love and thoughtful generosity.

As he basked in that warm, friendly feeling of self-contentment, the stewardess approached and introduced herself as Julia, asking him and the woman seated next to him if they would like a beverage before lunch.

The woman next to him nodded, no. He, however, wasn't about to abstain from celebrating his return to paradise, so he replied, "No use quitting now, young lady. I'll kick things off with a Bloody Mary. No telling when I'll be coming back this way again."

"Good choice," she remarked, trying to hide her amusement with the only one of her passengers who seemed friendly, and in good spirits. "What brought you all the way to the East Coast, Mr. Thomas, business or pleasure?" she asked, in an equally friendly manner.

"Neither, I'm sorry to say. I came here to say goodbye to an old buddy of mine who was killed in a boating accident a week ago. He met with a rather untimely, and somewhat mysterious, demise, I'm afraid. We were best friends and neighbors when I resided here with my family years ago. We managed to get into a lot of mischief together, just ask our ex-wives. They claimed it all came out of a bottle. Looking back, I guess it did. Oh, well, that was a long time ago."

Suspecting she had asked a question that might better have been left unasked, she expressed her sympathy for his loss and assured him that, under the circumstances, he was certainly entitled to a drink and hurried off to get him one.

When she returned he watched her graceful stride, captivated by how much her mannerisms reminded him of Vicky Daniels. When she handed him his drink, he asked, "You wouldn't happen to know a fellow flight attendant by the name of Vicky Daniels, would you?"

Julia's eyes widened with surprise. "Why yes," she replied, "Vicki and I are best friends. I'm taking her place while she's on vacation. Are you a friend of hers?"

"Vicki was the attendant on my flight from San Diego last Friday," he replied. "Would you believe she was one of the guests at my friend's wake? I had no idea she lived there. We recognized each other immediately and shared some laughs over the coincidence of running into one another. She told me she spent most of her vacation time there with her Mother. It's a long story, but as I remember the relationship from many years ago, her mother and my friend's wife have been neighbors for years. Small world, isn't it?"

"It certainly is," she replied, "and getting smaller all the time."

Since he and the woman sitting in the seat beside him were the last passengers served, Julia lingered for a few minutes, anxious to learn more about how her friend was enjoying vacation. "Did her ex-boyfriend ever show up?" she asked. "His name is Dan Hughes. Vicki told me he owned a boat and kept it at the marina there. She seemed confident that he would be attending Mr. Newman's wake and appeared very anxious to see him again."

Before he could respond, a passenger on the other side of the aisle interrupted with a request for a drink, which Neal eagerly seized as an opportunity to order another for himself. That done, he settled back in his seat, amused at how small the world had become in just a few days, unaware that it was about to get a good bit smaller.

During the short passing of time that followed, the woman next to him decided to break silence and volunteered a question. "Excuse me, sir. I couldn't help overhearing your conversation with our attendant, and her mentioning a man by the name of Dan Hughes. Are you a friend of his?"

Not knowing the woman, and somewhat surprised by her sudden breech of silence, he hedged around her question by answering, "Are you?"

"Not fair," she replied. "I asked you first."

"Fair enough," he conceded, wondering just how much he should tell his attractive travel mate. "Yes, I know Dan," he began. "I've known him ever since he was a baby. His family and mine go back a long way."

Keeping a watchful eye out for Julia to return with his Bloody Mary, he continued: " I flew in from San Diego last Friday to attend a wake that was being held for an old friend of mine by the name of Billy Newman. I stayed overnight with Dan's parents that night. They were also old friends of mine. Since the wake was being held at the beach where Billy's widowed-wife lives, we drove together and met Dan at the wake. I remained there as a guest of Mrs. Newman until today. She had grown up with my former wife and was a very close friend of our family over the years. Yesterday, Dan invited me to spend the day on his boat with him so we could get reacquainted. It was a lot of fun."

From the corner of his eye, he could see Julia returning, so he quickly asked, "Now, would you mind telling me what your connection is with Dan?"

"Well, for starters, I guess the proper thing to do would be to introduce myself."

Extending her hand, she introduced herself as Jessica Sterling. "I met Dan some years ago in Cuba under some rather bizarre circumstances. I've just returned from there recently and thought I would look him up for old times sake. Unfortunately, I was unable to make contact with him. Apparently, he was with you."

Without associating any significance to her name, he replied, "My name is Neal Thomas. It's a pleasure to meet you."

As soon as their hands separated, Julia turned from serving a passenger across the aisle and handed him his Bloody Mary, encouraging him at the same time to continue with his accounting of the Newman wake and her friend, Vicki Daniels.

Briefly, and without embellishment, he described the previous Saturday's events, trying not to provide too much detail regarding Dan and Vicki's relationship. He did, however, explain that they had met and appeared to be enjoying themselves until they were interrupted by a call on Dan's cell phone. "Shortly after that, Dan excused himself and left," he explained, "presumably for privacy, however, he didn't return until some time later. Harsh words were exchanged and he left again, visibly upset."

Satisfied with his condensed version of the weekend, Julia thanked him and left with a reminder that lunch would be served in a few minutes. Her departure opened another opportunity for him to question Jessica further about her relationship with Dan. Rather than beat around the bush with pointless conversation, he came right to the point. "How long have you known Dan?"

Collecting her thoughts for a moment, she wondered how much Dan had told Mr. Thomas about how they had met. Of one thing she was sure, Dan would not have told the stranger sitting beside her anything, had he not trusted him implicitly. So, she said, "If you believe that birds of a feather flock together, then I guess you could say that Dan and I were destined to meet one another at some point in time. The event took place on a deserted beach near the eastern end of Cuba. A sudden storm forced him to crash-land his plane on that beach. Lucky for him, it was me who found him. The rest is history."

"But you're an American," he remarked, quietly. "What in the hell were you doing in Cuba? And, what are you doing here now?"

Fortunately, the disruption of lunch being served saved her from having to respond immediately, and offered the opportunity to think more about what she was going to say. Her inquisitor, on the other hand, seemed a good deal more interested in his meal than he was in her answer, so she relaxed and tried to enjoy the only decent meal she had eaten in several days.

The silence that followed brought a welcome distraction from the unpleasant substance of his inquiry, because it invaded a part of her life that she would have preferred to remain private. On the other hand, the coincidence of meeting a total stranger on an airplane who knew a mutual friend did seem to demand some kind of meaningful response.

Following lunch, she felt she could no longer ignore the questions he had put to her earlier, so she answered them somewhat defensibly. "Why I was in Cuba is of little consequence, and too complicated to go into right now. Suffice it to say that when Dan recovered from his injuries, I arranged to get him off the island before the wrong people discovered he was there. I felt that, if I didn't, he would have been needlessly killed. I liked Dan. He was the first American I had seen in a very long time, and I didn't want to see him harmed."

While she sipped from a lukewarm cup of coffee waiting for him to comment, he began recalling bits and pieces of the story Dan had told him the previous day about his crash landing in Cuba. When all the pieces came together, he came to the conclusion that no matter how far fetched the coincidence seemed to be, he was sitting next to the woman who had rescued him. The woman her fellow soldiers had called, "Jess."

Watching her silently anticipating his next question, he reached into his hip pocket, pulled out his wallet and found the business card Sandy Sterling had given him, along with Jessica's old driver's license Dan had given him only yesterday, and placed them on her tray. "It would appear that you and these two items have something in common, wouldn't you say?"

The sight of her mother's name, and the old driver's license she had given Dan the night he left Cuba, sent a shock wave through her that drained some of the color from her face. She stared at them for a moment and then faced him, asking nervously, "Where did you get these?"

Her reaction convinced him that playing games with her emotions was inappropriate at that time, so he patted her arm gently, and smiled to ease the tension. "The card was given to me by a very lovely woman who sat next to me on my flight from San Diego to Washington last Friday. Her name is Sandy Sterling. The driver's license is yours, obviously. You gave it to Dan the night you said goodbye to him in Cuba, and asked him to get in touch with your mother to inform her that you were alive and well. I had no way of knowing how long Dan kept your license. But knowing Dan, I'm sure he never contacted her, and is just now getting around to it by passing the responsibility on to me, which I intended to take care of as soon I got back to San Diego."

Watching her staring nervously off into space, something in the physical characteristics of her face suddenly triggered a memory that transported him back to his flight from San Diego where, as now, he found himself looking into the lovely face of a woman in the seat next to him. As the two faces slowly began to blend into unmistakable likeness, he laughed at himself for not making the connection sooner. "Apparently, the Sandy

Sterling I flew across the country with last Friday is the same woman he wanted me to contact in San Diego. And, I think it's safe to say, the mother you haven't seen in twenty years. Correct me, if I'm wrong."

She was slow to respond, but after careful consideration decided nothing could be gained by avoiding the truth. Resting her head back against her seat she began to speak, effortlessly and with compassion. "No, you're not wrong. That is my mother. I recognize the business address on the card. My father owned his own publishing company before he died. His death really pushed me over the edge. Heartbroken and afraid to face the future without him, I foolishly turned to drugs. My mother, who I didn't get along with at the time, was quick to recognize the change in my behavior. She was continually on my case to get help, but I wouldn't listen. Frustrated and angry, I finally ran away from home."

With her brief but candid admission out in the open he was hesitant to pursue the subject any further, so he provided her with an option, by asking, "Do you want to talk about it?"

Her response was not immediate because the lifestyle she was used to rarely tolerated any round table discussion. She did, however, recognize the sincerity in his voice, and accepted the fact that if she ever expected to survive the emotional upheaval she was flying into, she would need a friend. "I'm not proud of what I did to my mother by running away," she admitted. "Nor am I proud of what I've become. It's taken me this long to learn that I made a monumental mistake, and I'll probably spend the rest of my life atoning for it. The truth is, what's done is done. Now it's time to get on with my life while I still can. Hopefully, my mother will forgive me and want to be a part of it. Although, I wouldn't blame her if she didn't"

"Have you talked with her?"

"Unfortunately, no. I was hoping to make contact with Dan before I left for San Diego so I could ascertain how my mother reacted to the news he was supposed to have delivered. That's why I went to Virginia in the first place. I did finally make contact with his parents, but they informed me that he was away for the weekend and didn't know when he'd return. I was hoping to at least talk to him, but I guess it just wasn't in the cards."

"Dan has a long history of irresponsibility," he commented, "I doubt very seriously if he ever gave any thought to contacting your mother, or that he even remembered saying he would until I came along and started asking questions about his past. He's a good-hearted person in many ways, but not very reliable, I'm afraid."

After pausing for a moment, she looked at him and sighed, "I guess I'm just going to have to rely on you then, since you unknowingly spent the whole day with my mother last Friday. What kind of an impression did she make on you?"

Unable to escape the directness of her question, and hoping his response would not put her on the defensive, he replied, "You're mother is a very attractive and caring woman who is going to be emotionally devastated when you show up on her door step without any warning. My concern is that you may be setting yourself up for one hell of a disappointment, considering the years that have gone by without any communication between the two of you. Have you considered that possibility?"

"Yes I have," she replied with conviction. "I would be a fool not to. That's why I wanted to talk to Dan. I could have at least gotten some feel for what to expect. Now I really don't know what to do, except to confront her and accept the consequences whatever they might be."

"Well, you have one thing going for you," he commented. "She did mention that the meeting she was attending in Philadelphia wasn't scheduled to begin until today, so she booked her return for Wednesday. That will give us time to plan a way for the two of you to reunite with as little emotional trauma as possible. Twenty years is a long time."

"Us?"

He knew immediately from the surprised expression on her face that he had once again inadvertently involved himself in someone else's business without being asked. Having unwittingly implied his willingness to become involved, there was little left for him to do but offer it. "Given these somewhat dubious circumstances, my dear," he replied, fatalistically, "you're going to need all the help you can get, want it or not."

The sincerity in his tired eyes made her aware that sitting next to her was someone genuinely interested in helping her. This was an awareness she had not experienced in a long time, and it pleased her. "It's been some time since anyone gave a damn about doing anything for me that didn't have a long string attached to it," she remarked, cynically. "As you so aptly put it, I'm going to need all the help I can get."

Before explaining how he intended to help he noticed Julia standing in her service cubicle observing the interaction that was taking place between the two of them, so he pressed the service button. Considering the commitment he had just made, he rationalized that it was as good a time as any to seal it with a drink.

When she arrived, he remarked, "I don't know about my friend here, but I could use another Bloody Mary."

Jessica looked at him, and then at Julia, hesitant to follow suit, but finally gave in.

"I'll probably regret this, but you might as well make it two."

Winking at Neal, she smiled and returned to her cubicle, whispering to herself, "You sly old fox."

While waiting for her to return, Jessica took on a look of puzzlement, and asked, "To satisfy my curiosity, just how are you planning to arrange this meeting between my mother and me? I'm starting to have serious reservations about whether or not I'm doing the right thing. What if she doesn't want to see me?"

"I don't think that's likely," he replied. "Unless I miss my guess, when she realizes you're for real, and all in one piece, you're going to get one hell of an ass-chewing for what you've put her through for the past twenty years. Then, I suspect, she'll break down and cry her eyes out."

"I've been chewed on by professionals," she remarked, halfway laughing. "Believe me, that I can handle."

"Well then, here's what I have in mind."

The words had hardly left his lips when Julia returned with their drinks. She didn't linger, having sensed that something sensitive was being discussed. Her hasty departure gave him the opportunity to continue his proposal. "Does anyone in San Diego know what you are planning to do?"

"No." she replied, sounding somewhat despondent over what was slowly developing into a more complicated situation than she had previously imagined. "I'd be a fool not to recognize that many of my friends will probably be scattered all over the globe, living their own lives and hardly concerned with my whereabouts. I was counting on my mother to bring me up to date on that subject. That is, providing she'd even talk to me. I'm doing this cold turkey, Mister Thomas. Flying blind, so to speak. And, I'm fully prepared to accept the consequences of my decision."

"Let's assume that your mother is still in Philadelphia," he suggested, "Where were you planning to stay when you arrived in San Diego?

"Believe it or not," she replied, "I did anticipate that eventuality and made advance reservations at a hotel in La Jolla where my parents used to take me for dinner. I planned to phone her from there, not just show up on her doorstep. I'm not that stupid!"

Recognizing that she might have already anticipated a negative response from her mother, and was reacting defensively to his inquiry, he softened his approach with a touch of humor. "I've met very few stupid women in my life, dear lady. Those who I erroneously thought were, are now spending their husband's inheritances."

His remark brought a chuckle to her beautiful face, and a calming affect to the perplexity that lay ahead. Still unsure of what he had meant by arranging a meeting, she pursued the matter further by expressing her own brand of humor. "I'm still not sure about how this is all going to come together. But this I do know; when you're all the way down, there's nowhere to go but up. So, point the way, Mr. Fixit, I'd follow you down the barrel of a cannon!"

"That's a girl," he replied, relieved that her mood had become more positive. "Go ahead and check into your hotel," he suggested, "but don't try to get in touch with your mother. Wait until after I've had a chance to do what Dan Hughes should have already done. Hopefully, I can convince her that your silence was all his fault."

"It was, in a way," she tried to convince herself. "Over the years, I've pacified my conscience by believing that Dan had been loyal to his promise and called her. I should have known better than to trust anyone involved in hustling drugs. But, then again, there are a lot of things I should have known. Kind of late to be blaming someone else for my own stupidity."

"Don't be too hard on yourself, or Dan," he said, comfortingly. "He's about as reliable as a flat tire. I'm sure you're familiar with that old saying about trusting others to do what you can do for yourself. Dan's heart is in the right place, but sometimes his head isn't. I can assure you, however, that all of this is going to work itself out. You and your mother are going to be reunited in a few days, and all of your concerns will disappear. Believe me, I will help you make it happen."

With less than an hour left before their flight landed in San Diego, Jessica turned thoughtfully away from the promise her newly adopted friend had just made, confident that his age and wisdom would help her recapture the love and forgiveness of her Mother, whom she had so foolishly abandoned twenty years ago.

Neal, on the other hand, looked with growing anticipation at the ever-approaching range of coastal mountains that beaconed the land of his childhood dreams. A place where movies were made and fantasies came to life, John Wayne country. Where beaches are literally strewn with beautiful women sunning their bodies, while surfers ride the breaking waves trying to attract them. A return to paradise, where anything can happen, and usually does.

Part 2
The Aftermath

Chapter 8

Welcome Home

As much as Paula wished she could turn back the hands of time, the first light of dawn crept relentlessly into the bedroom where she lay restlessly trying to deny Monday's arrival. The wakeup buzzer had already sounded, giving her another few minutes before she had to get out of bed to face another day's challenges. Somewhat relieved that Neal was not there to distract her into doing something she didn't have time for, her thoughts concentrated on the day ahead.

What came to mind first was her department head's insistence that she find someone other than herself to meet Neal at the airport that afternoon. As he had explained on the previous Friday, her attendance at the department's Monday staff meeting was absolutely essential, so she was compelled to ask Ron Barns to help her out. He said he would be glad to, commenting that although he hated going to the airport, he was anxious to hear about Neal's trip, and welcomed the opportunity to share a drink with him to celebrate his return.

Of equal concern was her speculation on what kind of shape he would be in after three days of partying? Predictably, he would be tired, hung over and uninterested in pursuing anything more than a couple of drinks in the Jacuzzi, a bite to eat and falling asleep in front of the television.

The more traditionally amorous homecomings she had looked forward to during the earlier years of their relationship would, regrettably, have to be postponed until after the recuperative period. Accepting the inevitable, she threw back the covers and walked lazily to the bathroom where the warm soothing water of a shower began caressing her anxiety away, making the beginning of her day seem just a little brighter and easier to face.

Refreshed, she began the process of applying her makeup while a cassette player in the bedroom played a tape of ocean waves breaking on a rocky shoreline, a sound that over the years had been the background for their more frequent moments of intimacy, she recalled. His putting the coffee on at the same time began a daily routine that repeated itself from the first day they began living together. It was a time when conversation between them covered everything from office politics to explaining the ending to whatever television program he had fallen asleep on the previous evening. Trivia was also addressed, and usually covered grocery items they were out of, cautions that wine and vodka levels were getting dangerously low, and general commentary on actions and activities of their respective children and friends, which – for obvious reasons – had to be carefully phrased.

For the most part, their conversations were light and jovial. There were times, however, when his unintentional preoccupation with what he had planned for his day vexed her to the point of exasperation. "Not remembering what I tell you is a dead give away that you are exercising that selective memory of yours again," she would scold on occasion.

He, of course, denied the accusation and would reply, in jest, "I am an innocent victim of Attention Deficit Disorder. You know, ADD. For example, when I am reading something, or performing a task of some kind, a totally irrelevant thought comes to mind that makes it necessary for me to re-read a sentence in order for it to sink in. I guess that's where the term, *slow reader*, comes from."

The smiling face she saw looking back at her from the mirror was a pleasant reminder that, regardless of his forgetfulness, the frivolity of his logic, or the voracious appetite he had for her, sexually, he was fundamentally a very kind, thoughtful and talented man, whose only fault was being a dreamer, and too easily taken advantage of by those who would call themselves his friends.

As her combing fingers primped and coaxed her hair into the style that had become her signature, she turned her attention away from Neal and concentrated more on what she was going to be confronted with at work that day.

For starters, she knew her boss – a man she had comically dubbed, "Doug the Hustler" – would ask her to brief him on questions he would be expected to answer at that day's staff meeting. Typically, she had learned over the years, that he was never adequately prepared for anything. Anticipating all of this, she had managed to obtain a copy of the meeting agenda from her friend, Susie, the City Manager's secretary. The agenda, and other data she was able to get from the city's central computer, would be enough information to prevent Doug from embarrassing himself in front of his peers. It had happened before and resulted in everyone's life at the office, and at home, being made miserable for days. Her personal commitment was never to let it happen again. Today, she anticipated, would be a test.

Putting aside her anxiety, she took comfort in the fact that Neal's presence in their home again would neutralize any negative thoughts she might take away from the meeting. How comforting, she thought, to know the abuses she had endured from her former husband during their child-raising years would never threaten her again. No more would she have to tolerate drunken behavior that included both verbal and physical harassment.

By comparison, she concluded, Neal was a piece of cake. The worst she could expect from him would probably be no more threatening than seeing him playing the piano when she arrived home in the evening, probably because he was fantasizing over some young woman he had seen at the beach that day. Amused by the picture, she concluded it would be silly to be too concerned over such adolescent behavior? To do so would be as ridiculous as scolding a teenager for enjoying all the attendant discoveries of puberty. Such discoveries were a normal part of the growing up process, which she had to admit, he had not yet completed.

For whatever reason, eating breakfast during the week had never been a daily habit for her. Neal, on the other hand, treated himself to a good breakfast every morning, one that would see him through until dinner. Because she preferred only to drink coffee and read the newspaper, he made a special effort to prepare something special on weekends, a treat that always pleased her with almost child-like enthusiasm.

Sipping her coffee while glancing at the clock, occasionally, she was suddenly chilled by the thought that he might not always be there for her; a reaction intensified by the gray, chilly marine layer that blanketed the coast, covering their home like a *Foggy Day In London Town,* as he might have musically referred to it. How strange, that on the day of his return she should experience such a gloomy forecast. One that had never expressed itself in all of the years they had known each another.

Lukewarm coffee and a quick glance at her watch, however, brought back the reality that she could no longer dawdle time away thinking about silly premonitions. Securing the house, she drove down the ocean highway to work, glad that he would be home that evening when she returned.

At the same time she was cautiously making her way through the dense fog that was everywhere, Neal was awakened from dozing by the Captain announcing that they would be arriving in San Diego in forty-five minutes. Anticipating that Paula would be waiting for him outside the baggage claim area, he rolled his head toward the seat next to him and observed Jessica staring thoughtfully at the ceiling. Suspecting that she might be a bit anxious about what lay beyond those forty-five minutes, he asked, "Are you getting a little nervous, now that you're almost home?"

"Nervous doesn't even come close," she answered, her gaze still fixed on the ceiling. "I'm having serious doubts about whether I'm doing the right thing as far as my mother is concerned. Maybe I should leave well enough alone and go on back to where I came from."

"And just where would that be?"

Realizing she had opened a door that was best left closed, she rolled her head toward his, and replied, "You really don't want to know."

Her reply made it difficult for him to ease her anxiety so he fashioned a different approach out of an incident a friend had shared with him not long ago. "One of my closest friends is a crazy Irishman by the name of John Pauley. He's the father of quite a large family. One evening after we had been drinking for some time, he told me that his wife had died of cancer early in their marriage, leaving him with all the children to raise and educate. He also told me that the oldest daughter, eighteen at the time, was so devastated by her mother's death that she left college and disappeared for over two years without telling him one word about where she had gone, or who she was with. The only thing that kept John from going crazy was his responsibility to the rest of his family."

Before he could continue, Jessica interrupted. "What you're telling me is all very interesting, Mister Thomas, but what does it have to do with me?"

"Just the coincidence, my dear," he replied. "You see, John told me that he had just about given up on ever seeing his daughter again when he received an unexpected phone call one day. When he answered, the tearful voice of his oldest daughter asked for his forgiveness and confessed she wanted to come home. Well, the sound of her voice and the knowledge that she was alive melted his heart like an ice cream cone on a hot day in July. Now she's the mother of three of his many grandchildren, and the apple of his eye. That incident reminded me of your current dilemma. I think you should be aware that running away from a situation doesn't fix anything. If you run, you'll be haunted all your life by never knowing how your mother would react to seeing you again. Facing her, no matter what the outcome, is still your wisest alternative. It's old advice, but as true as the first time it was given."

"You mentioned a little while ago that you wanted to help make this reunion happen," She remarked. "Do you have a specific plan in mind?"

A sharp reduction in air speed as the plane began to nose down gave notice that their final approach was only minutes away. Pressured to settle the matter before they landed, he began to outline a plan that would inform her mother that Jessica was alive and well without actually speaking to her. "Every year on the Fourth of July my lady friend and I throw a party for family, friends and people we do business with. There will be plenty of food, spirits and entertainment. It's the perfect setting for having a good time in the sun, and it's strictly casual."

"Whoa, slow down," she cautioned, placing her hand on his arm. "This still doesn't deal with the shock of my mother learning that I'm almost on her doorstep. How do you propose to accomplish that?"

"I'm getting to that," he replied. "Listen carefully to what I have in mind."

Before he could get the first word out, an announcement from the cockpit directed the flight attendants to prepare for landing. While they scurried about the cabin picking up empty glasses and waking passengers, he proceeded to explain his proposal, hoping it would provide the encouragement she needed to reunite with the unsuspecting mother she had run away from so many years ago. "In a few days I'm going to contact your mother and invite her to join me for lunch." he explained. "At that time, I will tell her about Dan Hughes and what he was supposed to have done after he left you in Cuba. Hopefully, her reaction to the news that you are alive and here in San Diego will tell me all I need to know about how wise your decision to come here really was. If she expresses a sincere willingness to meet with you, I will invite her to my party. The atmosphere there will lend itself to a less traumatic reunion for you both. If, on the other hand, she tells me she doesn't want anything to do with you, then at least you will have been spared the hurt and embarrassment of face-to-face animosity. In either event, you will have the satisfaction of having tried and can get on with your life, wherever it takes you."

For a moment he thought he saw tears starting to gather in her eyes, but she wiped them away before they could show themselves. "I guess the big question on my mind is, why are you going to all this trouble to reunite two people you hardly know? What's in it for you?"

"Absolutely nothing," he answered, watching San Diego's airport runway rapidly approaching. "Had Dan followed up on what you asked him to do years ago, your return today might not be such a shock to your mother. At least she would have known you were alive. Didn't you ever write to her? A Christmas card, a phone call, something?"

She hesitated a moment until the whining of lowering the landing flaps and wheels ended before answering. "To most people, my failure to communicate with my mother might be interpreted as an expression of cruel and unusual behavior. They would be right, I suppose. Someday, it may be possible for me to explain my behavior, but for now, I can't. Please know that I shall be forever grateful to you for whatever you can arrange in order to help bring my mother and me together again. Your proposal sounds reasonable, so just tell me how I can help"

They were on the ground taxiing toward the terminal when he reached under the seat for his briefcase and withdrew a business card he had designed to advertise his artwork. Placing it in her trembling hand, he looked into her troubled eyes and smiled. "Not to worry," he comforted her, "this will keep you in touch with me should the need arise. Call me in a couple of days when you're rested and we'll talk. Okay?

She nodded, affirmatively, and rested back against the seat. As they docked at the terminal, she turned to him and expressed her thanks for the help he had offered. To assure him that she was prepared to re-enter a world that she hadn't seen since her teen years, she said, "I have a car reserved in my name, and I'm sure I can still find my way around this town, so don't worry. I'll be fine. I will call you as soon as I'm settled."

Once inside the terminal, he remained with her until she was safely aboard the rental car shuttle. Then, bags in hand, he sought out a place to sit while he waited for Paula's arrival. Minutes had turned into almost a half an hour when he decided to call her office. Half way through dialing her number on his cell phone, a familiar voice rang out from the curb area directly in front of him. There, in the midst of all that turmoil, was an arm waving frantically from the all to familiar cab of Ron's pickup truck.

"Ah, hah," he mumbled. "There's been a change in plans."

Almost jogging, he reached the truck, placed his bags in the flat bed and slid into the cab alongside his frustrated buddy.

"Sorry I'm late," he apologized. "Traffic is exactly why I hate coming down to this place. It's stop-and-go all the way past the merge, both directions, so I brought you a couple of beers to sip on while we stop and go our way up the freeway. Now, lets get the hell out of this mess!"

Amused by Ron's impatience with matters over which had had no control, he settled back with his beer and enjoyed its calming affect. Considering the hangover that was gradually settling in, he was glad Ron didn't insist on him accounting for every minute of his time In Virginia. After thanking him for being there to meet his flight, he waited for as long as it took to exit the terminal area before asking, "What happened to Paula?

"Her boss insisted that she bring him up to speed on some meeting they had to attend tonight. It was going to take her all day to gather the information so she called and asked if I would do her a favor and pick you up. Now I ask you, how could I refuse?"

From the time they left the airport until the welcome sight of his home came into view, Neal remained virtually mute about the events that had taken place during his three-day absence. Coming to a stop in front of his garage, however, encouraged him to invite Ron in. "I know how you feel about drinking on a weekday," he remarked, "but how about joining me for a roader before you leave? I really do appreciate you picking me up."

Ron hesitated for a moment, recalling the three DUI citations that were already on his record. "Thanks, but no thanks. Tomorrow will be soon enough. You are coming down to shoot pool, aren't you? Everyone's anxious to hear about your trip."

"I'll be there, but I'm not taking any bets on my performance."

As the truck slowly disappeared behind the many trees that privatized the property, he walked to the front door and let himself in. The air inside was a little musty from being closed up all day so he set about opening windows and doors, allowing the refreshing scent of the sea to filter in.

Unpacking in the buff came next. Being naked made it quick and easy for him to slip into his swim trunks for a much-anticipated soak in the Jacuzzi. As he entered the kitchen, he noticed a magnet-held note hanging on the refrigerator door, and the light on the telephone answering machine blinking, so he pushed it. "Hi, Mister Thomas," the message began, "this is Jessica Sterling calling to let you know that I am registered at the La Valencia Hotel in La Jolla, room 201. Also, I want to thank you again for being so kind. I look forward to hearing from you soon. Hope you're having a great homecoming. Bye."

He could feel the perspiration start to pop out on his forehead, as he listened to the voice that prompted him to stiffen the drink he had already started to prepare. Reviewing the situation, he reasoned that there was nothing really unusual about getting a call from a female acquaintance. But trying to explain the hotel room number would be a hard sell, especially after just having come off a three day trip, so he erased it, glad that it had said no more than it did.

With his drink nearly half gone from the anxiety attack he had just experienced, he turned toward the refrigerator to read the note. It read:

Hi Curly,

Sorry I couldn't pick you up today. That jerk
I work for has me running all over the place
in order to prepare for a meeting tonight. I'll be late.
Grab a bite to eat and I'll see you in the morning.
Love you,
Me

Tossing the note into the trash compactor, he walked out onto the patio deck and turned the Jacuzzi on, grateful for the solitude and comfort its hot, swirling water would bring. A line from an old Beatles song came to mind as he lowered himself slowly into the water: "Alone again, naturally."

Fifteen minutes after soaking and mulling over events of the past four days, he rose up onto the redwood decking and let the soft ocean breeze dry his body.

Off in the distance, colors mixing in the sky over the horizon heralded the coming of night and gave birth to stars already twinkling in the darkening sky overhead.

While his towel-wrapped body made its way to the bluff to view the beach below, scattered silhouettes of people walked casually on the wet sand. It was while standing there on that little piece of paradise that he came face to face with the reality that his here-to-fore simple existence was now a thing of the past. Nothing, he feared, was ever going to be the same again. Rather than let the bizarre events of the past few days dampen his enthusiasm for what lay ahead, he reached upward, glass in hand, and spoke to the stars. "Here's to you, Billy! Thanks for the memories."

Walking back toward the housc he began thinking about what priorities he had to address that week. Of primary importance was determining whether or not Sandy Sterling had returned from her trip to Philadelphia. Nothing he had promised Jessica could take place until her return was verified.

Also of importance was preparation of the menu and guest list for his and Paula's annual Fourth of July party. Before he could give it the attention it demanded the phone rang. When he picked up the receiver he heard Paula's voice speaking to someone in her office whom had apparently interrupted her. His cheery, "Hello," however, recaptured her attention. "I'm sorry, dear," she apologized, "I was calling to make sure you were home safely when one of our more inconsiderate committee persons interrupted me with an absolutely stupid question about a dead issue. How are you?"

"Tired and hung over," he replied, "but you already knew that. I saw the note you left. Do you have any idea when you'll be home?"

"Not really, there's a mountain of paperwork I have to go over. Just go on to bed whenever you feel like it. I feel terrible about not being there on your first night home."

"Don't worry, there's no need trying to fix something that isn't broken. I doubt you'll find me awake whenever you do get home, anyway. I'll see you when I see you. Drive carefully."

"Thank you, dear. You can tell me all about your trip tomorrow. I bet you had a fabulous time. See you in the morning."

Putting the receiver back in its cradle, he looked at the clock and decided it was too late to mess up the kitchen when he wasn't really that hungry. In a gesture to put some finality to the trip, he fixed a nightcap, turned on the television and settled back in his recliner to view the evening news. He hadn't been watching long when the commentator's emotionally sterile presentation of what had gone on in the world that day lowered his eyelids as if they were window shades. He was asleep, a deep, snoring sleep.

Several hours later, and more tired than she could ever remember being, Paula pulled into the driveway, grateful that the horrible day she had struggled through had finally come to an end. The lights inside the house were still on, which could only be for one of two reasons; Neal was already in bed and had left them on for her. Or, as she was more inclined to believe, he was asleep in his chair.

Letting herself in as quietly as she could, the latter of her two suspicions was amusingly confirmed. Putting her purse and briefcase aside, she changed into something comfortable and returned downstairs to the kitchen where a much-needed glass of wine needed only the pouring. Though it helped to put the day behind her, his snoring remained ever mindful that reality was alive and well. After several futile attempts to wake him, she finally gave up, turned off the television and went to bed, consoled by the thought that he would eventually wake up and take his place beside her. Homecoming in the traditional sense, she pondered with some regret, would have to wait.

Six o'clock the next morning arrived as it always had, on time, abrupt and unwanted. After two, ten-minute intervals of snoozing, she finally accepted the message her clock radio was programmed to deliver and walked sleepily to the shower to avoid being snuggled into a compromising situation.

By the time she had finished showering, he had already made his way to the kitchen to prepare coffee. As he reviewed his daily routine, he came to the conclusion that being retired hadn't changed his habits that much. Even as a kid he was up at first light of dawn, eager to take on whatever the day had to offer. This day was no exception. Despite a lingering hangover, he had separated the newspaper and set out the cups when she arrived in her robe and slippers.

"Hi there, Curly" she greeted him with feigned enthusiasm. "I'm sorry I was so late getting home last night. I was hoping your first night home could have been a little more romantic, but I'm really not into waking the dead to achieve it."

"Good thinking," he remarked. "There's always tonight, tomorrow or whenever. I'm just glad to be home. Now, do I get a kiss, or do I carry you back to bed?"

"At the risk of you throwing your back out again, I think it would be more prudent if we just kissed. We'll discuss the other thing this evening in the Jacuzzi. Now… shall we?"

Hidden by the semi-darkness of early morning, he and Paula embraced in a lingering kiss that held all the passion of the first time they had kissed many years ago. Their bodies pressed tightly together and writhed in harmony causing Paula's robe to partially separate and expose the soft mounds of flesh that flattened under the pressure of his embrace.

It was Paula who quickly recognized the consequences of continuing their togetherness. Breaking away slowly, she patted his flushed face and asked, in a slow, sultry voice, "Is that a roll of quarters in your pocket, big guy, or are you just glad to see me?"

As always, he couldn't resist her knack for expressing humor at the appropriate time and began to laugh. Imitating the voice of his childhood hero, John Wayne, he replied in kind, "Well, yeah gotta cock it first, pilgrim."

The next hour passed quickly while they read the newspaper, discussed the highlights of his trip, and the usual trivia associated with her daily routine during his absence. On another note, she somewhat casually mentioned that their Fourth of July party would be coming up soon. "Have you given any thought to the guest list, or what type of food we should serve? Your smoked salmon was a big hit last year."

Until that moment his thoughts had been preoccupied with scattered events of the past weekend and shooting pool with Ron Barns and the guys that afternoon. Somehow, their annual party, and all the preparations it required, seemed too far away to demand any immediate attention, but her reminder brought home the message that it was, in fact, almost upon them.

Considering it a little premature to mention anything about inviting Jessica Sterling and her mother, he replied, "With a few exceptions, I don't see much of a change from last year's list, unless you have someone in particular you'd like to invite. I would, however, like to do something different, as far as food is concerned. What do you think about a big kettle of ranch style, beef chili, with beans and onions?"

The wall clock suddenly reminded her that, if she lingered any longer to discuss the party, she was going to be late for work. Not wanting to sound disinterested in his suggestions, she replied, "Let's save this discussion for the Jacuzzi tonight. I need to get to work to review my notes on last night's meeting."

The pressure she was under was understandable, so he motioned her to go and get dressed and walked to his studio with a fresh cup of coffee to read the unopened mail that lay waiting on his desk.

A short time later, she appeared in the studio impeccably dressed and asked him to escort her to her car. Before leaving, as was her habit, she hesitated momentarily to wish him good luck with his pool game, and to be mindful of how much he drank.

He nodded, affirmatively, knowing from experience that what she was asking was, in part, contradictory. As she turned to enter the car, he patted her on the backside and teased, "Hmm, nice buns!"

Back in his studio, he sat for a moment trying to decide how to best spend the day until it was time to journey south to join Ron Barns and the boys for another Tuesday afternoon of shooting pool. The large oil painting he had been working on for months seemed to be asking him to finish it, but a voice from within, and an unsteady hand, cautioned: *Better wait a day or two, old man. This is not a good time.*

Curious to see if he had received any e-mail messages during his absence, he left the easel and powered up his computer, waiting patiently for a familiar voice to announce, "Welcome. You've got mail."

As usual, there were messages from close friends, some relatives and a few air travel and vacation package solicitations, the usual Spam. However, at the end of the reading and deletion process he was attracted to the last letter's subject. It read: "*Thanks For The Memories.*"

Curious, he clicked it open. It read:

Hi Neal,

Sorry I wasn't able to come back to Nick's to wish you bon voyage. I'll make it up to you when I come to San Diego. Will keep you informed as soon as I work out the details. Best wishes to all.

Dan

After reading the letter several times, he clicked *delete* and shut the computer down, deciding it would not be a wise move to mention anything about it to Paula until after he knew when Dan was planning to arrive. The possibility of him showing up on or near their Fourth of July festivities was a bit un-nerving. That kind of a surprise, it goes without saying, would not be well received, especially by her.

The e-mail did, however, refresh his memory about contacting Sandy Sterling. After all, it was he who was keeping Jessica in a holding pattern until he talked to her mother. It was his responsibility to follow up on what he had promised, so he called information and got the number. After the third ring a woman's voice answered. "Good morning, Sterling Publishing," she said, pleasantly. "How may I help you?"

"My name is Neal Thomas. May I speak with Sandy Sterling, please?"

"Thank you," she replied. "I'll connect you."

Following a brief interlude of classical music, the receptionist's voice came back on line and said, regrettably, "I'm sorry, Mister Thomas, Ms. Sterling is on another line, but wants your number so she can call you back as soon as she's finished."

The number given, he hung up and walked leisurely into the kitchen, filled his cup with what was left of the coffee and shut it down. He had only taken a couple of sips when he realized that more coffee was a mistake, so he poured it in the sink, picked up the portable phone and walked out onto the patio deck. He hadn't been there thirty seconds when it rang. It was Sandy Sterling returning his call.

Following a mutual exchange of polite inquiries she laughed and remarked with noticeable enthusiasm, "Frankly, Mister Thomas, I'm both surprised and pleased to hear from you so soon. Are you responding to the offer I made you in Washington, or is this a social call?"

"Well, for starters," he replied, "please call me Neal. As far as my reason for calling is concerned, I'm having a hard time with where to begin, so bear with me."

"I'm listening."

"An old friend of mine, whom I met at Billy Newman's wake a few days ago, admitted to me that he had neglected to deliver an important message to you some years ago, and asked me if I would deliver it when he learned that you and I knew one another. It's too complicated to discuss over the phone, so would you be interested in joining me for lunch today to discuss the matter?

"I'm sorry, Neal, my whole day is booked solid, but tomorrow is open, if that's convenient for you."

"That's fine. My treat."

"Why don't you come to my office around one o'clock," she suggested. "That way we'll miss most of La Jolla's luncheon traffic. I know a quiet little spot near the ocean where you can deliver your message. I'll leave word with the parking attendant in our building tomorrow morning so you'll have a place to park. I'll drive."

"Thanks. I'll see you tomorrow."

Following their brief conversation he proceeded to his studio, exhilarated by how enthusiastically she had responded to his unexpected call. His excitement was short lived, however, when he reflected on how little he knew about her daughter's whereabouts for the past twenty years. There was only one way he could overcome that hurdle. He had to confront Jessica and intimidate her into revealing the truth about her past.

Convinced that there were no other options available to him, he picked up the phone and dialed the La Valencia Hotel and asked for her room. After six rings without an answer, he started to hang up until a panting voice on the other end cried out, "Hello! This is Jessica!"

"Hi, this is Neal Thomas. Are you okay? You sound out of breath?"

In a voice that giggled almost like a child, she apologized. "I'm sorry it took me so long. I was in the shower washing my hair when the phone rang. All I could do was grab a towel and rush to answer it. Fortunately, you can't see me standing here sopping wet and all covered with soap."

It took a moment or two for the image of her naked body to disappear before he asked, "Can you have lunch with me today? My treat."

"I'd like that very much. Would you like to come to La Jolla, or can I meet you somewhere?"

Since he was going to be in Del Mar that afternoon anyway, he suggested that she meet him at Bully's Restaurant at one o'clock, figuring that it was approximately an equal distance for both of them, and the atmosphere would be casual and relaxed. "It's right in the middle of town on Camino Del Mar, he explained. "You can't miss it."

"Believe it or not, I know exactly where it is," she assured him. "My Dad used to take Mom and me there for lunch on weekends before we went to the track. Don't worry, I'll be there."

For the rest of that morning he struggled to get back into his daily routine by scraping dried paint from a palette and selecting brushes and various tubes of paint that were essential to begin work again. His heart wasn't really in the effort but managed to accomplish a few things before time demanded that he leave. With renewed enthusiasm, he put his art work aside, secured the house and drove down the coast to unlock the mystery of Jessica's past, hoping all the while that he was doing the right thing for all concerned.

When he drove into Bully's parking lot a half an hour later there were no parking spaces available so he stopped at the valet parking sign and left his car with the attendant. While walking up the ramp to the street level entrance it dawned on him that the Del Mar Fair was in town, which explained the lack of parking spaces and the streets crowded with people.

Bully's was equally crowded. Scanning the bar, his attention was drawn to a waving arm and a pretty face beckoning him to join her. Getting there was another matter, however. It was a common practice – for single women and ladies of the night – to congregate at the high bar, making it awkward to pass them without making contact. Recognizing this hazard, Jessica left her stool and wiggled her way to where he stood waiting amused by the gyrations she went through to get there. "I figured leaving my seat would be a lot easier than you trying to get past all those drooling broads," she remarked, "Why don't we go out on the patio where there's some fresh air. I made a reservation in your name. We're number six in line."

As she led him to the patio area, he recognized a change in her that had softened her appearance. She wore a knee-length, all white, sleeveless dress gathered at the waist by a thin white belt. Her hair was tied up in a ponytail that hung from the opening in a white visor cap. Except for a light brush of pink blush on her cheeks, her only other makeup was a pale shade of red lipstick. White, high-heeled, strapless shoes graced her feet and gave rise to two beautifully shaped calves. Quite a makeover, he observed, from the western, blue-jean look she wore on the airplane the day before.

A drinking bar that stretched the entire length of the back patio provided a convenient place for them to wait and enjoy a glass of Chardonnay. It was Jessica who finally broke silence with a question he knew she was going to ask, and almost wished she hadn't. "Now, what's this lunch all about," she asked?

"It's about your mother. She's back from Philadelphia. I called her this morning and asked if she could join me for lunch today but she preferred tomorrow. She has no idea that you are here, or why. I did mention that I had a message for her from a friend of mine and invited her to lunch to deliver it. My friend, as you may have guessed, is Dan Hughes."

"I suspected as much. What are you going to tell her?"

Before he could answer, the public address system announced that their table was ready so they relocated to a booth inside the dining room. He could tell from the lack of animation she was exhibiting that the light and happy disposition she had greeted him with was slowly fading away.

"Well," she asked, abruptly, "have you decided how you're going to approach her yet?"

"Let me answer your question with a question," he began. "What would you want to know about a daughter you hadn't seen in twenty years? Wouldn't you be curious about why she left, where she went, and what she had been doing all that time without ever once writing or calling her?"

Her eyes shied away from his and looked thoughtfully into the glass of wine she held nervously in her hand, trying desperately not to react, emotionally. "What do you want from me, Mr. Thomas?" she suddenly blurted out. "Can't you understand that digging into my past could get us both into a lot of trouble? It's so complicated. Can't we just forget about that part of my life?"

Reaching across the table, he placed his big warm hand on hers and answered, "I can, but can she?"

It was difficult for her to reply, though in her heart she knew that what he had said was true and had to be addressed, regardless of the consequences. Glancing from side to side at the people around them, she whispered with words he could hardly hear, "I can't tell you anything in this place. Let's just enjoy our lunch and walk it off on the beach when we're done. It will be easier to tell you then."

After their food had been served, her personality seemed to revert back to the happy, almost carefree person she had been earlier. He speculated that possibly her change in attitude might have been attributed to the fact that the troublesome burden of her past was soon to be exposed, and for the first time in many years would be shared with someone she trusted, implicitly.

Following lunch, a short walk led them to a stretch of beach nearby that sprawled endlessly in either direction up and down the coast. Both had removed their shoes to allow the cold water to flow across their feet while they walked silently, side by side, each hesitant to speak. It was Jessica who broke the silence first, still a little hesitant to give him the historical ammunition he would need to confront her mother, but she did. "Unless you've actually experienced the loss of a loved one yourself, it's very difficult for most people to understand what another person experiences when they lose a parent, especially at such a relatively early age. My father's untimely death was devastating in a way only a teenager who had suffered through it could understand. It was as if the entire world around me imploded and crushed my emotional sensibilities, leaving me hanging somewhere in space without the desire or strength to do anything about it. The only relief from that kind of emotional upheaval is what you foolishly discover in the never-never land of whatever drugs you can buy or steal, both of which I did at one time or another."

"What was your mother doing during this heart breaking period?" he asked, almost stunned by her admission. "Surely she would have comforted you if you had gone to her."

"Problem was, I loved my father so much I became jealous of his affection for her. When he died I wrongly blamed her and have regretted it ever since. Only recently have the influences that once controlled my life disappeared, setting me free to make amends for the sadness and worry I have caused her all these years. My only wish is that she'll let me."

He didn't say anything right away, letting the ocean breeze and sunshine whisk away some of the anxiety she was so obviously trying to get rid of. It saddened him for a moment to witness the remorse she was experiencing so he changed his line of questioning to provide her the opportunity to be selective in what she wanted him and her mother to know.

"What do you want me to tell your mother tomorrow?" he asked, giving her the opportunity to be selective.

Thoughtfully, she replied, "I really am grateful for what you are doing for me. Regardless of how it all this works out, I just want you to know that I will be forever indebted to you. I doubt that anyone else on this planet would do what you're trying to do for someone you really don't know? As far as my mother is concerned, you can tell her it all began when I read an ad in the newspaper that offered five thousand dollars and all expenses to drive privately owned automobiles to various east coast cities, pick up another one and return it to San Diego. Somehow, it was all related to transporting cars belonging to military personnel from one coast to another, or so I thought."

She paused for a moment, looking thoughtfully out over the ocean, then continued:

"Sounds pretty straight forward, doesn't it? What a fun way to travel and earn money at the same time. Well, believe it or not, answering that ad turned my life upside down from the time I answered it until I met you on the airplane Monday."

Checking the time made her aware that even though it had been his suggestion to meet, she had already taken up far more of his afternoon than she had intended, and suggested that they head back toward Bully's. Along the way, she continued, sensing that his curiosity had not yet been satisfied. "Until I turned twenty-one, I was pretty much of a wandering Hippie-type, doing odd jobs, hanging out in hostels, smoking pot and trying to make sense out of senselessness. Even sex didn't make any sense, and there was plenty of that. Then one day, out of pure boredom and frustration, I picked up a newspaper one of my friends had salvaged from a garbage can and began reading the help wanted ads, hoping to find some escape from the lunacy I was pursuing. That ad, I thought at the time, held the escape I was searching for, so I answered it. I've rued the day ever since. But that's another story. As far as my mother is concerned, keep it simple. I'll deal with her, if and when the time comes."

When they reached Bully's parking she knew there wasn't enough time for her to finalize what she had started. She did, however, ask him to tell her mother that she sincerely wanted to meet with her and promised to answer whatever questions she might have at that time.

"I'm counting on you, to call me tomorrow and let me know how mother reacted to all of this. I will not leave my room until you do. It's that important to me."

He assured her that he would call and started to walk toward his car when her voice called out after him. "Thanks for lunch, and good luck tomorrow."

Smiling, he turned and waved goodbye. "Your welcome," he shouted back, "and welcome home!"

As he stood in the parking lot watching her car slowly disappear down the narrow alleyway that accessed the parking lot, he looked up into the deep blue sky above him and said, as if he were there looking down on him, "Well Billy, here we go again."

Chapter 9

Paving the Way

During the span of time it took him to reach Ron's house that afternoon, he found it difficult to concentrate on anything except his lunch with Jessica that day and tomorrow's meeting with her mother. Jessica's reluctance to go any further into her past than what she had told him that afternoon, although not the whole story, was enough history to confirm her existence. It would also provide some reasonable explanation for why her mother had never received any notification about her whereabouts or physical well-being. Dan Hughes, he hoped, would work out to be the perfect fall guy. That she was very much alive and staying at a hotel in La Jolla he knew had to be handled with some finesse, but felt he could pull it off without causing more emotional injury to either one of them. Inevitably, there would have to be a face-to-face meeting between the two woman he realized, but to fret needlessly over a situation of his own contrivance, and one over which he had no further control, seemed futile, so he pushed it from his mind and committed the rest of his afternoon to friends and the lighter side of involvement.

When he arrived there wasn't any place to park. Usually, he was the first to arrive, but his lunch with Jessica had lasted longer than anticipated. Unlike most Tuesday afternoons, he observed, everyone showed up on time including the seldom seen, Johnny Holland. Rationalizing that is was far safer to park around the corner anyway he did so and walked leisurely back.

Once the friendly round of hand shaking was over he went to the small and cluttered kitchen where he made himself a more than generous drink while Ron stripped the pool table of its cover and announced, enthusiastically, "Okay, gentlemen, pick a coin."

As explained to those infrequent, non-pool shooting friends who came by to watch and imbibe, the term "pick a coin" meant: six pennies with black dots on one side, ranging from one to six, were laid on a counter nearby, dots down. The number of dots on the coin you picked determined the partnerships and the shooting order, thus eliminating favoritism. Ironically, after a few drinks, the playing field usually became quite level.

Several games were played that afternoon and more drinks were consumed. Predictably, individual sensitivity levels increased when partners began advising one another on how the next shot should be played. The negative tolerance level for such coaching soon became proportional to the drinks each had consumed, and routinely resulted in someone's feelings getting hurt. In order to lighten the mood, Joey Siegel, who was Neal's partner at the time, asked, "Did anything interesting happen when you visited your old stomping grounds?"

In an attempt to dilute the tension that had built up between their three opponents, he went into some detail to describe the wake, the women he had met and his long day on the bay with Dan Hughes and his sexy friend, Donna. Wisely, he did not mention anything about his staying with Billy's former wife, Jennifer, or his coincidental meeting with Sandy Sterling and her daughter. He did, however, hint that Billy's death might not have been accidental and was still being investigated by local authorities as a possible homicide.

"Sounds like you walked into a can of worms," Don commented. "I hope you were smart enough to stay the hell out of it, friend or no friend."

The subject of Billy's questionable demise suddenly distracted everyone's attention from petty squabbling to a curious interest in his comment regarding the circumstances surrounding his death. There was just enough intrigue in the scenario to jump-start all of their collective imaginations into speculating on what might have happened.

Having heretofore refrained from venturing any comment on the subject, it was Ron Barns – a wee bit tipsy from too much gin – who suggested, almost sensibly, "A word to the wise, Neal, Leave it back there where it belongs. Besides, you're too far away to get yourself involved anyway."

That was good advice, he thought, but a little too late to be heeded, considering his growing involvement almost on a daily basis. Rather than mention anything further about the matter, he remained silent and left the group to use the bathroom before leaving.

When he returned it was Ron's shot. He and Neal had only one ball apiece left on the table. Ron's was blocked from being easily made by one of the center table bumpers. It could be made, however, or set up for the game winning shot, by banking it gently off the side cushion, rather than gambling on the winning bank shot. Predictably, Ron went for the set up and left the ball directly in front of the hole, virtually cinching the win.

Neal's ball, unfortunately, was only a few inches out of one corner at his end. Winning would require using one of the center bumpers to bank it in. The odds of that happening were not even close to fifty/fifty, and both players knew it. After studying the situation for a moment, he took a long swallow from his drink and walked slowly around the table where a shorter cue stick – that Ron had made and nicknamed, "Shorty" – stood upright against the wall. That stick was rarely used by anyone except when regular length cues became hindered by obstacles that surrounded the playing area, including a sliding glass door that opened into the front yard. So, with "Shorty" in hand, he lined up his shot, pulled back the stick and gently stroked the ball.

As soon as it hit the bumper and angled off, a loud, agonizing groan came out of Ron, who had been standing in line with Neal's ball and the hole.

"I'll be damned!" he shouted. "You've done it to us again!"

Johnny Holland, who had been Neal's partner for that last game of the day, slapped him on the shoulder and shook his hand. "Hell of a shot, partner," he told him, grinning from ear to ear. "Hell of a shot! That calls for a drink on me. Will you join us for one at Bully's?"

Before answering, he gave the invitation some serious thought. Considering what he had planned with Paula when he got home and his meeting with Sandy Sterling the next day, he decided that discretion was the better part of valor, and declined.

While the other three left, unceremoniously, Neal delayed his departure to chat with Ron while he went about securing his house. Standing at the sink rinsing his glass, he heard Ron say something he might not have said, had he not been drinking. "While we were shooting pool a little while ago I got the feeling your mind wasn't always on the game. Is something bothering you?"

He considered mentioning something about having had lunch with Jessica and his meeting with Sandy Sterling the next day, but thought better of it. As far as he was concerned at that point in time, it was nobody's business but his own, and was best left a private matter until everything was settled.

"Not really," he replied, matter-of-factly. "I'm still hung over from the trip. I'll be okay in a day or two."

Rather than question him further, he accepted his answer and said goodbye, feeling instinctively that Neal was holding something back.

Except for a brief stop at the super market, he arrived home a little past the time when Paula should normally have been there. Her car, however, was not in the driveway. Suspecting that she had probably been delayed at work, he dismissed her tardiness as matter of fact, anticipating that she would be home soon.

The first thing that attracted his attention when he entered the kitchen was the pesky red light on the telephone answering machine blinking away. After putting the groceries away he pushed the button and sat down to listen. The first message had been received following his departure earlier that day. The voice was a man's:

"Hi Neal. This is Dusty Lewis, your old friend and upstairs neighbor from Raleigh, North Carolina. My wife and I have just recently arrived in the San Diego area and would like to get together with you sometime to talk about what you've been up to all these years. Give me a call at the following number so we can work something out. Talk to you later."

He wrote down the name and number, recalling that Dusty had visited Jennifer's place at the beach while he was out on the bay with Dan Hughes. What a small world we live in, he thought, as the second message beeped in.

"Hi Neal, this is Dan Hughes. Give me a call as soon as you can. I need to talk to you. I'm at my parent's place."

"What now," he sighed in frustration, as the third beep sounded and Paula's tired and apologetic voice came on line. "Hope you had a good time with the boys. I hate to tell you this again, but I will be a little late getting home again. Look forward to joining you in the Jacuzzi as soon as I get there. Sorry about all this. I'll explain later. Love you."

After her call, he sat for a few moments weighing the significance of the first two messages. The advice of his friends only an hour ago seemed to confirm that there just might be some wisdom in what they had cautioned him about.

The time difference between the East and West Coasts made it too late to respond to Dan Hughes' call so he dialed the number Dusty had left. After four rings he was tempted to hang up when a pre-recorded message came on. He began to speak, giving his name and a brief message, when he was interrupted by an excited voice he hadn't heard for years. "Neal! How great to finally catch up with you. How have you been?"

For the next ten minutes, he and Dusty revisited the period of time when they were neighbors in a swinging, young couples condo just outside of Raleigh. As they both agreed, life then was carefree and unencumbered by the responsibilities and commitments of serious relationships from which Neal had divorced himself from at the time. It wasn't long, however, before their reminiscing ran out of funny things to talk about, so he asked him what had prompted him to leave the Raleigh area.

"Well, I got married, for one thing," he explained. "After a few rocky years working at the job I had when you were working here, I decided to do what I had wanted to do ever since I was a little kid, work for the CIA. I went to school and eventually got my shield. Fortunately, I was assigned to the Washington office and worked there until just recently when I was reassigned to the San Diego area."

"I understand you were in the Virginia Beach area last Sunday?" he remarked, trying to verify what Jennifer had told him. "Business or pleasure?"

"Yes I was," he replied. "I was looking for you."

"I know. Jennifer Newman told me late Sunday afternoon that you had paid her a visit. How did you know I was there?"

"Hey Dude, remember who I work for" he replied, humorously defensive. "You leave a trail a mile wide"

"Yeah, I guess so."

A moment of awkward silence passed between them before he recovered his wits enough to ask him if he and his wife would like to attend his Fourth of July party. His response was immediate and enthusiastic. "We'd love to. Can't wait to meet your lady friend. She and I had a nice talk when I contacted her over the weekend. Just for the record, my wife's name is Katie."

When he attempted to give him directions on how to get to his home, Dusty just laughed and kidded him about not paying attention. "Hey, Neal, remember? CIA? Believe me, I know where you live. See you at the party."

A quick glance at the clock made him nervously aware that Paula was still not home. It annoyed him that her job was beginning to demand such an unreasonable amount of her time. For lack of anything better to do, he turned the television on and flicked around the channels trying to find an old movie, or anything that would take his mind off the day's activity. During his search, he stopped momentarily on a news channel being broadcast from a beach community south of Virginia Beach. Curiously interested in the coincidence of something going on in the same area he had just left, he remained on the channel. A news reporter standing on the dock of what looked like the marina where Dan Hughes kept his boat, gave the following report: *"Good evening everybody, I'm Bob Sullivan. Local authorities have just released a statement that reclassifies the recent death of Tidewater resident, Billy Newman, from a boating accident to a homicide. No details are available at this time, but his former wife, Jennifer Newman, has agreed to give us a brief statement regarding the incident."*

Neal could hardly believe his eyes when Jennifer's image appeared on the screen and began her statement: *"I have never been convinced that Billy's death was an accident. He was too cautious a boating person to be as careless as investigators and the news media implied when the initial investigation took place. I have suspected foul play from the beginning, and was told this morning that results of an ongoing investigation by the local Harbor Police and Federal authorities have confirmed that. Hopefully, the perpetrators of this terrible crime will be identified soon and brought to justice. Thank you."*

Following her statement she turned immediately away from the reporter and left before he could ask any questions. Not knowing quite how to handle her abrupt departure, he reporter signed off, leaving the network anchorman somewhat amused while he searched through his notes for another news item.

Just at that moment, the sound of the garage door opening captured his attention. Relieved that Paula had finally made it home, he went to the kitchen, fixed her a glass of wine and returned to his chair, still reflecting on having seen Jennifer on major network television news.

When she entered the room, her expression left little doubt that any expectations he might have had regarding the Jacuzzi and an intimate evening, faded like the television screen when he clicked it off. He did, however, appreciate that she needed help and responded accordingly by relieving her of the packages she was carrying. In a goodwill effort to ease the burden of her obviously exhausting day, he tried a little humor. "Other than that, Mrs. Lincoln, how did you like the play?"

Having already heard him use that line on a number of previous occasions, she extended her arm and replied, without smiling, "Never mind about poor Mrs. Lincoln, Curly. Pour me another glass of wine."

For the rest of the evening they were content to share a light dinner and a couple of hours watching television. By ten o'clock, ironically, it was Paula who had already fallen asleep, prompting him to gently wake her so he could help her upstairs. Trying to remove her clothes, he decided, would be terribly awkward so he laid her on their bed, covered her with a light blanket and returned downstairs.

Normally, watching an old, black and white movie like *Gunga Din* would have put him to sleep in minutes. But the events of that day, and the uncertainty of what lay ahead for Sandy and Jessica Sterling, prolonged his dozing off until well after midnight.

When he finally did wake up, the sky outside was black and only one light in the kitchen was on which provided just enough light to guide his way upstairs.

Paula was still fast asleep when he entered their bedroom, causing him to reconsider getting into bed with her. After the day she had had, the last thing he wanted to do was wake her up. Reversing his path, he felt his way to the guest bedroom and collapsed under the soft moonlight that shone on the bed from an open window nearby.

During the few minutes prior to falling asleep for the second time that night, he pondered the urgency that Dan Hughes had expressed in asking him to return his call as soon as possible. Also disturbing was the anticipation of what was going to result from his meeting with Sandy Sterling the next day? It seemed the longer he thought about his growing involvement in their lives, the more he began to appreciate the wisdom in what his friends had tried to caution him about earlier that day. Despite the aggravation of it all, his eyes lids finally grew weary and closed.

Several hours later when the Eastern horizon began to lighten, he was wakened by the sound of running water coming from the master bedroom shower, an unmistakable reminder that, for Paula, a new day had begun. Still fully clothed, he walked barefoot to the kitchen, put on a pot of coffee and brought in the morning paper. Like it or not, he too was facing a new day, as yet unchallenged.

Not long thereafter, Paula made an unprecedented, fully dressed appearance in the kitchen and poured her usual black cup of coffee. Noticing the surprised look on his face she spoke before he could ask the question she knew was on the tip of his tongue. "Please bear with me," she began. "I don't know why, but the Assistant City Manager asked me to come in early today to discuss something important. I haven't got a clue what it's about. She did say it was private and confidential."

"Maybe you're finally going to get that promotion they've been promising you for over a year," he commented. "Lord knows you deserve it."

"Yeah, right," she replied, gulping down the last of her coffee. "In my dreams."

He didn't pursue the subject further because it was obvious she was in a hurry. Shrugging his shoulders to express indifference, he remarked, "Whatever. Do you need me to carry anything to the car for you?"

"No, I left most of my stuff in the car last night, except for groceries. Why don't you see me off?"

"You're already off," he joked, "but I'd be happy to see you to your car, Madam Butterfly."

It was a hasty goodbye, but they did enjoy a long embrace and a lingering kiss that rekindled a spark of what they both recognized as being a vital part of their relationship over the years. Watching her drive away he couldn't help thinking, *Ah yes, those were the good old days.*

Returning to the house, he went directly upstairs, shaved and took a shower. After putting on a fresh change of clothes he ate a light breakfast, while mulling over the order of events that would more than likely exhaust the rest of his day. Of primary importance was a call to Dan Hughes to determine why, all of a sudden, he was planning to come to California. Since it was already mid-morning on the East Coast, he poured a fresh cup of coffee and placed the call. The pickup on the other end was immediate, almost as if he were sitting by his phone waiting for it to ring.

"Hi, Dan. I got your message. What's up?"

"Did you see Jennifer Newman on television last night?"

"Yes I did, as a matter of fact. Can you tell me what's going on back there? What proof do they have that Billy was murdered?"

"Well, it looks like the crap is about to hit the fan, and I'm standing right in front of it. I need to ask you to do me a favor, if you will, Sir."

No sooner had the word "favor" cleared his lips than Neal began feeling uncomfortable. "I will if I can," he replied, wishing for the first time that he had never attended Billy's wake. "What can I do for you?"

Following what sounded like muffled voices talking in the background, he came back on line and explained his request. "I need to get out of this place for a few days, Mr. T. I also need to talk to you about a matter that I can't discuss over the phone. Are there any hotels or beach resorts close to you where I can get lost for a few days?"

In all good conscience, he could not deny Dan's request, even though he had a premonition that his being in such close proximity would create a problem for which he had no practical solution - the biggest being Paula. After a moment to assess how she might react to this sudden turn of events, he convinced himself that no news was good news. Besides, she really didn't have to know anything, at least for the time being. As far as he was concerned, Dan's request was little different than one from a relative who was coming to visit, so he replied on that basis. "You're in luck, Dan. There are a number of places within minutes. How much do you want to spend?"

"To hell with the money," he replied. "Just book me a reservation beginning the day before through the day after your party. Don't worry about picking me up. All I'll need are directions on how to get to the hotel from."

"I'll call you as soon as I confirm your reservations. I have a place in mind that's right on the ocean only five minutes from here."

After expressing his thanks, Dan hung up, leaving Neal somewhat befuddled over why his forthcoming party - that had seemed so simple a few days ago - was now fast becoming overly complicated by a few individuals, some whom he had only recently met. He shuddered at the certainty of eventually having to explain to Paula why these guests were invited, but decided he had better wait until after his meeting with Sandy Sterling before running the risk of compounding the emotional upset her job had already created.

During the hours spanning his conversation with Dan and leaving for La Jolla, he returned to his studio to continue work on the large painting he had neglected for over a week. Squeezing a few colors over those that had already hardened on the palette, he selected a small brush, not much bigger than the end of a toothpick, and began the painstaking process of detailing a wall of stone partially covered with ivy. As was so often the case, once the first paint was applied, his mind became completely distracted from the complexities of everyday life and drifted, as if in a dream, to childhood activities like playing sports, building model airplanes, foolish things he had said and done, all to the sound of music playing in the background. Those that remained most vividly were his emotional and physical relationships with girls of his own age. And some, he remembered with a little conceit, who were a little older.

He was still in a world of reminiscence when a glance at his studio clock reminded him that daydreaming was threatening to make him late for his appointment with Sandy Sterling. Showing up late would not be in his or Jessica's best interests, considering the seriousness of what he was attempting to do. Putting his brushes aside, he closed up the house and hurried to his car.

Traffic on the freeway, in addition to its usual congestion, was mixed with tourists, students on summer vacation and cars driving to the Del Mar Fair. To avoid becoming mixed in with them he took the off ramp at Carmel Valley Road and followed the lagoon west to Highway 101. There, he turned South, past the Torrey Pines Golf Course and followed the Scenic Drive into La Jolla. Traffic there was its usual mess, but the lunch hour was almost over, allowing him to arrive at the Sterling Publishing Company building with a few minutes to spare.

The building itself was a four-story structure whose ground level provided general and reserved parking. When he approached the security gate and identified himself, a uniformed attendant handed him a numbered pass and directed him to the space that had been reserved in his name. How accommodating, he thought, walking toward the elevators. Let's just hope it continues.

When the doors opened, he noted from the office listing next to the control panel that her office was located on the fourth floor. Where else, he thought, and pushed the button. The ride up was almost motionless and made pleasant by background music from a local radio station he recognized at once as "Soft Jazz." When the doors opened again he was impressed to find two attractive, stylishly dressed women preoccupied at two computer- equipped desks flanking an archway to a short hallway. Strategically placed around the area were beautiful, palm-like plants, while the walls boasted a large number of tastefully framed book covers.

Aware of his presence, the blonde woman on his right asked, "May I help you, sir?"

"Yes you may," he replied, politely. "My name is Neal Thomas. I have a one o'clock appointment with Ms. Sterling."

Trying to be nonchalant, the woman's eyes went directly to her office mate and quickly returned while she picked up her phone and gave notice of his arrival. A few seconds later she replaced the phone and said, "You're expected, Mister Thomas. Go straight down the hall. Ms. Sterling's door will be open."

Following the woman's directions, he walked down the wide hallway to a set of large double doors, one of which was open. Inside, sitting behind a beautifully handcrafted desk was his travel companion of only a few days ago, Sandy Sterling.

"I'd say welcome, it's been a long time," she greeted him in jest, "but it's only been a matter of days since I last saw you. How are you?"

During the few steps it took him to reach her desk, he became instantly aware of how differently she looked. Maybe it was her stylish clothes, the hair, the makeup or the animation in her voice, but she presented herself quite differently from what he remembered. Giving the devil her due, he thought, much more attractively. "I'm still trying to recover from last weekend," he replied. "I'm afraid I over did things a bit. Other than that, I think I'll survive. How are things with you?"

"Not too bad," she sighed. "That trip to Philadelphia was a waste of time, except for meeting you, of course."

She hesitated a moment, examining her thoughts carefully. "I truly am glad to see you again," she admitted, "however, I'm more curious about this message you say a friend of yours was supposed to deliver ages ago. What possible significance could it have after so long a time? And why are you, of all people, the messenger?"

The moment of truth had arrived, and he knew it. To avoid a lightening strike reaction by going directly to the subject of her daughter's sudden return, he used a chronology of events approach to answer her questions.

"As you know, the reason for my being on the same plane to Washington with you was to attend a wake being held for a dear friend of mine. When I arrived at the airport in Norfolk I was met by a man named Dan Hughes, the son of another friend of mine. During the three days I spent there, Dan and I shared a lot of time together. As a result, I learned a great deal about his personal life, and what he had been doing over the years since seeing him last. One particular incident involved crash- landing an airplane on a remote, uninhabited beach in Cuba, of all places. Fortunately, he was rescued and cared for by a small band of anti-Castro rebels. One of those rebels was an American woman, whom her fellow soldiers simply referred to as, 'Jess.' Her real name was Jessica."

Although she succeeded in not expressing any change in facial expression, Sandy did shift nervously in her chair when Neal referred to the nickname, 'Jess.' A moment later she encouraged him to continue, never taking her eyes off him for a second.

"According to what Dan told me, the American female who befriended him arranged a secret, night-time rescue operation that helped relocate him from Cuba to his residence in Puerto Rico, an act of selflessness that probably saved his life. Before they parted company that night, Jessica asked Dan to call her mother, if and when he ever got back to the U.S. He was to tell her that Jessica was alive and in good health, and not to worry. To verify all this, she gave him her outdated California Driver's License, which he still had and gave me last Sunday night. It was his way of helping me confirm everything I have told you here today."

Reaching for his wallet, he removed the discolored license and placed it in front of her. "Dan wanted me to express his regrets for not having contacted you when he finally returned to this country," he explained, "but having known him as a young man, and just recently being told of his nefarious past, I can understand now how he could have forgotten. I'm just glad he asked me to be his messenger."

Nervously, she reached across the desk and picked it up. After staring at the faded photo inset for a few seconds, she looked at him with sorrowful eyes, her lips twitching in an attempt to smile, and said, almost tearfully, "Better late than never, I guess."

Before he could respond, she rose up slowly from her desk, walked around behind him and closed the large door through which he had entered. From there she walked to a wall panel of four louvered doors and folded them back, exposing a fully equipped bar. Turning in his direction, she remarked, "If my memory serves me well, Mister Thomas, I believe you're a vodka person. Tonic okay?"

Neal replied, affirmatively, grateful that her reaction was not the lightening strike he had anticipated.

Pouring a more than generous glass of white wine for herself, she returned to her desk, handing him his drink as she passed. Several moments of silence followed while she made herself comfortable. With a feeble toasting gesture, she lifted her glass, looked across the table and said, almost uncaringly, "Please excuse me if I seem a little less than overjoyed by this news, but if that's all my daughter had to say after years of not knowing where the hell she was, or what had happened to her, you'll forgive me if I don't come apart at my emotional seams. I abandoned hope of ever seeing her again along time ago. I am grateful, however, for your effort on behalf of your friend, Mr. Hughes, to bring me this message, and I thank you for it."

The drink she had handed him was so strong it burned all the way down, leaving him momentarily speechless, but it did lay the groundwork for what followed next because he knew she wouldn't be prepared for it. "I wish that were all there is to it," he continued, looking anxiously ahead, "but I'm afraid there's more, which may not be so easily dismissed."

Before he could speak, the phone rang. She excused herself and answered it. "No, I don't need anything, nosey," she scolded, rolling her eyes. "And, yes, I'm fine. Tell anyone else who calls that I've left for the day, and to call back tomorrow. You know the routine."

Setting the receiver back in its cradle, she turned her attention back to Neal. "Now," she remarked without expressing any emotion, "you were saying?"

The phone call interruption gave him an opportunity to forego any further discussion about Jessica, deciding an office environment was not the ambiance that best suited what he had to tell her next, so he avoided the question by going to another subject. "Are you ready for some lunch?" he asked, "I'm getting a little hungry."

Once again, she rose from her chair, took both their empty glasses back to the bar and closed the doors, as if to say, *one's enough.* "Call it woman's intuition, if you will," she commented while returning, "but somehow I'm getting an uneasy feeling about that portion of your previous statement when you said, I wish that were all there was to it. If what you have to tell me is going to be more upsetting, I don't want to hear it in a public restaurant where I could embarrass myself. I suggest we continue the subject in the privacy of my home. We can have lunch there, if you're comfortable with that."

"That's fine with me," he agreed, hesitantly. "Will anyone else be there?"

She laughed. "Just the servants. Don't worry, I'm not setting you up for anything," she assured him. "Relax, you're in good hands."

Reaching for her phone, she excused herself and pushed one of the intercom buttons. A few seconds later she said, almost in a whisper, "I'm leaving on my private elevator. See you tomorrow."

At ground level, she suggested that he follow her in his car so she wouldn't have to bring him back. He agreed. The short drive led him to the residential hills overlooking La Jolla Cove where they parked inside the security gates of a very expensive looking, two-story home of sprawling elegance that one might expect to see on a Hollywood tour.

Beautifully landscaped, the house boasted one of the most beautiful ocean views he had ever seen. Inside was just as impressive, including everything from double spiral staircases, to elegant furniture, quality art paintings and a variety of in-door plants resting on classic pedestals throughout. They hadn't been inside very long when a middle-age couple came to greet them, introducing themselves as Ivan and Christina Olofson, Ms. Sterling's live-in servants.

Following their departure she led him to a large patio overlooking a swimming pool where she said lunch would be served. Comfortably seated, she asked Ivan to bring them each a drink, emphasizing that they were in no hurry.

For the first few minutes they were alone together, he purposely avoided any mention of her daughter so it would not cast a dark shadow over the beautiful setting in which he now found himself. It was she who reopened their previous office conversation. "I know you must think I'm quite an extravagant person to be living as I do, alone in a world of collections. Odd as it may seem, this is the only life I have. My daughter's grief after losing her father pales in light of what I experienced after his death. I hoped, at the time, that our mutual loss might have bonded us closer together. Lord knows I tried. When she disappeared I tried desperately to find her, but after years of searching brought no results, I finally gave up and concentrated on developing this property. As a publisher, I entertain frequently. My friends and guests are my family."

He hesitated making any comment when he noticed Ivan approaching with a tray in his hand, smiling as if he rarely had the opportunity to do so.

After setting the table, he turned toward Neal and said, "I hope you find everything to your satisfaction, Mr. Thomas. Call when you're ready for a refill."

When he was well beyond the sound of their voices, Sandy leaned forward and addressed Neal very seriously. "Now, getting back to why you're here, Mr. Thomas. Why don't you just tell me what you know about my daughter and stop tormenting me with your evasiveness."

Reacting with the same seriousness she had expressed, he sat his drink aside and told her what he hoped would crack the hard shell she appeared to be hiding behind. "During a conversation I shared with the flight attendant on my return flight to San Diego last Monday, a woman sitting next to me recognized the name of the man we were talking about. That man was Dan Hughes. The same Dan Hughes your daughter smuggled out of Cuba. The same daughter who confessed to me on that plane that she was returning to La Jolla, hopefully to reunite with her mother. A mother she hadn't seen in twenty years. What she didn't know, until I told her, was that Dan Hughes had never contacted you to deliver her message. Strange as it may seem, your daughter, Jessica, is waiting downtown at the Valencia Hotel for me to tell her whether or not her mother wants anything to do with her. That's why I'm here, Ms. Sterling."

He had barely finished when she buried her face in her hands in an attempt to hide the emotion that had suddenly overwhelmed her. Although he could see no tears, the pulsing of her upper body made it clear that she was sobbing, uncontrollably, like an injured child. Immediately, he tried to calm the emotional turmoil he had caused by rushing to her side to provide some measure of comfort, but she shied away from his touch. His persistence, however, eventually wore down her resistance and she collapsed willingly into his arms, exhausted and still sobbing.

The next few minutes were agonizing for him. He never suspected for a minute, given her professional resolve, that the woman he was beginning to perceive as being made of ice, was in fact a loving mother after all. With one arm still around her, he reached in his back pocket, pulled out a handkerchief and placed it in one of her hands.

She took it willingly, wiping her eyes and blowing her nose indelicately. When she regained what was left of her composure, she looked up at him with mascara running down her cheeks and remarked, humbly, "You'll have to excuse me. I was totally unprepared for this."

The manner in which she had excused herself was indication enough to convince him that the tension that had built up between them was no longer there. Releasing his hold on her, he replied, "I'm sorry for not using a gentler way to bring you this news, but there's a beautiful woman alone in a hotel room downtown waiting for me to tell her that her trip here was not in vain. What do you want me tell her?"

"Nothing," she replied, with stern resolve. "I'll tell her myself."

Her words were like music to his ears. For the first time since Ivan first served them, he was hungry. Helping himself to a little of everything on the table, he waited while she struggled to regain her composure. "Now that you've managed to reduce me to this pitiful state of humility," she remarked, half way in jest, "may I offer you another drink?"

"You may, but please promise me you will call Jessica immediately after I leave here today. She's probably a nervous wreck by now waiting for me to call, so don't let me down."

"Yes, yes, I promise! I'll even have her call you to let you know that we actually saw and talked with one another. Will that satisfy you?"

He understood that she was still a little testy from the embarrassment she had suffered, so he simply answered, "Of course."

The remaining time before he had to leave passed quickly. The relaxed atmosphere provided him the opportunity to extend her an invitation to his party, explaining that Jessica had already been invited. Her reaction was predictable.

"Let me get through this reunion business first, will you? I'll let you know how things work out. Where can I reach you? Do you have a business card?"

"As a matter of fact, I do. Please call me as soon as you can. I have a vested interest in all of this, you know."

On their way back through the house he insisted on saying goodbye to Ivan and Christina to thank them for making his visit a pleasant and successful one.

"You must visit us again soon, Mister Thomas," he remarked. "It's not often we have a man in the house to entertain that isn't a part of a crowd. It was a pleasure meeting you."

"Next time I'll do the entertaining," he replied. "I couldn't help but notice the beautiful concert grand piano you have in the living room. I'd love to play it for you some time."

"Oh, that would be splendid," he replied, enthusiastically. "Wouldn't it Ms. Sterling?"

"Yes, indeed it would," she agreed, taking Neal's arm while she escorted him to the front door.

On the way, she hesitated, momentarily and asked, "In your conversation with Jessica, did she ever mention specifically what she had done for a living all those years?"

"I'm as much in the dark as you are," he replied, avoiding the possibility of jeopardizing Jessica's option to tell her mother only what she wanted her to know. "I'm sure your questions will be answered when the time comes."

Once they reached the front entrance, both of them recognized that there was little left to say, so he hugged her affectionately for a moment and said, "Thanks for the afternoon. We've accomplished a great deal. "

Before reaching his car, he heard her voice call out after him, "Thanks for caring!"

It was the grim view of freeway traffic that convinced him to choose the Old Coast Highway as the more sensible route to take home. He was just North of Leucadia when it occurred to him that he had not yet made hotel reservations for Dan. Since his route led him directly in front of the Hilton Inn, he continued on up the coast until he saw its familiar façade basking in the late afternoon sun. According to the clerk on duty there were a number of rooms available at different rates, including those with ocean views. Reflecting for a moment on Dan's lifestyle, he selected one of the more luxurious ocean-view rooms on the top floor and made a tentative reservation in his name.

With only an hour remaining until Paula returned home, he decided to check out the cocktail lounge, appreciating that its ambiance would be of primary interest to Dan. He was not disappointed. Unlike most lounges he was familiar with, The Hilton was open and faced the ocean, allowing a steady flow of fresh air and beautiful sunsets to add to its guest's enjoyment. He was no sooner seated than an attractive young waitress approached to take his order. Her name, according to the tag she wore, was Maggie.

On top of what he had already had to drink that afternoon, the one she brought him took quick affect, and carried with it a playful mellowness that he hoped Paula would appreciate. Considering the emotional trauma he had been involved with for most of the day, it seemed relaxing to be alone for a while and watch the ocean undulating in the distance. Regrettably, it wasn't long before the last swallow rattled the ice in his empty glass, signaling it was time to leave. With the change from the ten-dollar bill he had given her still on the table, he waved Maggie goodbye as he stood to leave, promising to return when his friend from Virginia arrived.

Minutes later, he pulled into his driveway and noticed that Paula's car was already there. Usually, it was the other way around, he thought, so he quickened his pace to find her. It wasn't until after he had made a quick check of the place that he realized she wasn't there. That is, until a familiar voice from the patio yelled, "Hey Curly, is that you?"

"Yes dear," he answered, with a sigh of relief. "I'll be right there."

He couldn't have been more surprised, or amused, when, *what to his wondering eyes should appear,* but Paula's naked body in the Jacuzzi, with an open bottle of champagne within easy reach.

"Come on in," she motioned, slurring her words slightly. "I have a glass for you."

Amused by the scenario, and the carefree manner in which she was taunting him, he removed his clothing and joined her.

"Now, my sweet little cherub, what's all this about?" he asked.

Having already poured him a glass of champagne, she glided through the water to sit by his side, and asked, provocatively, "Haven't you forgotten something?"

The feel of her breasts floating against him, along with the underwater searching of their hands, brought a flashing glimpse of what would be the "welcome home" he had fantasized about for the past few days.

"Not for long," he replied.

Hesitating, momentarily, he asked again, "What's this all about? How come you're home so early?"

Sipping her champagne, and looking seductively over the rim, she replied, "Do you think this is proper conduct for the newly appointed assistant to the City Manager? What would he think if he could see me now?"

Jubilant about the news of her promotion, he kissed her tenderly, clinking his glass against hers. "Personally," he chuckled, "I doubt if he'd be able to think."

There was no dinner that night. It mattered little. The moon was full, the ocean sparkled and a soft summer breeze fanned the long overdue reunion of their eager and spirited bodies. All was right with the world, at least for the time being.

Chapter 10

Return To The Nest

Following Neal's departure from what she knew must have been a trying afternoon for him, Sandy stood in the doorway of her luxurious home watching his car disappear down the driveway. She lingered there in silence for a time wondering what the future held in store and how to deal with her daughter's sudden return from years of separation. Frustrated, she closed the door and returned to the kitchen where Ivan and Christina were tidying up, aware from the concerned expression on her face that something was seriously wrong.

A moment or two of silence passed between them before Ivan took the initiative and asked, caringly, "Are you all right, Ms. Sterling?"

"I'm really not sure, Ivan," she replied, sounding tired and confused. "I've just received some very disturbing news and I'm having difficulty determining what to do about it. The truth is, I'm afraid it's going to affect all of us."

The couple looked at one another, noticeably concerned by her statement, and waited anxiously for her to clarify it's meaning. When she didn't, Ivan asked, "Can we help?"

The lingering affect of the wine she had had that afternoon, and the emotional upset of learning about her daughter's return, made her feel suddenly lightheaded. She sat down at the kitchen table and tried to collect her thoughts, aware that Ivan and Christina were waiting nervously for her to explain herself. "The reason Mister Thomas came here today," she attempted to explain, "was to inform me that my daughter, Jessica, whom you know has been missing for years, is here in La Jolla and wishes to see me. Frankly, I'm totally flabbergasted by this devastating news!"

Although savvy to some American expressions, the European couple failed to grasp the meaning of the expression and continued looking at one another until Christina finally expressed herself with a statement that addressed the positive side of the situation. "Oh Madame, after all these years, to be able to see Jessica again. What wonderful news. Aren't you at all excited? I should be."

"Absolutely numb," she replied. "If you'll excuse me for a while, I m going to the library to make a phone call and do not wish to be disturbed by anyone. Is that clear?"

Recognizing the familiar resolve in her voice, Ivan replied, respectfully, "Yes, Ms. Sterling, we understand."

The Sterling home library was a room most men fantasized about. Walls were heavily paneled with dark, hand-rubbed wood. A massive stone fireplace, leather-upholstered furniture and bookshelves containing all types of interesting publications created an enviable environment in which to think and work.

A large screen, built-in television faced the classic wooden desk and high back chair where Sandy sat nervously contemplating the phone call she was about to make. It took some time for her to build up enough courage to pick up the receiver, but once she did, her resolve was steadfast.

When the desk clerk at the La Valencia Hotel answered, she took a deep breath and asked to be connected to Miss Jessica Sterling's room. Following only two rings, the receiver at the other end lifted and the unfamiliar voice of a woman answered.

"Is this Jessica Sterling?" she asked, almost afraid to hear the woman's answer.

"May I ask who is calling, please?" the woman replied.

"Jessica, this is your mother. I know you were expecting Mr. Thomas to call, but I convinced him that it would be more meaningful for both of us, if I did. He's a wonderful, caring man, but the bottom line is, you and I are the only ones who can determine whether or not we can re-establish our mother-daughter relationship."

She hesitated a moment, desperately trying to think of something that would relieve the tension, but found it difficult to say the words. For Jessica's sake, she took a matriarchal stance and continued: "If you have any concerns about my not wanting to see you, you're mistaken. It's been a long time, Jess, but I do want to meet with you. Let's not let the same mistakes we made twenty years ago stand in the way of a reunion so long overdue. Let's put the past behind us and meet each other half way. I'm willing, are you?"

Between wiping away the tears that were beginning to run down her face, and trying to blow her nose, she managed to regain some of her composure long enough to ask her mother to forgive her for all the misery and heartache she had caused. "I can't wait to see you, mom," she sniffled. "You can't imagine where I've been, or what I've been doing for all these years, but my life has been like some recurring nightmare that, at times, almost threatened my sanity. All that kept me going was the hope that some day, when my debt to those who were controlling my life was paid, I'd be set free to live again like a normal human being. Hopefully, today is that day."

Sandy's reaction stimulated about as much emotion as she might have experienced interviewing a new author. It was measured purposely to avoid any expression of false hope. Carefully choosing her words, she suggested that Jessica come to her home for lunch the following day, and offered to have her picked up at the hotel.

"That won't be necessary," she replied, somewhat relieved, but instinctively cautious. "I have a rental car, and I certainly haven't forgotten where we live."

Her words caused a flashback image of the house where Jessica had spent the first eighteen years of her life. Sandy realized in an instant how little her daughter knew of the changes and events that had taken place following her disappearance, including her mother's relocation to a new address. Describing the easiest route to her new address, she ended their conversation by encouraging her to call Mister Thomas that evening to put his mind at ease. "After all," she added, "had it not been for his genuine interest in both of us, we might not be talking to one another right now. We owe him that courtesy."

"I will," she promised, and was about to hang up when the words she thought had been lost forever in the insensitivity of her past suddenly overcame her. "I love you, mom."

Her arm froze. The words she couldn't ever remember hearing her daughter say almost prompted her to reply in kind, but she couldn't utter the words. Instead, she replied as enthusiastically as she knew how. "Thank you, Jessica. Those words mean a lot to me. I look forward to seeing you tomorrow."

For at least twenty minutes following their conversation, she sat quietly in the comfort of her library savoring the pride of ownership that came from having accumulated so many beautiful and valuable assets. Ironically, what captured her attention was a framed photograph of her daughter on the fireplace mantle. It had been some time since she last looked at it, and remembered when she used to view it daily during the days, weeks and months following Jessica's disappearance. As she rose from her chair and approached the mantle, her image came slowly into focus. She was wearing a varsity football cheerleader's outfit, and a smile that had already broken a number of hearts. The recollection of her rebellious behavior, at the time, caused a sudden apprehension over her return, and all the yesterdays that were coming with it.

Deciding that nothing constructive could be gained by speculating on tomorrow's reunion, she left the library and returned to the kitchen where Ivan and Christina were sitting at the table reading the newspaper and drinking tea.

Her sudden appearance after almost an hour brought the couple to their feet where they stood and waited for some hint of what she had been doing. Their curiosity, however, was short lived.

In the time it took to pour a glass of wine, she explained that she had invited her daughter to come to the house for lunch the next day, and admitted openly that she was, as she phrased it, "scared to death."

After breakfast the next morning, Jessica returned to her hotel room and decided it was time to call Mr. Thomas. A restless night had not provided much in the way of sound sleep, but it had restored her self-confidence enough to calm the anxiety she was experiencing about meeting her mother in a few hours. So, with his business card in front of her, she placed the call.

When his studio phone rang, he was busy preparing for his day at the easel, and fully expected it to be a junk call. "Hello," was all he volunteered.

"Hello to you too, Mr. Thomas," she greeted him, cheerfully. "This is Jessica Sterling. I just wanted to let you know that I have been invited to my mother's house for lunch today, and to thank you for all you have done to make that possible. It would appear that your efforts have not been in vane."

Elated that his previous day's meeting with her mother had resulted in something positive, he wished her well and invited them both to his Fourth of July party.

She expressed her thanks and said she would discuss it with her mother, explaining that there was a lot going on in their lives at present. Making plans of any kind would necessarily have to be dealt with on a daily basis.

He empathized with her reluctance to make any commitment, given the circumstances. However, as an added enticement, he mentioned that he had been asked by Dan to look into making hotel reservations for him in anticipation of his being able to attend the party. "Why don't you try to coax your mother into coming with you," he suggested. "Wouldn't it be exciting for you and Dan to see each other again after all these years?"

Mention of Dan's name resulted in an immediate response. "With or without her, I'll be there," she assured him. Following a brief pause, she added, "I'll call you after I have lunch with her today to let you know how things went. You can give me directions then."

"Fine, and good luck," he replied. "I'll look forward to your call."

Her eagerness to reunite with Dan reminded him that he needed to call Dan so he could confirm his hotel reservations with a credit card number. Placing a call to the cell phone number he had been given, he sipped his cold coffee and waited.

Within seconds, Dan answered, thanked him for getting back to him so quickly and commented once again on how anxious he was to leave the area. "There's a lot of stink coming out of this investigation into Billy Newman's death," he explained. "It's beginning to look like Pete Boggs and Miguel Ramirez are involved. They're the two guys you saw me leave with last Sunday night. Remember?"

"Yes, I remember, but I can't understand where you fit into all this. You didn't have anything to do with Billy's accident, did you?"

It was obvious from the long pause that followed that Dan was carefully choosing his words. "No, of course not," he finally replied, somewhat irritated by the inference. "I swear to you I had absolutely nothing to do with that." Hesitating again, as if he were talking to someone else, intermittently, he continued: "It all has to do with several packets of drugs that are missing from a shipment I delivered to Pete Boggs early last Saturday morning, before I went to Billy's wake. They think I stole them, but I didn't, so help me God. I've got a damn good idea who did, though."

Slowly, the missing pieces of the puzzle he had been trying to put together for days began to fall into place. Looking back, he pictured the transfer of items that was taking place during the early morning hours on the previous Saturday. He was about to tell him what he had seen when Dan interrupted and asked, "Have you made my hotel reservations yet?"

He told him that the local Hilton Inn had advised him to have Dan call the hotel as soon as possible, explaining that they needed a credit card number to hold the room.

"I'll take care of it right away, Mr. T," he assured him, pausing to sip what Neal suspected was a libation of some kind. "I really need to get the hell out of here for a few days. You got any problem with that?"

His immediate concern was how Paula would react. Especially on top of everything else he had avoided telling her. On the positive side, however, at least Dan had a place to stay and a rental car at his disposal. That alone, simplified matters considerably. "None at all," he replied. "As a matter of fact, Paula and I are having our annual Fourth of July bash in a few days. Hopefully, you'll be here to join us."

"Me too," he remarked with comic enthusiasm. "I'm looking forward to meeting Paula and seeing Janet and the girls again. It's been a long time."

Dan's enthusiasm wasn't really what he wanted to hear, but accepted it because he thought the time was right to inform him of the possibility that Jessica Sterling and her mother might be in attendance. "By the way," he remarked, "I think you should be aware of a situation that has developed out here over the past few days that indirectly involves you."

"How so?" he asked, puzzled by the implication.

"You're not going to believe this, but on my return flight to San Diego I sat next to the woman who saved your ass in Cuba years ago. Her name is Jessica Sterling. The same woman whose picture is on that California Driver's License you gave me last Sunday night. Remember? No thanks to you, she's preparing to reunite with her mother today for the first time in twenty years. Both may be attending my party, depending on how they hit it off at their reunion today. There's a hell of lot more to this story, but I'll save the details until you arrive. Just thought you ought to know what's going on."

After momentary silence, Dan replied in a manner he had not expected, considering what he thought would be very surprising news. "I'm glad you followed up on that," he remarked, hurriedly, as if something or someone were prompting him to get off the phone. "We'll talk more in a few days, but right now I've got to go. Donna just arrived. I'll call you when I get to the Hilton."

Somewhat disappointed by his blasé attitude, he hung up and returned to his easel, content that his personal effort on behalf of the two Sterling women had been a reward in itself. As for the future direction it would take, he hadn't a clue.

While he sat pondering the complexity of his ever-expanding involvement in the intrigue of his own contrivance, Jessica Sterling was stepping from a refreshing shower at the Valencia Hotel with Dan's name fresh on her mind. What a small world, meeting the same person she had unsuccessfully tried to locate in Virginia at a party in the home of a man she had only recently met. The coincidence fascinated her, sending a chill through her shapely body while she primped in front of the bathroom mirror. Moments later, while she dressed and groomed her hair, the clock alarm sent a warning that the time had come for her to face up to the inescapable reality of reuniting with her mother. An event that filled her with apprehension despite every effort she was making to remain calm and collected.

The day outside was blessed with blue sky and a warm, ocean scented breeze that brought back memories of vacation days she had spent on La Jolla beaches as a teenager. Smaller houses, she recalled, were built on both sides of the street back then, but had long since been replaced by larger, more expensive ones. Luxury of unparalleled splendor lay hidden in the beautiful landscaping that flanked both sides of the street now, especially the one at the address she had been given. Passing through the security gates that had been left open for her arrival, she marveled at the beautifully landscaped grounds that lined the driveway, and the almost Hollywood-like grandeur of her mother's estate.

"And I ran away from all this? she remarked, stepping from her car. "I must have been crazy!"

The sound of an approaching car alerted Ivan to the much-awaited arrival of the woman he now jokingly referred to as, "the lost lamb." Eager to carry out the instructions that had been given to him earlier, he proceeded to the front door and waited for the doorbell to ring. When it sounded, he opened the door to discover Jessica's smiling face looking up at him. Her attractiveness surprised him to the extent that he forgot the welcome he had rehearsed. Before he could regain his composure, she pre-empted his well-intended greeting by saying, politely, "Good afternoon, Sir. My name is Jessica Sterling. I'm here to see my mother."

Ivan's hand came up to his chest and rested there as he said, apologetically, "Please forgive me, Ms. Sterling, my name is Ivan Olofson. I'm afraid I wasn't prepared to greet someone so completely unlike the person I had pictured in my mind. Do come in. You're mother is waiting on the patio."

As they walked through the house, she thought about what he had said and decided to have a little fun with him. "That person you were expecting. Did she have horns and a long, pointed nose?"

"Gracious me, no," he replied with a hearty laugh. "That would be your Mother."

The spontaneity of his humorous reply ignited an equally hearty response from Jessica as they made their way through the kitchen and out onto the patio, stopping only to be introduced to Christina. When they arrived at the umbrella-shaded table where her mother sat looking out over the ocean, he stepped forward and announced her arrival, winking at Jessica as he turned and left.

While she stood there waiting anxiously for her mother's first words, Sandy rose and stared curiously at her daughter for what seemed a frighteningly long time. She finally offered her hand and remarked, with only a hint of a smile, "Well, Jessica, it would appear that you have charm to sooth the savage beast, as they say. I haven't heard that old fool laugh like that for quite some time. Do sit down. We have much to discuss."

Her mother's greeting was a far cry from what she had hoped for, but considering the circumstances, she knew she owed her some measure of humility. Sitting quietly across from her, she waited for her mother to open a dialogue.

"To be perfectly candid, Jessica, when Mister Thomas called and told me about your presence here in La Jolla, I suspected the worst and called local authorities to monitor this meeting. They have had you both under surveillance for the past twenty-four hours. You were followed here and are being watched as we speak. So, if you'll excuse me, I must call off the hounds. Even after twenty years, there's no mistaking your identity."

Although she had never considered that aspect of *returning to the nest,* she knew from her own background and training that in cases where a person had been missing for a long time, there was always an element of suspicion present when that person suddenly shows up. In a way, she was pleased to learn that her mother had considered the possibility of her being an intruder.

Leaving briefly to dismiss a detective who had been on surveillance just inside her home, she returned with a freshly opened bottle of champagne and two glasses. After they had each been filled, she raised hers and offered a toast, "I believe this occasion calls for something special," she proposed, finally smiling. "So, here's to your safe return. I never thought I'd live long enough to see this day. And much as I'd like to, you're too grown up to spank for what you've put me through all these years, but you do owe me one hell of an explanation. That said, welcome home, my dear."

Her Mother's sentiments were like the sound of music to her. For the first time since her arrival in San Diego she felt relaxed and better prepared to discuss the foolish and sometimes life threatening activities of her past without having to reveal the sordid details and confidentialities that she was pledged to honor. Thinking carefully about the chronological order of those activities, she attempted to explain them, hoping for an empathizing ear.

"When Dad died, it felt as if all the good in me was buried with him, leaving a heartless body full of anger and self pity behind, a perfect target for those who would introduce me to the addictive world of drugs and alcohol. For three years I spent most of my time bumming around warm climate states where shelters and communes were commonplace, working for whomever paid me enough to maintain my "hippie" lifestyle. Then one day I saw an ad in the newspaper that offered a lot of money to drive cars back and forth across the country. Supposedly, the cars belonged to military personnel. With nothing better to do, or lose, I applied and got the job. After a few crossings I managed to bank enough money to buy a small car, and I shared an apartment with a girlfriend when I wasn't on the road. I really thought I had it made."

Before she continued, Sandy interrupted and asked if she was hungry, suggesting that she could continue her story during lunch.

Jessica admitted she was famished, and most grateful for an opportunity to use the ladies room. When she returned Sandy had already instructed Ivan and Christina to serve lunch, and quite a lunch it was. Colorfully accented china plates offered hamburger-size, pan grilled crab cakes topped with a creamy Hollandaise sauce, Caesar Salad, and a mixed fruit cup. Both champagne glasses had been refilled.

Well into the meal that her daughter was obviously enjoying, Sandy paused a moment to rest, however, encouraged Jessica to finish her lunch, commenting that even if it took all night, she wanted to hear, "all of her story!"

There was hardly any mystery hidden in her mother's words. She knew without question that any attempt to shorten or edit out any detail would not be acceptable to her. Accepting that she had already bridged the river of no return, she nibbled on her remaining food, periodically, and continued.

"On one of my return trips to California I was traveling on a long, monotonous two-lane road mid-way through Arizona when I came up behind an open flatbed truck with a bunch of gardening tools laying loosely near the back. There was a car approaching in the opposite direction that was too close for me to pass the truck, so I waited. Just before the other car reached the truck, a short, three-pronged weed digger fell off onto the road in front of me, landing with the prongs sticking straight up. My front tires missed it when I swerved, but my left rear tire caught it and caused a blowout. Evidently, no one in the truck or the other car saw what happened and kept on going, leaving me stranded in the middle of nowhere."

"Dear Lord," Sandy gasped, "Did you have a spare?"

"Oh yeah," she replied, remembering what would turn out to be the beginning of her worst nightmare. "I had everything but good timing."

Sandy's eyebrows came together in a frown trying to figure out the timing connection, and then asked, "What timing?"

She realized in an instant that by answering her mother truthfully she would be unlocking the door to a part of her past she was hesitant to revisit, especially in the presence of her mother. But, because she had come there fully prepared to bear her soul, she continued, anxious to put the whole bloody mess behind her, once and for all.

"I had already opened the trunk to look for a tire jack when a Highway Patrol officer appeared out of nowhere and asked if he could help. When I told him I didn't have a jack, he used his to raise the axel. It was then that he noticed a white powdery substance trickling out of the puncture made by the weed digger. One sample taste was all the justification he needed to pull out his gun, handcuff and lock me in the back seat of his patrol car. I was absolutely terrified."

"What was the white powder? That patrolman certainly had no reason to treat you that way without an explanation. Where did he take you?"

Jessica giggled at her mother being so naive and replied, "Mom, when a police officer catches you red-handed with your tires packed with packages of cocaine he doesn't need to explain anything to you except your rights. After a wrecker came to pick up the car, he took me to the nearest town where I was held for questioning. Simple as that."

"What happened then? Surely you were able to clear yourself of any wrongdoing."

"I wish it had been that simple," she replied, vividly remembering the ordeal. "That little incident pretty well plotted the course of my life from that day forward, and there was little I could do to change it, until now."

"Go on."

"Because I was charged with transporting drugs across state lines, a DEA agent was called in on the case. Compared to the local Highway Patrol officer, I couldn't have asked for a more understanding and thoroughly professional person to interrogate me. The local lawyer who represented me was a nice guy, but way out of his league in this particular situation. He was the buffer, you might say, between the local police and me. Some of those characters were convinced that I was part of a statewide drug trafficking network and were after my hide. It became pretty intense for a while."

While she continued her story, Sandy made sure her daughter's champagne glass was never empty, having observed that the more she drank, the more animated and willing she became to open up and describe events in greater detail.

"How in the world were you able to get out of that mess?" she asked, feeding Jessica just the right questions to maintain the story's momentum.

"Well, it was DEA Agent Lewis who finally concluded that, if everything I had told them was the truth, there had to be a much larger network of dealers distributing drugs back and forth across the country. The information I had accumulated on my crossings, he pointed out to his superiors, was a hell of a lot more important than the crime I was being accused of, especially since he was convinced I was innocent. In other words, I had inadvertently become a key witness and an important source of information that could benefit them. Because of my first-hand knowledge of the overall operation, he had me legally remanded to his custody. I could have kissed him."

During the break in conversation that ensued, she drank several swallows from her water glass to help neutralize the champagne that tended to dry her mouth and thicken her tongue. Her mother noticed this and suggested she might enjoy something a little less bubbly, so she pressed the red button on a small, hand held electronic device that lay on the table nearby. Moments later, Ivan appeared and was told to clear the table and return with a drink of her daughter's choice. Jessica tried to decline, but her mother insisted, advising her that she need not be concerned about driving back to the hotel, because preparations were already being made for her to spend the night. She knew that to argue was futile, so she accepted her invitation and told Ivan she would enjoy a chilled glass of Chardonnay.

Ivan was well inside the house when she encouraged her daughter to continue her intriguing story, at the same time complementing herself on how cleverly she had maneuvered Jessica into spending the night.

"Do go on, dear," she insisted, "I'm absolutely captivated by your adventurous life so far. What an exciting life you have led."

Although she may have thought she had maneuvered her daughter into spending the night, Jessica was very much aware of what was going on, but decided there was little to be gained by refusing well-intended hospitality. Dedicated to pleasing her, she settled back and continued: "In order to thwart any escape I might have contemplated, Agent Lewis had me detained in jail overnight. The next morning he had a whole series of photographs taken of the car, and its contraband. Following that, he took me to the nearest airport where a chartered aircraft flew us to Washington, DC. Unbeknownst to me, my future was secretly being planned there.

The chilled glass of Chardonnay that Ivan arrived with was a vintage wine, and far superior to any she had ever tasted. To fully appreciate its quality, he invited her to savor its flavor before swallowing. Following his departure, she turned to her mother and grinned. "I know what you're up to, mother," she remarked. "I just want you to know how much I appreciate all this special attention."

"I'm glad, Jessica. It's been a long time since I've enjoyed this kind of company. Do go on."

"While I was being interrogated by Agent Lewis and his cronies in Washington, members of the drug organization that had hired me found out through an informant that I had been taken into custody by the DEA, along with the drugs. When news of this kind reaches underworld management it demands retribution. Based on similar events that have occurred in the past, my cooperating with the government placed me in a very precarious situation. One that could have very easily led to my being hunted down and killed."

"What ever happened to the Witness Protection Program?"

Jessica cringed at the mere mention of it, remembering her forced incarceration while she recounted every mile of her many trips across the country, delivering what she honestly believed was some GI's automobile. "What developed from the information I was able to provide was a map of the United States that pinpointed every cross-country route I had driven, and the location of every town and city where I had stopped to spend a day or two. Realistically, Agent Lewis speculated at the time, I was probably not the only driver that had been commandeered to unknowingly land-ferry drugs across the country. And there I was, right in the middle of it all. Or, to put it more tritely, up Crap Creek without a paddle. Not a very comfortable feeling, I can assure you?"

"Yes, I can imagine." she agreed. "But tell me, were you released from custody after you provided the DEA with all this information?"

"They couldn't." she replied, almost with anger. "It would have been like signing my own death warrant. Don't forget, the bad guys have their agents too. Unfortunately, they don't take prisoners."

"How frightening," she remarked, chilled by the thought. "I can't even imagine being in a situation like that. What in the world did you do?"

Before continuing, she held up her wine glass. "May I have another," she asked. "I can't remember when I've ever tasted better wine. Where did you buy it?"

"I have a friend who owns a winery in Temecula. He sends me a case every Christmas to remind me of the relationship we once had. He was dedicated to his wine and I loved this place, so the distance between us finally caused a meltdown and we stopped seeing one another. We're still friends, though. Please continue your story. Ivan will be here shortly."

"Agent Lewis was aware of the fate that awaited me if I were set free to wander back to California on my own. As an option, he offered me the opportunity to join the DEA as a special trainee. My future at that time was so unsure I came to the conclusion that his offer was the only chance I was going to get to dig myself out of the mess I was in, so I accepted his offer."

While her mother took a minute to digest the complexity of the situation her daughter had found herself in at such a tender age, Ivan approached with a full bottle of the wine Jessica had requested. "Will that be all, Madame?" he asked, appearing somewhat annoyed.

She waved him away with her hand and made a remark as he turned to leave, "Thanks for bringing the bottle this time, dear man. Makes it easier this way."

He left frowning, muttering something under his breath that she couldn't understand.

As she watched Jessica fill her glass, she wondered what was going on in her mind, and what strangely fascinating events from her past were yet to be revealed. The wine appeared to be slowly breaking down whatever reluctance she might have had earlier to venture beyond the barriers of privacy she had set for herself. To further penetrate that inner sanctum, she asked, "Were you ever romantically involved with Agent Lewis? How old a man was he?"

"Sorry to disappoint you, mother," she replied. "Everything between Dusty Lewis and I was strictly business. He was several years older and married, so that killed any attraction I had for him. We saw each other when I was in training, but those meetings were few and far between, and only to check on my progress. Once I became an agent, I transferred to our Miami office and never came in contact with him again."

"How did you like working in Miami? Were you there long?"

"Too long, I'm afraid," she replied, looking wistfully at the ocean shimmering in the late afternoon sun

"Unpleasant memories, dear?"

Realizing that she had left her mother hanging on a lead-in statement that required explanation, she returned to present day and addressed the question. "While I was in Miami, my partner and I were given an assignment to investigate a local businessman who was suspected of smuggling drugs into the United States from either Puerto Rico or Cuba, or possibly both. During that investigation, my partner and I became very close, and eventually intimate. There was even talk of marriage, but the case we were working took precedence over our personal lives, so we put it on the back burner until it was over.

Tragically, as it turned out, my partner was murdered during that investigation and I was seriously wounded. I recovered, but to avoid another attempt on my life, my superiors arranged to have me declared legally dead, and buried someone else's body in my place. While recovering in a guarded government facility, I was given a cosmetic makeover, a new Social Security number and drivers license. My pitiful little bank account was changed to a new name they had given me when they paid me off. Officially, I was now, Jessy Stuart. Nickname, "Jess."

"If I may ask, to whom am I speaking now?"

She laughed at the expression on her mother's face, and replied, "Not to worry, mom. I'm still your Jessica. I changed back to my birth name a month ago and retired from the DEA. "

Sandy glanced suspiciously at her middle-aged daughter and asked, inquisitively, "How did you manage that, my dear? "You're not old enough to retire."

She was about to reply when Ivan returned to make sure they were not in need of anything. Automatically, he reached for the wine bottle to fill their glasses. When it emptied after only half a glass was poured, he remarked, "Should I open another bottle, Madame. It would appear that this one has a hole in its bottom."

"What do you say, Jessica, shall we tie one on together to celebrate your homecoming? You still have a lot of story telling to do."

With what she had already consumed, she knew she was already pressing the envelope as far as remaining reasonably sober was concerned, but sided with her mother. "Why not. We're not going anywhere," she replied

Then, surprising the two with her boldness, she looked at Ivan and added, slurring her words a little, "Make sure the next one doesn't have a hole in it, will ya."

He enjoyed the humor and playfully examined the empty bottle as he turned and walked away, quietly commenting, "It would appear that this is not the only bottom we need be concerned with."

Until he returned, the two women remained silent, content to enjoy the sunshine that still lingered, along with the pleasant feeling of companionship that their reunion had given rebirth to. Moments later Sandy asked, "What happened between the time you acquired your new identity and the time you retired. That represents quite a number of years, or am I becoming too nosey?"

"Not at all," she replied. "Believe it or not, that period of my life was probably the most adventurous, and is now ironically linked to recent events that have brought us together again after all those years."

"I don't disbelieve anything anymore," she confessed. "Please go on."

Puzzled by where to begin and what to leave out for fear of over-shocking her mother she resumed her story:

"Because I had taken two years of Spanish in high school, and had picked up street Spanish in Tijuana that you and Dad were never aware of, I was selected to be an undercover agent for the DEA in Puerto Rico. My job was to report back on the drug activity there. My assignment was to search out and gain the confidence of one of the island's most notorious drug lords, a man by the name of Carlo Puzzi. It really wasn't that difficult a task because the man had a weakness for good-looking American woman, so I began hanging out in fashionable nightspots and gambling casinos waiting for an opportunity to meet him. By doing so, I gained quite a reputation around town. Ironically, meeting Carlo came quite unexpectedly late one Sunday morning when I decided to visit a local yacht club to enjoy their celebrated brunch. I was eating alone on the outdoor patio when a waiter came to my table and asked me to look at the man waving at me from a yacht moored not far away. When I asked the waiter in Spanish what the man's name was, he grinned and explained in his native tongue that the man's name was Carlo Puzzi, a very wealthy and powerful man who wanted me to join him and his friends. The waiter strongly urged me to accept the invitation, explaining that my bill had already been paid by Senior Puzzi, so I waved back, slipped the waiter a five-dollar bill and headed for the yacht."

While she took a breather to enjoy a sip of wine, she couldn't help but be amused by the look of bewilderment on her mother's face as she reached across the table and took her hand. "What a life you have led, my child. It's a wonder you're still alive."

"I almost wasn't a couple of times," she confessed. "I guess I'm just lucky, all things considered."

Reconsidering her earlier commitment to stay up all night to hear her daughter's entire life story, she asked, "Do you want to continue this tomorrow? You look a little tired."

She considered the suggestion but thought it best to finish the whole story so nothing would have to be carried over into the next day. After a long deep breath, she sat her glass down and continued. "That happenstance with Carlo began a comparatively long and intimate relationship, in contrast to the short term ones he was accustomed to. I really believed he saw something in me that none of his other romances offered. To tell the truth, the more I saw of him, the more I became enamored by his charm. He was an older man, probably in his late forties, and in excellent physical shape. He rode horses and loved the sea. At times he reminded me of Errol Flynn, a swashbuckling pirate with a touch of Fernando Lamas to bring out the passion in his hot, Spanish blood. But, like most Spaniards, Carlo loved his women, and I had a job to do. For that reason I redirected my interest toward a man who worked for Carlo by the name of Colonel Jason Ward.

Ward was a renegade, ex-Viet Nam commander who had been kicked out of the Army for reasons I'm still not sure of. He commanded an undercover group of Cuban commandos whose soul purpose in life was to get rid of Castro and establish Cuba as an export facility for distributing Columbia processed cocaine into the United States. I didn't like the man, but he was my ticket to Cuba. There I hoped to learn more about Carlo's operation. He feigned reasonable disappointment when I told him what I was planning to do, but wished me well with a promise that he would always be there for me if I ever wanted to return."

Shaking her head while looking at her in disbelief, Sandy remarked, "I'll say one thing in your favor, honey, you've sure got a lot of guts. Did you ever consider what consequences might develop from living among all those Cuban men? Why would Colonel Ward want you in his outfit anyway? Seems to me you'd be nothing but trouble."

"I was," she replied, smugly, walking unsteadily back and forth to exercise her legs. "I was also bilingual, which made me well suited for the intelligence work I was doing. In other words, I was a very important member of the team."

"Where did you live? Certainly there was some sort of private facilities available to you. You did bathe regularly, didn't you?"

"Certainly I bathed, mother. Maybe not as often, or as thoroughly as you, but I was clean and had my own tent. It zipped open and closed from the inside to insure my privacy. And, in case you're wondering about security, I slept with an AK-47. That's an automatic weapon I was trained to use, and very well I might add."

Recognizing that she might have hurt her daughter's feelings, she apologized for questioning her about her bathing practices and asked her politely to continue, promising not to comment or interrupt until she had finished.

Relieved that her mother was finally accepting her as a full-grown woman, and not the irresponsible girl she remembered as a child, she sat back down and continued talking in concert with a setting sun that was slowly disappearing beyond the horizon.

"There was a ten day period during the time I was in Cuba when Colonel Ward left our camp site on a mission, leaving three of the more reliable members of his command to watch over me. During his absence a freak storm came up out of the east and a small airplane crash-landed on a deserted beach near our camp. The pilot was hurt, but not seriously. His name was Dan Hughes, an American who flew drugs around the Caribbean for Carlo Puzzi. Ironically, the same Carlo Puzzi I had left in Puerto Rico.

When Dan was well enough to travel, I contacted Carlo and asked him, as a favor to me, to send a boat for Dan in order to get him off the island before Colonel Ward returned. I was convinced the Colonel would eventually kill him. What no one else knew, except my three watchdogs, was that I had accidentally stumbled onto the drugs Dan had dumped over the jungle before he crash-landed his plane. Convinced that I was going to need that plane someday to make my own escape, I hid it in the jungle, along with the drugs. There really wasn't that much wrong with it. Just a broken nose wheel and a bent prop that I knew could easily be fixed. When the boat arrived on the night Dan was to leave, I gave him my old California Driver's License so he could use it to find you and let you know that I was still alive and well. I only found out from Neal Thomas yesterday that Dan never contacted you. I can understand now how distraught you must have been all those years."

If nothing else, her story thus far began putting things in perspective and clarified what Neal had tried to explain to her the previous day. Along with that understanding came a deeper appreciation for what he had gone through to reunite a mother and her long lost daughter. People that, until a few days ago, he had never met. The coincidences of the whole situation fascinated her, and although she had promised not to interrupt, curiosity got the best of her. "I'm not clear on how you got from Cuba to my front door. Not that it will have any influence on what I have to say when you're finished, but I'd still like to know."

Her mother's inference that she had reached some conclusions from what had already been revealed thus far unnerved Jessica for a moment, but she continued in spite of it: "Soon after Dan Hughes left Cuba, Colonel Ward returned. He called me to his tent and told me he knew all about the American who had landed there, and that I had arranged for his escape. He was definitely not a happy camper and threatened to report the incident to Carlo Puzzi, not knowing that Carlo had arranged the escape at my request. To stall any attempt by the Colonel to take his anger out on me, Carlo summoned him back to Puerto Rico to attend what Carlo told him at the time was an emergency meeting. In doing so, Carlo had provided me with a window of opportunity to repair the airplane and make my own escape with the drugs that I had hidden inside. I was supposed to have sold the drugs and split the money with Carlo, but I never did. I fenced them through another source and banked the money in the States to finance my early retirement."

Sandy was smiling now, struck with remembering a time when Jessica had begun showing signs that her life would be adventurous. Though she had promised not to, she interrupted her to remind her of an incident that took place with her father when she was only a teenager. "I remember those frightening days when your father took you flying on weekends," she recalled. "I was a nervous wreck waiting for something to happen. The day you soloed was almost the death of me. I'm afraid you haven't changed much."

Jessica was tempted to point out that part of the problem between she and her mother at that time was her failure to accept her as a maturing woman with a spirit of her own, but she controlled herself and continued: "Fortunately, when Dan nosed his plane onto the beach that day, he was almost stopped. Damage to the props was minimal and easily repaired. The nose wheel, however, couldn't be retracted so I had my men jury-rig it with a piece of steel pipe in the locked-down position. All I had to do was lift off the beach and my troubles were over, or so I thought."

"Tell me truthfully, Jessica," Sandy asked, "weren't you just a tiny bit scared?"

"Down every foot of that beach until I was airborne," she replied. "I had already turned the engine over several times earlier to make sure everything worked. Luckily, Dan had landed with the gas tank more than half full. All I had to do was wait for the right time. It came unexpectedly the next day."

"What about all the men who were loyal to Colonel Ward? Didn't they suspect anything while you were repairing that airplane?"

"Not really. I lied and told them Colonel Ward had given me orders to get it fixed by the time he returned so he could use it himself. I was to be his pilot."

"What happened the next day to force your departure?"

"One of our outpost groups reported late in the afternoon that a large detachment of Castro's soldiers was heading in our direction which made it necessary for all of us to leave the area immediately. While all this flurry of activity was going on, I stole away to the beach that night with my three comrades, rolled the plane out onto the beach and took off, leaving them unavoidably on the beach to fend for themselves. The one thing I regretted having to do."

"But your home and safe now," Sandy remarked. "Surely you don't have any regrets, do you?"

"Not really, " she confessed, "especially after the serious wakeup call I experienced when I arrived in Puerto Rico."

Sandy poured what was left of the wine in each of their glasses before asking her to continue. "Do go on, dear. I know you're tired, but you wouldn't quit now, would you?"

Given the length of time she had been talking and the wine she had consumed, she was beginning to feel a little intoxicated and reluctant to continue. The wide eyes and expectant expression on her mother's face, however, forced her to continue, despite the beginning of what she knew was going to be one queen size hangover in the morning. "When I arrived at Carlo's private landing strip in Puerto Rico, I was picked up in a limo and driven directly to his estate. Carlo had already made arrangements for Colonel Ward to be returned to his troops so our paths wouldn't cross. Although he was pleased to see me again, he warned that there were those in his organization who suspected me of being an undercover agent for the DEA. Rather than having to face the unpleasant task of killing me, he ordered me out of the country and gave me a one-way, first class airline ticket to Miami that was leaving the next day. He also gave me a key to a post office box there that he said contained one hundred thousand dollars. It was his going away present in exchange for my promise never to return. Obviously, I accepted his terms and was on the plane when it left. The money was in Miami when I arrived just as he said it would be"

Wearily, she stood up to stretch, remarking in the process, "And that, dear mother, is what I've been doing all these years. Now it's your turn."

"I'm afraid my life's story would pale by comparison," she admitted. "My only concern is that yours might return to haunt you. Which brings me to the matter I wish to discuss with you, if you're not too tired to listen."

"Of course I'm not," she lied. "What is it?"

"As you may have already observed, I live here alone except for Ivan and Christina. They have separate quarters and enjoy an active life of their own. I have no idea what your plans are for the future, but I would be overjoyed if they included me. Until today, I was a lonely woman just growing older one day at a time. Now, I have an heir, someone to share all this with. Tomorrow you can check out of the hotel and into any one of the four empty bedrooms upstairs so we can spend a few days getting reacquainted. We still have so much to talk about. Sleep on it and we'll talk in the morning. Meanwhile, Christina has prepared a light dinner. She and Ivan are eager to welcome you back to the nest, so let's join them inside and make it a family affair, just the four of us."

The invitation was not what she had anticipated, nor wanted, but rather than put a damper on her enthusiasm, she walked around the table, took her in her arms and kissed her affectionately on the cheek, whispering softly, "Why not."

Later on that night, while she lay struggling to fall asleep in strange surroundings, she repeatedly kept hearing the words her mother had said just before dinner: "Now, I have an heir."

Chapter 11

Trouble's Messenger

Mid- afternoon on the day following Sandy and Jessica Sterling's reunion, Neal sat in his studio with little more on his mind than the same oil painting he had been trying to finish for months. After several hours of uninterrupted work, the urge to go for a relaxing walk on the beach encouraged him to quit. During in the process of cleaning his brushes and putting his studio in order the telephone rang. There was no mistaking the voice on the other end. It was Dan Hughes.

"Hi there, Mister T," he said in a voice that sounded as if it had been flavored with bourbon, "are you alone?"

"Just me and my radio," he replied. "What's up? Sounds like you're right next door."

"I'm at the Hilton Inn. Is that close enough."

The intermittent loss of his voice made it obvious that he was preoccupied with something, or someone, so he asked, "Are you alone?"

"No," he replied. "Donna's with me. Can you come over and join me for a drink? I need to talk to you right away."

Disappointed that he would have to postpone his beach walk, he agreed to be there in fifteen minutes, sensing that he was soon going to be asked to do something he would probably regret, one way or the other.

Driving into the hotel parking area a short time later, he asked himself three questions: *Why is he a week early? Why is Donna with him?* And, more importantly, *what's the urgency in talking to me now?*

Entering the lobby he suspected Dan was more than likely in the cocktail lounge, so he headed in that direction and found the solemn face of his friend waiting there with Donna sitting expressionless at his side.

As soon as he saw him, Dan rose and offered his hand, at the same time motioning to the waitress that he wanted to order.

After their order had been taken, he sat opposite the couple and confronted Dan directly. "What the hell's going on, Dan?" he asked. "How come you're a week early?"

He hesitated purposely for a moment as Donna stood up and excused herself. "I think I'm going to check out the pool," she remarked before leaving. "Come and get me whenever you've finished with whatever you two have to talk about. Nice to see you again, Mr. T."

Watching her hips undulating as she walked across the lobby, Dan turned to Neal and said, "If I had what she's got I'd be a millionaire by now."

"Thee and me," he agreed. "Now, do you mind explaining why you're here a week early."

Dan sat motionless looking at his drink for a moment and then reached into his pocket and pulled out a map. Handing it to Neal, he asked, "Do you recognize this?"

Neal took the map and unfolded it. As soon as he saw the marked circle around a portion of Back Bay's Eastern shoreline, he recognized it immediately. "That's the map you used to find Shark Hadley's place last Sunday. What's it doing here?"

"The bottom line is, I know how to find Hadley's place without a map, but you don't," he replied. "If anything should happen to me I want you to use it to lead the authorities there so they can pick up the evidence in that toolbox. Don't worry, I'll make it worth your while."

Still uneasy about what Dan was asking him to do, he refolded the map and tucked it into his hip pocket, assuring him that he could find the place. Out of curiosity he asked him why he kept referring to something happening to him. "Has somebody threatened you, Dan?" he asked without hesitation. "Is that why you're here?"

He admitted in a hushed voice that Miguel Ramirez had warned him about what could happen if he didn't come up with the three packets of drugs that were missing, and warned that he would be powerless to protect him from the consequences. "To tell the truth, I didn't know what to do, so I offered to pay Donna's expenses if she would keep me company while I hid from this bullet that's been chasing me around for days. I know who stole those drugs. They're the same two guys who delivered them to my boat early last Saturday morning. Like a fool, I was in such a hurry to get the stuff into my boat I never counted the individual packets. I'm almost positive Ramirez paid those guys to set me up because he knew I was making plans to leave the cartel. This tactic was his way of getting rid of me. Just like he got rid of poor old Billy Newman."

From movies he had seen about how Mafia boss's get rid of their unwanted, Neal recognized the logic in what Dan had deduced for himself, but couldn't reason why he thought coming all the way to California was going to solve anything. "What did you hope to accomplish out here?" he asked, questioning his reasoning. "The problem's back there?"

A weak but visible smile curled the corners of Dan's mouth as he attempted to explain the predicament he was in. "I'm a firm believer in that old axiom that claims there is honor among thieves. Two days ago word came to me through a friend in the organization that Miguel Ramirez had put out the word that I had stolen drugs. Afraid that Ramirez was going to have me killed, he suggested that I get lost for a few days while he looked into the matter. Since I was coming to your party anyway, I changed our reservations to an earlier flight that left this morning. We bought separate tickets just to make it appear as if we weren't traveling together, just in case."

"I can tell by your blood shot eyes that you haven't had a hell of a lot of sleep. Why don't I meet you back here around five o'clock. I'll have some interesting news to share with you then. In the meantime, you and Donna can get some rest."

On his way home he wondered how Dan would react to the news that Jessica Sterling was in town. Not telling him at the hotel seemed to be the safest alternative, especially with Donna there. What a strange day this is turning out to be, he thought, at the same time wondering if his early arrival was an accident looking for someplace to happen.

Entering the kitchen, his eyes were immediately drawn to the message light flashing on his telephone answering machine. Pushing it brought a message from Jessica Sterling, whose familiar voice informed him that she had left the La Valencia Hotel and if he needed to talk with her, she could be reached at her mother's home. Giving him the number, she emphasized that there was also an important matter she also wished to discuss with him.

The kitchen clock indicated that it was already mid-afternoon, so he placed the call. Several rings later, Ivan answered. Immediately recognizing Neal's voice, he praised him for his unselfish efforts to reunite Ms. Sterling and her lovely daughter. "I can't remember when I've been so impressed," he went on. "Please stay on the line while I locate her. I know Jessica is very anxious to speak with you."

In the time it took a pigeon to come to rest in one of Paula's wicker plant holders out on the patio, she came on the line. "Good afternoon, Mister Thomas, she asked in a tired, raspy voice. "How are you?"

"I'm okay, I think. Question is, how are you? Your voice sounds a bit froggy."

"Well, after being gone for twenty years there was a lot of explaining to do that lasted well into the evening," she explained, "And, if my mother has her way, there's going to be more of it today. That is, if my voice holds out."

Following several attempts to clear her throat, she added, "One bottle of champagne and two bottles of mother's private stock didn't help matters any. I really have a serious hangover."

"Believe me, you'll survive," he assured her. "Been there, done that. Now, what did you want to talk to me about?"

"Two things. First, mother and I would love to come to your Fourth of July party, so we'll need directions. Second, we'd like to invite you and your significant other to join us for dinner this Saturday evening. Kind of a get acquainted thing. Can you make it?"

His first impulse was to make up an excuse to decline because of Dan's early arrival, but his conscience dictated that he accept, considering all that was at stake. Ignoring *"Murphy's Law,"* he gave her directions to his house and then addressed the matter of Dan's premature arrival. "I am delighted that you and your mother will be coming to our party. There is, however, one bit of information that I feel obligated to tell you with regard to Dan's being there."

"And that is?" she asked, in a noticeably different tone of voice.

"Well, much to my surprise, Dan showed up here unexpectedly today with a female companion. I'm not sure why, but he's here, and may be leaving for home before the Fourth of July gets here.

Predictably, there was a pause. When she finally did speak, he was surprised by her attitude. "Not a problem," she assured him. "Bring them along with you Saturday. Should make for quite an interesting evening, don't you think?"

Without confirming it with Paula, he found nothing on their events calendar that would be in conflict with Jessica's invitation, but hesitated accepting on Dan's behalf, especially with Donna now in the equation. Diplomatically, he replied, "I will be seeing him in a little while. I'll ask him then if he would like to join us and call you back later this evening to let you know, one way or the other."

"Fine. I'll be here."

Time passed quickly following his brief but enlightening conversation with Jessica. Without realizing just how quickly, his watch reminded him that it was time to revisit the hotel. Hopefully, they had used their time wisely and would be rested when he arrived.

Before he could leave, however, the phone rang. Rather than run the risk of being delayed by some junk call, he waited for the message machine to kick in. It was Paula calling to inform him that she was joining the girls in her office after work to celebrate a birthday, and would not be home for dinner. That being a frequent occurrence in an office full of women, he took the message in stride and left to find out more about Dan's premature arrival.

When he entered the hotel he found Dan sitting alone in the lounge eyeing the only waitress on duty. He looked relaxed and somewhat more presentable. He had shaved. The clothes he had worn that morning had been changed to more easily fit in with California's casual lifestyle; sport shirt, shorts and beach sandals.

"You look like one of the natives," he kidded him. "Where's Donna?"

"She's having her monthly misery," he answered, waving his hand to get the waitress's attention. "You know, stomach cramps and a headache. Can I buy you a drink?"

Accepting the offer, he ordered a vodka tonic and waited for the waitress to leave before telling him about his conversation with Jessica Sterling.

His eyes got as big as hard-boiled eggs at hearing the news, and he stuttered some trying to respond. After gulping down what was left of the drink he already had, he blurted out, "Well I'll be damned! You actually made contact with her? I don't believe it."

"You'd better," he remarked. "We've been invited to join the two of them for dinner this Saturday evening. I told her I would check with you because I was unsure of your plans, having arrived here a week early. I told her I would call her back this evening after I had talked with you. Donna is also invited."

While Dan sat there shaking his head in disbelief, he continued: "And, just to bring you up to speed, she knows you never contacted her mother like you promised. You remember, the, *She's alive and well,* message."

For the next couple of hours he summarized all of the events that had taken place following his return to San Diego, emphasizing the need for him to do the gentlemanly thing and accept their invitation in order to put the matter to rest and appease his own conscience. "After all," he reminded him, "she did save your life."

Reluctantly, he said he would, providing Donna felt better and Paula was also going to be there.

He assured him that she would be there, knowing full well that Paula was completely unaware of the invitation, or that he and Donna were even in town. With his conscience growing heavier by the minute, he vowed to brief Paula on what had transpired when she returned home later on that evening.

To linger and watch Dan become progressively more intoxicated didn't appeal to him, so he finished his drink and reminded him that he and Donna were invited to join him for the Friday afternoon get together at Ron Barns' house the next day. That done, the two men shook hands and agreed to communicate the next morning about planning a few activities that were more orchestrated around Donna's entertainment than his. "After all," Neal pointed out, "she is on vacation too."

With an agreement in place, they patted one another on the back and went their separate ways, him returning home, and Dan trying unsuccessfully to score a hit with a thoroughly disinterested waitress.

The first thing he did when he returned home was to put Dan's map in his studio desk. Then he called Jessica to inform her that he and Dan would be arriving with their respective lady friends on Saturday, as planned. His only concern after hanging up was not having informed Paula earlier about his extracurricular activities. But, maybe that was doing more good than bad, considering what she was battling at work. Of equal concern was Saturday's unexpected dinner invitation. Would not knowing about it in advance upset her? Not that Dan's early arrival, or the circumstances surrounding it, were in any way disruptive or threatening, but in the back of his mind he couldn't rid himself of the nagging feeling that Dan's relationship with Donna was not a match made in heaven. Something he couldn't put his finger on triggered the premonition that Mr. Hughes was walking on thin ice and, for Paula's sake, as well as his own, he didn't want to be around when it gave way under the weight of the baggage he brought with him.

With time on his hands, and not much interest in resuming work on his painting, he sat down at the piano where, for just a little while, he escaped the reality of his topsy-turvy life and found solace in the fantasy of his music. He hadn't been playing long when the telephone annoyed him back to reality. Determined not to answer until he knew whom the caller was, he waited for the answering machine to kick in, hoping it was a junk call he could ignore. When the beep sounded, Dan's voice began leaving a message that he quickly interrupted by picking up the receiver. "Sorry

Dan," he apologized, "I thought it was just another junk call. What's on your mind?"

Once he started to speak, Neal new in an instant that he had continued drinking after he left him earlier and waited patiently while he slurred his way through a reply. "Oh, Donna's all pissed off at me again," he began. "Wants to do something besides sit around and watch me get bombed, as she put it so diplomatically. So, I'm taking her to Disneyland for an overnight getaway. I'll call you when we get back tomorrow."

With all the emotional conflict Dan was currently going through, Neal couldn't bring himself to lecture a grown man about what the consequences of getting a DUI in California, so he only cautioned him to be careful driving.

"No driving for me, sport," he replied. "We're taking the Amtrak! I understand they have a lounge onboard."

Uttering a sigh of relief, he encouraged him to have a good time. "Give some quality attention to Donna while you're at it, will you. And don't forget we're invited out to dinner Saturday."

"What time?"

"I'll be at the hotel to pick you up around five o'clock. Dinner's at six."

"Not to worry. I'll be ready."

Considerably relieved that the couple was going to be elsewhere until the next afternoon, he returned to his piano and continued playing for a while longer. Even after he finally quit, there was still some time to kill before Paula arrived so he decided to enjoy a relaxing soak in the Jacuzzi. Wrapped in a terry cloth robe she had given him for Christmas, he slipped into his sandals and returned downstairs, stopping in the kitchen long enough too mix a drink.

Moments later, while the hot, swirling water bubbled up around him like soft, massaging fingers, he thanked the stars that had just begun to appear in the gradually darkening sky for the few quiet hours he had enjoyed that afternoon. Unlike some people, who shuddered at the thought of being left alone for any length of time, he basked in it as he had as a boy, building model airplanes in the cellar of his home when winter's snow storms made a person glad to be inside.

Television as yet had not been invented, but radios came to life after school and in the early evening, bringing families together to enjoy the suspenseful drama and simple humor of such popular programs as Terry and The Pirates, Captain Midnight, The Shadow, Amos and Andy, and a host of others, as snow drifted by the foot in the stormy blackness outside.

Sunday newspapers brought entertainment to young and old alike in the form of such colorful characters as Dick Tracy, Batman, Popeye, Little Abner, Prince Valiant, to name a few. There were daily newspaper reports and radio broadcasts covering WWII battles, with graphic pictures showing our Allied Forces fighting in Europe and the Pacific to win the war that was supposed to end all wars – or so they prophesized.

Reflecting on the conversation he had shared with his intoxicated friend, Dan Hughes, only minutes ago, brought to mind a snowy winter's night in January when he was a young boy. He and his younger sister, Carolyn, were spending the evening at home with a girlfriend of his sister's, while their mother and father ventured out to attend a weekly dinner gathering with married friends. What a night that was, he recalled:

****

It was cozy and warm inside the house that snowy December evening. There was a fire in the fireplace, and all three were wrapped in blankets while they sat on the floor in front of the radio, eating freshly made oatmeal cookies dipped in milk. Sometime during the evening, it was Neal who thought he heard a car stop outside and went to the window to investigate. His suspicions were confirmed when he saw the glowing light on top of a taxicab that had stopped in front of his grandfather's house next door. Less then a minute later, the cab left. Had it not been for the streetlight hanging directly in front of the house, he might never have seen the shadowy figure of a man lying on all fours between two snow drifts, unable to get up.

Fearful that it was his grandfather who had fallen, and that he might be injured, he dressed for the bitter cold weather and ventured out to see if he could help. Arriving at the scene, he heard the downed figure singing in a slurred Irish voice, "Oh Danny Boy, the pipes, the pipes are c-a-a-l-l-i-n-g." The smell of his liquored breath made it immediately clear that the fallen figure was that of his drunken grandfather, John O'Day.

Helping him to his feet, he managed to guide his staggering weight to the front door, while the old man continued to babble on incoherently, instructing him repeatedly not to tell his mother.

Disadvantaged by not being strong enough to support the entire weight of his grandfather's body, and open the front door at the same time, he settled him back into the four feet of shoveled snow that lined the sidewalk so he wouldn't fall again, and turned to set about opening the snowbound door.

At first, the accumulated snow on the stoop held the storm door stubbornly closed. After a minute or two of chipping and scraping it away, however, he managed to force it half way open. Once the main door was accessible it only took a minute or two to assist his grandfather out of the snow bank and maneuver him awkwardly into the dimly lit house.

There was a single overhead light hanging from the kitchen ceiling that he managed to turn on without dropping the old man. It provided just enough light to guide him unsteadily into the adjacent bedroom where he laid him down on his brass bed, fully clothed. After covering him over with a worn khaki Army blanket, he kissed his forehead, affectionately, and returned to the kitchen to see if he could light a fire in the pot-bellied coal burner that sat like an armored knight in the middle of the room. Fortunately, the coal bucket was full. Unfortunately, it was frozen into a thin sheet of ice covering most of the floor and couldn't be moved. His dad explained to Neal later that the only water line entering the house had burst while his grandfather had been in town earlier that day.

For the first time since entering the house, he was able to survey the room in which he stood shivering trying to get a fire started. Aside from a wooden rocking chair, and a metal table by a window where his grandfather repaired watches and clocks, there was no furniture.

Part of his innocence wondered about the galvanized tub in which a number of beer bottles had frozen and exploded that day, leaving a film of sticky residue all over the place. Too young to understand the far-reaching consequences of his bizarre behavior, young Neal concentrated on the more important matter at hand.

Using some of the hundred or more newspapers that were stacked in the front room where fifty some clocks and grandfather clocks of all sizes and descriptions were stored, he managed to keep a flame alive long enough to ignite several pieces of coal. His patience during the next half-hour allowed him to nurture those few coals into a fire hot enough to remove the icy chill from the air and allow him to return home, hoping it would not burn out before his parents returned.

To say the least, his animated retelling of his heroic rescue was very disturbing news to his parents. They did, however, praise Neal for his quick thinking and thanked him affectionately for having prevented what could have been a tragic end to an otherwise enjoyable evening.

At his mother's insistence, just to be on the safe side, his father went to check on the old man and found him, as his son had described, sound asleep, snoring and fully clothed. Although he was tempted to wake him, he knew it wasn't worth the effort, considering how drunk he was. So, he stoked the fire, added more coal and cracked open a window to allow enough fresh air in to prevent him from suffocating.

Looking around the house's interior while he walked carefully over the icy floor on his way out, Neal's father couldn't help but wonder what the future held in store for his father-in-law. One thing was certain; John O'Day couldn't remain in that house for the rest of the winter. To let him stay there would certainly lead to his undoing.

During the few minutes his father had spent making sure the old man was safe, the wind and snowfall had increased to such intensity that it reduced visibility outside and rendered the streetlight near their two houses virtually useless. The pathway he had used to get there was now drifted over, making it difficult to return home using those same footprints. Even the side door to his own home was blocked when he finally arrived, requiring several minutes of hand digging to get it open. Once inside, however, heat from the cellar furnace provided a comfort zone where his father quickly shed his snow-covered clothing and rejoined his family by the living room fireplace.

Because there had been no radio announcement informing parents that school had been cancelled for the next day, the children were bundled off early to bed as usual. They hadn't been there long when voices from downstairs could be heard arguing over what to do with grandfather.

With the howling wind buffeting his bedroom window as he lay snugly buried beneath several quilted blankets, he prayed that his grandfather wouldn't have to go to the bathroom that night. The "Johnny," as it was called in those days, was a one-hole, wooden bench-like toilet, located in the corner of an old storage shed some twenty feet behind the house. Not a pleasant walk during the dead of winter.

The aftermath of that blustering winter night's adventure prompted his mother to make it very clear to her husband that she could no longer tolerate her father's drunkenness. In short, she had had it. Thus, her edict to the family dictated that grampa would move into Neal's bedroom, temporarily, where she could keep an eye on him. Neal would double up with his sister until warm weather arrived and allowed her father to return to his own home, such as it was. Plus, she added most emphatically, she had better not catch him drinking ever again.

Later on in the spring of that year, after the ruptured water pipe was repaired and the floor dried out, Grampa John O'Day returned to his home sober, and gave up drinking from that day on. Ironically, though, his sobriety had a humorous twist to it that showed up in the Sunday newspaper a few months later. The *Local News* section printed a large picture of him being followed by two, snow-white ducks, whom he had nicknamed after Neal and his sister. A short article accompanied the picture, and included some humorous statements made by Mr. O'Day in an interview at the time. Recalling his mother's reaction to what family and neighbors thought was very humorous, he remembered that incident as one of the rare occasions in his life when he had seen his mother cry, and couldn't understand why.

****

Looking out over the ocean, he could tell by the sky's color that Paula's arrival was imminent. To assist her if she needed it, he left the Jacuzzi, put on his robe and walked to the kitchen, water soaked and refreshed. He was in the process of refreshing his drink when the sound of the garage door being activated signaled her arrival. Anticipating that she would be carrying the usual paraphernalia he went to help, wondering on the way why she bothered bringing work home at all, since she never seemed to find time to work on it.

As they approached one another in the garage, she smiled, and with a hint of humor remarked, "If you're trying to tempt me with an offer you think I can't refuse, you're using the wrong bait, Mr. Wise Guy."

He glanced downward where Paula's eyes had been focused and realized his robe had partially separated, exposing his nakedness. "I just left the Jacuzzi a moment ago after hearing the garage door open," he explained. "I thought you might need a hand."

She laughed at him gathering his robe around himself and replied, "One with a glass of wine in it would have been nice."

Following an unemotional embrace and a kiss that was more expected than enjoyed, the two proceeded into the house where she tossed her handbag onto the sofa, sat down beside it and kicked off her shoes. "Now, would you please pour me a large glass of wine, dear," she asked. "I'm too tired to get it myself."

As he read it, the message couldn't have been clearer, though unspoken: *I've had a terrible day at the office,* and *no, I don't want to talk about it,* so he did as she had asked without comment.

Upon his return he attempted to lighten the mood, well aware, however, that he was approaching dangerous territory. "Guess who just arrived in town today?" he asked, casually.

"Please, Neal," she replied, resting her head back on the couch with her eyes closed, "no guessing games. I've been playing them all day. Just tell me it's not someone we have to entertain."

Realizing that Dan's early arrival had now made it necessary for him to reveal some of the specifics about what had taken place during and after his recent trip, he sank back into his chair and attempted to explain. "Dan Hughes called me several days ago and told me he wanted to get out of town for a few days. He asked me to make a reservation for himself and a female companion at any local hotel, so I made them at the Hilton Inn. Since their arrival coincided with our party, I invited them."

With only that much revealed, he waited for a moment to see her reaction, hoping for some clue as to how he should proceed, but there was none. Satisfied that he was still on safe ground, he continued. "The questionable good news is they arrived today. Which hints of there not being here for our party. And, I was informed by Dan less than an hour ago, they have made plans to go to Disneyland tomorrow and stay overnight."

"Why didn't you tell me about this when Dan first called?" she asked, somewhat annoyed at him for not confiding in her.

"What difference would it have made?" he replied, defensively. "They're not staying here with us. I just did him a favor because he said he needed to get away. He's a friend. Wouldn't you do the same for one of yours?"

Exercising restraint, she thought for a moment before answering, appreciating that the man she had been living with for almost ten years was merely reacting in a way she could have predicted. "How long do they intend to stay?" she inquired, hesitant to ask why they had come all the way to California just to get away for a few days.

"I never asked," he lied, knowing that revealing the truth about what Dan had confided in him earlier would only worry her more, and encourage questioning him further. "As a gesture of our hospitality, I did invite him and his lady friend to attend our party, if they were still here. Does that upset you too?"

Wearily, she stood up and walked to the kitchen to get another glass of wine. When she returned her mood had changed, realizing he had done nothing wrong or out of the ordinary. Not wishing to start the evening on a sour note, she gave him a lingering hug and answered, "No, and I apologize for acting like a bitch. I should learn to leave my job at the office."

"Well, the good news is," he added, hoping a night out would please her, "we've been invited out to dinner tomorrow night by friends of Dan's who live in La Jolla. You won't believe the circumstances that brought this all about, so I won't waste my time trying to explain it to you now. Just keep an open mind and a sense of humor. I can almost guarantee a night you'll never forget."

She stared at him, silently amused by the silhouette of him standing in front of the living room window watching the orange sun slowly disappear into the ocean as if he didn't have a care in the world. His blasé attitude irritated her somewhat, but she put her feelings aside, remarking, almost sarcastically, "Well, that will be a treat. I haven't had one of those in quite a while. What time are we expected?"

Rather than respond to her cloaked sarcasm with a remark that might reflect on the distance that seemed to be growing between them almost on a daily basis, he answered as if he were excited about the intrigue the invitation presented. "I told Dan we would be at the hotel Saturday afternoon around five o'clock, and offered to drive."

Prolonged silence under normal circumstances did not come naturally to her. So it was a little unnerving when he didn't provide some explanation about why they were going out to dinner with complete strangers. Unable to reach a satisfactory conclusion on her own, and frustrated by his silence, she finally asked, "What's going on, Neal? Why is Dan here? And who are these people in La Jolla?"

Her abrupt questions were indication enough for him to recognize that she had reached the limit of her patience. Nothing other than answering her questions truthfully, he had come to realize over the years, would be acceptable. Continuing to watch the sky darken, he gave her a daily accounting of his activities while in Virginia, and those that had occurred over the past few days. Content that there was nothing more he could tell her, he sat down in his chair by the fireplace and waited for her to respond.

At first, she sat motionless with her eyes scanning the ceiling as if there were something crawling around up there. Then, without any provocation from him, the corners of her mouth curled up into a funny little smile, as her head rolled slowly from side to side in frustrated disbelief. "I wish your mother was alive to hear all this," she finally remarked. "You know what she'd say to you?"

Her reference to his mother brought a thoughtful smile to his face, as he rose from his chair and walked toward the kitchen to freshen his empty glass. "Probably, fix me a drink," he replied, laughing a little.

Even though she was still upset by the senselessness of what she thought he was becoming needlessly involved in, she couldn't help being amused by his reply. "Damn it, Neal," she scolded, "You are one bad little boy! Behave yourself while I change into something more comfortable."

During her absence, one reoccurring dilemma kept bothering him; whether to continue on with his settled relationship with Paula, friends and family, or to run the risk of losing it all over a spur of the moment commitment he had made to Dan Hughes without considering the gravity of its consequences. Before he could identify the conditions that would force such a choice, she returned in her bathrobe and invited him to join her for a quick dip in the Jacuzzi. That her robe was hiding a naked body was quite obvious, but here intentions were not. After freshening his drink, he followed her outside wondering what was really on her mind.

Unlike their usual proximity to each another, she purposely distanced herself from him. Considerably more relaxed now, she asked, "Did anything happen while you were back east that you're not telling me about?"

"Why do you ask?" he replied, wondering what he had done or said that would have triggered such a question.

"We've known each other over ten years now," she replied, "and in all that time I've never had any reason to question you much about anything. You're so obvious and predictable I had no need to, but recently I sense that you've become preoccupied with something or someone you're not telling me about. Call it women's intuition or whatever, but you're not the same good old boy that left here a week ago."

His failure to respond prompted her to ask a question she had never intended to ask for fear of what the answer might be, but she did anyway. "Are you involved with another woman? Someone you met while you were back there, perhaps?"

Like a VCR in rewind, his mind flashed back immediately to the scene in Jennifer Newman's kitchen when she had so passionately kissed him. A voice from within warned: *Don't go there, stupid. The sand is quick beneath your feet.*

"Of course not, he replied, laughing out loud. "Who in their right mind would pay any attention to this old goat? Present company accepted, of course."

Not at all completely satisfied with the frankness of his self-image, she slithered through the water and came to rest at his side, content for the time being that her suspicions were ill founded.

Later on that evening she tested her earlier theory and fell asleep satisfied that the man lying next to her was still hers, at least for the time being.

The next morning her departure took place routinely and without any carryover from the previous evening's discussion, other than her parting words:

"I'll say one thing about living with you, my dear. There's never a dull moment."

With her at work, and Dan out of town, he put together a quick breakfast of leftovers and watched television to catch up on world and local news. Bored and upset with the political upheaval and military activity going on all over the world he switched channels to Turner Classic Movies and resumed work on his unfinished painting, relaxed and content with the progress he was making.

Around the time John Wayne met his end in the movie "The Shootist," he looked at his watch and was made aware that it was fast approaching the hour to start preparing for his Friday get together with Ron Barns, and whomever else showed up. He was in the middle of filling his plastic flask with vodka when the phone rang. It was Henry Hughes inquiring about Dan's whereabouts, explaining that Dan's mother had suddenly become very ill and had to be hospitalized.

Before answering Henry, he wondered what had led him to think that Dan was in California in the first place. He distinctly remembered Dan confiding in him when he first arrived that no one knew where he was going. After expressing his regrets over Polly's sudden illness, he asked, "What makes you think he's here in California?"

Expressing himself in the tone of voice that Neal recognized from having spoken with him only a week ago, Henry grunted, and said, "I called the telephone number of this woman, Donna, he's been dating lately, but she wasn't there. Because I explained about his mother's sudden illness, and the need for me to contact him right away, whoever the woman was who answered the phone told me in strictest confidence that she was vacationing in San Diego with a male companion. Need I say more?"

"No need to, Henry," he replied, a little embarrassed for not having given his friend a straight answer. "He's staying here in Carlsbad at the Hilton Inn, and Donna is with him."

"I figured as much. Can you give me his room number?"

"He won't be there, Henry. He and Donna left on an overnight trip to Disneyland and won't be back until five o'clock tomorrow afternoon. I'll make sure he gets your message, though, and will do whatever it takes to get him on a plane for home as soon as possible."

Briefly restating the seriousness of his wife's condition, he thanked him for his help and reiterated the importance of Dan making every effort to return home immediately, even if it meant his bimbo had to make separate arrangements.

"Don't worry, Henry, I'll make sure he gets your message."

Driving south on the freeway, he reviewed the only two options that were available to him. Obviously, trying to locate the two of them in Anaheim was out of the question, so he accepted the fact that he would have to wait until they returned the next day. Chances of booking a flight that same day would be highly unlikely, even considering the emergency. Assuming that to be the case, he hoped the news would not make it necessary to cancel the Sterling's dinner invitation, unless Dan was too upset to go. In any event, he and Paula could still attend and explain the situation. Considering all the preparations and manipulation that had taken place over the past few days in order to bring about their bizarre reunion, it seemed a shame for it not to take place. Preoccupied over the uncertainty he was forced to carry into the next day, he continued on to his friend's house hoping that Polly Hughes's illness was not terminal.

As was usually the case, Joey Siegel, Don Curtis and Ron were already gathered at the bar when he arrived. Unlike most Fridays, however, there was a noticeable lack of joviality and handshaking when he entered. Instinctively, he knew something was amiss, so he greeted everyone cordially and mixed a drink. When he returned to join the sullen group, Ron shook his hand and said, quietly, "Johnny Holland called from Scripps Hospital a few minutes ago and informed us that Phyllis had suffered a stroke. From what he said, I guess she's not doing too well."

That news, coupled with what Henry Hughes had told him less than an hour ago, had a depressing effect on Neal, making him almost wish that he had called ahead to tell them he couldn't make it today.

The gloom, however, didn't last long. It faded proportionately with the number of cocktails each of the four men had consumed until it degenerated, predictably, to watching television, fantasizing over several of the female anchor women, and speculating about how good they might be in bed. So engrossed were they in discussing the latter that they failed to notice a female figure approaching in the late afternoon shadows. It was Janice Burrows, a close and long time friend of the group who lived near Los Angles.

Her arrival was welcome relief for the group and brought with it the one ingredient that could remove the "yadda-yadda-yadda" from their afternoon gathering of senseless babbling; a good looking woman scented with perfume.

Of the four men, Neal was the most surprised to see her, in that he and Janice had dated occasionally in the early days following his divorce. There were hugs all around as she made her presence known, saving him until last so she could tease him with the soft curves of her shapely body. "Been a while, sport," she whispered in his ear, giggling like a tart. "Have you missed me?"

Somewhat embarrassed by her lingering embrace, and playful wiggling, he laughed and replied, conservatively, "Who wouldn't?"

For the next hour merriment rode un-harnessed down memory lane stopping only to replenish the liquids that were slowly threatening their good judgment and propriety. Much as he wanted to stay, the slight buzzing in his head reminded him that the time had come for him to leave before his affection for Janice tempted him into making a mistake. So, with her insisting that she accompany him to his car, he said goodbye to his buddies and left.

It was dark outside which made finding the door lock difficult. As he fumbled with the key, she seized the opportunity to comment, "I don't ever remember you having that much trouble finding me."

When the key finally did slide into the lock, he turned and gathered Judy into his arms as she had done with him earlier, and whispered, "The next time we're marooned on a deserted island together, my dear friend, I won't have that kind of trouble, believe me."

Before his car began to move she kissed him hard on the mouth through the open window and then stood back as it pulled away. She watched his arm waving back at her from a distance and yelled loudly after him, "Chicken!"

Further down the street he watched her image fading away in the rear view mirror and smiled with satisfaction as a brief recollection of his former romance with her flickered through his mind. The darkness, however, soon redirected his attention toward the headlight beams that were leading him safely home to the closing of another day.

The house lights were on when he arrived, giving notice that Paula had already arrived and was probably having a glass of wine while she read the day's mail. Checking in the mirror to make sure he was clean of any lipstick residue Janice might have wanted Paula to see, as a joke, he entered the house.

She was sitting on the patio staring expressionless out over the ocean. Aware of his presence, she advised him to get a drink and join her. "We have something important to discuss," she remarked, seriously.

He did as she had suggested without comment. Moments later he returned and sat down by her side, asking in a slightly slurred voice, "Are you alright?"

She hesitated for a moment and then replied, almost in tears, "After I returned home this afternoon I received a telephone call from our landlord, Mister Fahey. He explained that his relatives feel he should be in a long-term care facility because of his failing health. In order to afford that type of care, he will be forced to sell this place and is offering us an opportunity to consider buying it. Otherwise, he will be forced to put it on the market. He is giving us a week to respond, one way or the other."

Finishing the remainder of her half empty glass, she asked, sarcastically, "And, how was your day?"

With much of the booze he had consumed that afternoon still lingering in his system, the few swallows he had had while listening to her just served as a catalyst to activate them again. Struggling to comprehend the consequences of having to relocate again at his age, he stood up and leaned against the gazebo in an attempt to steady himself. When the first words he spoke made it obvious to her that he was in no shape to discuss the matter intelligently, she stood up and looked directly into his eyes for a few seconds and then said, almost angrily, "On second thought, let's discuss this in the morning."

Chapter 12

Cocktails and Dinner

When Neal woke up Saturday morning Paula's side of the bed was empty. Her not being there didn't come as much of a surprise, considering his previous day's activities and the almost devastating news that old man Fahey had dumped on her. Giving the devil her due, she had every right to be upset with him.

While he sat on the edge of the bed debating whether or not to take a shower before facing her, the aroma of freshly brewed coffee beckoned him to forget the shower, at least until after he had had a cup or two and determined what kind of a mood she was in. At least he figured that tack would provide him with some guideline on how to manage the remainder of his day.

Dressed in a pair of Levi shorts, a sport shirt and worn out sandals, he made his way downstairs and into the kitchen where she sat reading the newspaper. To test the water, he poured a cup and confronted the silence that hung in the air between them like early morning fog. "I assume from your absence in bed this morning that I snored you into the guest room again. Sorry about that."

"Don't be silly," she replied without looking up. "That old mattress of yours is still better than the one we sleep on every night. I enjoyed the change, as a matter of fact."

Silence continued between them for some time while she read and he drank coffee trying to find a diplomatic way to open a dialogue that wasn't going to be controversial. He was about to tell her about Henry Hughes' call when she pre-empted him with a statement that brought back a reminder of what she had tried to discuss with him the previous evening.

"We need to have a serious conversation about where we're going to live if we can't afford to buy this place. And, never mind telling me about Dan Hughes and all his problems. They're not yours so I don't see why you think you owe him a damn thing!"

All of a sudden he felt as if he had been thrust between the proverbial rock and a hard place. There was no mistaking the smack of reality she had just lowered on him, and he knew it. In order to show some serious appreciation for her concern, he told her that he would look into what kind of mortgaging was available through his credit union and the Veteran's Administration. Then, to put the subject on hold, he told her about the telephone call he had received from Dan's father, emphasizing that Dan and his friend Donna would probably be on their way back to Virginia as soon as he told him about his mother being hospitalized.

Having received similar news regarding her own mother several years ago, she became visibly upset and suggested that he cancel their dinner plans for that evening. "Certainly Dan and his friend will want to make immediate arrangements to return home."

He didn't argue the point, afraid that his insistence on going might aggravate her. Rather than cancel the invitation prematurely, he suggested that they wait until Dan returned and let him decide what was appropriate.

She had her doubts as to whether or not his proposal was reasonable but did agree that the decision was rightfully Dan's. She, on the other hand, expressed her own reluctance to attend based solely on the premise that she didn't think it was appropriate, under the circumstances.

With plans for that evening becoming more and more uncertain by the minute, she concentrated on a variety of different activities that temporarily distracted her from the anxiety of their domestic plight, and the disruptive effect his so-called friends were having on him.

Neal's approach to it all, however, was typically male, and wisely led him away from the potential hotbed of controversy that was threatening to explode to a nearby Costco to purchase supplies for their party. From there, on to Home Depot to amuse himself among the vast numbers of gadgets and tools that most wives jokingly told their children were their father's toys, and then drove home.

Shortly after his arrival the phone rang. It was Dan calling to let him know that he and Donna had returned from Disneyland and would be waiting for him in the hotel lobby at five o'clock. He was less than cordial, giving Neal the impression that he was already uptight about something, so he opted not to pursue the matter, or his father's call, until he could talk with him personally.

Because he thought Paula was trimming shrubbery near the bluff, he assumed she couldn't hear the phone ring, and for that reason decided not to mention the call to her right away. He figured, no use getting her upset again until he could determine how Dan was going to react to the news of his mother's sudden illness.

For much of the day that followed they purposely avoided coming in contact with one another, a tactic that had served them well throughout their relationship when emotions threatened to get out of hand. And on several occasions had been the mitigating force that had prevented serious confrontation. Later on that afternoon, however, he was compelled to remind her that it was time to stop what they were doing and dress for dinner. It was then that she informed him that she was in no mood to spend the evening trying to act like she was having a good time when, emotionally, she was a train wreck. "Make up whatever excuses you think are appropriate," she advised him firmly. "I'm just too upset to act like I'm not. I'll only embarrass you in front of your friends, and I don't want to do that."

Her attempt to hide that she was on the verge of crying made the seriousness of her emotional upset vividly clear to him. Realizing that she had a valid reason for not wanting to become involved in a situation that he knew intuitively was not going to end with Dan's departure, he put his arm around her and said, reassuringly, "I understand, dear, I'll take care of it."

Some moments of silence passed before she regained her composure enough to confront him with a question he wished she hadn't asked. "Why didn't you tell Dan about his mother when he called earlier?"

Surprised that she had heard the conversation, he side stepped the truth and replied, "I figured it would be more personal to tell him in person. After all, I'll be seeing him in less than an hour."

"Are you still planning on having dinner with the Sterling ladies, even if he says he doesn't want to?"

"I won't know until I talk to him," he replied, resentful at being questioned about the matter. "Maybe I will, and maybe I won't."

That was not the reply she wanted to hear, and although disappointed that he appeared to be insensitive to her emotional upset, she accepted his answer and seized the opportunity to take advantage of it. In less time than it had taken him to bathe and get ready to leave for the hotel, she had called her daughter and made plans to spend the night with her and the children, having found out earlier that her husband was on duty at the hospital that weekend.

Paula and her only daughter, Ellen, unlike most mother and daughter relationships, were more like sisters, sharing everything from underwear to experiences regarding intimacy. Energized by the thought of seeing her two granddaughters again, she joined Neal in their bedroom and told him calmly of her plans while packing a small overnight bag. Before he could say anything, one way or the other, she kissed him less than enthusiastically and shouted back at him as she hurried down the stairs, "See you tomorrow!"

As she drove away from the home she thought she would be living in forever, she expressed her resentment toward his selfish behavior, "Read my lips, Buster! Two can play this game."

Though her sudden departure temporarily solved the dilemma he had been faced with only minutes ago, it left him with a feeling of having created a situation that was destined to come back to haunt him someday. Something in the coincidence of having become inadvertently involved in Dan Hughes' screwed up life, and the untimely notice from John Fahey, seemed to indicate that the two events were somehow related. Grateful that he had been given the opportunity to deal with them separately, he secured the house with a new appreciation for the time worn phrase, *"nothing is forever,"* and left for the Hilton Inn.

Entering the lobby, he glanced immediately toward the lounge and saw Dan sitting by himself with a drink in his hand and an angry look on his face. Curious why he was alone, he asked the obvious, "Where's Donna?"

The look Dan gave him was answer enough; *Donna wasn't going.*

"Is Paula in the car," he asked? "Go get her and I'll buy us one for the road. We have time."

"It's just you and me, sport. Where's Donna?"

Dan invited him to sit down and motioned to the waitress that he was ready to order. When she arrived, Neal recognized her immediately as the same waitress that had waited on him the first time he came there to inquire about making Dan's reservations. "I told you I'd be back," he said, grinning broadly. "Your name is Maggie, right?"

"As rain," she replied, flattered that she had made an impression worth remembering. "What'll it be, guys?"

Both men ordered their preference and watched her walk away with each of them knowing what the other was thinking but remaining discreetly silent. When she was beyond hearing them, Neal got him back on track by asking, again, "Now, what's wrong with Donna?"

His reply wasn't immediate, but after she walked behind the service bar, he turned toward him and said, "Well, yesterday when we arrived at the hotel we had a few drinks and I tried to get a little cozy with her before going out to dinner. She told me she was having an unusually heavy period. That would have explained her not wanting to have sex, and, in general, the ornery disposition that went along with it. I told her I understood and left her alone. You know, win a few, lose a few, and move on. That is, until we went out to dinner."

He tried not to show amusement in Dan's willingness to accept Donna's excuse for denying him his primary motive in inviting her in the first place, but couldn't resist grinning a little when he remarked, "Sounds to me like someone didn't do their homework."

"Yeah, yeah, yeah," Dan grumbled, and continued: "The restaurant we went to last night was so crowded that we finally accepted an invitation to join a fun group that had two empty seats they said they'd be glad to share with us. Trouble was, they were on opposite sides of the table, but we sat down anyway and eventually got acquainted with everybody. I was really beginning to enjoy the arrangement until I noticed one of our waiters putting a major hit on Donna. The next thing I know, Donna excuses herself to go to the bathroom. Smelling a rat, I excused myself and followed her as if I had had a calling too. I hid behind a plant near the spot where they met one another. There was an exchange of small pieces of paper. Names and telephone numbers I suspected."

Neal was about to explode with laughter watching his face grow redder and more animated as his story unfolded, but he held it under control and listened attentively as he continued: "Then the son of a bitch kisses her and disappears into the kitchen while sweetie pie moseys into the ladies room, and eventually back to the table. Man, talk about being pissed off!"

As much as he wanted to remain there until he finished the rest of his story, Neal upended the remainder of his drink and motioned for Maggie to bring the check. "We're going to be late if we don't get on down the highway," he warned. "You can finish your story on the way."

He waited until they had made their way onto the freeway before encouraging him to continue. Dan was guilty of a lot of things, he thought, but being out of surprises wasn't one of them. He was sure he wouldn't be disappointed.

After taking a small swig from the flask he had hidden inside his jacket pocket, he continued with his sad, but humorous, tale of woe. "I waited until we got back to our hotel room before asking her to explain what she was up to. She denied any wrongdoing, of course, telling me that what they had exchanged on paper was only their names in case she should revisit the restaurant some day. When I asked her to show me her piece of paper, she went ballistic and locked herself in the bathroom, telling me that she wasn't going anywhere with someone who didn't trust her. That's where I left her."

Following the second swig, he put the small flask back in his jacket and remarked, "Yeah know, Mr. T, when I first invited Donna to come on this trip with me she was excited as hell. Anxious to see and do things she could never have afforded on her own. But from the time she met me at the airport until now, she's been nothing but one big pain in the ass, and I think I know why."

Before he could comment, Dan interrupted with an additional statement that puzzled him. "And, I'm not buying this menstrual business either. I've suffered through her periods before, but she's never acted like this. Something or someone got to her before we left Norfolk, but she won't talk about it. Does Paula ever act that way?"

Turning off the freeway at the La Jolla, exit, he thought about his ten-year relationship with Paula and realized that most of those years had passed without any serious, long-lasting emotional conflicts. Only since his return from Virginia had he given any thought to the possibility that her patience might be running out if he persisted in involving himself further in Dan's volatile lifestyle. With that thought in mind, he looked over at the brooding face of his friend and tried to inject some common sense.

"Right now I'm not thinking about anything but having a good time. If you've got any sense at all, you'll do the same. As far as I can tell nothing is broken, so why try to fix it. For whatever reason, Donna probably didn't want to come up here with you any more than Paula wanted to come here with me. Simple as that."

"Well put, Mister T," he replied. "I think this is going to be one hell of an interesting reunion for both of us."

Fifteen minutes later they drove through the gates of the Sterling estate, arriving just a few minutes before six o'clock. As they walked leisurely toward the main entrance, Dan asked, "What did you say these ladies do for a living?"

Smiling at the humorous implication of his question while ringing the doorbell, he chuckled and replied, "Something you can't afford."

Within seconds, one of the large twin doors opened and exposed the formally attired figure of Ivan Olofson. He greeted them, enthusiastically, and then led the way to the patio where their hosts were anxiously waiting for them to appear. Both were dressed in pastel colored, light summer dresses and matching high heels. Taking the initiative, Neal introduced Dan to Sandy first, and then turned to Jessica and remarked, "I don't think you two need any introduction, do you?"

"Not hardly," she replied, staring intently at Dan with her hand outstretched. "Nice to see you again, Dan. How's the life I saved doing these days?"

Even though the anger Dan felt toward Donna's behavior that day was still seething inside him, the feel of Jessica's warm hand and her friendly smile calmed him immeasurably. Remembering the advice Neal had given him only minutes before they arrived, he put Donna back where he had left her and replied, "Not too bad, thanks to you," he replied, feeling a little self conscious. "I can't believe how much you've changed…for the better, that is."

She smiled as she withdrew her hand and patted him gently on the cheek. "Thank you, but if it hadn't been for your unannounced arrival on that Cuban beach years ago, I might still be there pushing up daisies in the jungle. I'd say we both have a lot to be thankful for, wouldn't you?"

Before he could answer, Sandy interrupted. "I was under the impression that you two were bringing lady friends for dinner this evening. Was I mistaken?"

The two men looked at each other for a moment, each expecting the other to say something clever in the way of an excuse. It was Neal who finally took the initiative.

"Both ladies had prior commitments and asked me to express their regrets for not being able to attend. They were truly disappointed."

"Well, I guess we have you two all to ourselves then," she remarked, not at all convinced that there weren't other reasons for their absence, but she accepted his explanation. Motioning Ivan to come forward, she remarked, "Please bring our guests drinks of their choice. And tell Christina we'll dine at seven."

An awkward silence shrouded the small group of virtual strangers following Ivan's order taking, each trying desperately to think of something that would open a meaningful line of conversation. Sandy finally broke the silence. "Before this evening progresses any further, I would like to take this opportunity to express my sincerest thanks to you, Mr. Thomas, for your part in reuniting me with my daughter after twenty-some years of painful separation. The good Lord must have guided your footsteps, kind sir."

Some mixed chatter followed until Ivan returned with a tray of drinks, providing Neal the opportunity to respond by offering a toast. " Thank you for those kind words, Ms. Sterling, I'm not a very religious man… in the classic sense, that is. I do, however, believe there is a force in the universe that controls the interaction between its constituent parts and all living things. It is also my belief that that force defies human understanding because it is wise enough to know that we'd screw it up, given our history on this planet thus far. So, here's to whomever or whatever force brought us all together here today, As the saying goes, ours is not to question why, ours is just to do or die."

"Isn't he something?" Dan remarked, happy to be holding a drink again. "That's what an Ivy League education will do for you."

Everyone laughed, seemingly enjoying the humor in Neal's somewhat non-conventional approach to the meaning of religion and the mysteries surrounding the miniscule planet we live on. The ice had been broken, so to speak, and the *happy juice* had begun to flow. Wishing to capture Neal's undivided attention for a moment to discuss a private matter, Sandy suggested that Jessica take Dan on a quick tour of the estate before dinner, commenting that she knew they both had a lot of catching up to do and would probably enjoy some quality time alone. Jessica needed no prodding. She seized the opportunity, anxious to hear more about his post Cuban adventure and why he had come to California.

They weren't out of sight long when Sandy turned to Neal and confronted him with a question regarding the same subject. "I've had some very serious discussions with Jessica about her relationship with your friend, Mr. Hughes, and I need to know, is he a problem?"

Neal laughed and replied, "He was to his parents, but I can assure you he poses no threat to Jessica."

Confident that Dan would be on a plane back to Virginia the next day and out of everyone's life, possibly forever, he backed up his assurance with a postscript of humor. "From the little I know about your daughter, I would hazard a guess that she is more than capable of taking care of herself. As far as Dan is concerned, he's a character, but a harmless one."

While they continued to enjoy their time together, Jessica and Dan walked leisurely around the grounds exchanging memories relating to their Cuban adventure and the events following their separation. Considering it inappropriate to mention anything about his decision to cease involvement with the Tidewater Cartel, he asked her if she and her mother were planning to attend Neal's Fourth of July party.

"Mother and I have already accepted his invitation," she replied. "Are you and your lady friend planning to be there?"

"That's why we're out here," he answered, avoiding any hint of the real reason. "We'll be leaving for home as soon as it's over, though. Maybe we could get together for lunch before I leave."

"Will Donna be there?"

The memory of what he had endured for the past two days made his reply a guiltless pleasure. "I can assure you she will not, if that's a condition to your accepting my invitation."

Placing her arm in his, she said she would give him her answer at the party. As they turned and retraced their steps back to the patio, she looked out over the ocean and asked, "Why didn't you call my mother when you returned to the States?"

Although he had anticipated being asked the question, he had successfully avoided it thus far, but there it was, like a hangman's noose around his neck waiting for the horse to ride out from under him. I'm a dead man, he thought, trying to conjure up an excuse that would keep the horse from bolting. Filled with remorse for failing to do what he had promised many years ago, he stopped and turned Jessica toward him with both hands on her shoulders, and confessed. "I have no excuse other than my own thoughtlessness. All I can do is ask your forgiveness, and hope that you won't judge me too harshly. How does the song go? – "What can I say after I've said, I'm sorry?"

"Not much," she agreed, grinning a little, "except to say thanks to Mr. Thomas for being so caring. None of this would have taken place were it not for him."

"Amen to that," he replied while finishing the remainder of his drink. "I could use a refill."

Satisfied with their few minutes alone they returned to the patio where Neal and Sandy sat patiently waiting for them. According to Sandy's watch it was close enough to seven for her to suggest that she and Neal continue their conversation in the dining room, inviting Dan and Jessica to join them. After they were seated, Ivan appeared with a fresh round of drinks that gave Sandy the opportunity to once again toast the good fortune that had come into her life. "Before dinner is served, I think it is appropriate for all of us to express our gratitude for the new friendships that have been created here today, and to pledge ourselves to their growth and prosperity. May it always be that way… cheers everyone."

"Here, here," they replied in unison, each taking a generous sip.

Following her informal toast, she turned toward Jessica and gave a follow-up announcement that caught her completely by surprise. "Now that you have returned to the nest, I would like to make you an offer I hope you won't refuse. One that I hope will dissuade you from ever wanting to leave your home again."

For a moment there was dead silence. Neal and Dan's eyes glanced questioningly at one another, eager to hear what was coming next. Leaving the head of the table, she walked around to Jessica's chair, placed her hand on her shoulder and announced to the wide-eyed gathering, "For some time now I have considered hiring someone to manage Sterling Publishing so that I could retire. Of those who were qualified, none had that special quality I was looking for, until now. Though she's only just returned, and will need training, it gives me great pleasure to introduce my new Executive Assistant, Ms. Jessica Sterling. Effective immediately, if she'll accept the offer."

Her Mother's announcement shocked Jessica speechless. While she sat quietly trying to grasp the magnitude of responsibility the offer represented, Neal and Dan clapped their hands in approval, yelling for Ivan to bring another round.

Following the aftermath of her unexpected announcement, she added, in a voice quivering with emotion, "Now, I'm happy to say, the looking is finally over. I can train my own daughter to take over when I retire, something that I have been spending a lot of time thinking about lately."

Still a bit un-nerved, Jessica opted to wait until after their guests had left to respond to the offer. Nothing, she had learned the hard way, was ever accomplished under the influence of what was starting to look like an evening of marathon drinking, so she used a diplomatic ploy to put the matter aside until after their guests had gone. "Thank you for your confidence, mother," she replied with feigned embarrassment, "but I don't think we should discuss this matter when we have two charming and handsome men to entertain. Besides, I'm hungry!"

Sandy, though anxious for some positive response, agreed, and summoned Ivan to begin serving dinner.

An appetizer of jumbo shrimp was served first, followed by a shallow bowl of creamy lobster soup garnished lightly with parsley. Wine glasses were filled with Sandy's special reserve, energizing her to address matters of a more personal nature. Turning her attention toward Dan, she asked, inquisitively, "What brings you to California, Mr. Hughes?"

Dan smiled, realizing he was being diplomatically interrogated. "During Neal's recent visit to attend the wake of a mutual friend, he invited me to attend his annual Fourth of July Party. Never dreaming, I'm sure, that I would be in a position to attend. Well, as destiny would have it, I recently closed a real estate acquisition that made California the ideal spot to celebrate, so I accepted the invitation."

Looking sideways at Jessica, he added, "And, if I had known what a beautiful surprise awaited me, I surely would have come alone."

Examining the content of his reply, Neal recognized that he had very skillfully maneuvered the conversation away from the real purpose of his visit. In an attempt to lend some credence to his answer, he followed up with some additional support. "After the hospitality his family offered me during my recent visit, I was only too happy to invite him to our holiday festivities. Although, to be perfectly honest, I was quite surprised when he called a few days ago and said he'd be here."

Raising his glass in a toasting gesture, he added," Here's to Dan, a man of many surprises, and a dear friend. Welcome to paradise."

As the others responded similarly, Ivan entered the room pushing a mobile serving cart and announced, "With your permission, ladies and gentlemen, dinner is served."

"At last," Jessica blurted out, excitedly, "I could eat a horse!"

"I think you'll find the filet mignon much more to your liking, Miss Jessica," Ivan remarked, in jest. "Especially when topped with this delicious mushroom sauce Christina has prepared. It's an old family recipe."

"Sure beats the hell out of horse chops," Dan commented to everyone's amusement. "I'd rather ride'um than eat'um."

His expression, in a comically overstated western drawl, pretty well set the mood for the rest of the dinner. What had initially started out as a more formal affair now took on an air of liquor-fed joviality that prompted the others to contribute their own amusing comments. Even Ivan joined in the merriment with subtle comments made all the more humorous by his European accent. Despite the frivolity, however, Neal couldn't dismiss the nagging sting of reality that Paula, old man Fahey and Dan's father had contributed to his already turbulent existence. The booze helped to some extent, but not enough to pacify his apprehension over where the whole crazy mix was leading him. Without attracting anyone's attention, he let his eyes wander over to the large grandfather clock that stood majestically against the wall behind Dan and Jessica. The hands read nine-thirty. It was time to think about leaving.

Ironically, Dan had already come to the same conclusion. It had been a long and trying day for him, coupled with too much to drink. Not to mention facing Donna when he returned to the hotel, an event he was not particularly looking forward to. So, in support of what he already suspected Neal was thinking, he made his move. "Much as I hate to see this memorable evening come to an end, I'm afraid it must," he apologized. "I still have some unfinished business to attend to tonight, as does Neal."

"I understand perfectly," Sandy assured him as she rose from her chair, "but he made a promise to play the piano the next time he was here, so I'm holding him to it. Then you're both free to leave,"

"Fair enough," Dan replied, looking over at Neal. "Ready, maestro?"

He smiled and agreed to play, although somewhat surprised that she would have remembered such a promise made almost in jest.

On their way to the living room, Sandy stepped into the kitchen and invited Ivan and Christina to join them.

"Shall I serve everyone a brandy, Ms. Sterling?' Ivan asked. "Would do well after dinner."

"Why, yes," Sandy replied, suspecting that the suggestion was a ploy to include himself and Christina in the serving. "How thoughtful of you."

By the time she returned with Ivan and Christina at her side, Neal had seated himself at the grand piano while Dan and Jessica sat close by. When all was quiet, he relaxed into the luxury of the surroundings almost as if he were alone. A few seconds later his large, tanned fingers played a series of modern chord variations up and down the keyboard to test the sound quality he was so anxious to hear; a sound that only a concert grand piano could produce. From the instant he heard the crisp, clear tones of the upper register, and the mellow resonance of the long bass strings, any thoughts he might previously have had about leaving the estate without playing such a fine instrument disappeared.

Thirty-five minutes later and two more servings of brandy found four smiling faces still captivated by his music. Dan, however, had fallen asleep in his chair, powerless to fight off the fatigue that had plagued him for the past few days. Regretting the unpleasant message he still had to deliver, he left the piano and wakened him.

The goodbyes were warm and friendly, filled with promises that more than likely would never be fulfilled. Yet, on the other hand, sincerity was there in abundance. As far as he was concerned, that was all that mattered.

Traffic on the freeway was surprisingly light. Dan had drifted back to sleep, giving him an opportunity to plan the diplomacy he would use to explain his mother's sudden hospitalization. Paula's unexpected decision to visit her daughter made the task somewhat easier. But Dan, he anticipated, would surely confront him with why he hadn't informed him of his father's telephone call when he first returned from Disneyland. As lights of the Hilton Inn came into view, he nudged Dan to waken him. When he was sure he was at least half way alert, he broke the news. "First, I want to apologize for not having told you this sooner. Your father called earlier today to tell you that your mother became suddenly ill yesterday and had to be hospitalized. Since he had no way of knowing where you were, he told me, and asked that I give you the message. Regrettably, I held back telling you until now because you were already upset with Donna, and I didn't want to make matters worse. With all that has happened to both of us today, I thought having dinner with Jessica after all these years would put you in a better frame of mind. Besides, the chances of you getting out of here this evening were virtually impossible. To set things right with your father, you'd better call him first thing in the morning and tell him what your plans are. I'm sorry about all this. I just didn't think it was the right time to break the news to you."

"That's okay, Mr. T," he replied, still half asleep. "It's too late to call him now anyway. I'll do it in the morning."

While lighting a cigarette, he remarked, calmly, "Mom's been in and out of the hospital a lot lately. I'm not surprised that she's back in again so don't let it bother you."

Relieved that he no longer had to puzzle over the dilemma he thought he was in, he brought his car to a stop opposite the hotel entrance where he expected Dan to simply say goodnight and leave. Contrary to that expectation, he just looked at his watch and asked, "Got time for a nightcap?"

Although he was tempted to decline the invitation in favor of a good night's sleep, he parked the car and followed him into the lounge. Maggie, the attractive young woman who had waited on them earlier, was still on duty and came to their table immediately. After their order had been taken, Dan looked at him and said, as if struck with a rush of guilt all of a sudden, "Maybe I should call the room and invite Donna to join us. I sure don't want her on my ass tonight, especially after what you just told me. What do you think?"

He thought carefully for a moment about what Dan had proposed and was reminded of an old saying he had put to the test many times in his own hectic and sometimes unrewarding past. "You'd best let that sleeping dog lie," he advised. "But, let your conscience be your guide, my friend." She's your problem, not mine."

Dan got up slowly and walked to one of the service phones in the lobby. Several unanswered rings made it obvious that Donna was not in their room, so he hung up and made an inquiry at the desk to determine if there were any messages for him.

From where he was sitting Neal could observe his movements as he paced up and down in front of the lobby desk. The expression on his face convinced him that something had gone amuck. Following an animated conversation with the clerk, he returned, visibly upset. "That bitch checked out and hopped a limo to the airport while we were gone." he sputtered in a loud, angry voice. "I can't believe she did that!"

Although Dan was not at all amused by Donna's sudden and unexplained departure, he was. Unable to mask the smile that wrinkled his weathered face, he looked up and calmly remarked, "Well, Dan, look at it this way. One of your problems just went away."

Reflecting for a moment on the cost he had incurred just to have her accompany him on his ill-fated getaway, and the little she had contributed to it, he sat back heavily in his chair and said, almost comically, "Who was it said, a fool and his money are soon parted?"

"I'm sure it was a woman," he replied sarcastically, looking over the top of his glasses.

"Yeah," Dan countered, still somewhat peeved, "probably on her back wondering what color to paint the ceiling."

For the next hour he listened to Dan elaborated in more detail about his intimate relationship with Donna. The more he drank, the more revealing he became, unwittingly suggesting that he had suspected her recently of being an undercover informant for the notorious Tidewater Cartel. Continuing, almost bitterly, he once again referred to her change in personality when she arrived at the airport on the evening they left for California, acting almost as if something unpleasant had happened to her earlier that day.

During the next few minutes Dan sat quietly eyeing Maggie's movements around the lounge while Neal reflected on how impatient Donna's behavior appeared to have been when they first arrived in San Diego. It had begun in the lounge when he had asked him to explain the reason for their early arrival. Tired as he was, and longing for the empty quietness Paula had left him at home, he asked him if Donna knew anything about the map he had given him for safe keeping. "Come to think of it, she did," he replied. "She saw it when I unpacked my bag and asked me, sarcastically, was I going to try and use it to get around in California. Why do you ask?"

"Just curious," he replied. "Let me sleep on it. Give me a call in the morning and we'll do breakfast."

"Not too early," he remarked, as Maggie approached with the bill. "Who knows, I might get lucky."

"In your dreams," he replied, winking at her as he strolled out of the lounge.

Purposely, he took the long way home to clear his head and ponder where his life was taking him. The marine layer had just begun its intrusion, bringing with it memories of similar nights when he was a married man, scuba diving in Mexico with his buddies. Looking back, those weekend getaways offered the only escape he could afford in to get away from his troubled marriage, and provided a temporary loss of identity in which to hide his indiscretions and infidelity without conscience. Or so it appeared at the time. Now, it seemed as though those troubled and thoughtless years of *romancing the stone* were a foolish, expensive waste of time, and should have been spent with his family. There was no *stone*, he all too late realized, only the rewards that came from honesty and hard work.

Entering the driveway, his headlights followed the pavement and came to rest on the dark and lifeless house that Paula had left behind. Out of spite, he speculated, hoping to stir up some appreciation for the domestic situation that was confronting them. Spending the night at her daughter's home would not normally have been upsetting to him. On this particular occasion, however, it had left him with a sense of having done something wrong. In an effort to right the matter, he went immediately to the telephone, hoping that his expression of thoughtfulness would ease the tension between them. When he entered the kitchen the blinking of the telephone answering machine caught his eye, so he activated it, fully expecting to hear Paula's voice. It was Henry Hughes,' however, and had an angry urgency to it:

"Neal! Please contact Dan immediately. Tell him his mother has taken an unexpected turn for the worse and to fly home immediately. Hopefully, before she passes on. This is urgent! I'm counting on you, Neal."

After clearing the message, he called the Hilton and asked for his room. There was no answer so he asked the clerk to page the lounge. A few seconds later, Maggie's voice came on line. When he explained about the message from Dan's father, she hesitated a moment before telling him what he was in no mood to hear right then. "I've been trying to get him to go to bed ever since you left, Mister Thomas. He's getting pretty drunk. Maybe you should come back and get him. Otherwise, I'm afraid the night manager will call the police."

"I'll be there in ten minutes, Maggie. Tell the manager I'm on the way."

Cursing out loud, he called Dan a number of unflattering expletives as he hurried to his car and returned to the hotel. When he arrived, Maggie led him to the security office where they found Dan cuffed and sitting on a chair with his eyes half closed.

According to the night shift officer, Dan had threatened to jump in the pool if Maggie didn't take him to his room and kiss him goodnight, so she called security before he could make a fool of himself. The officer had every intention of locking him up for the night until she talked him out of it, explaining that a friend was on the way that would take full responsibility for him.

Visibly upset, and almost in tears, Maggie turned to Dan and said, "I'm sorry about your mother being sick, and I hope you make it back in time to see her alive, but do me a favor, will you, please don't come back."

Her parting remarks must have had some sobering effect on Dan because he looked at Neal and asked, "How'd my mother get into this conversation, Mr. T? What's going on here?"

"I'll explain everything when we get you to your room," he replied, angrily. "Just sit there and be quiet for a minute."

Apologizing to the officer for Dan's drunken behavior, he explained about the bad news he had just received. Reluctantly, the officer accepted his apology and let them go, advising Dan that any further attempt to harass Maggie would bring on the local police.

Leaving the office, he led Dan immediately into the elevator. By the time they had reached his room, he had given him his father's message, and emphasized the importance of getting some sleep. "Under no circumstances are you to leave this room tonight, unless you want to sleep it off in the slammer. Is that understood? Damn if I'll come and bail you out."

Dan promised he wouldn't and started to get undressed, admitting that Neal was right and thanking him for coming to his rescue. "I don't suppose there's any use in calling the airline tonight, is there?"

He looked warily at his blurry-eyed friend and encouraged him to wait until the next morning. Dan thanked him again and fell into bed while Neal went into the bathroom to relieve himself before leaving. When he returned, Dan was lying flat on his back snoring and, hopefully, out of harm's way.

On his way through the lobby he glanced into the lounge. It was empty, except for Maggie sitting alone at a table counting her tip money. *Nobody waiting for me at home,* he thought, as he walked in to tell her goodnight. "Can you spare me a dime, lady?" he joked.

"Better than that, Mister T," she replied. "How about one for the road… on me."

"Why not," he replied, "but just for the record, you don't owe me a thing."

Maggie folded the thick stack of bills she had finished counting, put them in her purse and walked to the bar. As she mixed and handed him a double vodka tonic, she remarked, "I can't thank you enough for coming back tonight. I was getting a little uneasy serving your friend. Is he always that aggressive?"

"He's carrying a lot of baggage." he replied after a moment of reflection, "and some of it's pretty heavy. I've known him ever since he was a kid. He hasn't changed much."

"What's he doing way out here in California if his mother's so bad off?"

"While I was back in Virginia attending the funeral of a mutual friend I invited him to attend a Fourth of July party I have every year. I really never thought he'd take me up on it. The fact that he showed up several days early has me convinced that some of that baggage he's carrying around has dirty laundry in it."

"I'd be mighty careful about how chummy I got with him," she commented, "He's bad news."

"He'll be gone tomorrow," he told her. "I'll probably never see him again."

Having finished his drink, he stood up while she dimmed the lights and prepared to leave, remarking somewhat cynically, "I hate to say this, Mister T, but with those kinds of friends, who needs enemies? Will you walk me to my car?"

"I'd be happy to," he replied, surprised by the friendliness of her request. "Where's it parked?"

"Not far, over there under that light," she replied, placing her arm in his. "Sometimes late at night I get a little nervous walking around out here alone, even under the light. It's comforting to have an escort for a change."

"My pleasure," he replied, holding her car door open when they reached it. "If you're not working on the holiday, come by my house for some food and drink. There'll be live music and a lot of interesting people gathered there."

"Thanks for the invitation." She replied. "Stop by and give me directions when you can. I'll buy you a drink."

"You're on!"

Tired and mentally numbed from the day's activity, he drove cautiously home and collapsed into the safe but empty comfort of his bed without noticing that the red button on his answering machine was blinking again.

Chapter 13

When Old Friends Get Together

Following a much needed shower that washed part of the previous day's overindulgence down the drain, Neal put on his casuals for what he hoped would be a fruitful morning of researching rental ads in the newspaper. Hopefully, the results of that effort would calm Paula down if she knew he had found a reasonably priced rental equal to the one they were being forced to leave. At least she would have to give him a measure of credit for making a serious effort to address the dilemma in which they now found themselves. Thus, with paper in hand, and a hastily prepared breakfast in front of him, he poured another cup of coffee and began the search.

The first half hour passed quickly without arousing much serious interest. Then, as his enthusiasm was about to lose its momentum, the bolded words, ***Must Sell!!!*** attracted his attention. Highlighting the ad with a yellow marker, he turned and reached for the phone, noticing for the first time that the message light had been flashing.

Assuming that Paula might have tried to reach him the previous evening, he pushed the button. Contrary to that assumption, the heavy southern drawl of Henry Hughes' aggravated voice identified the caller.

"Neal, if you know where Dan is, please tell him that his mother passed away early this morning. Although the urgency for him to return is no longer critical, we do expect him to attend the funeral, if it's not too much of an inconvenience, that is. Thank you, I'll be in touch."

For several minutes he sat reflecting on Henry's message and puzzled with how to break the disheartening news to Dan. Not a very pleasant way to start the day, he thought. While pouring the remainder of his coffee in the sink, and wondering if he should call him right away, the phone rang. It was Dan. From the sound of his voice Neal concluded that he was either drunk, or so hung over he sounded as if he were. "Just thought I'd let you know that I called my father early this morning to let him know what my plans were. He told me that mom had passed away and had called you to relay the message, so I thought I had better check in to let you know what my plans are. Evidently, he must have called yesterday while we were having dinner with Jessica and her mother. You did get the message, didn't you?"

"Not until this morning," he admitted. "I was just about to call the hotel when you called. Where the hell are you?"

"I'm at the airport. My flight leaves in thirty minutes, so I thought I'd give you a call to say thanks for everything, especially last night. Maggie must think I'm a real bone head."

"Don't concern yourself with her. You're a piece of cake compared to some of the characters she runs into. Besides, chances are you'll never see her again, anyway."

After a brief pause without any response, he asked, "By the way, how did you manipulate a flight out of here on such short notice?"

"I've been up most of the night. Couldn't sleep very well, so I thought I'd make better use of my time by bugging the airlines. Because of mom's death and dad's persistence, I was able to get a special circumstances seat on a flight leaving here in a few minutes."

"I'll say this about you, Dan, you're the only person I know who can talk the stripes off a tiger."

After the hesitation that followed, Dan asked, "Do me a favor, will you? The next time you see Jessica, explain why I had to leave so suddenly. I really liked her and would love to see her again, but I'm afraid the chances of her ever getting back East again are slim and none. Tell her to call me, if she does."

"Consider it done, my crazy friend," he replied, skeptical that any such reunion would ever take place. "She and her mother will be at my party. I'll express your feelings then."

"Thanks, I owe you one."

He was about to hang up when Dan added, "Oh, I almost forgot. Please give my best wishes to your family, will you? I really missed seeing them."

"I will," he promised, certain that Dan's final request was probably the only one he could realistically fulfill with any degree of certainty. Out of respect, he added, "Please let your father and sister know that my heart-felt sympathy goes out to all of you. Call me if I can be of any help whatsoever."

After his call, Neal sat for some time thinking about all the events that had taken place in his otherwise settled and uneventful life since attending Billy Newman's wake. It was mind-boggling how one seemingly normal act of respect could have initiated a chain of events that had all the early warning signs of seriously influencing his future.

Content with the rationalization that little could be accomplished by worrying, he decided that his time would be better spent pursuing what he had been doing before Dan called. What better place to do it than alone on the beach, he decided, so he gathered up the newspaper and headed in that direction, leaving his sandals behind.

It was a beautiful day. The feeling of cold, wet sand beneath his feet filled his mind with the same fantasies he had enjoyed as a boy playing on the sandy beaches of Lake Ontario.

A mild Santa Ana condition had flattened what would typically have been rolling surf, dampening the hopes of surfers who watched disappointedly from nearby bluffs. Much as he empathized with their frustration, he welcomed the solitude and went in search of a resting place where he could read without interruption. A large piece of driftwood heavily draped in dried kelp provided the perfect setting.

Almost an hour had passed when he realized with growing disappointment that the ads he had been reading so enthusiastically offered little hope of an affordable rental near the coast. His search had suffered a major setback. Frustrated and troubled, he sat staring at the ocean unsure of what to do next.

Had he not been so preoccupied he might have noticed that his privacy had been quietly invaded. Nearby, partially hidden behind an easel, was a woman he had never seen before sketching on a large pad. Although her upper torso was almost totally hidden, her legs were not. They were well defined and fell gracefully down from a pair of men's Khaki cargo pants into leather sandals.

From where he sat it appeared the woman was including him in whatever she was working on. Being an artist, his curiosity was suddenly aroused, so he rose in an attempt to view her work. He had not even taken the first step when the woman's anxious voice pleaded, "Oh, please don't move! I'm almost finished. Five more minutes?"

He waved his consent and returned to the log, laughing a little as he sat back down. While he waited patiently for the woman to finish, his mind's eye made a quick assessment of what little he had been able to see of her.

She was taller than most women. Wore a wide-rimmed, straw hat that showed all the signs of old age; frayed edges, knotted chinstrap, and a stained, maroon hatband that fell down and separated behind her neck. As she peeked out from behind the pad every so often, he caught glimpses of the short, auburn hair that poked haphazardly out from under the rim. A short time later she put down her charcoal pencil and beckoned him to, "Come and see!"

A gust of air parted the woman's smock as he approached and exposed the tank top covered breasts of an attractive woman whom he speculated was in her mid to upper fifties. "Thanks for letting me finish," she said, greeting him with a broad smile. "My name is Becky Parker."

He shook her charcoal-stained hand, replying with a friendly grin, "Neal Thomas, pleased to meet you. Now, let's see what mischief you've been up to at my expense."

"Please do," she replied, stepping aside to provide him with a better look. "After all, you are the subject of interest."

His reaction was immediate and unmistakingly one of approval. There on the sketch pad in surprising likeness was his image looking thoughtfully out to sea from the driftwood log he had been sitting on. What impressed him most was how quickly she had captured his image and the surrounding background detail. "I am truly impressed," he commented. "Do you do this professionally?"

"I do a number of things professionally, Mister Thomas, but this I enjoy," she replied.

Her answer, which he was tempted to inquire into further, had privacy written all over it, so he respectfully put his curiosity aside and changed the subject. "I spend most of my time painting and drawing too, now that I've retired. Keeps me from falling victim to the infamous devil's workshop, as the saying goes."

"Oh, yes," she remarked, amused by the analogy. "I'm familiar with that place, and the idle hands that work there too. In fact, I'm a charter member. Do you go to meetings?"

"Not on a regular basis," he countered, impressed by her quick and witty sense of humor. "Like everything else that's fun, it's sure to be bad for you."

"Speak for yourself," she joked in reply as her eyes searched the community of homes that lined the beach not far from where they stood. "I'd love to stay and continue this conversation," she added, nervously, "but I'm afraid I must go."

To determine what had prompted such a sudden urgency to leave, he looked in the same direction, but was unable to observe anything unusual going on, so he asked, "Do you live around here?"

"No, I'm visiting friends for a few days who live here."

Pausing for a moment to determine whether or not her reply was more evasive than truthful, he experienced a strange fascination toward the woman, and why she had selected him to be the subject of her sketch. Obeying his artistic, and sometimes overly romantic preoccupation with the workings of human nature, he threw discretion to the wind and sawed off the limb he was sitting on. "Every year on the Fourth of July I put on a bash at my home up there on that bluff," he explained, pointing in that direction. "We have food, an open bar, live music, and a happy gathering of a lot of nice people. It starts at three o'clock in the afternoon and you're invited, if you're still here. I'll even take you on a personal tour of my studio. I'd appreciate your appraisal of my work."

Contemplating how refreshing it would be to enjoy an afternoon in the company of people she didn't know, she glanced again in that direction, and replied, "Why not? I haven't had that kind of fun in so long I've almost forgotten what it's like. Thanks for the invitation. Don't be surprised if I show up."

While he watched the gathering up of her materials, she thanked him again and started to leave. Several steps into her departure she turned with one eyebrow raised and cautioned, "You may live to regret this, Mr. Thomas. Some would tell you I have a terrible reputation for having too much fun."

"I'll take my chances," he replied

Seconds after they both had turned and started to leave, she turned back and asked, inquisitively, "By the way, are you married?"

"Used to be!"

It took only a few minutes for him to reach the top of the bluff. Panting a little, he strolled toward the house, noticing along the way that Paula's car was parked in the driveway. Entering, he found her thoughtfully watching television and sipping a glass of wine, hardly conscious of his presence.

"Welcome home," he greeted her, enthusiastically. "How are Ellen and the kids?"

Her reply was disappointingly unenthusiastic. There was a noticeable despondency in her reply that hinted at her having experienced something emotionally upsetting. "Are you okay?" he continued to inquire feeling a little uneasy about where this poorly started conversation was going. "Anything wrong?"

She put off her reply for a moment and looked wistfully out over the ocean at the gradually darkening sky consume what was left of her day. After he had settled in his chair, she turned and addressed his questions. "Since leaving you yesterday," she began, obviously agitated, "I've spent most of my time talking to Ellen and Mike about our having to move, and your nutty friend, Dan Hughes. Our having to move they dismissed as a gamble everyone faced when they rented, but not the worst problem to solve. However, your relationship with Dan Hughes, they both agreed, is becoming foolhardy. They're concerned that you don't know enough about him to realize what you're getting yourself into. And, to be brutally frank, so am I."

The fact that Paula had discussed his personal business with her family irritated him to the point where he was tempted to say something caustic. Age, however, and the wisdom that sometimes comes with it, tempered his reply to only a snide comment. "Seems as though I'm being given a lot of advice by those who shouldn't be giving it because it's none of their business."

Not to be put aside by his flippant remark, she started toward the stairs in an obvious ploy to end their conversation in favor of a good night's sleep. "I think the message here is, don't say you weren't warned."

He waited until she had almost reached the top of the stairs before responding. "Dan's Mother passed away very early this morning from an illness he told me she had been fighting for some time. He left on the earliest available flight, if that's any comfort to you."

She stopped abruptly and stared down at him, her eyebrows raised in surprise. "That remark was uncalled for, Neal. I didn't know any of this. How was I supposed to?"

Shaking his head in frustration, he replied, wearily, "Go to bed, dear, we'll talk in the morning."

The next day arrived without its customary wakeup alarm. It was Monday, the third of July. Since the fourth had fallen on a Tuesday, Paula had planned to extend her weekend by taking the day off to help Neal prepare for their holiday celebration. There was plenty of work to be done, demanding an early start. No time to fall victim to the gentle hands that so often had delayed her good intentions. After their previous evening's disastrous homecoming, she doubted she would be a likely target for his affection. With as little body movement as possible, she slid out of bed and proceeded quietly to the kitchen. In less than a minute the coffee maker sat brewing and the newspaper lay unfolded on the table. The day, as far as she was concerned, had begun.

Sometime later, Neal also made his way to the kitchen, his tasseled gray hair and unshaven face bearing witness to what his generation commonly referred to as, the morning after the night before. Weary-eyed and blinking, he made his way to the downstairs bathroom, splashed cold water on his face and returned to the kitchen to find her shaking her head with that, *you did it to yourself,* look on her face. "I've seen better looking heads on totem poles, she remarked humorously. "What's your excuse this time, Dan Hughes again?"

The question was not amusing so he dismissed it as just another verbal character assassination that woman resort to whenever they feel obligated to express their dissatisfaction toward the heap of exasperating irresponsibility they had unwittingly chosen as a mate. Typically, on weekdays, their time together involved snips and chips of intermittent conversation designed to test his ability to recall conversations they had shared the previous evening. Therefore, it came as no surprise when she asked, "Would you mind explaining again what happened to Dan's mother. Somehow, what you attempted to explain last night got lost in translation."

For the next half hour he gave a complete accounting of all that had taken place during her absence, and assured her that it was very unlikely that their lives would ever be disrupted again like they had been during his untimely visit. "So far as I know," he explained in an attempt to close the subject, "Dan took all of his problems back to Virginia. He has no reason to come back here, so let's forget about him and concentrate on tomorrow. Right now, that's our highest priority. And I intend to make it a happy and memorable day. Hopefully, without conflict."

Although she felt some guilt for being overly critical of Dan, especially in light of his mother's passing, his departure came as a breath of fresh air to her, and she sighed with relief. The previous day's upset with Neal seemed to gradually subside as the day progressed and renewed a sincere interest in enjoying their families and old friends again.

With separate tasks to perform, much of their day was spent apart from one another until late that afternoon. Tired, but content with what had been accomplished, she suggested they relax in the Jacuzzi for a while before eating dinner, a suggestion he responded to with enthusiasm.

Later on that evening, while they laid beside one another watching the moon cast its light across their tired but satisfied bodies, he remarked with a little chuckle, "I really wasn't that hungry anyway."

By two o'clock the next afternoon all that they had struggled to accomplish the previous day had been completed. The catered buffet had arrived well in advance of the first guests and the bar was manned, ready for the onslaught of thirsty revelers.

Derek Stone, Neal's son-in-law, had just finished setting up his band of fellow musicians when the first guests began arriving. All members of the band, like Derek, were lawyers, and very much in demand when it came to local weddings, parties and special events. The vocalist, a Marilyn Monroe look-a-like whom everyone in the group had nicknamed, "Trixie," was a showstopper with her platinum hair, bright red lips and white satin gown. Her movie-like pantomime of the famous Hollywood star had gained her quite a reputation, adding to the band's already popular following, though probably not necessarily with the band member's wives.

Karen Stone, Neal's oldest daughter, sought out her dad immediately to embrace him and ask, "Where's Paula? She must be frantic!"

He laughed and nodded toward the house, cautioning her as she hurried away, "Remember, honey, she's not your mother."

Shortly after she disappeared into the house another familiar car pulled into the driveway and parked next to Karen's. It was his youngest daughter, Laura, and her husband, Paul. They emerged in a storm of laughter, each carrying a bottle of wine. It made him smile to see how happy they appeared as he remembered the day he presented himself at their wedding as father of the bride. What a monumental day it had been.

"Hi, Pops!" Paul greeted him. "We brought you something to help fortify the bar."

Looking as if she had just stepped off the cover of Vogue Magazine, Laura arrived a few steps later in her hyper mode of almost Disney-like animation and hugged her father, affectionately. "Hi, Daddy! Can you believe it? We're actually on time. Have Susan and Marty arrived yet?"

Hugging her slender body while he kissed her on the cheek, he stepped back and replied with regret, "No, I'm sorry to say. You're sister called early this morning to tell me that she and Marty both have colds. They were afraid of passing it on, so they decided to stay at home. That hug was partly from them."

"Bummer," she remarked, noticeably disappointed. "I haven't seen her for weeks. Guess I'll have to wait until the next holiday."

"I'm afraid so,"

During the following two hours, while the band filled the air with a continuous flow of lively music, a steady stream of guests continued to arrive until every square foot of the back yard and patio was occupied. Some had gathered inside, but they were, as he had so long ago classified them, the serious talkers.

The outsiders were not. Typically, they were more inclined to drift among familiar faces and tell them the same stories they had heard many times over, with subtle changes added or omitted, depending on what level of sobriety they had managed to exceed.

Without question, the most predictable grouping was made up of those who never strayed too far from the bar. They were mostly single men and women of all ages who probably would have been sitting on a bar stool someplace watching televised golf, had they not been invited to the party. It was a strange mix, and included all of Neal's closest friends.

Surprisingly enough, Sandy and Jessica Sterling were among the early arrivals. In doing so they provided a timely opportunity to enjoy more than just a few minutes of quality time with their host to discuss a few personal matters, one of which was why Dan Hughes wasn't there.

Saddened by the news that Dan's mother had passed away, Jessica's eyes began to show signs of tearing, causing her to turn away briefly to dab them with a tissue, while Sandy politely encouraged him to greet his other guests. Jessica, however, restrained him briefly and assured him that, even though it was her intention to accept her mother's job offer, there were matters back East that needed her attention, during which time she would make every effort to contact Dan. "Now, go have some fun," she ordered, still sniffling a bit. "Mother and I have already introduced ourselves to your significant other. That's what women do, you know. She's a lovely, gracious lady."

How nice of them to have sought her out by themselves, he thought, walking toward the bar. How typically female to seek out the object of his affection to see if she measured up to their expectations. Evidently she had, based on Jessica's appraisal.

As far as he could tell from casually looking around at his guests, he was apparently the only person there without a drink in his hand. Determined to rectify that situation, he continued on his way to the bar and ordered a double vodka-tonic. "In a real glass, Danny," he told the bartender.

Seconds later, the young man handed him his drink, and remarked, "I've had it waiting on ice for almost half an hour, Mr. T. Where've you been?"

"Taking care of business, young man," he replied with a wink. "Monkey business, if you get my drift."

Danny shook his head and laughed as he handed him his drink. "Why am I not surprised?" he joked.

As Neal turned and left to mingle with more of his guests, a familiar voice shouted from a spot near the bluff. "Hey, Neal! Over here!"

Looking in that direction, he recognized his friend, Dusty Lewis, and a woman he assumed to be his wife, motioning for him to join them. Instant flashbacks to the time when he and Dusty had been neighbors in Raleigh flickered through his mind as he made his way through the crowd to greet them and apologized for not having met them when they arrived.

"Don't worry about it," Dusty replied, "I'd like you to meet my wife, Katie. She's really impressed with the band. Where did you find them?"

After a brief introduction, he replied, "They're my son-in-law's group. They call themselves, The Briefs. All lawyer's, except for the vocalist. Isn't she something?"

Dusty was about to make a comment when Katie interrupted.

"Yeah, she's something alright. Look at those old geezers over there near the bar with their eyes bugged out. I guess they're the origin of that old saying, there's no fool like an old fool."

"Careful now," Neal cautioned. "I resemble that remark."

"My apologies," she replied, blushing slightly. "Present company excepted, of course."

Before either of the two men could express themselves further, she remarked, unemotionally, "If she's the only person you two old goats feel compelled to talk about in my presence, I'm going to get another glass of wine. Can I bring either of you anything?"

Both smiled and respectfully declined. After she was beyond hearing distance, Dusty looked at Neal with a puzzled expression on his face and whispered, "One of your female guests looks vaguely familiar but I just can't remember where or when our paths might have crossed."

"Which one? There's a lot of them here."

"That attractive dark-haired woman standing with an older woman near the bar."

He didn't have to search very long before realizing that he was referring to Jessica Sterling and her mother. Given the nature of Dusty's profession, he felt it would be inappropriate to go into too much detail about any of his guests, so he decided to satisfy his question with a question. "Is this an official inquiry, Agent Lewis?"

Dusty smiled, realizing that his host was not about to tell him much of anything without some justification, so he apologized, explaining that his government service came with a certain trained curiosity that he admitted could be interpreted by others as improper or intrusive. "Of course not," he insisted. It's just that she has this uncanny resemblance to someone whose name I can't remember. I'm usually pretty good remembering names and faces, but that woman has me baffled."

"Oh?" Katie interrupted, having overhear her husband's remark upon her return, "and you met her where?"

" Her name is Jessica Sterling," Neal interjected, in a diplomatic gesture to get Dusty off the hook. "And the other woman is her mother, Sandy Sterling. You'll find this hard to believe, but I met them both recently when I flew back to Virginia and discovered we have a mutual friend. That friend was supposed to be here today, but had to fly home unexpectedly due to the sudden death of his mother."

Before any further conversation could take place, Katie interrupted and said she had a message Paula had asked her to give Neal. "She said a woman by the name of Jennifer Newman called a little while ago and wants you to call her as soon as possible. Paula thinks you should tend to it right away."

Her message aroused Neal's curiosity almost immediately. Try as he might to set it aside until later, he felt an irresistible urge to find out why she had called, so he excused himself and started to leave. A few steps away he heard Dusty call after him. "Talk to you later, sport. I just remembered where I met your friend, Jessica Sterling."

Neal threw him a thumbs-up and wove his way through the noisy crowd toward the bar. When he arrived, Danny had already prepared him a fresh drink and said, "I saw you coming, Mister T. You'll need this one. Ms. Dillon is looking for you and appears to be upset about something."

"What now?" he sighed, searching the sea of faces for some glimpse of her. Frustrated, he started for the house thinking that she might have gone inside, but was distracted by the silhouette of a woman standing at the top of his beach access stairway. Because the late afternoon sun was masking her identity, he felt he had to make sure she wasn't a stranger crashing the party. At the risk of irritating Paula further, he walked hurriedly toward the woman and discovered her to be the one who had sketched him on the beach. "Welcome, Becky," he greeted her, "What a pleasant surprise. How long have you been standing here?"

"Long enough to question whether I should be here at all," she replied. "I don't recognize a soul."

"Nonsense," he said, as he took her by the hand. "There's a couple over there who don't know any of my guests either. Let me introduce you to them."

Reluctantly, she followed him to where his friends were seated and stood awkwardly by as he introduced her, telling the three of them to get acquainted while he went to find Paula. "Get Becky a drink will you, Dusty. She looks like she needs one. I'll be back as soon as I find out where Paula is."

"Take your time," he replied. "We'll take good care of her."

As both men parted and went in different directions, Becky looked at Katie and whispered, visibly embarrassed, "What's our host's name?"

"Neal Thomas," she replied, amused by her embarrassment. "He and my husband met when they were both bachelors years ago. Obviously, you haven't known him long?"

"Not really. We met yesterday on the beach and discovered we have a mutual interest in art. I came here today solely to view his work." Pausing briefly, she looked at the activity going on around her and remarked, "If, there's an opportunity to do so, that is."

On the way through his crowded house, Neal was approached by his daughter, Karen, who told him that Paula had gone upstairs for what she assumed was a chance to freshen up a bit, but she hadn't come back down yet. Concerned, she asked him to go check on her to make sure she was all right.

When he entered the bedroom he knew immediately that something was wrong. She just looked up at him with an expressionless face and said, "Jennifer Newman called a little while ago so I took the call up here because of all the noise. She wants you to call her tomorrow morning, and emphasized that it was urgent."

"Did she say why?"

"No, she just said it was important, and not to call her back tonight because she wasn't at the beach."

Sensing that Jennifer's call was in some way connected to his recent involvement with Dan Hughes, he sat down on the bed and put his arm around her. As she relaxed and gave in to his comforting caress, he kissed her tenderly and chuckled, "Hey! Somebody's having a party downstairs and they're wondering where the hell we are. You don't want them to think we've snuck off to get a little, do you?"

She raised her head until her eyes could see the silly grin on his face and laughed in spite of herself. "You should be so lucky, you silly citizen."

Strolling arm in arm toward the stairs to rejoin the party, he patted her gently on the soft, round curves of her shorts and whispered, "Hmm, nice buns."

Unable to resist the affable charm of the man she had fallen in love with for what seemed a lifetime, she patted him back affectionately, and whispered, "Sweet cakes to you, Buster."

It became immediately apparent when they entered the back yard that the activity level and noise had reached an all time high. The band was playing a familiar rock and roll number that was being enjoyed by young and old alike while their bodies gyrated to the beat. Even the sometimes stuffy, Dusty Lewis, was in full swing with his wife and Becky Parker, forming a swinging trio for the amusement of everyone there.

When they reached the crowded bar, he ordered drinks for both of them and then they sat down to watch the fun. A short time later, the music suddenly ended, surprising everyone. With the vocalist's microphone in hand, his son-in-law, Derek, quieted the crowd and made an announcement. "On behalf of The Briefs, I'd like to take this opportunity to thank all of you for your enthusiasm, and to indulge us for a few minutes while we take a much needed potty-break. During that time, and with a little encouragement from the audience, I'm sure we can coax my father-in-law into entertaining us by playing a couple of songs on the keyboard."

The applause was immediate and unrelenting until Neal was finally forced to take his place at the electronic keyboard, an instrument which was much like his own. After selecting a Bossanova beat, combined with orchestral violins, he began to play a song he had composed for Paula's oldest granddaughter when she was only four years old titled, "Sophia Marie." Many there had heard it before, and sang along to its lively beat. The cheering and clapping that followed was all the encouragement he needed to continue, but not before announcing that his next selection was a new melody he had composed for his own daughters titled, "My Three Girls."

The audience response was most gratifying, especially when he noticed Karen and Laura applauding in the background and blowing him kisses. Rising from the keyboard when he saw the band returning, he caught a glimpse of Sandy and Jessica waving from a crowded spot nearby. Because he was still very much caught up in the drama of their recent reunion, he picked up the microphone instead and announced, "Before the band starts playing again I would like to introduce you to two lovely ladies who have just recently been reunited after almost twenty years, a truly amazing story. How about a nice hand for Sandy Sterling and her lovely daughter, Jessica."

As clapping persisted and heads turned inquisitively, Sandy took Jessica by the hand and walked over to him, asking for the microphone. When the noise subsided she began to speak. "What our dear friend, Mr. Thomas, failed to tell you is, I might never have seen my daughter again had it not been for the selfless effort he put forth to personally bring that reunion about. For his dedication to that end, I shall be forever grateful. Thank you, Neal, from the bottom of our hearts."

The hand clapping, whistle blowing and fractured sounds of musical instruments paying tribute left him speechless. He knew that if he remained there a moment longer he would lose it, so he left quickly to hide his tearing eyes, waving his arm in a gesture of thanks until the growing darkness beyond the noisy gathering had swallowed him up.

A crescent moon hung high in the indigo sky, sparkling the incoming tidal waves with diamond-like reflections as they curled and crashed onto the beach below. Their noise and almost hypnotic affect lulled him into a sense of almost hypnosis, dulling any consciousness of the woman who was approaching him from behind. "You're quite a remarkable man, Mr. Thomas," the woman remarked. "Mind if join you for a moment before I leave?"

Startled by her voice, he turned abruptly to discover Becky Parker walking toward him somewhat unsteadily.

"Damn!" he gasped with relief. "You scared the hell out of me."

She remained silent for a moment, grinning like a bad little girl. "Sorry," she apologized, slurring her words a little, and hiccupping, "I can assure you it was quite unintentional."

He couldn't help being amused by her moonlit face looking up at him with her eyes blinking and her body trying desperately to maintain its balance. "That's okay. "I was just caught up in a little night dreaming and you startled me. Are you alright?"

"Fit as a fiddle and ready for love, "she replied, giggling a little. "Oops, no pun intended."

"None taken," he assured her. "Can you make it home by yourself? I can walk with you if you'd feel safer."

"Well," she replied with some hesitation, "ordinarily that would be a pretty good idea, but if I just scared the hell out of you, what's the point?"

"Be serious!" he scolded. "It's dark down there."

After removing her sandals, she straightened up and replied in an obvious attempt to sound sober. "Thanks for asking. I should have known you'd be a gentleman too."

Hesitating a moment to brush the wind-blown hair from her face, she gazed blurry-eyed out over the ocean and spoke, almost philosophically. "The night is my friend, and I am never alone. So, worry not for me, my friend. The moon will take me home."

Before he could repeat his offer to accompany her, she had already started down the stairs to the beach below. Halfway there, she turned and yelled back over the ocean's roar, "I loved your artwork! Your friend, Dusty, took me on a tour of the house! I'm jealous!"

Still not sure that he had done the right thing by not insisting that he walk her home, he lingered on the bluff until he could no longer see her.

Hoping that she had made it home without incident, he walked casually back toward the revelry that was gradually toning down. He had just stepped out of the darkness when Paula spotted him and approached. "And, just where have you been, Mr. Host? Guests are beginning to leave."

Rather than explain, he simply replied, "I've been on the bluff getting a breath of fresh air. Who's leaving? It's still early."

"Some of our guests have to work tomorrow," she replied, somewhat irritated. "People are anxious to get home. It's getting late."

Though he wanted to deny the party's ending, he knew realistically that it was over. The band members had already begun to pack up their instruments, and leftover food was being given away to anyone who wanted it. So, not having had anything to eat that afternoon, he filled a paper plate, thinking, *better late than never.*

During the next half hour the majority of guests had bid them goodnight and left. Those who remained were predictably the last to leave and represented the hard core of his closest male friends. The surprising exception was Dusty and Katie Lewis. They had formed a jolly group of four with Sandy and Jessica Sterling and appeared to be having another reunion of sorts. Curious about what the unlikely group had in common, he walked over to join them. When he got there Dusty grabbed his arm and said, excitedly,"I told you I thought I knew this remarkable woman," he blurted out. "She's Jess Sterling, one of the DEA's most outstanding agents, code name, Vixen."

"Was," she corrected him, watching Neal's mouth drop in surprise. "Thank God I am no longer cursed with that unfortunate distinction."

As an agent himself, Dusty elected not to pursue the subject any further for reasons he felt were personal and possibly confidential. Glancing at his watch, he reluctantly announced that it was time for him and Katie to leave.

The usual well intended promises to stay in contact with each another followed, but each knew, realistically, that such promises were rarely ever kept. When the hugging and handshaking ended, the two couples left to go their separate ways, leaving Neal with unanswered questions regarding the past, present and future of the intriguing and highly complex Jessica Sterling, as well as his infamous friend, Dan Hughes. Though puzzling, none of those concerns were serious enough to interfere with joining his die-hard friends for a nightcap.

Ron Barns, Joey Siegel and Don Curtis were still standing at the bar talking controversial political gibberish when he arrived. That Danny had had his fill of them was quite obvious. Handing him a fifty-dollar bill, and praise for a job well done, he patted him on the back and told him to get lost.

Though tired and emotionally out of phase with Neal because of his unpredictable behavior of late, Paula joined the men just long enough to finish her glass of wine and say goodnight. That done, she made her weary way up the stairs and sat in her darkened bedroom for a few moments to reflect on the day's activities.

What hadn't taken place was the opportunity to tell Neal what she had learned from old man Fahey earlier that day regarding his asking price for the house. On the other hand, she reconsidered, it was probably better that she had held back telling him, given his preoccupation with family, friends and entertaining. There was always tomorrow, she conceded, not noticing where the hands on her tiny wristwatch were positioned as she placed it on the night table and climbed into bed. Had she noticed, she would have realized that tomorrow had already arrived.

It wasn't long after Danny the bartender left that Neal's three buddies admitted they had had enough and left without ceremony, leaving him alone at the bar. Still emotionally wound up from the day's activities, he decided to take one last look at the ocean to end what had been a very tiring and thought provoking day. Why he wasn't tired he did not know. Maybe the intrigue of discovering that Dusty and Jessica had had common ties at one time was partly at fault. Or, was it Becky's poetic remark on the bluff before leaving that left him baffled. It was neither, he concluded.

Moments later, as he lay in bed listening to Paula's heavy breathing, he realized that the real culprit was Jennifer Newman. What was so important that it required calling him on a National Holiday without any hint of purpose? Unfortunately, the dark blanket of sleep that crept over his weary eyes denied him the answer.

Chapter 14

Missing

The following morning ushered its way in on the sound waves of Paula's wakeup alarm. Unfortunately, the snooze control only forestalled the inevitable and soon forced her to sit up on the edge of the bed and curse the dawn.

Neal's corpse-like body lay motionless beside her in a state of half-consciousness, de-energized to the point where any attempt to exercise his usual modus operandi would be futile. Her conclusion couldn't have been more accurate. It became a certainty when he felt the mattress respond to her departure, obviously having concluded the same thing.

Much as he desperately wanted to lie there to give his aging body a rest from daily routine, he raised his head sluggishly off the pillow and came to a sitting position. The image that greeted him in the mirrored closet door opposite his side of the bed was the only picture he needed to remind him of how much he had enjoyed the previous day, other than the irritating voice within his throbbing head that kept reminding him that it was he who had shot himself in the foot.

Drinking coffee and reading the newspaper proceeded with little conversation between the two of them until just before it was time for her to leave for work. While they walked to her car and chatted about every day matters of little significance, she asked, "Please try not to get yourself involved with anyone tonight, will you? I have something important to discuss with you that will require your undivided attention. Promise?"

As bad as he felt, he couldn't imagine anything that could detour him from doing absolutely nothing for the rest of the day. "Nothing short of an earthquake is going to get me involved with anything, or anyone," he replied. “My soul purpose in life today is to tidy up this place and relax. I only wish you could be here to do the same thing.”

“Me too,” she remarked, sliding in behind the wheel. “Then I can count on you having your wits about you when I get home this evening?”

“Don’t press your luck, Tootsie. I’ll be here.”

During the hour that followed he noticed a piece of stick-on notepaper attached to the telephone receiver. It read: *Don’t forget to call Jennifer Newman.*

Amused by her business-like reminder, he peeled it off and went to his studio to make the call, wondering again why she wanted to talk to him. Jennifer answered after three rings. After inquiring about the usual family related subjects she came straight to the point. “I wish there were some easier way to tell you this, but I’m afraid something has happened to Dan Hughes.”

Suddenly, all the pseudo-wisdom he had been given about becoming involved in other people’s problems hit him like a sledgehammer. “I don’t understand,” he stammered. “Dan called me from the airport yesterday morning just before he left. He knew about his mother’s death and seemed anxious to return to be with his family. I can’t imagine what could have happened to him.”

“Well, evidently something has,” she responded with a tone of sarcastic skepticism. “Henry called me yesterday thinking he might have come down here to pick up his boat before coming home, so I drove to the marina and checked. It was still there.”

The thought that Dan might have fallen victim to the same untimely demise as Billy Newman dampened Neal’s forehead, causing him to seek the cooler environment of his patio where he asked, “Has Henry notified the authorities?”

“Yes he has. The airline confirmed his arrival in Norfolk and the police have an investigation already under way. Henry told them that Dan was returning from California, and that you were probably the last person with whom he had had personal contact. I’m giving you a heads-up on all this so you’ll be prepared if they contact you.”

“Prepared for what?” he asked, noticeably irritated. “Hell, you know more than I do.”

“Calm down,” she replied, just as irritated. “There’s a lot going on back here that you’re not aware of. The DEA is convinced Billy’s death was not an accident, and may be linked to drug related activities that Dan may have been a part of. His sudden departure to California has raised some questions that they think you might be able to shed some light on. It would be in your best interest to cooperate.”

In his tired and hung over condition he realized that he had over reacted. "I'm sorry," he apologized. "My head isn't screwed on as straight as it should be this morning. We had a large gathering here to celebrate the holiday and I'm afraid I overdid it a wee bit."

"Oh, really. I can't imagine," she remarked, sarcastically. "Good to hear you're still that happy go lucky man we all grew to know and love."

A brief pause ensued while he struggled to come up with some meaningful reason why the DEA might think he knew something about Dan's disappearance. Before he could respond, Jennifer asked, "Was Dan alone when he came to California?"

"No," he admitted. "He brought his friend, Donna, the girl who showed up at his boat late Saturday evening after the wake. I had no reason to question why she was there, other than the obvious. She was also onboard his boat the next day when we cruised the bay. Why, is that important?"

"Could be," she replied, pausing momentarily. "Even so, I don't think we should be discussing this over the phone right now. Just be aware that the local authorities, and the DEA, are very much interested in talking to you."

"Do you know when?" he asked, starting to feel uneasy.

"Soon," she replied, "so, be prepared. I'm just letting you know now so you won't be caught flat-footed. If I hear anything more, I'll call. Otherwise, you're on your own. As they say, too many cooks spoil the soup."

All he could think of after she hung up was, *out of the frying pan, into the fire.* She had left his befuddled mind swimming in the murky waters of not knowing what to do next. It was painful enough that his head was threatening to go into orbit, but now having to explain to Paula what the substance of Jennifer's call implied was somewhere he didn't want to go, at least for the time being.

On the surface, there appeared to be little he could do but wait until the DEA made its move. To help solve the immediate problem he went to the medicine cabinet to get an Alka-Seltzer, convinced that ridding himself of a nagging headache was the first crucial step toward getting his brain back to thinking straight. It was a wise move. Within minutes the hangover began to weaken, giving him some improved recollection of those persons and events that might provide some meaningful clue as to Dan's whereabouts.

The first order of business, he decided, was to review the map Dan had given him. After memorizing the specific coordinates where the inlet to Dan's hideaway was located, he proceeded to a file cabinet he kept in the garage. There, among the many folders filled with tax records and miscellaneous material, he knew the map would be safe. As a precaution he had never exercised before, he locked it and hid the key.

After thoroughly reviewing all that had transpired over the past few days, he came to the conclusion that the only person who could possibly shed any light on Dan's whereabouts – other than Donna – was Jessica Sterling. She had spent time alone with him at the Sterling estate and might recall him mentioning what his future plans were. Picking up the phone, he dialed the Sterling residence. After several rings, Ivan picked up. "Sterling residence."

"Ivan, this is Neal Thomas. May I speak with Jessica?"

Apologizing for her not being there, he explained that she and Ms. Sterling had gone to the office to introduce Jessica to the staff. "Part of a get acquainted with the business visit, I should say," he remarked. "I'm sure you can catch them there, if you call straight away."

Neal thanked him and placed the call. Following a short delay, Sandy's pleasantly formal voice came on line. "So soon, Mr. Thomas?" she remarked. "Jessica and I are still in recovery mode, thanks to you. What a wonderful party. What can I do for you?"

"Something I hope Jessica can help me with, if she's there?"

"As a matter of fact, she's standing right here. I'll put her on."

"Good morning, Mr. Thomas," she groaned. "I'll have you know I'm holding you personally responsible for the miserable headache my dear mother seems to find so amusing. Good party, though. Seeing Dusty Lewis again was a coincidence I could never have anticipated. Where in the world did you meet him?"

'That's a whole other story, Jessica," he replied. "I hope I have the opportunity to tell you all about it sometime. Right now, however, I have a more serious matter to discuss with you that involves Dan Hughes."

He had anticipated the silence that followed and waited patiently for her to respond.

"I'll do what I can, Mr. Thomas, "she finally replied. "What has that poor misguided fool done now?"

"Evidently disappeared, from what Jennifer Newman told me a little while ago."

"Disappeared! Would you mind explaining that, please."

Hesitating a moment to formulate a carefully worded inquiry, he explained the purpose of his call. "He left here unexpectedly yesterday morning to return home for his mother's funeral. She passed away from an illness she had been plagued with for some time. For whatever reason, he never made it home. According to Jennifer, his boat is still at the marina where he left it before coming out here, so we know he hasn't used it to leave the area. Jennifer also informed me that the DEA has been called in to investigate his disappearance, and has expressed an interest in questioning me about his visit here. Before they do, however, I need to know if Dan talked to you about anything that might be useful in determining why he's not where he should be."

"One things for sure," she cautioned, "we can't continue this conversation over the phone. Why don't we meet at Bully's in Del Mar where we had lunch last week? We can continue this conversation there. Mother, by the way, is definitely in favor of that suggestion, if it's all right with you. "

"A glass of wine and something to eat sounds pretty good to me. How about one-o'clock? Most of the lunch crowd will be gone."

"See you there."

After the call, he strolled out onto the patio, laid back in his deck recliner to try and make some sense out of this strange new development in the ever-changing saga of Dan Hughes' life, and tried to comprehend the mental anguish his father must be experiencing. To lose a wife, and discover at the same time that your only son had disappeared, was more than he could imagine and it frustrated him. Not that he could have done anything to prevent either of the two occurrences, but he was suddenly overcome with empathy for the two men, and vowed to honor his friendship with them, regardless of the consequences. Try as he may to put the puzzle together, the mental anguish and lingering effects of the previous day's revelry were more than his brain could handle, causing his weary eyes to close without notice.

Two hours later, the sound of a message being recorded on his answering machine woke him. It was his daughter, Karen, calling to tell him that she had had a lengthy talk with Paula about Mister Fahey's asking price for the house, but the message ended before he could intercept it. Still groggy from being awakened, he glanced at his watch to discover it was eleven-thirty. "Damn," he shouted, upset with having napped into a time-crunch to meet Jessica and her mother. Reasoning that he could replay the message later, he splashed some water on his face, secured the house and drove hurriedly along the coast to Del Mar.

Pulling into Bully's parking lot he was surprised to discover that only *Valet Parking* was available. Even though he was still concerned about being late, he need not have been, because there was a small group of customers still waiting at the entrance, two of whom he recognized immediately, Jessica and her mother.

"I guess this means I'm not late," he remarked, making his way past others in line. "Thanks for saving my place."

"So much for your luncheon crowd theory," Jessica commented, laughing at the surprised look on his face. "This place is packed."

Embarrassed, he shrugged his shoulders and accepted the playful intent of her criticism. "Hey," he replied, "You can't win'em all."

Seconds later, while looking intently over the heads of those in front of him, he saw the familiar face of his friend, Tommy Camillo, the restaurant's manager. A quick, overhead wave of his three-fingered signal finally caught Tommy's attention. Smiling back in recognition, he disappeared just long enough for the loudspeaker to announce: "Thomas! Party of three."

Inside, the two men gripped hands and embraced in a manly expression of friendship. As they exchanged male trivia and laughed like two old college buddies, Jessica and her mother looked at one another with blank faces as they waited to be introduced. Their wait was short lived.

"You never cease to amaze me, my friend, " Tommy remarked in broken English. "Always with such beautiful women."

Shortly after introductions were exchanged, Tommy motioned an attractive waitress standing nearby to escort his friends to their table, commenting as he patted her gently below the waist, "These people are not customers, Carmen. Treat them like family."

When their wine orders arrived, Jessica raised her glass and said to Neal, "How long have you two been going together?"

He laughed, but wasted little time in addressing the subject of Dan Hughes' unexplainable disappearance. Looking at her seriously, he asked, "When Dan and I visited you and your mother last Saturday there was a period of time before dinner when you two were alone together. Did he mention anything then about why he had come to California?"

Looking back at him just as seriously, she replied, "Under ordinary circumstances I'd say that was privileged information, especially now that the DEA has become involved. Having been a former agent in that organization, I can tell you that their involvement complicates matters considerably."

"It's already complicated," he remarked, "and I'm right in the middle of the whole damn thing. I need some information that I can use as a wild card if I become more involved than I already am. I know things about Dan Hughes that no one knows. Why he picked me to confide in I'll never understand, but he did. And, to be perfectly honest, I'm becoming a little concerned about what I'm being dragged into, friendship or no friendship."

To restore calmness, Sandy interrupted with a comment. "It seems to me that both of you know more about Dan Hughes than anyone, including his family. Wouldn't it be wise to pool your resources and try to figure out what happened to the man on your own? Based on what I've been reading in the newspapers recently, I wouldn't trust any Government Agency any further than the length of my nose."

In support of her mother's observation, Jessica remarked, "She has a valid point, Neal. Like the man said, two heads are better than one. Having walked the walk and talked the talk, I'm inclined to agree with her assessment of government intervention. After all, Dan could just as easily be somewhere goofing off on his boat, for all we know."

"According to Jennifer Newman, his boat is still at the marina. How do you account for that?"

Jessica had anticipated that he would continue to press for an admission that Dan had confided in her, so she decided to meet him head on. "I don't know what reason he gave you for being here, but he told me that he had come to California because he was afraid to remain in Virginia and was waiting for a friend to let him know how serious the situation was. He also confided in me that you were the only person he knew, other than myself, that he could trust. So much so, that he showed you information that would incriminate all the persons responsible for the distribution and sale of narcotics in the Tidewater Area, including a map that showed the location of where the evidence was hidden. All that information in the hands of someone the Cartel couldn't identify he hoped would keep him safe when he quit the organization. Looks to me like that someone is you!"

"This is becoming more and more like a Tom Clancy thriller," Sandy remarked, glancing at her watch. "I hope you two are keeping notes on all this."

"Let's solve the mystery first," Jessica remarked. "This story needs an ending."

Neal grunted and wiped his lips. "Let's hope it isn't mine."

One could see by the blank fixation of Jessica's eyes that her thoughts were lost for a direction in which to continue. As she lifted her glass and swirled its contents, she turned to him and spoke in a half whisper, "So far as anyone knows, you are just an old friend of Dan's family that he contacted while here on a vacation. For the time being, that's all the DEA needs to know until they find him."

"What about Donna, and the map?" he asked. "Shouldn't I volunteer that information?"

She paused before answering his question, knowing from personal experience that providing more information than asked for is a mistake.

"Respond truthfully to questions with yes or no answers, as much as possible. And don't volunteer anything. It could come back to haunt you. Right now you're just an innocent bystander who may or may not have information they can use. Call me after they've contacted you. Then we'll know what to do."

An awkward silence followed until Jessica followed up with one last bit of advice. "Be careful what you tell Paula. No need to alarm her needlessly until the DEA contacts you. After all, they may already have located Dan, so let's just wait and see what develops."

Satisfied that all the strategy she had suggested made good sense, he excused himself to use the men's room, more as a diversionary tactic to prevent Sandy from picking up the check than actually having to use the facility. It thus came as an unexpected surprise when he learned from Carmen that the bill had already been taken care of by Mr. Camillo. When Neal confronted him about it on his way back to rejoin the ladies, Tommy explained that his gesture had a string attached to it. "Ron Barns showed me copies of some of your artwork recently. He suggested that you might consider painting something for the restaurant to promote your work, and make a few bucks in the process. Would you accept my generosity as a down payment?"

Neal beamed with surprise and shook his hand. "Of course I will! As a matter of fact, I'm currently working on an oil painting that would really add some class to this place. If you like it, I'll finish it as soon as I can and we'll talk about the price then."

The matter was settled. While he made his way back through the still crowded dining room, he reflected on the many times Ron Barns had tried to persuade him to approach Tommy about displaying a piece of his art in the restaurant. Funny how things work out, he thought, approaching the two ladies with a silly smile still on his face.

"Everything's taken care of," he remarked. "Shall we go?"

When both ladies were in Sandy's car, Jessica lowered her window and advised him to deal with the situation one day at a time, and to call her after he had talked to the DEA.

"Remember, don't volunteer any information. Absolutely nothing!"

Following their departure, he stood in the parking area for a moment pondering what to do for the rest of the afternoon. Ron Barns' place was only minutes away so he tipped the attendant, slid into his car and headed in that direction.

As he expected, Ron was sitting in his easy chair with several televisions tuned to a variety of different stations while he read one of the many novels that lay in numbers al. over the place. "To what do I owe this untimely intrusion, Mr. Thomas?" he asked, without looking up. "You're a little early this week, aren't you?"

"I think I may have stepped in it this time, old buddy," he replied as he shook his hand and passed on to the kitchen to fix a drink.

"How so?" he asked, closing his book. "You haven't fallen in love again, have you?"

"Nothing quite that simple," he replied. "The DEA wants to talk to me about Dan Hughes. Seems he's disappeared."

During the hour that followed, he outlined the history of events that had led up to the current predicament in which he now found himself hopelessly involved. "I think I'm up to my ass in alligators with no way to drain the swamp," he admitted. "And to make matters worse, Paula hasn't got a clue about any of this. I shudder to think what she'll do when I tell her about the DEA getting into the act."

Ron shook his head in disbelief and replied, "Seems to me I recall advising you not long ago that getting involved in other people's personal business was not a wise thing to do. Evidently, you weren't listening."

"Yeah, I guess so. Paula tells me that all the time. I hate a smart-ass."

Ron chuckled, knowing he had struck a nerve. Rather than let him suffer in silence, he broke a precedent and fixed himself a canning-jar-size martini and returned to his recliner. "I shouldn't do this," he remarked after the first swallow, "but as the old saying goes, misery loves company. Cheers!"

By the time the two men had finished their drinks, Neal's conscience was nagging at him to leave for home. With Ron's caution to keep a weather eye out for patrol cars, he bid him goodbye and headed for the coast highway. According to his watch, it was still too early to expect Paula to be home so he relaxed and enjoyed the scenery while his mind sifted through the ashes of his firestorm of activity over the past twenty-four hours.

Whether it was the pseudo-clarity that sometimes accompanies a few drinks, or the awakening of a dormant memory, he couldn't help being preoccupied with Dan's lady friend, Donna Sanders. Taking into account her first hand knowledge of where Dan's Back Bay hideaway was located, and the map she had had brief access to, the thought struck him that she might have played some not-so-obvious part in whatever happened to him, directly or indirectly. To satisfy his curiosity and eliminate her as a possible suspect, he drove directly to the Hilton Inn in order to check their registration records. Hopefully, the hotel might still have her home address and phone number on file.

When the hotel manager informed him that registration records were confidential and couldn't be accessed without an official warrant, he went directly to the patio lounge where he hoped Maggie Jyles would still be working. She was there and greeted him warmly. "Sorry I couldn't make your party," she apologized. "I had to work."

Ordering a drink and giving her a few highlights of the party, he motioned her to come closer and whispered, "Can you do me a favor?"

She smiled and replied without hesitation, "You can always ask, Mister T."

"I need some information about the woman who stayed here with Dan Hughes this past weekend," he explained. "I can't tell you why I need that information right now, but it's important that I learn if she gave a home address and phone number when she registered. Her name is Donna Sanders."

"No problem," she assured him. "I know how to access the guest registration files. Come by tomorrow afternoon about the same time and I'll give you whatever information I can find. Though I doubt your friend would have registered her by name. More than likely," she added with a flavor of sarcasm, "he probably checked in as Dan Hughes, and guest."

She was probably right, he thought, paying his tab and leaving, but it was still worth a try.

When he reached home the kitchen clock indicated that Paula would be arriving soon so he relaxed and prepared himself for whatever it was that she had emphasized would require his undivided attention. Under ordinary circumstances, that expectation would have been considered wishful thinking, but in this instance he vowed to listen attentively to whatever she had to say.

The ice had barely struck the bottom of his glass when the sound of her car gave notice that she had arrived. As a gesture of gentlemanly consideration he poured a glass of wine for her and waited. Given the exhausting aftermath of their previous day's partying and having had to work all day, he expected her to be somewhat less than energized when she greeted him. However, much to his surprise, her entrance was animated and eager for the libation he had waiting for her. As was her routine, she changed quickly into something more comfortable and came to join him in the living room where he sat watching television. Without the slightest hesitation, she reached for the clicker and pushed the mute button, explaining that she needed his undivided attention. True to his promise, he did the wise thing and listened.

"Your daughter, Karen, called me at my office today and invited me to have lunch with her. Seems her dad didn't returned the message she left for him earlier this morning, which brings up the question, where were you all day?"

He admitted he had fallen asleep, but rather than explain what had taken place the rest of the day, he made the excuse that he had become preoccupied with other matters and had planned to call her in the evening when he knew she would be home.

Paula accepted his explanation with a grain of salty skepticism, and continued with what she had originally intended to say in a manner that left him with the impression that he was in no way – at least for the time being – off the hook. "Karen has convinced Derek that the only way she can spare you the trauma of ever having to move again is to buy this place from Fahey and rent it to us. Which, I don't mind pointing out, is a far more generous expression of sibling affection than most people have a right to expect. I was dumbfounded!"

Even though he knew in his heart that any one of his three daughters would have done the same thing were it within their means, he felt a deep sense of personal pride in Karen's maturity and selfless generosity.

"She is her father's child, my dear. Guided by emotion, sometimes victimized by reality, but a survivor, none-the-less. I am truly blessed."

"Yes you are," she remarked. "I don't know what force continues to steer you out of harm's way, considering your tendency to poo-poo religion, but yes, you are blessed."

"Maybe so," he replied, with a touch of reverence, "but I doubt that being a churchgoer has influenced much of anything if you've read the newspaper lately. I damn sure wouldn't want to be the Pope."

Recognizing that she had gone somewhere she shouldn't have, she changed the subject. "Karen asked for Mr. Fahey's telephone number during our lunch today. She and Derek want to talk to him right away since he's given you first refusal. Derek says he can save a considerable amount of money if he can deal directly with Fahey and not a broker. Makes sense to me. What do you think?"

He agreed, wholeheartedly with the plan, relieved that Karen's timely intervention had saved him from having to explain his involvement in Dan Hughes' life because of his sudden disappearance. "By all means, " he replied. "Call her back right now and tell her we'll go along with whatever deal they can work out with Fahey. And please, emphasize how much we appreciate their generosity."

While Paula placed the call and talked at some length with Karen, he left the room and walked leisurely out to the bluff behind what he hoped would soon be a home he would never have to leave. There, in the rapidly fading light of another busy day, he forced himself to concentrate on what needed to be attended to the following day. Sending flowers to the Hughes's residence was a must. Calling Henry for an update on whatever news was available concerning Dan's whereabouts was another. Meeting with Maggie Styles, though he doubted her search would uncover much of anything, had to take place, if for no other reason than to eliminate Donna Sanders as a possible conspirator in Dan's disappearance.

He was about to return to the house when the dark silhouette of someone standing in shallow water on the beach caught his eye. Moments later the figure turned and walked back to the sand, disrobed and ran back into the water, unaware that anyone was watching. The scene mesmerized him, bringing on a broad smile as the naked figure revealed itself to be a woman. Amused, he murmured out loud, "Now that's my kind of woman."

When he returned to the kitchen he found Paula still talking on the telephone. The image of what he had just witnessed taking place on the beach slowly faded away, bringing in its place the reality of what he had to deal with the next day. Hoping that Paula's conversation with Karen had sidetracked her from pursuing any further discussion regarding his current activities, he refilled her wine glass, refreshed his own and walked out onto the patio deck. Moments later, remembering the happy, carefree days of his youth, he discarded his clothes, turned on the Jacuzzi and slipped into the soothing water, regretting that he couldn't take part in the spirited abandon taking place on the beach less than fifty yards away.

Paula in the meantime had concluded her conversation with Karen and looked around curiously to determine where he had gone. Illuminated mist rising from the Jacuzzi betrayed his whereabouts. With some question as to whether or not she should follow his lead, she pulled a deck chair close to where he sat naked and half submerged.

"Had a busy day, soldier?" she asked, poking fun at his ever optimistic expectations.

"As a matter of fact, no," he lied. "I'm just boiling away the physical and emotional residue of yesterday's overindulgence. Why don't you join me?"

She threw back her head and laughed, uncontrollably. "I don't know what you had in mind for dinner, sport, but I'm definitely not on the menu. I could use something to eat, though."

Dripping wet, he rose from the Jacuzzi and stood motionless for a few moments letting the balmy night air dry off his body. Paula, on the other hand, returned inside not in the least bit intimidated by his little-boy nakedness. Her insensitive departure only dramatized how physically and emotionally distant they had become recently. Granted, his past and current activity could hardly have been compared with the comparative tranquility of TV's, *The Andy Griffith Show,* but he had tried to be responsive to her problems, regardless of how trivial they may have seemed at times. Possibly, she might have suffered more upset from the recent threat of having to relocate than he realized. In any event, something that had physically bonded them throughout their relationship was gradually disintegrating and it disheartened him. He had only reached the halfway step on his way to their bedroom when her voice questioned him from the living room. "By the way, what did Jennifer Newman have to say?"

He froze. Reality had once again reared its ugly head as his mind struggled to respond. Realizing that sooner or later the question would have to be answered, he simply replied, "I'll be down in a minute."

The short time it took to put on something casual was just enough for him to realize that he could no longer avoid telling her about the situation in which he was about to become unavoidably involved. If whatever was dying in their relationship was ever to come alive again, it had to begin with the truth, he concluded. Telling her the truth was the least he could do to make up for keeping it from her. Entering the living room, he began to speak before she had a chance to distract him with something unrelated. "The reason Jennifer called was to inform me that Dan Hughes has apparently disappeared. Combined with newly uncovered information regarding Billy's death, his disappearance has now prompted a Federal Investigation. Because he came all the way out here to see me, the DEA is curious about what he said and did during his stay."

"When do they want to talk with you?"

"I don't know," he replied. "Possibly within a day or two, or maybe sooner."

"Have you any information for them?" she persisted.

His thoughts went immediately to Jessica Sterling's parting comment earlier that afternoon and dodged the question by answering, "I won't know until they contact me, now will I?"

Frustrated with his glib and uncanny ability to avoid giving a straight answer when he was obviously trying to hide something, she surprised him by not pursuing the matter any further, other than one final comment: "I'll say one thing for you, Neal. There's never a dull moment when you're around." Walking to the kitchen to refill her glass, she sighed and asked, "Now, can we eat?"

Just then, the telephone rang. He considered letting the answering machine handle it, but reconsidered for fear that whomever was calling might leave a message he didn't want her to hear. Setting his TV tray aside, he returned to the kitchen and picked up the receiver hoping it was a telemarketer he could easily dismiss. After a short period of intense listening, he reached for his pen and began writing, repeating everything verbally as he did so. The only words she heard after the conversation ended was, "Okay, Dusty. I'll be there tomorrow at one o'clock."

"What was that all about?" she asked when he returned and slumped heavily into his chair. "You look like you've just talked to a ghost."

"A ghost I'd welcome," he replied, solemnly. "That was my DEA friend, Dusty Lewis. He and his wife, Katie, were at our party yesterday. Remember?"

Paula thought for a moment. "Vaguely," she said, still searching to recollect. "Isn't he the guy who knew Jessica Sterling from somewhere?"

"Exactly! This is the very reason Jennifer called yesterday, to make me aware that the DEA might want to talk to me. Well, damn it, she was right. Agent Lewis asked me to come to his office tomorrow to discuss Dan's visit."

"What the hell is there to discuss, other than his poor choice in women," she remarked sarcastically. "You could have told him that over the phone. Why a special trip downtown?" Pondering the situation for a moment, she looked at him suspiciously and asked, "Am I missing something here?"

Again, Neal sidestepped an informative answer by replying, "Well, dear, I guess we'll just have to wait until tomorrow to find out? I have no idea what he wants."

With his cold dinner sitting nearby, and his interest in heating it up destroyed by the unexpected call, he opted to spend whatever was left of the evening wallowing in the bottled euphoria that sat on his bar only a few feet away.

Paula, on the other hand, recognizing the uselessness of trying to converse with him when he was so sullenly quiet and preoccupied, ate her dinner and bid him goodnight, perfectly content to read a book, or work a crossword puzzle until her eyes grew weary and closed.

Chapter 15

Prelude To Discovery

Because she had been asked to provide copies of confidential documents prior to a scheduled meeting the next morning, Paula had reset her clock to alarm one hour earlier than usual. Neal, she suspected, would not be up to his usual routine, so she wasted little time in getting dressed and leaving before he began to stir. It was easier, she decided, to buy a Starbuck's black coffee and a cream cheese bagel along the way than run the risk of falling victim to her companion's harmless groping.

Having purposely pretended to be asleep in order to camouflage his own personal agenda, Neal leaped out of bed at the sound of the garage door closing and put on a fresh pot of coffee while he showered and dressed for his day of unforeseeable consequences.

With nothing but the surf breaking on the beach to distract him, he began his day as he had hurriedly planned it. After ordering flowers for Polly Hughes's memorial service, he placed a call to the Hughes residence hoping that someone might have received some positive news of Dan's whereabouts. Several rings later a recorded message began that made him question why no one was home, especially under the circumstances. Following the last of several beeps, he began his message. He had only spoken a few words when Henry's only daughter, Mary Ellen, came on line and greeted him rather despondently, "Hi, Mr. T. It's good to hear your voice again."

He smiled at the mind's-eye image of her child-like face as he listened to the mature voice of the woman he had known as a child. "Hello, Mary Ellen. Terribly sorry to hear about your mother," he said compassionately. "Is your father there?"

"Sure is. Sorry about the message machine. Daddy told us not to answer unless it was a member of the family, but I'm sure he'll want to talk with you. Hold on."

Following a brief pause, Henry's tired voice spoke across the thousands of miles that separated them. "I'm glad you called, Neal, although I'm afraid we have no news regarding Dan's disappearance. At first, I wasn't worried, mostly because he's done things like this in the past. But when a DEA Agent showed up here recently, I realized the situation was far more serious than I had suspected. I'm sure they'll want to question you too."

The temptation to say something that would raise his hopes almost prompted him to reveal what Dan had confided in him before he left San Diego, but he thought better of it and replied, "The DEA has already contacted me. I have an appointment this afternoon to meet with one of their agents who just happens to be a friend of mine. I'll know more after I talk with him, so just sit tight. With all that's going on in your life right now, I'll wait till I have something meaningful to tell you before I call. I'm so sorry for your loss. Polly was a wonderful lady."

The silence that followed made it obvious that Henry was struggling to maintain his composure. In an attempt to reassure him that all was not lost, he let out a little laugh and said, "Your son is probably the craziest person I've ever met, but he's no fool. He's alive, somewhere. I'm pretty sure of that. I'll find him."

The sound of his own uninhibited boldness rattled around in his brain like a persistent echo that asked the question, *now just how do you propose to do that?* "I think someone close to Dan has betrayed him," he theorized. "When we find out who that person is, we'll find Dan."

"I can't imagine who that could be," Henry replied, "but I wish you every luck in finding out. I'll be waiting to hear from you. Soon, I hope,"

Unable to concentrate on much of anything following his unrewarding call, he turned to thoughts of little consequence. The reality of Dan's disappearance, however, persisted like an emotional hangover from a bad dream. Frustrated and angry for having allowed himself to become a victim of his own stupidity, he sought solace in the warm sun that beckoned him from the beach below where worry and seriousness to most people the world over was non-existent.

Looking up and down the almost deserted beach, a thought came to him that he hadn't walked here by himself for quite some time so he headed north for no other reason than to kill time until his meeting with Dusty Lewis.

A mild Santa Ana condition had flattened the offshore water to the extent that surfing by any stretch of the imagination was uninviting. It was, however, appealing to those who found it particularly pleasing to feel the wet sand beneath their feet and the occasional lapping of water around one's ankles. How fortunate I am, he thought, May it ever be so.

Reaching the lifeguard stand that he frequently used as a turning around point, he stopped for a moment to rest and wipe the perspiration from his forehead, unaware that a woman was approaching. She asked in surprise, "Is that you, Mr. Thomas?"

Turning abruptly, he laughed when he recognized her. "Damn it, Becky Parker, that's the second time you've snuck up on me. What are you doing here?"

"I might ask you the same question," she replied. "You seem to be the one who has strayed away from home."

"Yeah, I guess so," he admitted. "I thought a long walk on the beach would do me some good. I've had a lot on my mind lately. I'm sure you can appreciate the need to be alone, occasionally."

"Indeed I can," she admitted. "The part that hurts is not being able to share your thoughts with anyone. How could they possibly understand?"

"They can't, my dear. But, sometimes talking does a body good. Do you have something you want to get off your chest?"

"No more than you do," she replied, somewhat indifferently. "Maybe someday."

"Fair enough," he conceded, glancing at his watch. "I better get back home. I have an appointment at one o'clock. Until we meet again?"

She shook his hand firmly and watched him turn to leave before remarking, "I don't know where I'll be for the next week or two, but I have your number. I'll give you a call when I return. Maybe we can do lunch or something."

Waving his willingness to participate, he turned and walked away, quickening his pace a little to allow for a quick change of clothes. It was noon when he finished, just enough time to grab a bite to eat.

As he had expected, the DEA office was much like any number of government offices he had seen on television. A receptionist greeted him cordially and led him to a waiting area where coffee and soft drinks were available. Having chosen to sip hot coffee, he made himself comfortable with a magazine and waited. Some minutes later the receptionist approached and invited him to follow her to Agent Lewis' office.

Dusty was seated at his desk with a phone in his hand when they entered. He motioned for Neal to sit in the seat across the desk from him, smiling at times, scowling in between. What was being talked about made little sense, but he waited patiently and looked around the office to assess its furnishings.

Minutes later he hung up the phone and apologized for keeping Neal waiting. He was smiling now and greeted him warmly, remarking, "I'll give you credit for one thing, my friend, you do throw one hell of a party." Shuffling a few papers around on his desk, he said more seriously, "Now, down to business. Our Washington office has directed me to ask you some questions on the subject of your relationship with a man by the name of Dan Hughes, who I believe is a friend of yours, right?"

"Yes," he replied, with Jessica Sterling's caution still fresh in his mind.

Dusty looked at him intently for a moment with his hands clasped together in his lap before continuing. "Relax, Neal," he advised him in a friendly manner, "you're not here as a suspect."

There was a file lying on the desk in front of him that bore the stamp, *Confidential.* He paused briefly to review its contents, and then continued. "From the information we've been able to gather so far in our investigation into the drug-related activities of Mr. Hughes, it would appear that he is still actively involved. Were you aware of that?

"Yes, but only recently."

"Who informed you?"

"My daughter, Karen, brought the matter up several days ago when I told her Dan was coming to visit. She did not mention anything about him being seriously involved in distributing the stuff, though."

"Do you know why he came to California?"

"All I know is, he closed a real estate deal for his father recently and had made enough money to justify a much needed vacation. Having never been here before, he chose California because I had invited him to the same party you and Katie attended when I was back in Virginia a little while ago. He said he'd be here. Simple as that."

"Not quite," Dusty remarked. "There's more to his story than you may or may not be aware of. So, I'm going to quit playing games with you and explain just what's going down here."

Pausing briefly to close the confidential file he had been referring to while questioning Neal, he continued: "Whether you know it or not, you may have inadvertently gotten yourself involved in a situation that could put you in harm's way, and possibly others, so listen closely to what I have to say."

If there was any previous notion in Neal's mind that his seemingly coincidental involvement in Dan Hughes' disappearance was just simply going to go away, the look in Dusty's eyes told him he was seriously mistaken. Nervously attentive, he replied, "I'm listening."

"We now know that the death of your old buddy, Billy Newman, was no accident. We also learned from a personal interview with his former wife, Jennifer, that she suspected Dan, or people he knew, of being responsible for Billy's fatal accident. She also told us that Billy had been subpoenaed to testify before a Grand Jury on another drug-related incident, which she said you couldn't have known anything about. In your defense, she insisted that you couldn't have been involved in any of Dan's affairs simply because you hadn't seen him in years. She did mention, however, that while you were here to attend Billy's wake, you, Dan, and a female companion by the name of Donna Sanders spent all the next day together on Dan's boat. Is that correct?"

Neal shifted uneasily in his chair and replied. "Yes. But if you already know all of this, why are you asking me?"

"Several reasons," he replied, rising from his chair and stretching. "But first, let's take a coffee break, then we can continue."

The break came as welcome relief from what Neal suspected was going to be an all day question and answer session. Despite the fact that Jennifer had blessed him with some degree of absolution, he anticipated Dusty was using the coffee break as a softening ploy prior to hitting him with a full frontal assault. So far, though, Jessica Sterling's counsel was well advised and working.

Back in his office Dusty took the lead aggressively. "After looking at all the facts we have to conclude that what you saw and heard during that Sunday cruise with Dan, and his sudden decision to go to California, are in some way connected. So, let's concentrate on the cruise first. Where did he take you, and what did you see and hear that could be construed as out of the ordinary?"

Mulling the question over for a moment, being very much aware that his answer could open a floodgate of further questioning, he put the ball back in Dusty's court by countering with a question of his own. "Has anyone talked to Donna Sanders yet? Since you know she was with us all that day, and accompanied Dan when he came out here to visit me, it seems to me she's the one you should be questioning."

"I agree," he replied, conceding the point. "The problem is, our people in DC can't locate her. She's not registered with the DMV or the Social Security Office. Even if she did have a driver's license, or a card, it's probably a fake. Dan is probably the only person who knows anything about her, so until we find him, or her, you're it."

That he was now the key source of information in the DEA's investigation made it all the more important that he fulfill his promise to Dan and lead them to the evidence that lay uselessly hidden in his hideaway; a place that, without the map Dan had given him, the DEA would never be able to locate. With renewed confidence, and a sense of power he hadn't felt since his football days as a quarterback, he relaxed and called the game's first play: "You'd better get this on tape."

Dusty looked over at him, smiling in a way that conveyed a message Neal should have already figured out on his own. "It's been on since you arrived."

Somewhat humbled by his own naivete, he continued: "Dan Hughes came to California because he was told by an informant within the Tidewater Drug Cartel that he was suspected of stealing drugs from shipments he was being paid to deliver. Dan denied having stolen anything, but thought he was being set up because he wanted out of the cartel. After all, he had already established himself as the highest paid salesman in his father's real estate business. He didn't need the money any more, or the hassle."

"Was he dumb enough to think he could just pick up and walk away from that kind of operation whenever he felt like it?" Dusty asked in astonishment. "Talk about stupid!"

"With the evidence he had gathered over the years entrusted to someone they didn't know, yes he did, crazy as it may seem."

"What evidence?" Dusty asked with renewed interest.

Though the discovery of evidence could plunge Neal deeper into a situation that was escalating by the hour, he answered anyway, with one reservation: "If I tell you where it is, will you promise me you'll do what you can for Dan, if and when we find him. Certainly you owe him that much for information that can help you bust one of the biggest drug operations on the East Coast."

"You know I can't make any deals or promise anything," he replied. "Have you considered how much trouble you can get yourself into by withholding evidence? Now, tell me what you know before I lose my patience."

Recognizing the dead seriousness that had suddenly taken over Dusty's demeanor, he continued, despite the cautions Jessica Sterling had given him. "Dan has a hideaway on Back Bay that no one but myself and Donna Sanders knows anything about. He took me there the day after Billy Newman's wake and told me he had inherited the place from an old fisherman by the name of Shark Hadley whom Dan had befriended many years ago. While we were there, he showed me a tool box hidden away in a closet that contained detailed records of his drug shipments, photographs and a personal diary; enough information to put a lot of people away for a long, long time.

"How long were you going to keep this information a secret?" he asked, somewhat annoyed. "You could be considered a co-conspirator, you know."

"Now, hold on, old chum. At least give me a chance to explain."

"I'm still listening."

Despite Jessica's veteran council, he knew it was time to reveal all, lest he become the innocent victim of a system for which he had little, if any, respect. "On several occasions during my brief encounter with Dan, he expressed a concern that others in the drug cartel might be trying to get rid of him for a number of reasons. The primary one being that he was stealing from them. Trumped up or not, they wanted him dead. Because I was the only person he felt he could trust, he gave me a map that showed the exact location of the hideaway Shark Hadley had willed him. He further asked me to promise that I would lead the authorities to the evidence he had stashed there if anything should happen to him."

"When were you going to do that?" he asked, still not convinced Neal was telling all there was to tell.

"Right after I gathered all the information I could," he replied with some agitation. "Hell, I only just found out myself that he was missing! I too have a life, you know."

"I know," Dusty sighed, finally relenting. "What other information is there?"

Neal's half-empty cup of coffee was now cold and distasteful, so he asked if he could take a break and pick up something from the street vendor he had seen on the way in. Dusty agreed, and volunteered to go with him, admitting that he too was in need of a little nourishment. When they returned, Dusty went straight to his last question. "Now, tell me about this other information you've come up with?"

"Dan stayed at the Hilton Inn near where I live while he was here. There's a waitress there by the name of Maggie Jyles who has agreed to go into the hotel's computer files and get me a printout of Dan's registration. Hopefully, it may have included a home address and phone number for Donna Sanders, the woman he brought with him. If there's anyone who knows where Dan is, I believe it's her."

"You know, we've already discussed her lack of registered identity. When will you have this new information," he asked, eager to explore Neal's theory.

"I'm to check with her later this afternoon. I'll know then if we have anything we don't have now and will call you sometime tomorrow, probably in the early afternoon. Okay?"

"Fine," Dusty replied. "I'll be waiting for your call."

The two men shook hands and were about to part when Dusty held Neal back for a moment and asked, "If push comes to shove, are you available to assist our agents back East if Dan can't be located and is presumed dead?"

"Yes," replied, hesitantly, "but I hope it doesn't come to that."

Lingering doubts as to whether or not Maggie would be able to come up with anything more than they already knew regarding Donna Sanders, bothered him all the way to Ron Barns' house. Accepting that whatever lay ahead was now beyond his control, he went in to have a quick drink and chat a bit, aware that his time was limited.

"Have you lost track of what day it is again, Mister T?" he asked, with a note of friendly sarcasm. "Fix yourself a drink and we'll shoot a game or two of pool."

"Sorry, old buddy, I can't." he replied, apologetically. "I'm due at the Hilton Inn in forty-five minutes, but I sure need a drink before I get there."

"How so, more company?"

"No. I have some information waiting for me there. I just hope it's what I'm looking for. Otherwise, I may have to go back East again. And, believe me, that's the last place on earth I want to go right now."

Ron continued to sit quietly studying the screen on his laptop computer until Neal seated himself at the bar, and then made an unexpected remark that caught him off guard. "I know it's none of my business, but quite honestly, Neal, you've changed. Did anything happen to you while you were back East? Something you'd like to share with an old friend?"

"It's that obvious? Paula asked me the same thing," he grunted in reply, aware that his best friend's observations were well founded and demanded some kind of an explanation. Ignoring the fact that he could be severely criticized by the DEA for revealing confidential information, he repeated the crux of what had been said in Dusty Lewis' office only an hour ago, confident that Ron would never let it go any further than the distance between them.

While he talked, Ron smiled and shook his head, unable to comprehend the jeopardy in which some people were willing to place themselves to honor a promise. Thus, it was with some degree of exasperation that he commented on Neal's situation. "You certainly have a knack for getting yourself involved in the craziest situations. What is it with you, anyway? Do you have a death wish?"

"Don't ask. You'd think with an Ivy League education I'd know better. Maybe that's the problem." Half way out the door he turned and remarked, jokingly, " Must be something in the water!"

Thirty minutes later, and a good deal more relaxed than he had been all day, he parked his car at the Hilton Inn and headed straight for the lounge. Maggie recognized him immediately and brought a drink to his table. "Hi there, Mr. T," she greeted him, enthusiastically. "I have something for you."

Her smiling face and an outstretched hand presented him with a copy of Dan's official registration form. To his disappointment, there was no reference to Donna Sanders, by name. However, as Maggie pointed out, a double asterisk by the room number indicated that something had been left behind in the room that she thought might prove helpful. The item, as a matter of hotel policy, was being kept under lock and key for thirty days until the owner claimed it. If not claimed, it would be disposed of or given away. Further, it could not be released to anyone without proper identification. She was, however, permitted to note its description, and any identifying markings that were visible.

"Well, what was it," he asked, looking wide-eyed and excited.

Using the pencil she held in her hand, she slipped it under the registration form and flipped it over. Her notations read: *Car keys – if lost, mail to M. Ramirez – c/o The Surf Club, Va. Beach, VA.*

Impulsively, he reached up, cupped her face in his hands and kissed her full on the lips. "Maggie," he whispered, "what cloud did you fall from?"

"Nine, I hope," she giggled, puckering her lips for another. "Can't fly on one wing."

Without hesitation he pressed his lips softly on hers as he might have with any of his three daughters and said, "Thanks, baby, I owe you one."

While he sat parked in his driveway a short time later, he looked back at where his day had taken him and wondered how he would explain his newly developed situation to Paula. The possibility that he might be asked to help in the investigation, and how it might affect his relationship with her, were foremost on his mind. Certainly, he expected, it would not sit well, regardless of how valuable he might have become to the DEA. Resigned to take whatever materialized in stride, and with as much humor as the situation allowed, he entered the house and waited for her return.

After turning on the television to catch up on the news, he noticed the red light on the answering machine blinking once again. There were two messages. The first was from Paula, informing him that she would be late getting home again and advised him to eat dinner without her.

The second was from Dusty Lewis, asking that he call him at home that evening, regardless of the hour, so he did just that. As he suspected he would, Dusty answered within seconds. "Glad you called back early," he remarked. "Was your waitress friend able to come up with any information on the person we discussed earlier this afternoon? It's important that I know right away."

He understood Dusty's reluctance to mention Donna Sanders by name, so he simply answered, "Yes."

"Good," he remarked, unemotionally. "My office tomorrow? Same time?"

"Yes."

Without Paula there to keep him company, and ask questions she already knew the answers to, time passed slowly for him so he wrote and answered e-mail until it was time to prepare something to eat. One incoming letter in particular captured his curiosity. It was from *BParker@aol.com.* It read:

Hi Neal,
Just a quick note to say thanks again for inviting me to your party, and to remind you that I will be out of town for a while. Stay safe. I will contact you when I return.
Becky (on the beach)

He was tempted to reply but thought better of it, given the probability that she had already left town, so he hit the *Delete* command and shut down the computer. Remembering the coincidental circumstances under which they had met in the first place, he left his studio puzzled by the question he had been asking himself ever since they first met: *who is Becky Parker?* Faced with the frustration of having no other clue than her skill as an artist, he chased the question from his mind and listened to the evening news, while preparing a sandwich he intended to have for dinner. Both were interrupted, however, when the phone rang. It was Jennifer Newman. "Has the DEA contacted you yet?" she asked, obviously irritated. "They sure have been pestering the hell out of me, lately!"

Some people never change, he thought, remembering the good old days when he and Billy were in more trouble with their wives than they were out of it. "Yes," he replied. "As a matter of fact, I have to meet with them again tomorrow. Why? Is anything wrong?"

There was a slight pause before she responded, which he suspected was to take a swallow of whatever she was drinking. He knew the sound of ice rattling around in a glass and the sound of her voice well enough to recognize that she was. "No, not really," she admitted. "I just thought you ought to know what you're getting yourself into before they hand you a bunch of crap about what they think they know. The truth is, their entire investigation hinges on what you know. They haven't got a clue, so keep that in mind when you're talking to them."

That she thought he hadn't already come to that conclusion tickled him. Rather than dampen her well-intended advice, he replied, half seriously, "Better change the sheets and check your supply of vodka, dear heart. I have a funny feeling you're going to have a house guest real soon."

"I'm prepared for that, "she replied with a giddy chuckle. "You know where the key is."

He laughed, remembering her offer of hospitality the evening of Billy's wake. "Keep a light on in the window, love, I'll be in touch."

Following her unexpected call, he resumed preparing his sandwich, poured a glass of milk and settled down in front of the television, only to be interrupted again by another phone call. This time it was his daughter, Karen, informing him that she and Derek had reached a selling price agreement with Mr. Fahey. "This means you and Paula will never have to move again," she continued, excitedly. "Isn't that great?"

For the first time in his sometimes hectic and emotionally troubled life, the threat of never having to suffer the turmoil and physical demands of relocating were a heartache he would never have to endure again. "Yes, it certainly is, sweet girl," he replied, almost in tears. "Words cannot adequately express how grateful I am for what you and Derek have given us. You've certainly made our day. Paula will be thrilled to death."

Outside, the evening was warm and balmy. What better place to celebrate the event than enjoying his favorite of all past times. Humming along with the outdoor speakers that quietly filled the air with soft jazz, he shed his clothes and slipped into the Jacuzzi, happy for the first time in quite a while.

Though the threat of having to change his residence had been forever removed, the frustration of not knowing what was going to result from his meeting with Dusty Lewis the next day was not. He could only hope that Paula would recognize the seriousness of the situation and support whatever the DEA might ask him to do in order to remedy a situation that could only get worse if not fixed as soon as possible. For whatever reason – possibly the complexity of it all – he was reminded of a time in his working career when he had proposed a solution to a serious problem that the engineering department where he worked was having a difficult time trying to solve:

****

After construction of the world's first nuclear-powered aircraft carrier had been completed and commissioned into service, it was discovered that one of the reactor plant steam generators was leaking small amounts of primary coolant into the secondary plant steam generating system. A decision was made by the Navy to replace those specific generators when the carrier returned to port for its first refueling availability. Because the generators in question were supposed to be designed to operate for the ship's lifetime, no consideration had ever been given to removal of the multi-ton behemoths in case they had to be replaced. Obviously concerned, the Navy directed the contractor to develop such a procedure. Its design fell heir to the Atomic Power Division of the contractor's organization, where many hours of serious investigation were spent developing proposals to remove the huge components, none of which proved to be practical, given the unit's size and weight. That is, until a young designer by the name of Neal Thomas became intrigued with the problem. Confident that his creative imagination, and knowledge of the overall propulsion plant system, could come up with an innovative removal procedure, he took the problem home to solve it on his own time.

For several weeks he worked tirelessly into the wee hours of the morning to develop a series of sketches that simulated the removal sequence, and defined the equipment that would be required. Some of that equipment already existed, but the major pieces he innovated himself. When finally convinced that his preliminary procedure was sound and doable, he entered his boss' office one morning and presented him with the proposal, along with its supporting sketches. It didn't take his boss very long to recognize its feasibility and immediately presented it to the Division Manager. He, in turn, complimented the concept and authorized the young designer to develop a scaled drawing that would illustrate the step-by-step procedure to the Navy. They authorized it almost immediately.

Several years later, when the carrier returned for her refueling availability, Neal stood on the flight deck and watched with pride as the handling procedures he had developed removed the ailing generator carefully from the reactor compartment, and laid it down on a shipping skid as gently as if it were a baby.

Talking about the event with friends and colleagues later on in his career was always exciting to him. When asked how it felt to see his imagination develop into something real, he would joke, "I guess it could be compared with a woman having her first baby!"

****

It was dark now, except for the glow of light that illuminated the water in which he soaked. His drink had long since bottomed out, and the callings from his stomach were craving satisfaction. Dripping wet, he stepped up onto the patio deck where the cool night air dried him in minutes and sent him upstairs for something casual to wear. It was from their bedroom that he saw the lights of Paula's car beam their way up the driveway and shut down. Eagerly, he hurried back downstairs to help her, hoping that the long day had still left her sense of humor in tact. "I've got some good news, and some bad news," he joked, "so get comfortable and I'll tell you all about it."

By the time the "get comfortable" ritual was finished, he had a tall, iced-down glass of wine waiting for her. The chatter that usually took place between them during the process, however, was missing. After kissing him on the cheek, she sank onto the living room couch and asked, "What's the good news?"

Though her somewhat less than enthusiastic response had stolen some of the wind from his sails, he refused to be deprived of the elation his daughter's phone call had given him. "Maybe hearing the news that Karen and Derek have bought this place from old man Fahey will help cheer up your day," he replied. "It sure made mine!"

"I know, "Paula sighed, smiling to feign an interest. "She called me this afternoon too. It is wonderful news."

Following two continuous swallows of wine that drained her glass, she asked, without emotion, "Can we save the bad news until morning? I'm exhausted."

"Sure," he replied, though disappointed with her lack of enthusiasm, "It isn't all that bad, anyway. Go on to bed."

The goodnight kiss she left him with was more an act of procedure than affection, and left him alone and a little despondent. Watching her trudge wearily up the stairs he thought, *Isn't it ironic how we humans struggle to achieve something that eventually robs us of the energy and passion it takes to enjoy life, realizing too late – unfortunately for some – that they were better off without it.*

Chapter 16

Gone Fishing

When Paula woke up the next morning Neal was not beside her. The familiar sound of snoring from the guest room, however, reassured her that he was safe and had probably opted to take advantage of the guest room rather than run the risk of waking her.

She had no way of knowing when he finally decided to go to bed, but suspected his daughter's good news had given him all the incentive he needed to celebrate the event. Had she to do it all over again, joining him would have been the preferable way to go, she thought, but the prospect of what the day held in store justified the decision not to.

As quietly as possible she went about her usual early morning routine, thinking as she dressed how romantic and physically exciting mornings had been when she and Neal first began living together. A far cry from what was now developing into complicated lives that appeared to be drifting further and further apart every day. Possibly, she hoped, Karen and Derek may have unwittingly provided them with a basis for revitalizing their relationship by giving them the domestic security they so richly deserved. Or, had they already passed that infamous point of no return?

Not until she tiptoed past the guest room door and peeked in did she become aware that he wasn't there either. The scent of freshly brewed coffee, however, betrayed his whereabouts, bringing a smile of relief to her face as she made her way downstairs and entered the kitchen. "Sorry if I woke you," she apologized. "What time did you finally go to bed?"

"I have no idea," he yawned. "David Letterman was interviewing some celebrity when I finally woke up. My neck hurt, I do remember that."

Amused, she poured a cup and began thumbing through the newspaper while he stood silently by the window looking dreamily out over the ocean. "Sorry I wasn't much company last night," she finally admitted. "And, I'm as happy as you are about Karen and Derek buying this place, and have already expressed my thanks to her, personally."

Following a brief moment of awkward silence she asked, "Do you want to tell me the bad news now, or wait until this evening?"

It was now his turn to test the water. "Yesterday's visit with my friend, Dusty Lewis, resulted in him asking me if I would be willing to assist in the investigation of Dan Hughes' disappearance."

"So, what did you tell him?" she asked, apparently undisturbed by the consequences of what she had already concluded was going to be a positive reply.

Surprised by her almost bland acceptance of what his so-called bad news was going to be, he continued. "Well, Jennifer Newman called me yesterday to inform me that the DEA is relying heavily on my cooperation to tell them about what I saw and heard when Dan took me out on his boat that Sunday, as well as what he said and did out here. Hell, how can I not cooperate?"

Without commenting right away, she poured another cup and returned to the table, then remarked, quite matter-of-factly, "Based on what you just told me, I guess that means you're going to take another trip back there. If that's what it takes to find out what happened to your friend, do what you have to do. Don't worry, I can look out for myself."

Hearing her accept the situation so understandingly made it clear to him that she was not going to get upset about the matter, and appeared to be almost intrigued by the whole scenario. Could it be that she was a far more understanding person than he had given her credit for, he asked himself. Or, was there something on her mind that took precedence over the importance he had placed on his own predicament. "I have a meeting with Dusty Lewis today to review some newly received information," he explained. "Hopefully, that information will eliminate the necessity of me having to fly back there again. Honestly, I really don't want to do that."

Moments later, as they walked together to her car, she patted him on his backside and said, "See you tonight, Curly. Maybe you'll get lucky!"

After she disappeared down the road he returned to the house and gave serious thought to the possibility that the DEA might insist on his presence in Washington to help them plan whatever covert operation was necessary to recover the evidence from Dan's Back Bay retreat. Based on that possibility becoming a reality, he went to his studio to retrieve the map. After studying it for a moment to implant the coordinate locations Dan had circled, he placed it in the false-bottom compartment of his briefcase along with the information Maggie Jyles had given him. Setting it conveniently by the front door, he returned to the kitchen and began preparing breakfast when the phone rang. Somewhat irritated by the interruption, he answered, wondering, who would be calling him at that hour?

Dusty Lewis' voice provided the answer. "Can you be in my office at ten o'clock this morning," he asked. "The Washington office has suddenly become very much interested in the evidence I told them you have. If you can bring it here at that time, I can review the information and report back to them before their quitting time. Is that possible?"

"Do I have a choice?" he asked, knowing full well that he didn't, but determined to express his annoyance with the imposition.

"Look, it's very important that this information get to Washington as soon as possible so it can be used in support of the investigation that's going on. They're counting on you, Neal."

"They'd better be," he remarked. "I'm all they've got. And yes, I'll be in your office at ten o'clock."

"Good man, I knew you wouldn't let me down."

With less than an hour before he had to be on the freeway, he finished his breakfast and dressed for the meeting, already anticipating that it would not be to his liking. As the southbound miles to San Diego slowly registered on his odometer, he reflected on Paula's earlier words: *"Do what you have to do."*

A short time later the familiar building where Dusty's office was located came into view. Briefcase in hand, he left the parking area mulling over in his mind all the possibilities that might result from this. The fact that Dusty had called him that morning to move up the original time seemed to imply a sense of urgency. Possibly, his superiors were applying pressure on him to ascertain whether or not the information he had was of sufficient importance to initiate a plan of action. That action, he feared, would more than likely include him now. Paula was right… again.

In contrast to his previous day's visit, the atmosphere in Dusty's office seemed to be bustling with activity. The receptionist, he observed right away, seemed to be friendlier and more accommodating, almost as if she had been prompted to appear that way. Smiling pleasantly, she led him to Dusty's private office, while the eyes of several other individuals followed him with curious interest.

Inside, the two men sat opposite one another with hot coffee already in place. Following a friendly greeting, Dusty sat comfortably back in his chair and opened the conversation. "First, I want to thank you for coming here earlier than we had originally planned. This matter of Dan

Hughes' disappearance has come to the attention of the DEA hierarchy in Washington. They have received word from an undisclosed source that Dan is seriously suspected of having been involved with drug distribution in and around the Tidewater Area. Because you may be the last person to have communicated with him, I have been asked to determine if the information you said you have is vital to our investigation. If it is, I am authorized to arrange for your return to Washington. There, a special task force of highly trained operatives will be waiting for your guidance in helping to locate Dan for questioning."

In less than a heart beat Neal realized that he had just crossed over the line into a total and irreversible commitment. Accepting his fate, he opened his briefcase and withdrew the map and the hotel reservation form that lay hidden within. Placing them on the desk in front of Dusty, he remarked, "These two pieces of paper don't look like much, but you'll have one hell of a time finding Dan Hughes without them."

Dusty fingered the two items curiously and then opened the map. "I'm guessing this circled area is where Dan's hideaway is located. Right?"

"That's it," he replied, "but the place is a hell of a lot harder to find than you'd think, from just looking at the map."

"How so?"

With as much detail as he could recall, Neal explained how Dan was able to locate the hidden inlet once he had reached the circled coordinates, emphasizing how important it was to locate the white Styrofoam marker that would appear and disappear with the tide.

Dusty was duly impressed with the ingenuity of its creator and surprised to learn that the idea may have been the brainchild of Dan's benefactor, old Shark Hadley himself. "I'd have a hard time swallowing this story," he commented, "if I didn't know you had actually gone there yourself."

Putting the map aside, he turned his attention to the Hilton Inn registration form. After reading the notations Maggie Jyles had made on the reverse side, he asked, "What do these car keys have to do with anything?"

"Plenty," he replied, leaning forward in his chair. "They link Donna Sanders to Miguel Ramirez. According to what Dan confided in me, Ramirez is a major player in the drug cartel. I met him briefly on Dan's boat the night of Billy Newman's wake. Donna Sanders is the woman who was with us the next day when Dan took me out to show me his hideaway. She's the same woman Dan brought with him when he came out here to visit me. I'm convinced she knows where he is. The fact that she's driving around in a car that belongs to Ramirez tells me she's someone you really need to find and talk to, difficult as that may be now."

Without saying another word, Dusty hit a button on his interoffice phone and told his secretary to call Washington and get Director Raymond Bronson on the line. Apologizing for having to ask him to leave while he talked with Bronson alone, he suggested that Neal freshen his coffee in the outer office and relax until he called him back. He obeyed, grateful for a respite from the tension that was gradually building.

Except for the receptionist who had originally greeted him, everyone else in the outer office seemed preoccupied. For this reason, he took Dusty at his word. After freshening his coffee he relaxed in a chair near the woman whose identification tag bore the name, Ginger Spyce.

"I guess you get a lot of ribbing about your name," he commented, attempting to open a conversation.

"Yeah," she replied, turning in her chair to face him. "I don't know what my parents were thinking, or drinking, when they pulled that one out of the hat. I've gotten used to it, though. Actually, it gives me some identity."

He tried not to laugh but couldn't hide his amusement. Pardoning himself, he remarked, "From where I'm sitting you appear to have plenty of that."

Laughter and friendly conversation followed for several minutes until Dusty's personal secretary approached to inform him that Agent Lewis wished to see him in his office, so he excused himself and left.

Dusty wasted little time in making him aware that Director Bronson wanted him in Washington as soon as possible. Looking at Neal with empathy written all over his face, he said, "I don't think I have to explain to you what this means, Neal. We could put you on a redeye flight tonight, but I know you have matters to put in order before you leave. How about a non-stop flight out of here around noon tomorrow? Can you live with that?"

"That's as good a time as any," he replied, accepting the fact that his destiny had already been charted. The journey there, he was forced to accept, would follow the direction the DEA wanted, regardless of whatever reasoning he could present to the contrary. However, and for no other reason than to hear himself express a minor objection, he looked across the desk at Dusty's furrowed brow and asked, "Isn't anyone going to ask me if I want to do this?"

Dusty's eyes widened in surprise. Hoping not to offend, he replied in as politically correct a way as he could, given the delicate nature of the task in which Neal was being asked to participate. "It is no longer a matter of whether or not you have an option. The United States Government is asking for your help in exposing a drug operation that is responsible for the deaths and addiction of untold numbers of Americans, including children of all ages. What we are asking of you is no less important than what you were asked to do as a soldier in the Army, serve your country."

He stopped talking for a moment to let his words eat away at Neal's inherent sense of National pride and responsibility, observing that they were already having a visible effect on him. "Besides," he added, "wouldn't it make Paula and all of your family and friends proud to know you were instrumental in busting up a major drug operation and helped us solve the mystery of Dan Hughes' disappearance? Think of what you'd be doing for his family."

"You really know how to hurt a guy, don't you," he finally remarked, weary of resisting the inevitable. "Call me this evening when you have my travel information. I'll be ready."

Smiling, Dusty stood up and approached him, offering his hand and patting him on the shoulder. "Oh, by the way," he mentioned as they parted company, "stop by the receptionist's desk on the way out. She has something for you."

The sound of his office door closing behind him gave Neal the peculiar feeling of having been set adrift – like when he was a kid in a rowboat going fishing with his Grampa John. More to keep him company than anything else, he remembered. Fishing had nothing to do with it. He didn't like fishing in the first place, but went anyway.

So, what's new? Neal asked himself, amused by the irony of it all. You're going fishing again!

When he approached Ginger's desk she reached for a letter-sized envelope that lay in the middle tray of her in-basket. "Take good care of this," she advised, "It contains your tickets for tomorrow's flight. Also included is enough cash to cover meals and incidental expenses. Save all your receipts. You'll have to fill out an expense report when you return. There's also information regarding ground transportation and directions on where to go when you get there. It's just our way of making sure you're well taken care of."

"That will have to wait," he flirted, placing the envelope in his briefcase. "Right now I'm a little pressed for time, but thanks anyway."

When he turned to leave, she winked and replied, "You're welcome. Have a safe trip."

Heading home on the freeway, he became increasingly apprehensive about the direction his life was taking. Having served in the Army for two years brought home the reality that once he arrived in Washington his individuality would disappear in the bureaucratic quagmire of the government's way of doing business. All things considered, the likelihood of actually finding Dan Hughes alive, knowing what his enemies were capable of, was gradually beginning to fade. On a more positive note, however, the opportunity to see his brother, Joel, again gave him the impetus he needed to fulfill his promise to Dan, and get on with the rest of his life.

In what seemed to be a trip of a thousand miles, he arrived home shortly after noon and began the methodical process of preparing for his next day's journey. Because Paula had already predicted what the outcome of his meeting with Dusty would be that day, he couldn't resist the temptation to call her so she could gloat a little in the name of women's intuition.

"I knew it was coming," she admitted matter-of-factly, "And, you needn't act like you're disappointed. This is that adventure you've been fantasizing about ever since I've known you. Just remember what's been said many times before, Curly; be careful what you wish for, you just might get it. We'll talk about this over dinner tonight. My treat."

It was mid-afternoon when he put the last few items of travel clothing neatly into his suitcase and carried it downstairs. With only a few hours left until Paula returned home, he decided it was a convenient time to contact Jessica Sterling and fill her in on what had resulted from his meeting that day.

Although she could not be reached at Sterling Publishing, or at home, she had given her cell phone number to Ivan with instructions to give it to Neal, if he called. Seconds after dialing that number, Jessica's familiar voice answered. Without going into too much detail, he summarized what had taken place and promised to get in touch with her as soon as he returned.

"Isn't that a coincidence, "she laughed. "I'm sitting here in La Jolla booking a reservation to do the same thing. I've decided to accept my Mother's job offer, but I need to clean up a few loose ends back East before I can seriously commit to that responsibility. Maybe we'll run in to each other."

"I doubt it, but here's my cell phone number, just in case."

After recording the number, she asked, "Have you heard anything from Dan?"

"Nothing yet, but I'm hoping this DEA investigation will come up with something."

"Don't get your hopes up," she cautioned, "and watch your back. These guys don't take prisoners."

"Thanks for the warning. I'll be in touch."

No sooner had he hung up the phone than it rang. It was Paula apologizing for having to attend another meeting after work that would interfere with dinner plans that evening. Despite his attempt to convince her that he could wait until she got home, she insisted that he go to bed early and get some rest. Being alone for a while, she added, would give him time to organize his thoughts. "By the way, Mr. World Traveler," she asked in closing, "how are you getting to the airport?"

Disappointed, and a little irritated with her reluctance to draw a hard line between her personal and professional life, he accepted her work ethic and replied, jovially, "Well, now that I have a kitchen pass for the evening, I think I'll have a couple of drinks with Ron and ask him to take me. I can leave my car at his place tomorrow and pick it up when I get back."

From Paula's end of the line the conversation shifted to muffled words that sounded as if she were talking to someone in her office. Then she replied, "Sorry about that, dear. I'm sure Ron won't mind taking you. He's been very generous in that respect." Hesitating a moment to put another interruption on hold, she added hurriedly, "I have to go. Don't be late, and don't drink too much."

For someone who lived every day free of interruption, the thought of returning to the chaotic life he had left only days ago seemed inconceivable. Disgruntled by the thought, he hung up content that the rest of the day was his to enjoy any way he pleased.

He began by opening his briefcase to examine the envelope Ginger Spyce had given him. He noticed with some surprise that the airline tickets it contained were designated First Class. A smaller envelope contained five hundred dollars in cash and a note that read: *Don't spend it all in one place.*

Also included was a short list of names, titles and phone numbers. Director Raymond Bronson was the only person he recognized. Following the names, a note instructed him to proceed directly to the Airport Security Office upon his arrival. An agent there would escort him to a nearby hotel where he would spend the night under protective custody until he met with Bronson the next morning.

With nervous hands and growing anxiety over how militarized traveling had become, he put the items back into his briefcase, wishing for the first time that Jessica Sterling could be accompanying him on his flight to Washington. Somehow that thought brought to mind his promise to call Henry Hughes. Putting his briefcase aside, he made the call.

Though it was late in the evening back there, Henry answered right away and expressed his gratitude for Neal remembering to call. His voice seemed noticeably less distraught than on the previous day, almost as if he was trying to convey a message, but was hesitant to do so.

For the sake of brevity, Neal went straight to the chase and told him about the recent developments that were requiring him to return to Washington. Further, he expressed his wish to visit with both he and Jennifer Newman before returning to San Diego.

"Good," he replied with measured enthusiasm, "we have much to talk about. Please contact me the minute you arrive at Jennifer's and I will join you there."

Although he could just as well have called Ron Barns to confirm his willingness to drive him to the airport, he decided not to waste his freedom hours by sitting alone in front of the television. Considering what he was going to be faced with for the next few days, a little bit of the lighter side of life seemed in order.

Needless to say, Ron showed a measure of surprise when Neal drove up in front of his house and entered a few moments later. "What's the matter?" he remarked, offering his hand, "Paula kick you out, or have you forgotten what day it is again."

Neal laughed and replied, "No, she hasn't kicked me out, and yes, I know what day it is. I'm here to ask you if you can give me a lift to the airport tomorrow. I have to go to Washington again."

"Doesn't your brother live there?" he inquired. "Is he okay?"

"Yes, but he's not the reason I'm going. Truth is, the DEA wants me to help them with their investigation into Dan Hughes' disappearance. I really don't want to go, but I'm afraid I don't have much of a say in the matter. Seems I've been reminded of my patriotic duty."

Having already expressed his opinion on a number of occasions regarding the predicaments Neal seemed prone to getting himself into, Ron remained silent, preferring to listen for the time being until he heard the rest of what his friend had to say.

"I know you think I've lost my mind," Neal remarked, finally breaking silence, "but I have no other choice. Can you give me a lift to the airport tomorrow morning?"

Shaking his head in quiet disbelief, he said he would, but commented as he rose from his chair to use the bathroom, "I'm tempted to call you the dumbest s.o.b. I've ever known, but I have this premonition that someday I'm going to need your help. I just hope you're still around to give it." On the way back he added, "In answer to your question, yes, I'll take you to the airport."

After Neal had fixed a drink and returned from the kitchen, Ron had second thoughts about what he had just said, and apologized. "Sorry if I offended you a minute ago. I just don't want to see you get hurt. Those characters back in Washington couldn't care less about what happens to you once they've gotten what they want."

"Don't worry, I'm not offended," he assured him, gulping down the remainder of his drink. "I plan to be around for a long time, so ask for my help any time you need it. In the meantime, I better go home and get a good night's sleep. I have a feeling I'm going to need it. See you tomorrow."

It was still early enough to watch the sun sinking slowly below the crimson horizon when he merged onto Old Coast Highway. By the time he had passed through the few communities that dotted the coastline along the way, all that remained of the beautiful sunset was a crimson glow reflecting off the Hilton Inn's façade. As he approached the hotel, he decided the time was right to enjoy a nightcap with Maggie Jyles, so he parked and headed for the lounge, speculating as he walked in whether or not Paula would be at home when he got there.

Fortunately, many of the people gathered in the lounge that evening were coupled at tables, leaving a few smaller ones near the windows unoccupied. Though busier than usual, Maggie saw him enter almost immediately and scurried off to mix him a drink. When she returned, her curiosity got the better of her and she asked, "Did the information I gave you help any?"

"I guess it all depends on your definition of help," he replied. "Those car keys are responsible for putting me on a plane to Washington tomorrow to help the DEA find Dan Hughes. He's been missing ever since he left here."

"You're kidding," she uttered in surprise. "Why Washington?"

Deciding that whatever he told her wouldn't make much sense unless she knew all the people involved, he gave her the condensed version. "I've convinced the DEA that the woman Dan brought out here with him knows something about his disappearance. Unfortunately, no one seems to know anything about her, except Dan and me. The name on the car key's I.D. tag that was left behind in their room, however, bears the name of a man who is linked to an East Coast drug cartel. I suspect she's on his payroll as an informant, and may have set Dan up for some foul play when he got back there."

"Maybe that's why she got so upset with him that afternoon when they returned from Disneyland, so she could use it as an excuse to leave without him."

"Could be. I guess we'll just have to wait until we find her. If we find her."

During their conversation he noticed several customers were looking in their direction and appeared irritated. The reason was obvious so he finished his drink, placed a five-dollar bill in her hand and attempted to leave.

Maggie, however, held on firmly and said, most insistently, "No, no, Mr. T, my treat. Have a safe trip and come see me when you get back. I want to hear the ending of this story."

He smiled, closing her fingers around the money. "Keep it, dear, and thanks again for your help. I'll see you in a few days, hopefully."

During the time it took to drive home, he attempted to second-guess what questions he might be asked when he came face-to-face with DEA Director Bronson. He was certain that the search for Dan's hideaway would be his main focus because of the evidence that was hidden there. Review of that evidence had to take place in order to bring charges against Miguel Ramirez. Once his guilt was established, he harbored little doubt that Ramirez would plea bargain in exchange for information leading to the whereabouts of both Dan and Donna Sanders. If all went well, the mystery of Dan's disappearance would solve itself and allow him to return to whatever normal life he had left. Or so he thought.

Turning into his driveway, the sense of futility that comes from trying to second-guess the unforeseeable gradually broke down the enthusiasm his logic had attempted to create. The letdown reminded him of an excerpt from a book about the Second World War that his former wife, Janet, had given him many years ago. It prophesized, in essence, that regardless of all the painstaking preparations that go into planning for war, it all goes to hell in a hand basket as soon as the first shot is fired, leaving Dame Fate in charge.

Reflections from the taillights on Paula's car greeted him when he reached the garage. Puzzled why she had arrived home earlier than she told him she would, he entered quietly and found her asleep in his chair. An empty glass of wine and the remnants of a salad sat on a tray in her lap. Rather than disturb her, he carefully picked up the tray and took it into the kitchen, dimming the lights as he left. With nothing better to do until she wakened, he thought a moment or two of quiet reflection on the bluff might calm his restless mind. As his hand reached for the doorknob, a voice flavored with a pinch of sarcasm asked, "Leaving again, Mr. Gadabout?"

Startled, he spun around and found Paula entering the kitchen. "Damn!" he exclaimed. "I thought you were asleep"

"I noticed you have your travel gear by the door," she commented, smugly. "Going someplace?"

Recognizing the, *I told you so,* expression on her face, he admitted, "You were right all along. The DEA wants me in Washington tomorrow. Sorry about that. I really hate leaving you alone again."

"Don't beat yourself up over it, dear heart," she yawned. "I received a call from Ellen today. Mike's leaving tomorrow to attend a two-day seminar in Palm Springs, so I thought I'd leave right after work to keep her and the children company while he's away." Pausing briefly, she added, "Ellen also mentioned that she and Mike have met an elderly man who is looking for someone to run his greenery business when he retires. They thought it might be wise for me to look in to it while I'm there."

"Why not?" he replied naively. "You've always been good at that sort of thing. Who knows, it might just open a new window of opportunity for you to get out from under that train wreck of a job that's driving you crazy most of the time."

Rather than continue the conversation and prematurely admit that she was the interested party, she cleverly took advantage of his vulnerability by turning off the lights and disrobing. As her robe fell in a heap on the floor, she pressed herself against him and whispered, seductively, "I think its time for a nice relaxing Jacuzzi, don't you?"

An hour later, as pale moonlight highlighted the curves of their naked bodies, she rested quietly back on her dampened pillow and whispered, "I'm going to miss you, Curly."

The previous evening's wanton frivolity had been costly in terms of paying attention to matters of routine. She had forgotten to set the alarm. Had it not been for the sound of seagulls spiraling over the bluff beyond their bedroom window she might have overslept, but their squealing forced her sleepy eyes to open.

Though the digital display indicated that there was some cause for alarm, she snuggled up against his back and whispered, "Hey, Mr. Lucky, it's wakeup time. Momma needs her coffee."

Before he could react, she slid quickly out of reach and sought the privacy of her bathroom, giggling a little as she closed the door behind her. Knowing that he was in no less of a hurry, he followed her lead and went to his own bathroom, well aware that the day ahead – at least for him – allowed little margin for time spent in pursuit of further frivolity. As his mother had counseled him so many times during the days of his youth, there was a time and place for everything.

Were it not for the urgency that heralded in each of their days, there may have been leisure time to indulge in meaningful conversation, but time was of the essence. Not wanting to sound too much like the mother he sometimes accused her of being with him, she held back her thoughts until she was in her car about to leave. "It goes without saying that you are no longer a little boy, so I'll spare you my motherly words of wisdom. Telling you to be careful assumes you don't know how, but that's another issue. Just come back in one piece, will you. I need your half of the rent."

Following a lingering kiss that said all there was left to say, he backed away and joked, "And what was your name again?"

In less than an hour after her departure his bag was packed and sitting beside his briefcase at the front door. Satisfied that his home was secure he left for Ron Barns' house, uneasy about what lay ahead.

Ron was standing outside motioning him to pull into the driveway when he arrived. That accomplished, and his bags resting securely in the back of Ron's truck, they got in and started toward the freeway. Halfway to the airport, Ron broke the silence that neither of them thought would last that long. "Well my friend, I still think you're nuts, but who am I to judge. I know you'd do the same thing for me if my ass were in a sling. I just hope that knucklehead, Dan Hughes is alive so he can thank you."

"Oh, he's alive, Ron, I can feel it in my bones. Question is, where?"

Little more than that was said on the subject until they reached the airport terminal. Because the traffic seemed unusually congested at his curbside check-in, Neal made a suggestion that Ron was only too happy to accept. "I can make it on foot from here, old buddy. No use you getting tangled up in that mess up ahead. Thanks for the lift."

Ron agreed and nodded appreciatively as he left the truck. "No problem. Call me when you're ready to come home. I'll pick you up."

Within minutes Neal had checked his one suitcase through to Washington and passed through the security checkpoint with only one minor delay. As he walked down the concourse to his departure gate, he was reminded of a day not long ago when he had walked the same concourse on his way to attend Billy Newman's wake. In retrospect he hoped the trip he was now about to embark on would not result in complicating his life as much as that one had. *Damn you for that, Billy,* he cursed to himself. *You're more trouble dead than alive.*

Time passed quickly while he waited restlessly in an open bar nearby. Soon the attendant announced boarding for First Class ticket holders, a select group of parents with small children and one handicapped senior woman in a wheelchair. Gulping down the last swallow of a Bloody Mary he had been passing the time with, he moved quickly toward the boarding gate and down the loading ramp, anxious to be finally on his way. He hadn't been seated very long when he noticed a female flight attendant busying around in the forward service cubicle who looked familiar, but she stepped out of sight before he could make a positive identification.

Settling back in his seat, he rested comfortably while watching the balance of passengers pass by, bumping and stumbling down the aircraft's narrow passageway. Thanks to helpful flight attendants who aided in the process, baggage was stowed efficiently and order restored before the massive jet maneuvered away from the gate and out onto the taxi runway. Forward movement began almost immediately, but slowed intermittently because of other planes waiting in line ahead of them.

During the stop-and- go process he had an opportunity to observe the flight attendant as she moved casually about the cabin tending to passengers and checking seat belts. Sensing his preoccupation with her, she let her eyes drift slowly over the seats until they locked onto his. Self-consciously he attempted to look away but was drawn back suddenly by a smile that beamed like a Steinway Piano keyboard. Almost instantly, the evening following Billy Newman's wake flashed before his eyes and restored the memory of a kiss; Vicky Daniel's kiss.

Offering her hand in a friendly gesture, she greeted him with genuine enthusiasm.

"Welcome aboard, Mr. Thomas. It's good to see you again. Would you like a drink after we're airborne?"

Neal's reply was somewhat delayed because of his fascination with the way she carried herself, body movement that had not changed since the first time he saw her. "If you can remember what I ordered the last time we flew together, yes I will," he challenged.

"You've got Bloody Mary written all over your face," she replied, certain of her choice. "You're as obvious as a fly in the soup."

"You have a remarkable memory, my dear. Whenever you're ready, except please, skip the soup!"

Before turning away she leaned over and whispered, "That's not all I remember, Mr. T."

Almost immediately as she left to be seated for takeoff, a voice from the cockpit announced, "Flight attendants prepare for departure."

As she had done so many times in the past, Vicki strapped herself into a small fold-down seat near the forward hatch and waited expressionless as the fully loaded aircraft lumbered onto the runway. In less than a minute the ocean beyond Point Loma could be seen shimmering in the sun as the aircraft continued its slow climbing turn toward the East. Of the many boats he could still see moving on the ocean below he wondered how many of them were actually going fishing that day?

Chapter 17

Chasing The Goose

Forty-five minutes after takeoff the *Fasten Seatbelt* indicator light above Neal's head turned off. Unlike his previous trip to the East Coast, the person seated next to him was not an attractive, middle-aged woman in the publishing business, but a young man intensely preoccupied with his laptop computer. Every so often, however, he turned briefly toward the window and gazed nostalgically at the beautiful cloud formations passing below, and then returned again to continue typing. Minutes later, when Vicki appeared from behind her cubicle, the young man shut the computer down, placed it under the seat in front of him and lowered his tray. Apparently, just as much interested in watching her move down the aisle as Neal was.

After serving the young man a soft drink, she handed Neal his glass of ice, mix and vodka, remarking before leaving, "Come and see me when you're ready for a refill. The exercise will do you good."

He laughed and replied, "That obvious, huh?"

"No, silly," she giggled. "I have something personal I want to discuss with you."

Her graceful movements were only a few steps away when the young man remarked, "Pretty, isn't she?"

Surprised by his outspoken breach of silence, he hesitated for a moment trying to think of something appropriate to say, but not the young man. In a voice too mature for his age, he added, glibly, "Now I've seen first hand what my colleagues mean when they joke about young women being attracted to older men. It would appear they weren't joking."

Amused by the young man's observation, he replied, "I wouldn't buy any stock on that notion just yet, young man. The market's too unpredictable."

"Yeah, I guess you're right. But she is pretty."

Neal smiled while he recalled the many pretty women he had met in his lifetime that had affected him in the same way. Intending to pass on some wisdom, he turned toward the young man and told him, "When I was a kid, my Grandfather used to counsel me about pretty woman when he had had too much to drink. He'd look at me with his furrowed gray eyebrows and whiskey-breath, and say, "Boy, pretty is as pretty does. Trouble is, he never explained what pretty did."

Now they were both laughing; Neal, because he thought he had thoroughly confused the young man, and the young man, because he had listened to his father all too often refer to the same old bromides. Not to be outdone, he replied, in kind. "Beauty is only skin deep, right? And, how about, you can't judge a book by its cover? You remind me so much of my dad. He used to lecture me all the time about the consequences of becoming too seriously involved with women, pointing out how different we were, especially with respect to our plumbing."

"Those are words of wisdom, young man," he commented, reflectively. "Not heeding them can lead to very costly consequences sometimes."

"Yes sir, I'm well aware of that."

He could sense from the change in expression that the conversation was approaching a sensitive area, so he offered his hand and introduced himself. "Neal Thomas, and your name is…?"

"Sean Peterson. Pleased to meet you, Mr. Thomas"

Now that the silence between them had been pleasantly broken, and his Bloody Mary needed refilling, he excused himself to use the rest room and stood up to leave, but not before Sean got in a friendly dig, "Tell her I'm next."

Proceeding to the front of the cabin he cornered Vicki in the service cubicle and asked, "Now, what's this personal matter all about?"

"I understand Dan Hughes visited you in San Diego a few days ago," she replied. "How's he doing?"

The question shouldn't have come as a surprise, but it did. Excusing himself, he retreated into the privacy of the cramped men's room to think of something to say that wouldn't alarm her. When he returned she eyed him in a way that let him know she was still waiting for an answer. "Is he back yet?" she asked, seriously.

"I'm really not sure where Dan is right now," he admitted, truthfully, "but I have business in Washington that may shed some light on that. Hopefully, in a few days, if I'm lucky."

"He's not in any trouble, is he?"

Just the way she asked the question seemed to imply that she knew more than she cared to reveal, so he took the same tack. "Vicki, Dan's been in trouble of one kind or another ever since he was a kid. The question now is, what kind?"

"Let's talk further when we get to Washington," she whispered. "I have something to tell you that I can't discuss here. Wait at the terminal gate. I'll meet you there, okay?"

Promising that he would, he returned to his seat and found Sean sound asleep with his head resting comfortably on a pillow pressed against the cabin bulkhead. Making every effort not to wake him, he lowered himself into his seat and sat there quietly sipping his drink while Vicki's innuendo buzzed around in his head like a pesky fly.

Maybe she and Dan had gotten together before he left for California, he speculated, raising the question; did he mention anything to her with regard to why he was leaving so suddenly? Or, had she talked with Jennifer Newman. Was it possible that Jennifer had said something that aroused her curiosity? In either event, the search for Dan could not get under way until the DEA examined the information he would soon be leading them to. Without it, he feared, Dan's whereabouts might remain a mystery forever.

Three hours and an in-flight movie later, he heard the jet engines begin to decelerate and the cabin angle dip slightly for the aircraft's downward approach into Washington. Except for Vicki's presence onboard, and an occasional exchange of conversation with Sean, the flight had been relaxing and uneventful. He eventually did volunteer that he was returning home from college after having earned a Master's Degree in Political Science. When Neal asked about his professional goals, he told him that, ultimately, he wanted to be President of the United States. Given his somewhat negative feelings about the integrity of politicians in general, Neal swallowed his prejudice and bid the boy good luck. As they shook hands and said goodbye in the terminal, he remarked, somewhat honestly, "I hope I'm around when you run for office. I'd like to give you my vote. What side of the aisle are you?"

"Why tell you and ruin a perfectly good relationship," he replied, grinning coyly. "Let's just say the winning party and leave it at that."

"Good answer," he replied, wishing he were as young and full of such high hopes. "Good luck!"

The young man's departure left Neal standing alone near the gate waiting for Vicki to arrive. In less time than he had expected to wait, she appeared, pulling her carry-on travel bag behind her. "Come on, I'll buy you a drink," she insisted. "I sure could use one."

"Thanks anyway," he replied, apologetically, "I was directed to go straight to the security office as soon as I landed. Can I have a rain check on that offer?"

She looked a little disappointed, but respected his decision and replied, "Sure, no problem. As a matter of fact, we can talk while we're walking in that direction. It's on the way to where my car is parked. This is probably a wiser choice, anyway," she remarked. "One never knows who's listening over your shoulder in a bar."

They had only walked a few yards when she scanned the surrounding area and began to speak quietly. "I saw Dan at the Norfolk airport when he returned from California. I was on my way to the parking lot to pick up my car when I saw him standing alone near the shuttle parking area talking on his cell phone. I gathered from the language he was using that something, or someone, had really made him mad. I went over to offer my assistance in case he needed a ride somewhere. When he saw me approaching he said a few quick words and then put the phone back in his pocket. His greeting was cordial, but I could tell he was still upset and kept looking around as if he were expecting someone. It wasn't until after I asked him if he needed a lift that he explained what had happened."

Neal chuckled and remarked, "I've got a pretty good idea what took place, but go on."

"Well, when Dan took the shuttle over to the long term parking facility after his flight landed, he said his car was gone. Ironically, the car his travel companion drove was still parked in the space next to his."

"Let me guess," he interrupted. "That car belonged to Donna Sanders."

"Yes!" she blurted out in surprise. "He told me she had followed him there so she'd have her own car when they returned from San Diego."

"Then why did she take your car? And, how did she get your keys?"

He chuckled again, and tried to explain. "Obviously, he must have trusted her well enough at one time in their relationship to tell her where his hide-a-key box was located in the event of an emergency. They had a bad argument at the hotel last Saturday night and left while Dan and me were having dinner with mutual friends. When she arrived back in Norfolk and discovered her keys were left in the hotel in California, she took Dan's car, figuring she could return it before he got back."

"Sounds plausible," she admitted, "But there's more."

"More?"

"Oh, it gets better, believe me," she replied, wide-eyed and excited. "I offered to give him a lift to the marina, but he said he had already called a friend who was on his way to pick him up. When I suggested that he call his friend back, he broke down and confided in me that he was in a serious trouble."

"What kind of trouble?" he asked, becoming increasingly more interested. "Where is he now?"

"I honestly don't know," she answered, nervously, "but here's what happened: When he called this person to pick him up, he informed Dan that his travel companion, Donna Sanders, had been beaten up by Miguel Ramirez for leaving the keys to one of his cars in San Diego, and had actually threatened her life. Dan seemed genuinely concerned for her safety and didn't want to make matters worse by getting me involved, so I took his advice and headed for the beach by myself."

Neal shook his head in disbelief and finally asked, "Have you had any contact with Dan since then?"

"Nope, but I know someone who has."

"Go on, don't just leave me dangling here."

"When I arrived home that same evening, I noticed Jennifer Newman's kitchen lights were on when I drove by, and my mother's car was parked out front. To stretch my legs and catch a breath of fresh air, I walked back to find out what those two old broads were up to. It was a warm night, so the front door was open when I got there. Standing outside where I couldn't be seen, I was surprised to overhear Jennifer tell my mother that Dan Hughes had been there earlier and had asked her to be sure to give you a message whenever you returned."

"What was the message?" he asked, watching the security office door come slowly into view.

"When mother asked her the very same question, Jennifer told her that Dan had left it in a sealed envelope that she was to give to you in person. That's when I knocked on the door."

A few paces from where they would soon part company, he turned to her and said, "Well Vicki, I don't know what to make of all this, but from what you've just told me, I believe our mutual friend, Mr. Hughes, has been able to stay one step ahead of whomever is chasing him, for the time being. Let's just hope he doesn't trip and fall. Bless whatever celestial manipulation has seen fit to bring us together today. Hopefully, we can meet again when I finish this dreadful business with the DEA. Until then, thanks for confiding in me."

She stood motionless for a moment looking up into the tired blue eyes of the only man she had ever known who would have honored a friendship the way he had. "You're a fine and noble person, Mr. T. My only hope is that someday Dan will realize that too. I'm on standby status right now, so I'll be hanging out at the beach for a few days. Call me if you have time to share."

Inside the security office, business appeared to be moving along as one might expect; slow and slower. Uniformed officers were involved in conversation relevant to the day's activities while they prepared to change shifts. A large black woman sat at a desk nearby. Judging from her demeanor and the stack of folders she was arranging in a file cabinet, she appeared to have some managerial authority. Approaching her, he asked, "Excuse me miss, my name is Neal Thomas. I'm supposed to meet a DEA agent here this afternoon. Has he arrived yet?"

"Ah, hah," she remarked, her sudden smile revealing a mouthful of beautiful white teeth. "So you're the mystery man we've all been waiting for. Have a seat while I let Mr. Miller know you're here."

Moments later, two men appeared; one in uniform, and the other in civilian clothes. After shaking hands, the man in uniform returned to his office, while the other approached Neal and offered his hand. "Welcome to Washington, Mr. Thomas. We've been expecting you. I'm Agent Miller, Charlie Miller."

A brief identity verification exchange followed before the two men left the office and proceeded to a reserved parking area where a chauffeured limousine was waiting. Not until they were safely underway did Agent Miller open a dialogue. "We have only recently become aware that you have a brother here in Washington who lives fairly close to the airport. Director Bronson felt sure you'd feel far more at home staying overnight with him, rather than alone in a hotel, if that's acceptable to you."

Neal shook his head and asked the obvious, "Have you discussed this with him?

"Yes we have. In fact he is looking forward to your visit and is eager to help in any way he can."

"Does he know why I'm here? I don't want him involved in anything that could possibly compromise his safety. "

"There is no danger," Miller assured him. "In fact, one of the reasons for this change in plans was implemented because of your brother's background. He knows the system and can be trusted."

In what seemed to him a relatively short period of time after leaving the airport, Neal was let out of the limousine in front of his brother's two-story town house. Agent Miller's parting words were few, but to the point. "Get a good night's sleep. I'll pick you up at seven o'clock sharp tomorrow morning.

As he watched the limo's tail lights fade away into the hot, humid night, he heard his brother's voice call out from an open door behind him, "Hey, Bro! Welcome to the big city."

Although tired at the end of his own long and emotionally challenged day, Joel wasted little time in making his brother feel at home by giving him a short tour of his small but tastefully furnished home.

"The girls are both out of town this week," he explained when they returned to the living room, "so relax and fill me in on what the hell is going on with you and the DEA. Knowing how they operate, I believe only about half of what I've heard and less about what I've seen, so why don't you bring me up to speed on the nitty-gritty."

The update took about an hour and only addressed specific events following Billy Newman's death, including how that single event had pulled him into the quagmire of Dan Hughes' nefarious past, present and questionable future. When he finished, Joel shook his head slowly in silent disbelief and offered a comment: "If I weren't so bogged down at the office, I'd take some time off and go with you on this wild goose chase, but I can't. My only hope is that you and the DEA find Dan before the Cartel does. Believe me, they'll kill him if they get to him first. In the meantime, let me fix you a bite to eat before you turn in. I have a feeling tomorrow's going to be a very long day for you."

A ham and cheese sandwich and a can of beer was all it took to induce almost falling asleep in his chair. So, formalities aside, he bid Joel goodnight and climbed the stairs to take advantage of a much-needed rest.

Though his brother's advice was well intended, sleep that night was destined to be restless and often interrupted by foreign sounds emanating from the unfamiliar world outside. Thus, his brother's footsteps were clearly audible when he approached and entered his bedroom the next morning. Before he could speak, Neal rolled over and let him know in a raspy voice, "Never mind with the words and music, Joel, I'm already awake. So much for a good night's sleep."

A quick shave and a hot shower, however, seemed to restore some of the vitality he had lost the previous day and hoped it would help him make it through the day that lay ahead, regardless of the outcome. By the time he finished dressing and descended the stairs with his suitcase in hand, the smell of freshly brewed coffee drifted up to meet him.

Joel was spreading cream cheese on bagel halves when his older brother entered the kitchen and remarked, with a touch of humor, "I hope you get up this early every work day, brother mine. Otherwise, I could qualify as one big pain in the ass!"

"We're right on schedule," he replied. "We're just going in different directions. Just be glad the girls aren't here.... talk about a mad house!"

The large hand of the kitchen clock was only two minutes away from the seventh hour when the doorbell rang. Eyeing each other with mutual understanding they rose and walked to the front door. Agent Miller stood waiting patiently outside, along with the all to familiar limo waiting at curbside. Opening the door to acknowledge his arrival, Neal shook his brother's hand and pledged he would return as soon as the search for Dan came to an end, one way or the other.

"Good hunting, Bro," was all Joel could say as he watched his brother descend the steps and enter the limo. Then he shouted after him, "Watch your back!"

Several miles into their journey to the airport, Neal observed that the limo was not headed in the reverse direction it had traveled the previous day. It must have been the curious look on his face that prompted Agent Miller to offer clarification. "If you're puzzled about why we're not headed for Dulles Airport, it's because Director Bronson wants us to meet him at Andrews Air Force Base. He has arranged for us to be flown to a Naval Air station near Virginia Beach where a helicopter is being readied for us to conduct the search you've been sent here to help us with."

Confused, Neal slumped back in his seat with an *I don't believe this* expression on his face, and finally asked, "Don't you guys ever tell a person what's going on before the fact?"

For the first time since he had met Agent Miller, he saw him smile. Not a warm, friendly smile, but one that lets a person know he enjoyed the power that came with knowing more than the other person. "That would take away our advantage," he replied, his eyes still focused on the road ahead. "We couldn't have that now, could we?"

"Lighten up, will you!" Neal remarked with mounting agitation. "I'm the guy holding all the aces. You need me a hell of a lot more than I need you."

Agent Miller finally turned his head away from whatever he had been concentrating on and replied, still grinning, "Dusty Lewis said you were a feisty old geezer, but you do have a point, however, much as I hate to admit it. So let me give you a well-meant word of advice: be wary of Ray Bronson. He's a feisty old geezer too."

There had been times recently when the coincidental events of his everyday life had seemed a little too far-fetched to be taken seriously. That is, until the limousine in which he was now a passenger passed through the Andrews Air Force Base security checkpoint and parked next to the small jet Agent Miller had explained would be waiting for them. Stepping into its cramped interior made it abundantly clear that the real world was sending him a serious message: *Welcome to the point of no return.*

He and Agent Miller had not been buckled in long when Neal observed another car approaching the aircraft. A man of average height with thick gray hair and a ruddy complexion emerged. As he walked across the tarmac, Neal was struck by his resemblance to Spencer Tracy, a favorite movie star of his since Hollywood's 1940 release of the film classic, "Northwest Passage."

"That's our Director, Ray Bronson," Miller informed him when Bronson entered the aircraft. "He can be very intimidating so watch what you say, and how you say it."

The Director's somewhat serious expression changed to a pleasant smile when he saw Agent Miller. Stopping for a moment where they were seated, he said pleasantly, "Hi, Charlie. I take it this is our man Thomas?" Shaking Neal's hand firmly, he remarked, "When we get some air under us we'll talk more. In the meantime, relax and I'll get this show on the road."

To say that Neal was pleasantly surprised would have been a mild understatement, considering Agent Miller's earlier comment, so he rested back in his seat and watched Bronson give the pilot a thumbs-up for takeoff.

Shortly after reaching cruising altitude, Bronson unfastened his seatbelt and approached the two men. The cordiality was gone. "Here's what's going down as soon as we get to the Naval Air Station, gentlemen. The Navy has a chopper standing by for us to use to cruise the coordinates you've provided, Mr. Thomas. If there's a cabin hidden in that area, we should be able to spot it from the air. The Navy has also provided us with an armed surface craft that we can transfer to once the waterway to the cabin is visible. Should we run into any trouble, the Navy will handle it. We are not to interfere. Is that understood?"

Both men nodded their understanding, followed by Neal remarking, "I hope someone checked the tide table. No one's going anywhere if it's low."

Bronson's furrowed brow returned as he addressed Neal's comment. "That's why we left Washington so early. According to the Navy's table, high tide should crest about three hours after we arrive. Time-wise, that will allow us a few hours to get to the cabin and back again. Hopefully, with the information you have assured us is hidden there."

Neal remained silent for a moment, and then replied. "Well, Director, unless some creature from the black lagoon has swallowed it up, the cabin should be right where it's supposed to be."

"For your sake, let's hope so," Bronson remarked before returning to his seat.

With Agent Miller dozing restlessly beside him, and Bronson preoccupied with documents a few seats away, he rested his head against the seat and tried to make some sense out of the puzzling events Vicki Daniels had described to him. So far, he concluded, they hadn't provided much useable information other than there being a message from Dan waiting for him when he got to Jennifer's place.

Following their arrival at the Naval Air Station, a brief meeting was held in the Flight Operations Headquarters. It was there that Director Bronson briefed the helicopter and boat crews on their specific responsibilities. Following the meeting Bronson, Agent Miller and Neal were transported to a secured area where a helicopter gunship was parked and warming up. Its awesome presence sent a shiver through Neal he had not experienced since his own two-year tour of duty as an infantryman in the U.S. Army. How fortunate, he thought, never to have had to witness the violence of combat, and heartache that came with it. Although he was not proud of electing to play football for the remaining half of his tour, the memory of so many of his comrades having lost their lives in Korea made that choice seem a wise one.

Fortunately, it was a blue-sky day for flying and provided crystal-clear visibility to aide in the impending search. They were airborne for what seemed to be only minutes when shimmering water from the relatively calm Back Bay came into view, signaling their presence with a moving shadow skimming across the water.

At matching speed below, the Navy's gunboat followed their lead in pursuit of the coordinates Director Bronson had given them. Time passed quickly. In minutes the helicopter hovered like a humming bird over the designated area, while the gunboat waited protectively just off shore.

In an instant, the sum total of what Vicki Daniels had confided in him at Dulles Airport the previous day suddenly came together like scattered pieces of a puzzle. The picture they created made it vividly clear why Dan had decided to go to the marina instead of home. He had left his mark in the shape of a black-rimmed hole in the heavily overgrown area directly below the chopper. It bore all the characteristics of what an intense fire must have created, and had destroyed any possibility of retrieving what they had come for. In a desperate move to make sure the structure had been completely destroyed, Director Bronson motioned the pilot to go as low as he could. The strong downward flow of air from the chopper's blades parted the burned out overgrowth and exposed the charred remains of what had at one time been Dan's secret hideaway. Shocked and disappointed, Bronson directed the pilot to return to base, and radioed the gunship to do the same.

Fortunately, the noise generated by the helicopters engines made conversation during the return trip more difficult than was worth the effort to pursue, so he remained silent and reflective, as did Bronson and Agent Miller. Back at Operations Headquarters, however, conversation resumed, but not in the tone that Neal had been anticipating, considering the futile outcome of their mission. It was Bronson who opened the conversation. "I understand you have friends in this area, Mr. Thomas," he began matter-of-factly, while stuffing documents back into his briefcase. "It might be a good idea for you to spent some time with them before you return to California." He hesitated a moment and then added, sarcastically, "Who knows when the Government's going to finance another wild goose chase like this one?"

Neal took the implication seriously, but rather than confront him directly with a similarly sarcastic reply, he chose a more diplomatic response, anticipating that their paths would cross again in the near future. "This day may have been a wild goose chase for you, Mr. Bronson, but I have every intention of making sure it hasn't been one for me. And, yes, I do have friends in the area. I'll let you know when the crow is ready to eat."

"Well said, sir, I'll look forward to your call. In the meantime, drinks are on me at the Officer's Club."

Although their parting words were not affable, they were respectful. Agent Miller was particularly gracious in his expression of optimism regarding Neal's intention to pursue his quest to find Dan Hughes. Bronson, however, remained skeptical, and remarked as he and Agent Miller boarded their jet an hour later, "Dan Hughes is probably so far away from here by now even the CIA couldn't catch him. But, good luck anyway!"

It was late afternoon when Bronson and Agent Miller left for Washington, so Neal returned to the Headquarters Office to ask one of the clerks if he could use the phone to call a taxi.

"Where to?" the young man asked in a Southern accent thick enough to spread on corn bread.

"Sandbridge," he replied, quite amused by the young man's friendly demeanor.

"If you're not in a hurry, I can drop you off on my way home," he replied. "I live there."

While the young man busied around putting his office in order, Neal decided the time was right to let Jennifer Newman know he had arrived. Her phone rang long enough to suggest that maybe she wasn't at home, but was answered just about the time he was ready to take his chances on arriving unannounced. Because he had known her and Billy for so long, it didn't take Sherlock Holmes to conclude that she had been drinking. "I'm b-a-a-c-k," he joked. "Have you made the bed?"

She hesitated a moment to control her irritation with him, and then replied, "Neal Thomas, you get your ornery butt over here right now. I've been sitting around here all day waiting for you to call. Where the hell are you, anyway?"

By the time he finished giving her a brief explanation, the young clerk whose uniform bore the name, *Jenkins,* signaled that he was ready to leave. Growing impatient with her continued questioning, he told her he would be there shortly to explain everything, and then hung up.

Under ordinary circumstances, his estimate of "shortly" would probably have been more accurately stated as thirty-five to forty minutes. Driving in a souped-up, fender-less convertible with over-sized tires, however, placed him in front of Jennifer's in less than twenty- five minutes. A record, he estimated, taking his bag and briefcase from the back seat. "Thanks for the lift, Jenkins," he said in parting, "and good luck at Indi."

The young GI looked up with a big smile and said, "I hope I didn't scare you, Mr. Thomas. I built this car from scratch, and it's kind of hard not to drive her on the edge."

"I've been scared before, son," he replied, "but it was never this much fun. What's your first name?"

"Todd, Sir."

"Please to meet you, Todd. Just remember, fast is exciting, but slow and easy does it every time."

He laughed and revved his engine, unconsciously. "That's what my girlfriend keeps telling me, Sir. One of these days I'll have to slow down, I guess. But till then, I just light the fire and kick the tire. See ya."

Waving his hand with youthful vigor, young Mr. Jenkins' hand-built jalopy disappeared down the beach until the sound of his engine became lost in the noisy surf breaking on the beach across the street. Smiling in envy, he turned and ascended the stairway to Jennifer's cottage, eager to learn how the drama of his traumatic afternoon had affected her day.

"Who was that?" Jennifer asked as she came over to greet him.

Closing the screen door behind him, he put his bag and briefcase aside and accepted the hug that lay waiting in her outstretched arms. Her body was warm and generously close, making it unmistakingly clear that she had little on beneath her robe. To avoid what he was unprepared to pursue – at least for that moment – he drew politely away and replied, "A nice young man stationed at the Naval Air Station who lives here. He was kind enough to give me a lift when I told him I was coming here to visit a friend."

"You should have invited him in for a drink," she remarked while refreshing her own. "What would you like?"

"Make it plain water for the moment," he replied. "I need to keep my wits about me until after you tell me when and why Dan Hughes came to see you?"

Mentioning his name triggered a reminder that he had promised to call Henry as soon as he arrived, so he asked if he could use her phone and explained why.

"I've already taken care of that," she assured him. "I talked with Henry briefly after Dan left here yesterday. I told him I was expecting you to show up sometime today and would be spending the night. He's planning on coming down to see you tomorrow morning."

"Did Dan mention anything about why he hadn't contacted anyone when he returned from California?" he asked, puzzled by the apparent secrecy in which Dan and his father were cloaking themselves.

"He was in too big of a hurry to say much of anything," she replied. "However, he did mention that he was on his way to the marina to pick up his boat and asked me to give you this."

A small envelope had been lying on the table but went unnoticed until she picked it up and handed it to him. It was sealed and addressed simply, "Mr. T." Puzzled and curious, he opened it and withdrew a folded piece of notepaper that read:

Check your P.O. Box as soon as you return home, Mr. T. My gratitude is inside. Good luck, D.

After staring at the words for a moment, he placed the note back in the envelope and put it in his briefcase, saying, "I'll have that drink now."

While she attended to his request, he sat pensively watching the day disappear into darkness until a woman's figure passing beneath a streetlight attracted his attention. Recognizing the grace with which she walked, he asked, "Guess who the First Class attendant was on my Washington flight yesterday?"

"Vicki Daniels," she replied, matter-of-factly. "She called to tell me you were on the way. Sweet girl."

Neal laughed and shook his head. "Talk about coincidence! She told me she had run into Dan at the airport, unexpectedly, when he first arrived from San Diego. When she offered him a ride down here, he told her he had already made other plans. He was in a big hurry then too, according to her."

"Dan's on the run, I'm convinced of that," she replied. "Why else would he have gone to California all of a sudden? More importantly, why didn't he go straight home when he got back, especially after hearing that his mother had become seriously ill and died? The answers to my questions came when he showed up here yesterday to deliver this note and pick up his boat. Obviously, he's on his way somewhere."

Soon after she returned to the table with what he thought was an overly strong drink, she listened intently while he summarized all of the various events that had taken place before and after Dan's visit to California, including the disappointing discovery that he had obliterated his hideaway, for whatever reason.

"How did the DEA react to all this?"

"Well, let's just say I'm not a likely candidate for their good guy of the year award and let it go at that."

"Not to change the subject, but when were you planning to return to California?"

"As soon as I talk to Henry, I guess. The DEA gave me a prioritized, open-ended ticket just in case our search for what we hoped to find at Dan's hideaway was successful. Since that's a bust now, I should probably leave the day after tomorrow. Can you put me up until then?"

"You're welcome to stay as long as you want. However, I have to leave here tomorrow morning for a couple of days. Just lock up the house when you leave. There's some fresh crabmeat in the refrigerator, if you're hungry. I've already eaten, so help yourself."

"I'd like that. Maybe I can talk Henry into spending the night so he can drop me off at the airport on his way home. I suspect he could use a little R&R after all he's been through."

"Down here?" she gasped. "In your dreams! You'd have better luck at a church picnic. Besides, I hardly think he's in the mood for what you're looking for."

Following a few inquiries into the health and whereabouts of some of their old friends and relatives, she excused herself, unceremoniously, and went to bed, leaving him to nibble on crabmeat and ponder why she hadn't exhibited any of the sexual innuendos that had made his previous visit a memorable one. Oh well, he thought, retiring to the guest room, nothing is forever.

Although he hadn't expected to, he did sleep well. The certainty of returning home, as well as the opportunity to talk with Henry before he left, made the outlook for his day look particularly inviting. Once dressed he proceeded to the kitchen where Jennifer was busy preparing one of her more popular breakfasts: soft-boiled eggs over pan-browned crab cakes, topped with creamy Hollandaise sauce. She turned as he entered the kitchen and greeted him cordially. "Good morning. Looks like you really needed a good night's sleep. There's fresh coffee in the pot so help yourself while I fix our plates. We have a little time to talk before I have to leave. Henry should be here around ten o'clock."

As they sat enjoying the tantalizing tastes of her cooking, she opened the conversation with bits and pieces of information relating to her husband's demise that she thought he ought to be aware of. "Even though the authorities can prove Billy's death was no accident, they still don't have a suspect. Miguel Ramirez, however, is high on their list, though they have no proof that he was directly involved. Dan Hughes swore to me he had no part in killing Billy, but knows who did. Otherwise, why would he all of a sudden take a trip to California? To go to your party? I don't think so. Something happened that forced him to put some distance between himself and Ramirez, but his mother's death messed up his plans and forced him to return prematurely."

With the tale of events that Vicki Daniels had revealed to him at the airport still fresh in his mind, he asked, "How much do you know about a girl by the name of Donna Sanders? She's the woman that accompanied Dan to California."

She remained silent for a moment while clearing the table, and then replied. "Only that she's the main reason behind Dan's breakup with Vicki Daniels. Authorities here think she is in some way linked to Ramirez and his suspected affiliation with the local drug cartel." She was about to excuse herself in order to freshen up before leaving, but hesitated a moment to add a parting comment: " I assumed Dan was alone when he dropped off that envelope the other evening. When he left, however, I remember watching him enter the passenger side of what I thought was his car. Apparently, someone else I couldn't see had driven him here."

When she left to complete her final preparation for departure, he walked out onto the patio to relax until Henry arrived. Though the air was heavy with humidity, a strong on-shore flow brought enough relief from the sun to make it tolerable, allowing him a few minutes to relive memories of similar days long gone by. The daydreaming was short-lived, unfortunately, when Jennifer approached from within and bid him goodbye with a friendly hug. Half way down the stairs she turned to give him a parting reminder. "Let me know as soon as you find out whatever happened to Dan, will you? I really am interested."

"I will," he promised. "If I'm still alive!"

"That's not funny," she scolded. "I've already lost a husband. I don't need to lose a good friend."

Her car had only traveled a short distance when Henry's Cadillac approached from the opposite direction. Following a brief exchange of conversation through open windows, she continued on her way while he joined Neal on the deck. "Good to see you again, my friend," he said after shaking Neal's hand. "What I have to tell you won't take long. I just hope we're still friends after you've heard what I have to say."

Neal stood up immediately, deeply concerned. "My God, Henry, what's wrong?" he asked. "Can I get you a drink?"

"No thanks. I have to drive back shortly," he replied. "Unfortunately, Polly's passing has left me with a mountain of will-related complications that require my immediate attention. Aside from that, I couldn't let you leave without personally apologizing for my son's outrageous disregard for your privacy and safety. Imposing on our friendship with his drug-related problems was unforgivable. He did, however, show me the courtesy of a visit recently to apologize for the errors of his past, and to assure me that he would soon cease to be a burden to me, or anyone. I haven't seen nor heard from him since, and I'm convinced he's left the area for good."

"Did he mention anything about where he might be going, or if he planned to take anyone with him?"

"No he didn't, and truthfully, after all the worry he has caused his mother and me, I really don't give a damn where he goes! Son, or no son, enough is enough."

All Neal could think of at that moment was his final words to Raymond Bronson after he made his, "wild goose chase," remark when they parted company at the Naval Air Station. With Dan apparently resigned to leaving the area, possibly for the rest of his life, he felt a sudden sinking sensation as he asked him, "Did Dan express any intention of getting in touch with me before he left?"

"I asked him the same question. The answer he gave me was, and I quote, that's been taken care of. I just assumed you two had been in touch with one another recently. Were you?"

"No, not recently," he replied, with growing doubt that he would ever hear from Dan again. "But I'm sure I will, sooner or later."

When Henry looked at his watch for the lack of anything further to say, Neal recognized the time for parting had arrived. Offering his hand, he smiled and assured him that their friendship would always be in tact no matter what their crazy kids did. His departure left Neal saddened and wistfully looking out over the ocean, muttering to himself, "Now, damn it, how in hell am I going to get to the airport?

As he considered his options, a car approached the driveway and turned in. From the driver-side window the familiar face of Vicki Daniels appeared, and she hollered, "Where's Jennifer?"

"She had to leave town for a couple of days," he shouted back. "Come on in, I'll buy you a drink."

"You're on!"

As he watched the shapely Miss Daniels climb the stairs, he couldn't help considering the possibility that *Dame Fate* had just stepped in to solve his dilemma. What a stroke of luck, he thought, as the lyrics from one of Frank Sinatra's most popular recordings suddenly came to mind, *Luck Be A Lady Tonight.*

Chapter 18
Redemption

Vicki's unexpected arrival came as a welcome touch of timely coincidence. Thus, he wasted little time in laying the groundwork for enticing her to drive him to the airport the next morning. His ploy disguised itself as a dinner invitation to celebrate his departure to San Diego. "Would you consider having dinner with me tonight in exchange for a ride to the Norfolk Airport tomorrow morning?" he asked. "I have to be in Washington by noon to arrange for my return flight to San Diego."

"You're in luck, Mr. T," she replied, wide-eyed and smiling. "I was notified an hour ago that I am no longer on stand-by status. I have to be at the airport early tomorrow morning myself, so I'd be grateful for your company."

He excused himself for a moment and returned with his briefcase. Studying the itinerary briefly, he explained that his return trip was open-ended. Handing the paper work to her, he asked, "How do I handle this?"

After briefly reviewing the electronic ticket, she led him inside like a little boy and told him to relax while she placed a call. Seconds later her face lit up when a familiar voice on the other end answered. "Michelle?" she inquired, with almost child-like enthusiasm. "This is Vicki."

Small talk followed briefly, and then she explained the purpose of her call. "I have an open-ender here who needs a flight to San Diego tomorrow arriving early evening. His ticket is First Class and has a Government priority code stamped on it. See what you can do and call me back at this number."

That done, she replaced the receiver and said, "As soon as I get you squared away, I have to leave for a little while, but I'll be back by three o'clock. We can talk about dinner then."

Almost half an hour of casual conversation passed before the call they had both been waiting for was returned. Quickly, Vicki grabbed a pencil from a beer mug bearing Billy Newman's name and wrote down the data, winking at Neal, occasionally, to convey her assurance that all was going well. Following an enthusiastic, "Thanks, Babe," she hung up and repeated the good news to her anxious listener. "Pays to have friends in this business," she remarked. "Michelle has you scheduled to arrive in San Diego at seven o'clock tomorrow evening, California time. To get you to Washington in time to make that flight, we've got to leave here by six a.m. tomorrow. How's that for service?"

Relieved and grateful, he gathered her in his arms and thanked her. "You are a wonder, my dear. I'm really looking forward to taking you out to dinner tonight. Thank you so much for your help."

"You're worth it," she replied, walking provocatively toward the door. "See you around three."

Immediately after she left, he picked up the phone that still bore traces of the perfume she had on and called Ron Barns to give him the particulars of his flight. At least Michelle had minimized the imposition on his friend's generosity by getting him home when the worst of freeway traffic would be over. That alone, he thought, would surely please his friend.

With his travel plans effortlessly taken care of, and a few hours to kill before Vicki's return, he was lured into such a feeling of contentment that he felt it surely should be rewarded. Humming as he searched Jennifer's refrigerator and cabinets for the proper ingredients, he concocted a Bloody Mary that went to the soul of satisfaction and put the unforeseeable on hold – at least for a little while.

When Vicki returned that afternoon the ice had long since melted in his half-empty glass. The edge of his upper lip was lined with what must have been the tomato juice residue from his last sip before falling asleep. Thankful that a slowly developing cloud cover had prevented his face from becoming sunburned, she aroused him from his slumber with a gentle touch and asked, "Do you always fix a drink before retiring?"

"Only when I'm expecting company," he replied, sleepily. "What time is it? And how long have you been standing there?"

"I just arrived. It's three o'clock, and I'm thirsty. Why don't you take a quick shower while I fix you and me a drink, then we can relax and discuss dinner."

Grateful for her sense of humor and welcomed suggestion, he left for a refreshing shower that heightened his enthusiasm to pursue the subject of her relationship with Dan Hughes. A relationship that he suspected had not yet been finalized, despite what he had seen and heard during his previous visit. Her reaction to the mere mention of his name seemed less hostile than before, almost as if she had experienced a change of heart regarding his sudden and unexplained trip to San Diego with Donna Sanders.

Before he could open a dialogue she suggested that they adjourn to the patio deck and take advantage of what was left of the sun. When they were both comfortably stretched out beside one another his curiosity got the better of him. "What puzzles me is why Dan didn't take advantage of your offer to give him a lift to the Marina, since you were coming here anyway."

The visor of her sun cap was resting on the rim of her sunglasses, shading the direction in which her eyes were focused. He sensed they were fixed on him so he continued, hoping to arouse a comment. "Something life threatening must have scared Dan into hiding. I believe the cartel has put a price on his head and he's trying desperately to escape the inevitable. I might be able to help him if I only knew where he was. But, unfortunately, that seems highly unlikely now. I'm afraid he's gotten to that point where he trusts no one, and leaving town is his only option. What a shame."

Vicki rolled her legs over onto the deck and stood up. Taking his empty glass she finally broke her silence. "Let me freshen your drink. I believe I can shed some light on Dan's predicament that may alleviate some of your concern."

The tone of voice in which she addressed him was calm and unemotional, causing him to feel a little guilty for having brought the subject up in the first place. Out of courtesy, he came to his feet when he heard her footsteps approaching and addressed her somewhat apologetically. "If you'd prefer not to discuss your relationship with Dan any further, so be it. And, I apologize for continuing to ask questions. It was not my intent to make you uncomfortable. Please forgive me if I have."

"Don't worry about it," she replied, turning slowly to focus on the mass of gray clouds moving steadily in their direction. "I think the reason he didn't accept my offer was to avoid exposing me to what he suspected might have been a dangerous situation. He even had reservations about asking his friend to take him to the marina, but took a chance that honor among thieves, as he put it, was still a viable ethic." Pausing for a moment, she spun around and suggested, "Just for the hell of it, why don't we check out the marina to see if he really left in his boat? Maybe somebody knows something we don't."

"Well, according to Jennifer, that was his specific purpose in coming here yesterday. But, as you suggested, maybe he said something to someone about where he was going. It's worth a try? Lead the way, my dear."

As she drove hurriedly down the beach road, Neal took serious notice that the storm they had been watching develop was now overhead and threatening a down pour at any moment. To avoid getting caught in it, they quickened their pace toward the slip where Dan's boat would usually have been tied up. There was a boat there, but it wasn't Dan's.

"Well, that solves part of the puzzle," he remarked, with noticeable disappointment. "Maybe the Dock Master knows something."

Because of an earlier weather forecast, a fairly large number of local residents – mostly older men – had come to the marina to secure their boats in preparation for the storm front that had now arrived. Many were gathered at the building's small bar to drink and converse when Neal and Vicki walked in, drawing curious glances from most.

"I'm looking for the Dock Master," he announced. "Any of you guys fit that description?"

All he received in way of a response was continued silence, until a younger man rose up from a table in the shadows and asked: "That you Mr. T?"

Squinting his eyes, he looked through the bluish haze of cigarette smoke hanging in the hot humid air and recognized Carl Newman, Billy's son, walking casually across the floor to greet him.

"Well, I'll be damned!" Neal blurted out as the two men approached one another and embraced. "What in the world are you doing down here?"

"You asked for the Dock Master didn't you?" he answered, grinning broadly while glancing at Vickie. "What can I do for you?"

Looking somewhat bewildered, Neal replied, "Didn't you tell me you had your own scuba diving business the last time I saw you?"

"That's right, Mr. T, and I still have it. I'm just filling in here part-time while my boat's being worked on. The regular Dock Master's in the hospital getting some tests done. We're buddies, so I told him I'd help him out. Now, what can I do for you two?"

For the next half an hour the threesome sat outside on the dock while Neal explained why he had returned to the area and asked him if he had seen or heard from Dan recently. His reply was proof that Vicki's suggestion to check out the marina was the best advice he had received since his arrival. It was beginning to add credence to what DEA Director Bronson had called his attempt to find Dan's hideaway; "a wild goose chase."

Though disappointed, he continued to listen in gloomy silence as he described what had taken place yesterday when Dan stopped by his mother's place before leaving the area, apparently for good. "Dan came by here a few days ago in a car driven by a guy I had never seen before, who left immediately after Dan got out. Dan came directly to the office, paid his bill in full and gave me a hundred dollar tip. When I refused to accept it, he insisted, saying that I had been a good friend. I asked him where he was going, thinking he was moving out of his parent's home to get his own place. All he said was, over the rainbow. After leaving me, he went directly to his boat and started his engines. Then, a funny thing happened."

"Go on," Neal encouraged him.

"Shortly after Dan started his engines, another car arrived. Wheeling a large suitcase behind her, an attractive woman got out and went straight to his boat. She hadn't been there long when I saw them arguing. Curious about what was going on, I walked down the pier and stood in the shadows to listen. The woman was crying and pleading for him to take her with him. Evidently, some guy by the name of Miguel Ramirez had beaten her up and threatened to kill her for not doing what he had paid her to do, and for losing the keys to his car. Still crying like a baby, she finally admitted that she had taken his car from the airport parking lot because she had left the keys to this guy Miguel's car in San Diego, whatever that had to do with anything."

"I'm beginning to see the light," Neal remarked. "What next?"

"In the faint light that dimmed his cabin, I watched Dan take the sobbing women into his arms. After holding her for a moment, he laughed and said, "Donna, we're a couple of losers who deserve each other, so before those bastards catch up with us, lets get the hell out of here. I have a plan. The next thing I knew Dan released his mooring lines, pulled out of the slip and faded away into the night with whomever that woman was. I haven't seen nor heard from either of them since."

"Well, I guess that pretty well puts a wrap on things," Neal commented, realizing that any further pursuit of the elusive Dan Hughes was purposeless. "Thanks for clearing up the mystery of his disappearance for me. I'm sure his father, and other interested parties, will be greatly relieved. As for me, I'll be spending the evening at your mother's place tonight and plan to leave for San Diego early tomorrow morning. Once again, thanks and good luck."

"Good seeing you again, Mr. T," he replied, "Give my best wishes to your family." Turning toward Vicki, he remarked, "I've heard my mom mention your name, Vicki. You're Trisha Daniels daughter aren't you?"

"Yes I am, but I'm not here very often. Mostly just weekends now and then," she explained, bringing closure to the conversation.

Carl sensed her reluctance to continue any further conversation, so he bid them both goodbye and returned to the marina building to join his friends. The door had no sooner closed behind him than boats began heaving on the churning water beneath their tethered hulls. Proof positive that the storm had arrived.

Likewise, when Neal and Vicki returned to Jennifer's patio deck, the menace of the storm was upon them. Making no effort to retreat inside, she picked up the two empty glasses that sat beside their two deck chairs and thrust her hands toward him, grinning playfully. "Your turn! Might as well have some fun while we're at it."

When he returned, scattered drops of rain had begun to speckle the redwood decking and her face as she stood looking skyward. "Man, does this feel good, or what?" she sighed. "I could stand here all night."

"Go ahead," he jested. "I doubt you'll melt."

Lowering her head, she opened her eyes and asked, "When was the last time you did something crazy like this?"

Watching the raindrops splash in his drink, he thought for a moment and then replied, "I was in the sixth grade playing sandlot football after school with a motley group of my friends. My team was behind one touchdown when it started to rain, but no one wanted to quit, so we kept on playing until the score was tied. The field had already turned into a sea of mud. Several plays later we were all soaked and laughing so hard the principal heard us. Aggravated, he donned his slicker and broke up the game, telling us all to get our muddy butts home. That's when the fun ended."

"Caught hell, didn't you?"

"Big time," he remembered. "Poor mom. Those were the days of tub and wringer washing machines. Took her half an hour to get the mud out of my clothes before putting them in the machine, and then they had to hang all night near the coal furnace to dry. When my Dad came home that evening she told him what I had done, and he sent me to my room without any supper. Later, she felt sorry for me and brought me a sandwich before I went to bed. What really made me angry was hearing them both laughing downstairs before I fell asleep."

By the time he had finished his story the rainfall had increased to the point where their shirts were clinging to them like wet paper towels. Hers left little to the imagination and she sensed he was undressing her with his eyes. Obviously, he was pleased with what they were doing and made no attempt to seek shelter. Instead, he just sat back and enjoyed the view.

"I can see where you might have been a very mischievous little boy at times," she remarked. "But, you know, sometimes a little mischief can be good for you."

After pausing purposely to see how he would respond, she realized he wasn't going to, even though she was encouraging him to do so "Any comment?" she finally asked.

By that time they were both so wet there was little point in going inside. Stretching out on the recliner beside her, he replied, rather philosophically, "My dear young lady, mischief is all a matter of interpretation. Webster defines it, in part, as *irresponsibly playful,* which would account for my playing football on that rainy afternoon. And, my parent's laughter when they thought I was asleep. On the other hand, having a little too much to drink and groping a women would be considered irresponsible by some, however, playful by others. Getting one's face slapped, or punched out by some jealous boy friend would be considered highly irresponsible and certainly not playful. In my case, I prefer not being taken seriously, because I think of myself as amusingly playful. No one gets hurt, and some actually enjoy the playfulness. End of comment."

"My turn!" she giggled, rising with both their empty glasses and walking toward the door. Holding it half open with her hip, she looked back and remarked, mischievously, "Time to get playfully amusing, as you say."

Watching her maneuver her way into the house he took notice of a slight unsteadiness in her walk that almost suggested they should wait for a while before having another drink. But, by his own definition, he was enjoying her playfulness and remained silent. After all, he rationalized, how much trouble could a person get into just playing in the rain?

Her return, as usual, was blessed with the body movement that was her signature, made all the more pleasant by the wet clothing clinging to her, as if painted on. "While I was inside, I had a thought," she remarked, handing him his drink and sitting down. "When we finish these, why don't we towel ourselves off a bit and have one at Nick's. I don't feel like dressing. We can go there just as we are. Afterwards, I'll fix something to eat here. Is that playful enough for you?"

"Sounds good to me," he replied, slurring a word or two. "I'll buy some shrimp and a bottle of wine at the market while we're there."

Not long thereafter, toweled almost dry, they were laughing in unison at the crazy spontaneity that was taking place as she parked her car in front of the restaurant. Jogging quickly through the relentless rain, they entered and proceeded directly to the bar, observing as they waited that the place was nearly empty.

The sound of their raucous entry distracted the bartender from the newspaper he had been reading and brought him to his feet to take their order, glad for a break in the monotony that was making him sleepy. They had only been there a few minutes when headlights from another car pulled into the parking lot. Moments later, two men entered and sat near them. After they had been served, one of them looked in their direction and smiled as if amused by the wet clothing they had on. Several minutes passed before the same man rose and approached Neal. "Good evening, Mr. Thomas," he said, bowing slightly to both of them. "My name is Miguel Ramirez. I believe we met on Mr. Hughes' boat recently."

Although the sudden appearance of a man he knew only by reputation un-nerved him, Neal maintained his composure and introduced him to Vicki.

She accepted his hand, but offered no conversation other than politeness, having heard more than she had wanted to hear about the infamous Miguel Ramirez during her stormy relationship with Dan Hughes. Her only thought was: *What's that bastard doing here at this time of night?"*

"Are you here on business or pleasure, Mr. Thomas?" he persisted. "I seem to recall you are from California."

Neal recognized Miguel's way of opening a dialogue as an obvious attempt to question him about the whereabouts of Dan Hughes. Determined not to open that door, he simply replied, "Business in Washington brought me so close to old friends in this area that I thought I would visit as many as I could before leaving tomorrow. Who knows when I'll ever have this opportunity again?"

"Have you seen Mr. Hughes during your visit?" he inquired, more aggressively. "I'm sure he would be disappointed if you didn't make the effort."

"Well, unless he shows up here in the next couple of minutes, I'm afraid I'll have to save him for another time." Upending the last of his drink, he placed his arm around Vicki's waist and nudged her to stand, remarking in a tone of finality, "And now, Mr. Ramirez, if you'll excuse us, I'd better call it an evening and ask this lovely lady to take me home. I have an early flight."

Miguel did not make any attempt to bow or shake either of their hands as he watched Neal place a five-dollar bill on the bar. As they turned to leave he remarked, dryly and without expression, "Should you see or hear from Mr. Hughes this evening, please mention that I would like to talk to him."

"I certainly will. Good night."

Outside, the rain had lightened to a warm mist. With no wish to stay there any longer than he had to, Neal purchased some shrimp and a bottle of Chardonnay from the market next door, while Vicki remained outside searching for some indication that there would be a sunset that evening. Unfortunately, the prospect was not good.

During the time it took them to reach Jennifer's home, Neal remained silent. Because she knew how upset the unexpected meeting with Ramirez had left him, she too refrained from speaking until they were safely inside. Then she asked a delicately phrased question that she hoped would trigger a positive response. "Would you object to me spending the night here? No one's home at my place, and seeing Ramirez has me a little on edge."

"I'm sure Jennifer wouldn't mind," he replied, without thinking, "but what about your clothes?"

"Everything I need is already in my car, including an alarm clock. I'll go get them while you pour us a glass of wine. Then I'll start dinner."

During her absence, he went into the guest room and removed his wet clothing, quickly replacing them with dry shorts and a sport shirt. He was standing in the kitchen pouring their wine when she returned. Seeing him already changed surprised her, so she chuckled and asked, "Who are you, anyway, Speedy Gonzales?"

The reference amused him, not having heard it for many years. "You'd better get out of those wet clothes too," he advised. "There's a dryer in the laundry room downstairs. I'll dry our clothes while you fix dinner."

Glass in hand Vicki pulled her flight bag down the hall and into the guest room where Neal's bag went un-noticed in the half-light entering from the hallway. In minutes she had changed into a knee-length Teddy and returned to the kitchen where she searched through Jennifer's refrigerator for something to compliment the shrimp. To her surprise, she discovered a bowl of deliciously seasoned macaroni salad topped with deviled eggs.

"Eureka!" she exclaimed excitedly as she removed the find. "Thank you, Jennifer!"

While their wet clothing tumbled in the dryer, he returned upstairs and lingered outside on the deck to enjoy the warm ocean breeze with his wine. He hadn't been there long when he heard the screen door open behind him. "Dinner is on the table," she mentioned as she came closer and stood by the railing. "You'll love the presentation."

Turning his head, he noticed that all the lights inside had been turned off, but candlelight from the dining room table cast a soft shadowy glow from within.

"I found them in one of the kitchen drawers," she explained. "Kind of romantic, isn't it?"

Whether the sudden urge to hold her came from the fragrance she was wearing or the wine, or a combination of both, he was too overwhelmed by the combination of her almost transparent attire and the ambiance she had created to resist, and succumbed without hesitation or remorse. For a moment he was afraid he might have misinterpreted her provocative innuendos and had jeopardized their friendship, but his anxiety was short-lived. Spontaneously, she placed her hands on either side if his whiskered face and gently drew his lips down to hers, erasing all fear that he had done anything improper.

Later on that evening while he lay restlessly in bed listening to her cleaning up the kitchen, he noticed for the first time that she had placed her travel bag in the guest room too. Moments later, as he puzzled with the dilemma of whose room he was in, he heard a light switch plunge the house into darkness, followed by her almost invisible silhouette entering the room and compressing the empty mattress beside him.

"Now, my sweet Mr. T," she whispered, trying not to giggle, "Don't you think we ought to take Mr. Webster at his word by getting a little irresponsibly playful?

Like the shocking sound of someone dropping a plate, Vicki's travel alarm shattered the pre-dawn silence the next morning sending them both to finish waking up in the overly large shower in Jennifer's bathroom. He couldn't remember the last time he had showered with a woman, but it didn't matter. Now was now, and she was determined to made it fun and irresponsibly playful.

In less time than they would have liked, two cups of coffee had been mutually enjoyed and their bags were packed. While he carried them to the driveway below, she made one final check of the house to insure that Jennifer's home was safe and secure for her return. Satisfied that everything was in order, she locked the front door and joined him in her car.

The sky above the horizon was gradually showing signs of daylight when they backed out of the driveway to begin their relatively short trip to the airport, each looking forward to traveling their separate ways, regretting nothing.

When they arrived, she insisted on accompanying him to his departure gate to bid him a fond farewell, and express her gratitude for all he had put himself through to help Jennifer find her husband's killer, not to mention the troublesome Dan Hughes. They were drinking coffee in a fast-food shop when she finally expressed what had been on her mind since leaving the beach. "The brutal reality of all this is, when you walk through that gate over there, I'll never see you again. What makes accepting that fact a little easier is the beautiful memory you're leaving with me. I know both Jennifer and Dan would have shared that thought with you, were they here. So, I'm speaking for all of us when I give you Bob Hope's memorable goodbye with all the love and friendship I can give; thanks for the memory."

Hearing her sentiments expressed so beautifully made his effort to express his thanks an awkward one. She saw his struggle and the sparkle of tears begin to gather, so she reached across the table and placed her finger on his lips, whispering comfortingly, "S-h-h-h, you don't have to say anything. Finish your coffee. I really must leave now."

While he struggled to regain his composure, she stood and kissed him on the forehead before turning to leave, but hesitated. Looking back with a happy smile on her face, she remarked, "Oh, about that up close and personal thing last night. I just thought you'd like to know that some little girls like to play in the mud too. See you, big guy."

He managed a weak smile as he dried his eyes and watched her disappear down the crowded concourse, convinced that he had seen her beautiful face for the last time."

The flight to Washington was uneventful, giving him some leisure time to examine his expenses, which, except for a couple of drinks and a few shrimp, were hardly worth reporting. Thus, he decided to return the money the DEA had given him, concluding that it might minimize the ass chewing he was going to get from Dusty Lewis when he returned. An event he was not looking forward to. And, there was his brother, Joel, whom he had promised to spend some time with before he left. Now made impossible by the hasty reservations Vicki's co-worker had arranged for him. Although he knew his brother would understand, he wasn't so sure about, Dusty Lewis, whom he expected would be waiting to talk with him with baited breath.

True to his word, he called his brother's office and, as expected, received a generous portion of understanding when he explained why his mission had failed. In reply, Joel commented, "Having known Dan Hughes during my younger days, I find it difficult to believe that he hadn't covered your butt before hauling his out of the country, if that's where he is. My guess is that he has a trump card up his sleeve and is holding it to capture an ace, not a deuce."

"I hope you're right, Bro, I'm running out of time."

With the nagging thought that Dan Hughes had planned his own disappearance still on his mind, he walked directly to the lounge where he and Sandy Sterling had lingered following their arrival in Washington almost two weeks ago. There in welcomed solitude he sat alone trying to figure out what Dan was trying to tell him in the sealed note he left with Jennifer Newman. Obviously, there was a purpose behind leaving it with her, but his mind was so cluttered with everything else that had taken place, he decided to give his brain a rest and let time suffer with it. That settled, he finished his coffee and headed for the shuttle, anxious to be on his way home again

Fortunately, the return flight to San Diego was uneventful, providing him an opportunity to get some much-needed rest, but the anxiety resulting from his failed mission taunted him frequently, rendering restful dozing impossible. Eventually, he gave up and passed time by watching an in-flight movie until the mountains east of San Diego made their presence known. With renewed optimism that his return would be rewarded in some unexpected way, he watched the horizon as if in a trance until the airport's runway beckoned in the distance. He was home.

As expected, Ron was waiting patiently at curbside when he left the baggage claim area, and wasted little time getting back on the freeway once his friend was in the truck. To avoid lingering at his place to fill him in on the details of his trip, he summarized the major events, proclaiming that only a death in the family could force him to go back East again. "It's a great place to be from," he remarked as Ron pulled into his driveway. "Let's just leave it at that."

Shaking Ron's hand, he expressed his thanks and excused himself, using the premise that he had several stops to make on the way home.

Ron recognized the urgency in his voice and waved him off, asking, "You planning on being here Friday?"

Hesitating a moment to transfer his bag and briefcase into his car, he shrugged his shoulders and replied, "Depends. I need to talk to Paula first, but I'll be in touch soon."

Still unable to dismiss the ever-present enigma of Dan's written message, he drove directly to the Post Office and opened his box. Given his history of never receiving anything but junk mail, he expected to find much the same thing. However, he was surprised to find two unexpected and apparently unrelated items there. One was a numbered key that meant he had received a package too large for the box. The other was a small package slightly larger than a postcard. Placing the small package in his hip pocket, he proceeded to the larger box bearing the key's number. Viewing its contents, the mystery of what Dan had so cleverly orchestrated presented itself in the form of a wooden crate equal in size and weight to a hand-carried toolbox. It had been shipped from his family's home address.

Still sitting in the Post Office parking lot, he delayed his departure long enough to open the small box he had placed in his pocket. It contained a cassette tape labeled: *A Message For Mr. T.*

Driven by a sudden and exhilarating sense of purpose, Neal drove home as rapidly as traffic would allow, convinced that the two items he had received contained clues to the mystery surrounding Dan's disappearance. His elation, however, was short-lived.

In attempting to unlock the front door, he discovered it had been locked from the inside in such a way as to prevent it from being opened. Close inspection of the casing revealed that someone had forced the door open and had broken the lock. His immediate reaction was that Paula had misplaced her key and had to resort to breaking in. But why, he asked himself, she usually came in through the garage. When he was forced to do the same thing, the answer was frighteningly clear. He was stunned by the realization that someone, other than Paula, had broken in. Closet doors were left open, along with drawers in every piece of furniture in the house, upstairs and down. Angered by the intrusion, the thought suddenly struck him that whoever broke in was looking for something other than household items, or other valuables. Nothing had been taken or broken. Even Paula's jewelry was still in her dresser drawer. Returning to the garage, his suspicions were confirmed. Standing against the wall with its drawers pried open was his file cabinet, its contents strewn in disarray on the floor.

"The map!" he shouted in anger. "They were after that damn map!"

It took over an hour, but fueled with the energy generated by his anger, he managed to restore the domestic order that he knew Paula would be expecting to find when she returned. Only then did he notice the blinking red light on the telephone answering machine. Weary and frustrated he pressed the button and waited. Paula's subdued and sometimes broken voice began to speak. "My dearest Neal, by now you will have begun to appreciate how frightening it was for me to return home and discover that someone had broken into our home. I called the police, but their investigation turned up nothing. I couldn't find anything missing, so I signed an incident report to document the break-in. Before they left, one of the officer's nailed the door shut, but I was so afraid to stay there alone, I packed a bag and returned to Ellen's. Call me after you get this message. I have something serious to discuss with you. Hope your trip went well.... Bye."

"Now what?" he blurted out loud when the message ended.

Still frustrated by the break-in, and the out-of-character seriousness of Paula's voice, he decided to wait until after he had had a good night's rest before taking on what she said she wanted to discuss with him. With a crowbar he had picked up in the garage, and Dan's cassette beginning to play in the background, he began to disassemble the wooden crate as Dan's message began. "Hi there, Mr. T. By the time you listen to this tape, Donna and me will be safely on our way out of the country and you'll have all the proof the DEA needs to initiate a full investigation into Miguel Ramirez's affiliation with the Tidewater Drug Cartel. I am truly sorry for having involved you in all of this, but I just couldn't run the risk of Ramirez finding my hideaway before I could mail you the toolbox, so I picked it up in my boat right after I got back from California and torched the place. Maybe someday that evidence will help absolve me of some of things I have done in my foolish past and I can come home without the fear of being killed, until then, stay in touch with my dad. I've already made my peace with him, my sister and Jennifer Newman. Your reward is in the box. Be sure to save this tape. It may come in handy in explaining my bizarre behavior of late and will help document how you obtained the evidence. Thanks again, my friend, and good luck."

By the time the message ended, he had succeeded in removing the all-to-familiar toolbox from its shipping crate, but it was locked. Puzzled, he searched the crate thoroughly for some sign of a key, but was unsuccessful until he concentrated on the box itself. Only after turning it on its side did he notice the outline of a key underneath a piece of duct tape that had been placed inconspicuously on one of the bottom corners. Peeling it carefully back, the old, partially rusted key became visible. He laughed while removing it and said out loud, "Danny boy, you are some piece of work."

Inside the old and somewhat tattered box – along with all the documents, photographs and microfilm he had remembered seeing weeks ago – sat a package Dan had addressed to him. With nervous hands and an aroused curiosity, he carefully removed the thick, watertight wrapping and gasped in awe at its contents. "Oh my God!" he exclaimed in disbelief. Stacked in the package were twenty bound bundles of fifty, one hundred dollar bills, totaling one hundred thousand dollars. The shock of seeing all that much money opened a floodgate of mixed emotions, none the least of which asked the question: *What the hell does one do with this much loot?*

Perplexed on the one hand, and deliriously happy on the other, he sat for several minutes contemplating the ramifications of revealing to Paula that his persistent loyalty to values embedded in honesty, friendship and commitment had at long last been rewarded. Ironically, by the least likely person he could have imagined. The irony of it all mouthed a chuckle and a serious thirst to celebrate his bizarre inheritance. Leaving the cache where it lay, he went to the kitchen and mixed a drink, determined to pursue his destiny with renewed spirit and self esteem. After noting the time, he decided that although it was getting late in the day, establishing contact with Dusty Lewis to tell him he was in possession of the ill-fated evidence was his highest priority. By doing so, Dusty would hardly be in a position to deny seeing him, especially when he learned that his expense money was being returned as a bonus.

Although diplomatic, Neal could sense a tone of calm indifference in his voice when he answered. Rather than toy with him, as he would have liked to, he came right to the point, reinforced with the knowledge that he was now Dusty's ticket to a possible promotion. "Call Bronson in Washington tomorrow morning and tell him I will be in your office here in San Diego at nine o'clock sharp, and not to eat any lunch. Mention that I will have a large portion of crow for him to munch on instead. He'll know what I mean."

"What the hell's going on?" Dusty snapped. "Am I missing something here?"

"You sure are," he teased, "but I can't talk about it over the phone."

"Damn you, Neal!" he yelled in frustration. What are you up to?"

"Tomorrow, old buddy. Nine o'clock."

He hung up before Dusty could pursue the matter further, smug in his confidence that tomorrow would be a turning point in what had heretofore been a life of settled and modest comfort. With that thought in mind he withdrew a single packet of bills from the money-laden package and placed it in one of the rarely worn UGG Boots that sat in his bedroom closet. The balance he took to the garage where he puzzled over a suitable place to hide it, since his broken filing cabinet no longer offered any security.

The place that finally satisfied his need was a leather travel bag that had belonged to his grandfather. It had been stored, inconspicuously, on a shelf in the garage ever since they moved there. What better place, he thought, climbing a ladder to bring it down. Inside the bag, a false bottom provided a hidden compartment usually used to store cash and other valuables whenever one traveled. Once the package was carefully concealed, and the bag returned to its seldom-visited storage place, he turned his attention toward the toolbox. After careful consideration, he decided the safest hiding place was upstairs under his bed where no one could get to it without first having to deal with him, and the revolver that was also hidden there.

Sitting alone in his easy chair with one hundred thousand dollars of hidden money to bolster his slowly dwindling assets, he decided he would rest easier that night if he touched base with Paula so she would be apprised of his safe return, and to ease her mind about the break-in. After several rings the phone picked-up and a sleepy voice answered, "Hello?"

"Sorry to call this late," he apologized. "I got your message and thought you might appreciate knowing that I am back and unscathed. It took awhile, but I managed to restore things back to normal. As far as I can tell, nothing appears to be missing. I'll put a new lock on the door tomorrow so don't fret over that. How are you, by the way?"

"How nice of you to ask," she replied, sarcastically. "I'm fine, and you?"

Her tone of her voice conveyed all he needed to know about what kind of a disposition she was in. To continue the conversation any further, he concluded, would not be in the best interest of maintaining civility, so he suggested that they defer any discussion about the break-in until after she returned. She agreed without argument and remarked, "Thanks for calling. I'm glad you're home safely, and I'll see you tomorrow."

Much as he hoped the cliché, *things will look better in the morning,* had promise he couldn't deny a gut feeling that promised to the contrary. Since the front door had already been nailed shut he lugged the toolbox upstairs and slid it under his bed. With the alarm set for six o'clock the next morning, he collapsed without undressing onto the unmade bed Paula had left behind in her hurry to leave. Sleep came quickly, calming the anxiety that had built up during the day, and provided some measure of rest before it would began all over again in only a few hours.

Despite being tempted to ignore what had alarmed him from a restless sleep the next morning, he silenced the irritating buzzer and accepted the message it had so rudely delivered. Swinging his legs lethargically over onto the floor he made his way clumsily into the bathroom and began the daily routine of waking up. On other occasions of lesser importance, the process might have been more enjoyable and taken more time. This morning, however, was energized by his desire to confront Dusty Lewis with the heretofore-considered mythical information that had almost cost Neal his credibility.

With Dan's toolbox in hand, and only one cup of coffee and an English muffin to fuel his growing excitement, he left through the garage and proceed Southward to vindicate his bruised sense of self-esteem. At least this time, he reassured himself, he would have enough tangible information to convince the DEA that what he had led them to a few days prior was not the "wild goose chase" Director Raymond Bronson had branded it. As his car ate up the miles one by one, his mind kept repeating over and over, the day of reckoning has finally arrived. Gloating a bit, he mumbled out loud, "I just hope you like crow, Bronson."

Ginger Spyce was sitting alone at her desk when he entered. "Thanks to you," she scowled with disapproval, "I was told to be here when you arrived. If I may ask, what's so important that it couldn't wait until nine o'clock?"

"I'm sorry," he apologized, sitting the toolbox down on the chair beside her "I'm here to deliver this goose."

"Goose?

"Yeah. The one Ray Bronson thought he was chasing back in Virginia. Or, haven't you heard?"

Before she could answer, the door he had just entered through opened again and in walked Dusty Lewis with three large containers of coffee. Handing one to each of them, he greeted them cordially and continued on toward his private office, inviting Neal to follow. Picking up the toolbox, Neal turned toward Ginger and remarked, with a wink, "I'll explain about the goose on my way out."

Ginger hand-motioned him to get going and replied, almost laughing, "You'd better!"

Inside Dusty's office the two men sat silently facing one another for a moment while they tended to their coffee. After his first sip, Dusty opened the dialogue. "I spoke with Ray Bronson briefly this morning. He wasn't all that happy to learn that I was meeting with you again, and is expecting a full report from me as soon as this meeting is over. Now, tell me what the hell is this all about, will you?"

For the next several minutes he described in detail what had taken place following the so-called "wild goose chase" Bronson had accused him of leading him on. He further described what was waiting for him when he returned to San Diego the previous day, however, purposely avoided any mention of the cash Dan had sent him. Placing the toolbox on his desk, he handed Dusty the key and said, rather haughtily, "There's enough evidence in this toolbox to hang every member of the Tidewater Drug Cartel in Virginia, and maybe some others. If Bronson has any doubts about where it came from, tell him I have a cassette tape that Dan sent me to authenticate what I've just told you. That, my friend, is what the hell this is all about."

Dusty opened the toolbox and carefully inspected every item of its contents. When he finished, he slumped back in his chair and struggled for the right words to say, but could only admit, "I don't know what to say. I am truly humbled by the magnitude of what this evidence represents. I'm speechless, and a simple thank you just won't cut it, but what can I say? I'm sorry for doubting you? Okay, I'm sorry!"

Impatient to be on his way, Neal stood to leave. Dusty knew he had no reason to detain him any further, but cautioned him not to discuss the matter with anyone. Extending his hand in friendship he said, "Though it sounds terribly shallow now, I'd still like to say, thank you. I will personally make sure that Ray Bronson is made aware of what you and Dan Hughes have contributed to this investigation. As for me, I can assure you that your efforts will not go un-rewarded. And that's a promise."

Satisfied that his promise to Dan had been officially satisfied, he said goodbye and left Dusty in the process of placing a call to Director Bronson. Stopping momentarily, he looked back and remarked, "When you get a hold of Bronson, tell him crow tastes better if the feathers are removed."

Still gloating, he stopped at Ginger's desk before leaving and opened his briefcase.

"Here," he said, placing the expense money envelope on her desk. "Except for the airline tickets, I haven't spent anything."

Visibly surprised, she took the envelope and asked, suspiciously, "I guess I shouldn't ask if you cheat on your income taxes, should I?"

"I refuse to answer on the grounds that it might incriminate me," he replied, trying to get a rise out of her.

"Never mind, I already know the answer," she assured him. "Now, what's all this "goose" business about?"

He smiled, closed his briefcase and winked, "Ask your boss."

With a lightness of heart he had not experienced for some time he left the city's congested streets and headed home, stopping only to purchase a new front door lock and handle assembly. He hadn't engaged in many do-it-yourself projects for quite some time, so the menial task gave him a sense of purpose and the opportunity to mentally prepare for Paula's return that night.

He had only just started to replace the broken fixture when the phone rang. Laying his tools aside he went to answer its persistent ringing and was pleasantly surprised to hear Jennifer Newman's voice on the other end. "Just checking to make sure you made it home all right," she began. "And to thank you for all you've done. I would love to have spent more time with you, but I'm sure Vicky Daniels made up for my absence."

Realizing she knew more than she was going to admit, he took the initiative and explained, "As a matter of fact, she came by the house shortly after you left and suggested that we go to the marina to see if anyone there could shed some light on where Dan might have been going when he left. Guess who filled me in?"

"My son, of course," she replied. "He told me that you and Vicki had inquired about Dan. Have you learned anything since then?"

What Agent Lewis had cautioned him about came immediately to mind. Knowing that Dan was already on this way out of the country didn't seem to have much to do with anything any more, so he simply replied, "All I can tell you is that Dan is alive and safely on his way out of the country with Donna Sanders, of all people. What he left behind will eventually avenge Billy's death. Trust me on this one, Jennifer, justice will be served."

"I get the message. Thanks for all your help."

A short pause followed that falsely gave the impression that she was about to hang up, but she came back on the line to have the last laugh by interjecting a humorous comment. "By the way, lover boy," she remarked, "the next time you and Vicki use my dryer, don't leave her underwear in it!" The dial tone ended all there was to say.

Noon was approaching when he completed installing the new front door lock. Hunger pains signaled it was time for lunch, but the thought of eating alone on a day that had started out with such promise was not all that exciting, so he put his tools away and considered his options. The search ended when he remembered he had promised Sandy and Jessica Sterling an update on Dan's whereabouts during their last luncheon meeting at Bully's. Excited by the prospect of seeing them again, he called their office and asked to speak to Ms. Sterling, Senior. Elevator music held him captive for a moment until her familiar voice came online. "I was beginning to think you had disappeared," she remarked. "How are you?"

"I'm fine. How would you and Jessica like to join me for lunch at Bully's? I'll fill you in on all the details then."

"This is awfully short notice. Let me put you on hold while I check my schedule."

Automatically the familiar piano styling of Oscar Peterson filled his ears while he waited for her to return, but was soon interrupted by her enthusiastic voice asking, "How about two o'clock?"

"Great, I'll see you there."

Following their brief conversation, his conscience reminded him that his preoccupation with the affairs of others had resulted in neglecting his own everyday responsibilities. Thus, he used the next few hours putting his financial business in order and reading neglected mail. Having come into the added resources that Dan Hughes had so generously endowed him with made the task considerably less bothersome. As far as what he had planned to do in the way of a serious art project, he decided to put his luncheon date to good use by taking the oil painting he had been working on to Bully's, so Tommy could judge whether or not it was suitable for the restaurant. Both interests he hoped would convince Paula that their future together was back on track, especially since the prospect of there being any further fallout from the aftermath of Dan Hughes's unexpected intrusion was highly unlikely. Armed with that certainty he removed a one hundred dollar bill from the UGG Boot in his closet and drove down the coast to enjoy a few hours of well-deserved relaxation.

Contrary to the usually crowded interior he had expected to find, Bully's was only partially occupied, making it easier to show Tommy the painting he had brought with him without causing customer curiosity to soar. He chose a corner booth for that purpose and asked the waitress to escort Ms. Sterling and her daughter there when they arrived. He had already ordered his second glass of wine when she entered the restaurant alone. Recognizing her immediately from her previous meeting with Neal, Tommy met her just inside the door and personally escorted her to his booth. "Your charming guest is here, Neal, he announced congenially. "Would you care for a drink, madam?"

"Yes please. I'd like a glass of that delicious Chardonnay you served the last time I was here."

"Ah, you remembered, dear lady. Thank you. I'll take care of it myself."

After Tommy was beyond hearing distance, Neal turned toward her and asked, "Where's Jessica?"

"She called me this morning from Virginia to inform me that the business matters she went there to take care of were finished, and she would be returning home tomorrow. Evidently, she made an attempt to contact Dan Hughes, but was unsuccessful. She sounded a little disappointed because I think she really liked that man."

To provide her with something she could pass on to Jessica that might put a positive note on that particular subject, he said, "Given his somewhat questionable past, his questionable whereabouts, and who knows what kind of a future, I'd say he did her one hell of a favor by not being there. Unless, of course, she's into his type of lifestyle."

"Hardly," she remarked, somewhat offended by his uncalled for insinuation. "Not after what she's been through."

Before the conversation could progress any further, their waitress approached with two fresh glasses of wine and Tommy following close behind. Pulling a chair over to join them, he excused himself for intruding and explained, "Ron Barns was in here the other day and presented me with a computer-generated portfolio of your artwork. I was so impressed I made up my mind right then to commission you to create a painting I could hang on that blank space right over there. Any ideas?"

Neal looked in that direction and immediately visualized the painting he had brought in with him hanging there. "Call it fate, coincidence, or whatever," he said,"but right here beside me is that oil painting I told you I was working on the last time I saw you. It's finished enough to determine if you think it's what you want to hang there. Would you like to see it?"

"You didn't bring it here not to show me, did you?

To provide suitable space for viewing, Sandy moved several feet in the semi-circular booth, while Neal pulled the stretched canvas out of one end of its paper wrapping.

It took a few seconds for Tommy to react, but when he did there was no denying his feelings when he did. "My God! My customers will think they're looking through a picture window," he said, excitedly. "How large is it?"

"Twenty-four by thirty-six inches. Framing is up to you, unless you want me to have it done. I've got a friend in the business."

"How much when it's finished?"

"I'll call you tomorrow."

"Fair enough," he replied. "Ron has already filled me in on your fifty percent down payment. I'll cut you a check the next time you come in, deal?"

Offering him his hand in agreement, he replied, "Deal. Did Ron also explain my work schedule?"

Tommy laughed and replied, "Yeah, I know. It's done when it's done. I'm in no hurry, but can you give me an approximate date?"

Neal assessed the approximate hours he had already spent. Taking into account that completing the work could be full time, now that Dan Hughes was out of the picture, he replied, "How about a month from now?"

"Perfect! Enjoy your lunch, and don't forget to call me about the total price." Turning toward Sandy as he stood up to leave, he remarked, flirtatiously, "Always a pleasure Ms. Sterling. Come back soon."

While Neal's concentration was still focused on the wall space where Tommy had planned to hang his painting, Sandy slumped back against the booth and sighed: "Well he sure took the wind out of my sails."

Confused, he turned and asked: "What wind?"

During the lunch that followed, Sandy explained that she and Jessica had just recently reviewed the entire history of her past, including her relationship with Dan Hughes, up to and including Neal's involvement. Both had agreed that such a story had the potential of becoming a best seller, especially with the ending promising such a dramatic conclusion, and with the possibility of other books to follow. "We were hoping you could be persuaded to author the book," she added, with a hint of disappointment. "But, I gather from what I just heard, your time will be pretty well dedicated to Mr. Camillo's project for the next month, or longer."

Overwhelmed by her proposal, he stopped eating long enough to digest the importance of the opportunity he had just been offered. He was on the verge of saying that he could handle both projects when Sandy continued: "Of course our offer carries an up-front commission of twenty-five thousand dollars, and the usual contractual options following publication."

Unable to determine the personal demands her proposal would impose on such short notice, he pushed his plate aside and signaled their waitress to bring another round of wine. Sensing that his recent gratuity from Dan Hughes, and the financial benefits that her offer represented were all part of some crazy dream, he excused himself and went to the men's room, wondering on the way if she would still be there when he returned. She was.

Faced with the reality that destiny had just placed a fork in the road of his life overnight, he returned to the table with his answer to Sandy's proposal already formulated. "I've been working more than one job all my adult life, my dear Ms. Sterling," he remarked, with more than just a little pride, " but at least I'm retired now and have the option to chose whether or not I want to continue doing that. Looking at the long term rewards, however, I am forced to ask, when and how much?"

Before going their separate ways, he agreed to sign a contract in her office the next day in exchange for a check in the amount she had mentioned. As far as they were both concerned, it was a done deal and their paths separated shortly thereafter.

He chose the Coast Highway route home, rather than spoil the high he was experiencing by mixing it with the anxiety of fighting traffic on the freeway. Part of his elation came from the anticipation of telling Paula about what he had accomplished that day. Certainly, he reassured himself, all of his good fortune was bound to have a calming affect on whatever anxieties she might still be harboring as a result of the recent break-in. With only a little over an hour left before she would be retuning home from work, he decided to enjoy his good fortune in the company of his favorite bartender, Maggie Jyles.

The lounge was virtually deserted when he entered. Maggie, as he had anticipated, was on duty and greeted him with her usual vivaciousness.

"How'd your trip go, Mr. T? Did you ever find out what happened to that crazy friend of yours?"

Without going into details she wouldn't understand anyway, he summarized trivial events and concluded with a joking remark that he thought she would appreciate. "Let's just say Dan's been able to bypass harm's way and wanted me to convey his fondest regards and sincerest apologies for being such an ass while he was here."

"I'd like to believe he was that considerate, Mr. T, but thanks for cleaning up his act, anyway. I hope he finds what he's looking for. Lord knows it wasn't out here."

Surprised by her insight, he raised his eyebrows and opted not to comment. After a few minutes of idle chatter that didn't seem to be going anywhere, he finished the last of his drink, tipped her and started to leave.

Expressing her thanks, she kidded him as he turned to leave. "Leaving so soon? Who's the lucky lady?"

Hesitating for a moment, he turned and faced her as the high he was still flying on challenged his aggressiveness. The ultimate temptress, she just stood there smiling with both hands gripping her tray, as if to say, *you'll never get a better chance,* so he made his move. With both hands holding her shoulders, he drew her to him, mating his lips with hers for just an instant then backed away. As he turned to leave, she giggled and asked, "Were you trying to tell me something?"

Grinning, and very much pleased with how effortlessly she had responded to his embrace, he waved goodbye and replied, "Next time let's try it without the tray."

With Paula's car already in front of the garage when he pulled into the driveway, he glanced at his watch and noticed his arrival was later than he had intended. Anxious to put the Dan Hughes affair behind him and surprise Paula with the two new projects he had acquired that day, he activated the garage door opener and stepped out of his car. Exactly at the same time he heard her voice call out as she approached from the bluffs. "It's about time you showed up, Mr. Fix-it," she remarked, sounding irritated. "Do you realize I don't have a key to that new front door lock?"

"Where's your garage door opener?" he replied, surprised by her sudden appearance, and apparent anger. "That's the way you usually come in. I must have forgotten to put the new spare key where we always keep it. Sorry about that. I had no idea you'd be home before I got here."

"I'm not blaming you," she apologized. "I came home early from work hoping to get here before you went down to The Pub. I wanted to discuss a matter that I've been reluctant to bring up before now, because

I wasn't sure how you'd react. It's going to have serious repercussions on our relationship. The last thing I expected was that my garage door opener wouldn't work. Maybe it's the batteries. I guess I'm just a little peeved because you weren't here when I expected you to be. Where have you been, by the way?"

Rather than fuel the already burning fire by telling her too many details, he hedged the question with a generality he hoped would put the matter to rest. "After I replaced the front door lock, I went to buy some oil paints I need to complete the oil painting Tommy Camillo is buying to hang in Bully's Restaurant.

"Uh huh," she remarked, suspiciously. "That would explain the lipstick, right?"

"Must have been the waitress at Bully's," he lied, reaching for his handkerchief. "I went there to discuss the painting with Tommy earlier, had a drink and then left. They all kiss me goodbye. No big deal."

"Don't bother explaining," she remarked, seemingly unconcerned about whether or not he was telling the truth. "I'm sure whoever put it there doesn't have any more sense than you do, so let's get on with the more pressing issue before us. Although I know you've already had a few, I suggest you fix another one while I explain what has taken place since the last time I saw you. And, please, don't interrupt!"

As they entered the house together, he became chillingly aware that he was about to be told something that his intuition warned him would not be to his liking. Something about Paula's sudden dispassionate behavior dispelled whatever elation he had built up throughout the day and left him suddenly fearful about what she had to say. As she had suggested, he fixed another drink and sat opposite her in the living room waiting for her to speak. After her eyes made an almost melancholy sweep of the room, she lowered them and said, "I'm sure you can understand how frightened I was the other day when I came home to discover that our home had been broken into. I had to assume that the break-in had something to do with your involvement with Dan Hughes. Obviously, whoever broke in was after something other than valuables, because nothing had been taken. I made up my mind right then that I would not stay in this house until after you returned. I packed a few clothes and stayed with Mike and Ellen, who both expressed their concern about the break-in. They offered me sanctuary until you came home, or longer if need be. Coincidentally, something did take place while I was staying with them that forced me to take a hard look at my life and where it was going. That's what I want to talk to you about."

His eyes had remained continually fixed on her throughout her entire statement. With every word he began to decipher the verbal code that he sensed was slowly becoming a prelude to the ending of their long and intimate relationship. "A discussion usually involves one or more persons, my dear," he remarked in an effort to reduce the tension he felt was building. "Am I released from your mandate to remain silent?"

"Not just yet," she replied, aggressively. "You still haven't heard what I'm planning, so hear me out."

"Carry on, Madame Floor Person," he remarked, sarcastically. "You have the floor."

"Thank you, Mr. Chairman," she replied in response to his humorous attempt to disrupt her train of thought. "I think the time has arrived when I can no longer endure the day-to-day petty politics and mismanagement that have now become an intolerable part of my job. My promotion and financial responsibilities have prevented me from seeking other job opportunities as a consequence. While I was staying with my family, however, I made the acquaintance of a flower nursery owner by the name of Franklin Potter who is a neighbor and good friend of Mike and Ellen's. He confided in me that, because of his age, he was no longer able to keep pace with the physical demands that his business required, and has decided to retire as soon as he can find someone to manage it for him. The more we talked about my background, the more interested he became. The next day he called and presented me with an offer I couldn't refuse, given the limitations that are currently imposed on my career. For these reasons I have decided to spend my weekends with Mike and Ellen until such time as I feel competent to run Mr. Franklin's business. Running my own nursery is something I've wanted to do. If I don't do it now, the opportunity may never come my way again. If I prove myself to be a competent manager, he will consider giving me an option to buy the business. You can't imagine how much that possibility would mean to me."

While he silently tried to evaluate the personal ramifications of her decision, she went to the kitchen, poured another glass of wine and continued. "I want to assure you that my decision has nothing to do with you, personally. Although at times, recently, while you were involved with Dan Hughes and all of his nefarious activities, I have questioned your sanity, but that's just you. You do what you feel you are morally obligated to do, regardless of the consequences. And now, for those same reasons, so must I."

His failure to interrupt, which he was occasionally guilty of whenever she wanted to discuss something that was of particular interest to her, came as a surprise. To assure herself that he was paying attention, and understood the consequences of her decision, she leaned forward in her chair and said, "Please tell me that you understand what I'm saying. Talk to me!"

"Phew," he sighed, relieved that her decision was far less serious than he had anticipated. "I must admit you had me worried there for a minute. I was almost ready to conclude that you wanted out of our relationship."

Despite her desire to maintain a climate of seriousness, she could not dismiss being amused by his total misinterpretation of what she was trying to say. Caught up in the realization that she may have unintentionally caused him undue concern, she replied, "Are you kidding? I still need your half of the rent, as you so tenderly phrased it not too long ago."

He laughed and replied, "How touching. However, let me ease your mind by assuring you that I have always been conscious of your hidden passion to achieve more than your present job could ever offer. Because I was possessed with that same passion many years ago, I uprooted my family from a way of life they were perfectly content with in order to fulfill that same dream. I did it, why shouldn't you? Though I shall miss you during the week, I cannot, in all good conscience, selfishly permit my personal needs to deny you a future that has already been granted me. So, do what you have to do. I'll survive. Besides, between the artwork Tommy Camillo has commissioned me to do, and the book Sterling Publishing wants me to write, I doubt we'd see much of each other anyway. So, what's new?"

Hesitating long enough to freshen his drink, he added, with a tone of foreboding, "To further complicate matters, I'm not so sure I won't be called back to Washington in the near future to testify for the DEA in their case against the Tidewater Drug Cartel Dan was mixed up with. I have this premonition that my knowledge of his past is soon going to place me before a Grand Jury. Now, isn't that something to look forward to?"

In a futile attempt to hold back the flood of emotion that was slowly blurring her vision, she covered her face not knowing whether to speak or laugh.

Neal, on the other hand, experienced an unexpected feeling of release now that their feelings were freely expressed. As if shedding a wet suit, he walked confidently over to where she sat wiping her eyes, drew her up into his arms and confessed: "I hate to tell you this, Tootsie, but you may have just done me a huge favor, so dry your eyes. We can't fix something that isn't broken."

Still sniffling a bit and wiping the tears from her watering eyes, she backed suddenly away from his comforting embrace and shouted, "A favor!"

Recognizing his poor choice of words, he made light of the faux pas and explained, "What I meant dear was, I'm a tired old man, and getting more tired every day. Your new challenge will give us both an opportunity to do what we have to do without having to live up to some pseudo level of performance we have grown to expect from each other. Now, we won't have to. I can do what I want, when I want, and you can do the same. After all, it's not like we're newlyweds."

"Well now, there's an enlightening observation," she remarked. "Even though I don't believe you for one minute. You're just using your age as an excuse for not doing what you don't want to do. It's a guy thing. What's with this saying, *you're only as old as the woman your with?* Well, I'm a hell of a lot younger than you are, so get with the program.

Chapter 19

Journey's End

The morning following Paula's return found Neal lying restlessly in bed thinking about the two projects that would be demanding his full attention during the months ahead, and the emotional upset that Paula's decision to accept Franklin Potter's offer to buy into his business had caused him. Those thoughts, in addition to his fear of getting an unexpected call from Dusty Lewis regarding some new development in the Dan Hughes matter, made falling back to sleep only wishful thinking.

For Paula, his constant tossing and turning finally ended her desire to continue snoozing until the alarm sounded. Rather than the two of them just lying there brooding over the inevitable, she coaxed him out of bed to fix coffee while she showered. "I don't know what's on your mind," she remarked, "but I do hope you get it figured out soon, or I may be forced to begin sleeping in the other bedroom on a permanent basis."

Disgruntled and sleepy-eyed, he strapped his sandals on and headed for the kitchen, however, not before poking his head into her bathroom and playfully asking, "Want a cookie, little girl?"

Stepping quickly behind the frosted glass protection of her shower door she laughed and scolded him for his juvenile preoccupation with her naked body, replying sternly, "That coffee better be ready when I get out of here, Mr. Cookie man, or you're going to be the guy sleeping in the other room. Now, get out of here and make yourself useful."

By the time coffee began dripping steadily and the newspaper had been brought in Paula was sitting at the kitchen table in her bathrobe. He could tell by the expression on her face that a question was forthcoming. "Last night you mentioned that you were starting two new projects. Do you mind telling me again what they are? I'm afraid I wasn't paying much attention at the time. "

As briefly as he could, he explained how Ron Barns had gotten Tommy Camillo interested in commissioning Neal to paint a picture for the restaurant, and the additional project of authoring a novel for Sterling Publishing.

"I guess you'll be very busy," she commented. "Maybe I won't be missed around here as much as I thought."

"Don't be silly. We'll still have our evenings and maybe dinner out every now and then. Let's just play it by ear and see what happens. "

A short time later while they walked to her car, she looked at him in a curious way and questioned, "Are you sure you're not taking on more than you can handle? After all, you're no spring chicken, you know."

"Don't you worry about me," he replied, confidently. "There's still plenty of spring left in this old chicken."

Smiling, she shook her head, got in the car and started the engine, leaving him to puzzle over why she hadn't made an attempt to kiss him goodbye. Before he could remind her, she eased the car into motion and waved goodbye.

"See you tonight, Curly," she shouted back. "Try not to get into any more trouble!"

Rather than return immediately to the kitchen he strolled out onto the bluff to enjoy a breath of fresh morning air and review his agenda for the day. Only two commitments demanded his immediate attention: signing on the dotted line with Sterling Publishing, and giving Tommy a price for the painting. Convinced that neither of the two required any real brain sweat, he strolled back inside, fixed a light breakfast and then placed a call to Sterling Publishing. In less than a minute he had secured a one o'clock appointment to finalize that commitment.

Tommy's painting was a no-brainer because it was already more than half-finished. Time to complete it was no less in scope than a similar work he had painted for another client which he had priced at three thousand dollars. Thus, he concluded that five thousand dollars was a more than generous price to charge Tommy, considering its size and complexity.

Estimating a completion date for the Sterling book, however, was a far more difficult task to predict. For one thing, the story's ending still depended on whatever action the DEA took following their review of Dan's evidence. On the other hand, the DEA would certainly have finalized that part of their investigation before he actually needed it. Based on those parameters, he was confident that a first draft could be completed in approximately six weeks, working four to five hours, every other day.

Finishing the painting, which required far less concentration, could be accomplished on the odd days and still leave a few hours to spend with Paula. The emotional demands of such a schedule, however, made him hesitate to re-examine what Paula had reminded him of. Granted, he was no spring chicken, but the die had been cast, and he wasn't about to let his friends down after they had expressed so much confidence in him. So, accepting the reality of what his two commitments represented, he took a deep breath and vocalized a famous old WWII declaration of courage from a movie he remembered seeing as a young man: "Damn the torpedoes, full speed ahead!"

For the rest of the morning he concentrated on writing notes in chronological order to document all the events that had taken place following Billy Newman's demise. Those notes, he explained to Sandy Sterling during their one o'clock meeting, represented the story's outline, from which he would begin writing the text within the next day or two. After signing the contractual agreement and receiving her company's check, he asked if she would care to have lunch with him. She politely declined, explaining, "Now that our business is concluded, I have to pick up Jessica at the airport. Won't you ride along?"

"I'd love to," he replied, "but I'm meeting Tommy Camillo at Bully's right after I leave here to settle up on that painting he wants me to complete for the restaurant."

"Ah, yes, I remember. Please convey my fondest regards to Mr. Camillo. I liked him."

"I will," he promised, "Tell Jessica I'm glad she's back home again."

She assured him his sentiments would be expressed and suggested that the three of them get together on a regular basis to discuss how the book was progressing, and he agreed. As he stood up to leave, she asked, "By the way, have you thought of a title yet?"

"No," he admitted, "but it's been on my mind. I'll be in touch."

Heading north along the coast he came to grips with the sacrifices he was about to make, both in terms of less time with friends and family, and a consciousness that his relationship with Paula was slowly beginning to lose its fiber. Could it be that he had created the monster that would eventually destroy him? Only time would tell.

His arrival at Bully's soon dispelled any notion that he had committed to tasks beyond his ability to achieve. After discussing the time element for completing the painting, Neal quoted him the price, which Tommy was more than pleased with and left immediately for his office, returning with a check minutes later. "I hope this will tide you over for the time being," he said, handing Neal the check. "I'll give you the balance at the unveiling

I'm planning to have when it's finished. Hopefully, its presence here will stimulate more business for you. I have a feeling you're going to become somewhat of a celebrity around here in the future."

"Don't you mean, more of a pain in the ass? Neal joked.

Tommy doubled over with laughter and replied, "You said that, not me."

After a quick lunch, he thanked Tommy and his staff for their support and left the restaurant, his self-confidence so reinforced that his first thought was to drive directly home and begin work. Just past the stop light at Fifteenth Street, however, traffic heading toward the racetrack had backed up, leaving him stranded momentarily in the north- bound lane in front of Del Mar Plaza. During that brief period of immobility his eyes wandered in and out of shop windows along the sidewalk until they came to rest on a painting being displayed in the window of a prestigious art gallery. "Why does that painting look so familiar?" he muttered out loud. The answer came in a heart beat. "I'll be damned, that's me!"

Continuing to gaze in awe at the beautifully rendered oil painting, his memory brought into focus the attractive middle-aged woman who had sketched a portrait of him sitting on a large piece of driftwood at the beach not long ago. "Betsy Parker!" he spoke in a whisper, as a *"beep"* from the car behind him startled him into motion. Embarrassed by having held up traffic, he moved forward until the Plaza's underground parking entrance allowed him to turn in. Once parked, he entered the gallery's rear entrance and spoke to an oriental woman whom he assumed from the name of the gallery was the owner.

"Excuse me, Madame," he asked respectfully, "I'm interested in that painting you have on display in the window of a man sitting on a driftwood log. I believe the artist's name is Parker."

"Well, you do have the name right," she replied, courteously. "Actually, she's not from this area, but visits Carlsbad, occasionally. She prefers to sell her work in Del Mar because of its celebrity. She's done an excellent job of capturing your likeness. Did you model for her?"

"Not exactly," he replied. "I was unaware that I was being used as the subject until I started to leave. I couldn't refuse her request to stay until the sketch was completed, never realizing that I would wind up in your gallery."

"Are you interested in buying the painting?" she inquired. "It's a remarkable likeness."

"As a matter of fact, I am," he replied. "But first, can you give me her address, or a phone number?"

"I'm afraid that's privileged information, Mister.....

"Thomas," he replied, "Is she in town?"

"I couldn't say. Ms. Parker brought that painting in a few days ago and said she would get in touch with me when she returned. Her visits here are sporadic and vary in duration. She's quite unpredictable."

"Well, just in case she does show up, here's my business card. Tell her to give me a call." He had already started to leave when a thought struck him, so he returned. "Please don't sell that painting to anyone," he pleaded seriously. "I'll be back tomorrow with cash. Okay?"

"Be sure you do," the woman cautioned. "I can only hold it for twenty-four hours."

"Fair enough," he replied. "I'll see you tomorrow."

He was almost ready to exit the gallery when her voice called out after him to come back. "I just remembered asking Ms. Parker what attracted her to this area when she brought in that painting, and she said, getting away from the Bay Area was good therapy. I assumed she meant the San Francisco Bay Area, if that helps you any."

"Thanks, yes it does," he replied, and left to continue his drive north.

Leaving the plaza behind, he continued on up the coast with his mind tumbling with mixed emotions like clothes in a dryer. Despite all efforts to concentrate on the projects that lay ahead, his thoughts strayed to the coincidence of coming face to face with his image painted on canvas by someone who, by any reasonable standard, was a complete stranger. He couldn't dismiss the premonition that Becky Parker, no matter who she was or where she came from, was destined to impact his life. Hopefully, not to the extent that Dan Hughes had.

It was a warm afternoon and not very well suited for the type of undivided attention his projects demanded. Rationalizing that he could put off until tomorrow what he was too tired and distracted to attempt that day, he mixed a drink and decided to relax. Taking a beach chair from the garage, he settled down on the bluff with a newspaper and fell asleep almost immediately.

Sometime later when the sun had lost its warmth to a slowly developing marine layer, he was wakened by Paula's gentle touch and encouraged to come inside for dinner.

Surprisingly refreshed from his nap, he suggested a cocktail and a few minutes in the Jacuzzi might heighten their appetite. She agreed, however cautioned him that she was not in the mood for anything beyond that. "I haven't felt well all day," she complained, "and if my nose is any judge, I'm probably coming down with a cold, thanks to my two grand-daughters."

Discouraged from pursuing anything other than a hot soak and dinner, he lied and assured her, "It had never entered my mind."

Predictably, as was so often the case recently, the remainder of the evening after dinner was spent watching television until one of them dozed off and had to be encouraged to go to bed. This night was no exception. Because of her fear of passing on a threatening cold, she opted for the guest bedroom and went to bed unopposed.

As he had promised, he returned to the gallery in Del Mar the next day and purchased Becky Parker's painting. Rather than having to explain its background to Paula, he had it wrapped and took it to Ron Barns' place to store until he could figure out what to do with it.

When he unwrapped it, Ron made the comment that the painting was so well done that his daughters would probably fight over it when he died. "Why don't you just give it to Paula," he suggested. "She's been a dear and loyal companion to you for over ten years."

Reflecting on the suggestion, he agreed and returned the painting to his car, hopeful that such a gift might soften the strained relationship that their individual quests for identity had created. When he returned, Ron was waiting for him with a drink in each hand. "Here, have one," he insisted, thrusting out his arm. "Tommy Camillo told me last night that he had commissioned you to do a painting for the restaurant. Congratulations!"

"Thanks to you," he acknowledged. "I really appreciate what you told him."

"Don't thank me," he said, turning away and dropping clumsily into his chair. "All I did was show him some of your work. Enough said."

For an hour, the two men drank while they watched television and, occasionally, vocalized their opinions concerning world politics, dumb commercials and women in general. Especially with respect to the clothing they seemed to enjoy almost not wearing. They joked back and forth about what life might have been like if such exposure had been as prevalent when they were growing up as it was now. Without debate, they both agreed that if such were the case, they would both be either dead, or in jail.

One of the news-related programs that appeared regularly on at least one of the three televisions that ran continuously reminded Neal that if he didn't leave soon he would be forced to endure late afternoon, stop-and-go traffic on the freeway. Finishing the remainder of his last drink, he bid Ron goodbye and left for home, grateful that he had reminded him of what a dedicated friend he had in Paula.

One hour after arriving home he had successfully completed hanging Becky Parker's painting over the fireplace in place of one of his own.

He wondered when he heard Paula's car enter the driveway how long it would take her to notice the exchange. Turning on the television to give the appearance of life as usual, he waited for her to arrive.

The less than exuberant greeting that followed within a matter of minutes said all that needed saying about the kind of a day she had had, so he relieved her of her burdensome paraphernalia, poured her a glass of wine and asked, humorously, "How's my little road warrior doing this afternoon? Bend any fenders?"

"That's not very funny right now," she replied, in a less than jovial tone of voice. "Some jackass jerk almost ran me off the freeway when I tried to exit. I honked my horn and cussed at him, but all he did was give me the finger and kept right on going. I was so upset I almost wet my pants."

Whatever enthusiasm he might have had for a pleasant homecoming vanished like the ice melting in his glass, causing him to question whether the surprise of discovering Becky's painting was poorly timed. Before he could respond with something to distract her until she calmed down, she fondled the glass of wine he had brought her and asked, sarcastically, "And, how was your day, Mr. Retiree?"

"Well," he sighed, "up until a moment ago I was doing just fine. I was hoping you'd be in a better mood, but maybe a glass of wine or two will help calm you. Go sit down and I'll join you in a minute."

Purposely allowing her a few moments alone to discover the painting on her own, he purposely took his time in the kitchen before walking into the living room. To his surprise, he found her standing motionless in front of the fireplace looking intently at the painting. Sensing his presence, she remarked, "It's very good, Neal. Who's the artist?"

"Her name is Becky Parker. I met her on the beach one day, after I became aware that she had been sketching me while I sat like a bump on a log reading the newspaper. At my invitation, she showed up at our Fourth of July party and sat with Dusty and Katie Lewis for a while and left fairly early. I think she's from San Francisco, but has friends here that she visits once in a while. The actual painting must have been done later from the sketch she drew of me on the beach that day," he explained further. "I saw it yesterday in the little art gallery near Bully's and decided to buy it for you. Something to remember me by."

"Why? Are you planning on going somewhere?" she asked, surprised by the implication in his statement.

"The question is, are you?" he replied, looking over the top of his glasses.

"Not to worry, Curly," she assured him, "you'll be the first to know when I do."

During the many weeks that followed, schedules and commitments that they had set for themselves seemed to turn the little time they had together into an emotionless vacuum where intimacy had all but disappeared. Neither of them seemed to place any significance on the matter because they were too tired at the end of each day to care. On a positive note, however, Neal did complete Tommy Camillo's painting on time and delivered it without ceremony a few days later. Also of importance was his certainty that the first draft of his book manuscript was nearly finished, an event that promised a vacation unencumbered by anything associated with work of any kind. Something to look forward to.

One Tuesday afternoon during that hectic period, Neal returned home from his pool shooting with Ron and the boys to find the red light on his answering machine blinking. The message was from Dusty Lewis, urging him to watch CNN's six o'clock news that evening, and get back with him as soon as he could, hopefully the next day.

With little else to do, and the wall clock registering almost six o'clock, he clicked on the television and went immediately to the CNN channel where the Anchor Person was presenting a live interview with the Director of the Drug Enforcement Agency regarding recent developments in an ongoing investigation into drug activity centered in the Tidewater Area of Virginia. Captivated by the announcement, he sat mesmerized as DEA Director Raymond Bronson was introduced and made the following prepared statement: "Based on recently obtained information, the DEA has taken several individuals into custody who are believed to be actively engaged in the distribution of drugs in and around the Tidewater area of Virginia. Efforts are currently underway to bring these individuals to trial, and if proven guilty, will be prosecuted accordingly. To those individuals who have assisted us in this effort – and you know who you are – the Agency extends its deepest gratitude and assurances that, as you once hoped would come to pass, the goose has come home to the nest, and the featherless crow has been eaten. Thank you."

Not content with waiting until the following day to acknowledge having seen the broadcast, he called Dusty immediately to discuss it with him. Katie answered, however, and informed him that Dusty had not yet come home, but did take the time to ask him if he had seen the broadcast, which he confirmed he had. Before hanging up, he asked if she would tell Dusty to call him as soon as he came home, whatever the hour.

"Anything wrong?" she asked.

He assured her that there wasn't, but mentioned that he wanted to ask her husband a favor. She promised she would relay the message, but suddenly asked him to hold, remarking that she thought she heard his car enter the garage.

Moments later, Dusty came on line and asked, "Well, what was your reaction?"

"I'll say one thing about your boss," he replied, "I never thought he'd be that cool. You know, about the goose and the crow. I'm glad Dan's toolbox contained enough lures to catch the big fish without getting me involved. Please express my gratitude to Director Bronson for being so discreet. It sure made my day."

"I will," he promised. "Now, Katie said you needed a favor."

"Do you remember me introducing you to an attractive woman by the name of Becky Parker at my Fourth of July party?" he asked. "She sat with you two when she first arrived."

"Do I!" he snapped back instantly. "Katie gave me hell all the way home for being so attentive to her. Be careful about favors in that particular area, Neal. I'm a little gun-shy."

"No problem," he assured him. "Let me explain."

In a matter of seconds he revealed the history of his brief encounter with the mysterious Ms. Parker, and the painting she had done of him. In particular, the anonymity she had requested from the gallery owner. "Based on what the owner had hinted, Ms. Parker is from the San Francisco Bay Area, but vacations not too far from my place at various times during the year."

Reluctant to ask the question he was sure Dusty was expecting, he said, "I think she's someone other than the person she portends to be. Is there a way to find out?"

Checking to confirm that Katie was elsewhere in the house, he replied in a hushed voice, "I'll deny under oath that you ever asked me that question, Mr. T. But I will share with you whatever my own curiosity might stumble upon, if you catch my drift?"

"Understood." He replied. "I'll look forward to hearing from you soon."

When Paula returned home that afternoon she went to his studio and greeted him more affectionately than she had at times recently.

"You never did tell me how Tommy liked your painting?" she remarked, greeting him affectionately with a kiss on the cheek. "I'll bet he was impressed with the finished product?"

"He was," he replied, surprised by her interest. "So thrilled he's having an unveiling party at the restaurant to celebrate the hanging. Promises to be quite an affair."

"You're kidding? She replied, excitedly. "I can't wait to see it on the wall. By the way, how's the book coming along?'

"The first draft is almost finished," he replied. "Then I'm going to take a month off and get the hell out of here for a few days." Surprised by his own words, he spun Paula around by the shoulders and asked, enthusiastically, "How would you like to spend a week in Palm Springs with me? Just the two of us!"

Her response wasn't at all what he expected. She remained silent for a moment, and then replied, a little disappointedly, "I've wanted you to take me to Palm Springs ever since we first met. How ironic that after ten years of waiting, I have to turn you down."

His eyebrows curled up slightly with recognizable surprise. "Why not?" he blurted out. "You've got more vacation time than God!"

The moment of truth had finally arrived. Despite her emotionally painful urge to delay revealing what she had held secret for several weeks, she replied, "I received a telephone call from Mr. Potter a few days ago. He told me he was in town on business and wanted to meet with me to discuss a recent development that has put a new sense of urgency on his plans to retire."

"I could tell by the way you've been acting lately that something was bothering you," he remarked. "Why didn't you tell me? I suspected that our less than intimate relationship lately had something to do with Potter. I take it he's satisfied with your trial performance and wants you on a permanent basis now. Can't say as I blame him."

Holding back her impulse to admonish him for habitually interrupting her, she asked, calmly, "May I continue now, or do you already know what I'm going to say?"

"Sorry," he apologized, sheepishly, "It's a bad habit. Even my closest friends find it irritating."

"Thank you. I'm glad to hear I'm not the only one," she replied. "May I get you a drink?"

"I guess you'd better," he replied with a chuckle. "Isn't this the part where the condemned man gets his last wish?"

Try as she may to maintain the seriousness with which she had begun their conversation she was amused by his sense of humor. Even in the face of his own personally upsetting experiences he had always used it to shield himself from the pain of disappointment that others wore more visibly. She wondered with her own painful uncertainty what really went on inside such an emotionally charged man. Returning to the living room, she handed him his drink, at the same time smiling and shaking her head in silent wonder. Seated in the chair opposite him, she raised her glass and said, "Make it one for my baby, and one more for the road."

He returned the gesture and took a swallow that watered his eyes, bringing him upright in his chair choking for air. "Holy mackerel!" he gasped, "I was only kidding. I'm too young to die!"

Only slightly amused, she waited until he recovered before continuing: "Mr. Potter has been recently diagnosed with prostate cancer, making it imperative that he undergo treatment as soon as possible. For that reason, he has asked me if I could make arrangements to take over management of the nursery as soon as possible. I told him I would."

"I figured as much," he admitted. "Any more surprises?"

"I've given my boss two weeks notice. Mike and Ellen are currently fixing up the guesthouse for me so I won't have to commute from here. Staying with them will allow me to save the rent money I'm paying here."

Hesitating a moment to make sure that what she was about to say next wouldn't sound selfish or impersonal, she explained that Mr. Potter had offered her an opportunity to buy into the business. His terms provided a profit-sharing arrangement that built up equity over time, and provided a weekly income to live on.

"How long do you figure it will take you to accumulate a controlling interest," he asked, somewhat skeptical about the plan.

"Let me finish," she replied. "As I explained before, he has no heirs, and he truly does like me....like a daughter, that is. So, he said the business would be mine as soon as I had saved fifty-one percent of its current value, or he died, whichever came first. How can I lose?"

Neal had to agree that Potter had offered her a chance of a lifetime opportunity. Had it not been for Dan Hughes' generosity, he might not have accepted losing half the rent payment so gracefully, but he dismissed the loss as something he could deal with, especially now that the prospect of his book earning additional income at some point in the not too distant future was a better than average possibility. As an expression of gratitude for her loyal and ever-helpful companionship during their relationship, he took her into his arms and said in a kind, and almost fatherly way, "I couldn't be happier for you, my dear. If anyone ever deserved an opportunity like this, it's you. Unfortunately, as we both realize, you and I won't be seeing much of each other any more, but I am hopeful that we can get together every now and then."

Several awkward moments passed while they pondered over the realization that the future would never bring them together as close as they were at that moment. It was Paula who acknowledged the impending finality of their relationship and whispered ever so suggestively, "Why don't we just skip dinner tonight, Curly."

Breakfast the next morning came with eager appetites. Conversation was light and bore no traces of regret over what each had accepted as destiny's journey to new and uncharted waters. For the first time in weeks they were happy and content with one another. Using the opportunity to outline her plan for moving out, she said, "For the next two weeks, I will be in and out of here after work to pick up all of my clothing. I'm sure you will make good use of the closet space I am leaving behind. Lord knows I've occupied more than my share over the years."

He laughed, and remarked in jest, "I'm already experiencing an empty feeling."

"Always the comedian," she remarked, "I'm going to miss your humorous anecdotes, but don't get too cocky. I'll be back after I get settled to pick up my personal belongings and some of my furniture. I don't think you'll ever be completely rid of me."

"I hope not, " he sighed. "I still have an interest in that crazy family of yours. You will call me on my birthday won't you?"

"I'll never let you forget how old you are, Curly. You can buy stock on that promise."

For the next few minutes he helped her load her car with the bare essentials she would need to close out her last two weeks on the job, remarking as she was about to leave, "Won't it be wonderful not having to spend an hour dressing for work every morning?"

"You can say that again, honey," she replied with glee. "Liberation City, here I come!"

He laughed, remembering his own feelings of liberation on the day he retired.

"Wait here a minute," he remarked, turning toward the garage. "I want to give you something before you leave."

Accessing the storage area where he had placed his grandfather's suitcase, he withdrew twenty thousand dollars worth of bundled bills and placed them in a plastic Zip-Loc bag. Returning to the car, he told her, "Dan Hughes wanted me to give you this money to make up for all the trouble he brought into our lives, so take it and run. He'll never miss it."

Cautiously accepting the bag, she looked at him blankly when she realized what it held and whispered without expression, "I don't know what to say."

"What's to say? Just be sure you invite me to the grand opening of your nursery. Now, go. You'll be late for work."

Clutching the money in one hand, while the other encircled his neck, she crushed her lips on his and held them there a few seconds as tears of joy gathered and a trail of mascara trickled down her cheeks in their wake.

With a look that brought a lump to his throat, she broke away and opened the car door in an attempt to leave, but he held it closed and asked, "Aren't you going to take your painting?"

"Take care of it for me, will you," she sniffled, "I'll pick it up after I get settled, I promise."

"Fine, It'll be there."

With her gone now, he buried himself in his writing to fill the emotional void her decision to leave had created. Frustrated at times, he would leave the house occasionally to clear his head on the beach, but that offered only temporary relief. As the final pages of the book's first draft were being written, however, a gradual sense of accomplishment began to re-energize his enthusiasm, and reinforced the self-confidence that had carried him through the completion of Tommy Camillo's painting. Curious about when the unveiling was to take place, he called him at the restaurant.

Elated to hear from Neal, Tommy told him that he had placed a large notice on the wall where the painting would be hung that scheduled the, *Come one, Come all,* unveiling ceremony for the following Sunday at three o'clock. He also explained that having given the event some further thought, he decided to reserve the outside patio for special guests of his and Neal's where they would have privacy and access to free hors-

d'oeuvres and live music. He was deceptively cautious, however, not to mention that a keyboard was also being provided in the hope that Neal would entertain, thinking as he talked, *how can he refuse?*

When the following Sunday arrived, the view from Neal's bedroom was partially obscured by a layer of coastal fog that added to the already depressing awareness that he was alone. To escape its dreariness, he sat up quickly and proceeded to the kitchen to put on a pot of coffee to drip while he showered. By the time he had finished, the first signs of the sun's arrival came in the brightening whiteness that flooded his bedroom. Fueled by the excitement that the afternoon unveiling promised, he dressed and returned to the kitchen to begin preparation for what promised to be another day of predictable overindulgence.

His hastily prepared breakfast was only half eaten when the phone rang. It was Paula calling to inform him that Mr. Potter's health had taken a sudden turn for the worse and made it impossible for her to consider attending the unveiling. She apologized profusely, explaining that it was just too far to travel, under those circumstances. She did, however, express her sincerest thanks again for the money he had given her, commenting before hanging up, "I never believed for a minute that the money you gave me came from the goodness of Dan Hughes' heart. I don't know where you got it, but thanks anyway. I can't tell you how grateful I am. Enjoy yourself. All the girls send kisses."

Although disappointed that she would miss seeing his painting unveiled on Bully's wall, he gave her credit for the loyalty she exhibited in turning down the invitation to fulfill a commitment she had made to a terminally ill old man. Her priorities were, as they had always been for as long as he had known her, in proper perspective. She would be missed.

By the time he had finished his cold and unappealing breakfast, it was time to dedicate a few hours to his as yet untitled book. Concentration, however, was distracted by a number of things, the most trivial of which was his curiosity about the type of frame Tommy was having custom made for the painting. Even though Neal had offered to have it framed for him, Tommy had insisted that he had an expert to do the work, so he put his curiosity aside and concentrated on the book until the hour to depart forced him to shut down his computer.

Arrival at Bully's was timely. Early enough to guarantee a parking space so he would have time to view the painting before the place got crazy. He had hardly passed through the front door when Tommy spotted him and took him aside to tell him that he had already hung and draped the painting to dramatize the unveiling. "I wanted it to be as much of a surprise for you as anyone," he remarked, excitedly, "So relax with your friends and have a good time. I know your evening will be rewarded in many ways. I can feel it in my bones."

Accepting his plan with measured skepticism, Neal walked toward the high bar where his buddies were gathered, motioning him to join them. "The first one's on me," Ron insisted, then asked, "Where's Paula?"

"She won't be here," he replied, without conveying disappointment. "It's a complicated story, so let's just leave it until Tuesday's game. I'll explain it all then."

Amidst the joking and cross talking that ensued, Neal became too preoccupied to notice Sandy and Jessica Sterling enter the restaurant. They hesitated near the dining room entrance hoping one of the men would notice them. Ron was first to make the connection and tapped Neal on the shoulder. "Hey Neal," he whispered, "I think a couple of your guests just arrived."

Both women were almost to the point of laughing when he turned and saw their faces. "Why didn't you pinch me or something?" he joked. "I am so glad to see you two again." Looking around for the hostess, he finally gave up and took them both by the arm and said, "Come on, you two, follow me."

As he led them out onto the patio where a small group of friends had already gathered, he explained, "This patio is reserved for special guests, so relax and let your hair down. I'll find a waitress and join you in a few minutes."

While Jessica waited for her mother to join her at the small table she had selected, Sandy walked back into the restaurant's interior and made note of the framed artwork and photographs that hung everywhere. After her curiosity had been satisfied, she returned to the patio and remarked to Jessica, "With all the hodge-podge already hanging in here, what do you suppose Mr. Camillo commissioned Neal to paint?"

"I can't imagine," Jessica replied, seemingly disinterested in the subject. "I'd be more interested in how he's coming along with that book we're paying him to write."

Her remark had just ended when Neal returned with one of the waitresses. After their order had been taken, Jessica took the opportunity to comment, "I know you have a lot going on right now, Mr. Thomas, but could you give us an update on the progress you're making on our book while we're all still sober?"

Caught off guard by the sudden switch from a fun and games type atmosphere to a business-like inquiry, he replied, "I'm glad you asked. I was going to call you tomorrow but since you're here, I'm pleased to report that the last chapter of the first draft is almost complete. I should be able to give you the whole manuscript in a couple of weeks. I'm alone now and without distraction, so my entire effort will be in that direction."

The two women looked at each other with wide-eyed surprise, uttering in unison, "Alone?"

His attempt to comment further was momentarily interrupted by the return of their waitress. Before she left, he took her aside and whispered, "Put everything they drink on my tab, will you please. I'll settle with you later."

Returning to the table, he took an overdue swallow from his drink and offered an explanation for his former statement. "Just recently Paula was offered a once-in-a-lifetime business opportunity that requires her presence elsewhere. She won't be living with me any more, but with her family, until she can afford a place of her own. I fully support her in this decision, and wish her well in pursuing whatever professional goals she has. We are still good friends and will remain so, no matter what the future throws in our paths."

Standing to leave, he paused and looked down at their puzzled faces and said, reassuringly, "Don't worry about the book. After all the three of us have been through to reach this juncture, you can rest assured that the preliminary draft will occupy my every thought until it is finished and on your desk. That, my dear ladies should take place by the end of next week, I hope. Now, let's all have some fun. I'll stop by every now and then to check on how you're doing. I know it's going to get crazy here in a little while, but promise me you won't leave without telling me good-bye. Order what you want, you are my guests."

Comfortably assured that their investment was in good hands, they stood and embraced him, promising that they wouldn't leave without saying good night.

Returning to the high bar Neal found Dusty Lewis idly chatting with Ron Barns and the boys. Placing a hand on his shoulder to get his attention, he said, "Welcome aboard, old buddy. I was beginning to think you had gotten hung up on the job."

"I almost did, thanks to you," he replied in a raspy voice. "Is there someplace we can talk? I just received the information you were interested in, and I don't think you want to share it with anyone in this place."

"Yeah, sure," he replied, excusing himself to the group and walking outside. "Now, what's this information you have that's so secretive?"

Assured that they were safely beyond being overheard, Dusty withdrew a folded piece of paper from his inside jacket pocket and handed it to Neal. "I have a friend in San Francisco who operates his own investigating business," he explained. "In response to my asking him if he knew anything about your friend, Becky Parker, he sent me this e-mail reply just before I left my office. Its contents prompted me to contact him for more information. That's why I'm a little late."

Neal unfolded the e-mail letter. It read: *In response to your inquiry: Yes, I'm acquainted with the woman in question. Suggest you call me for further information. Tell your friend he's made the big time. Ben.*

Neal stood looking at the piece of paper for several seconds before asking Dusty to explain its significance.

Smiling, Dusty put his hand on Neal's shoulder and chuckled. "Your friend, Betsy Parker, just happens to be Gloria Donaldson, one of San Francisco's most wealthy and socially prominent widows who, incidentally, just happens to be a very gifted artist. She prefers to sign her paintings using a pen name in order to achieve a certain degree of anonymity, rather than being given favorable critique because of her celebrity. She has a reputation for being somewhat of a kook. But then again, who isn't?" Scanning the immediate surroundings again as a quirk of habit, he placed his face close to Neal's and spoke, almost in a whisper, "You haven't heard anything yet, sport," he continued. "According to my source, she's suspected of being matriarch to an equally wealthy group of younger women in the Bay Area who have formed a coalition to provide escort service to traveling dignitaries and business executives. Reportedly, the list of satisfied customers stretches all the way to Washington. You don't want to know what that service costs."

Shaking his head in disbelief, Neal folded the e-mail and stuffed it in his pocket, remarking as they re-entered the restaurant, "I guess this pretty well validates the notion that one should not judge a book by its cover, doesn't it?"

Dusty laughed, and agreed.

For the next hour he put aside the bitter taste of disillusionment Dusty had laid on him and mixed with friends and acquaintances. As five o'clock grew closer, a steady increase in the arrival of early diners began to take place. Realizing that seating would soon be a problem, Tommy announced over the loudspeaker that the unveiling would be taking place immediately, and encouraged those who had come to the restaurant specifically for that purpose to gather in the main dining room. After a reasonable level of quiet had been achieved, he began to speak. "Some time ago, my friend and most loyal customer, Ron Barns, showed me examples of artwork created by his closest friend, Neal Thomas, whom, I might add, I only knew as a friend of Ron's and a frequent flier here at Bully's. Not as the talented artist whose work we are about to unveil."

After the whistles and clapping that followed died down, Tommy continued: "Ron suggested that I commission Neal to create a painting that would fill that empty spot on the wall over there, so I approached him on the matter and he agreed to accept the challenge...for money, that is." Laughter and loud conversation continued while Tommy walked to the wall area he had pointed to and removed the tablecloth that covered the spotlighted painting, remarking with pride, "And here, ladies and gentlemen, is the result of that challenge."

For a few seconds the entire restaurant remained silent, each person straining to take in the exquisitely applied detail of the landscape that had been unveiled. So photo-realistic that it begged for movement in the shallow stream that flowed beneath the stone bridge crossing over it. By any standard, it was masterfully created realism. Then slowly, as the lifelike beauty of the colors created an almost three-dimensional image, clapping hands could be heard from all over the room, sending a clear message that at least one of his challenges had been successfully achieved. In response to their enthusiasm, he stood and bowed in a clown-like fashion to hide his embarrassment and the intense feeling of pride that had overwhelmed him. Then, as he feared they might, the familiar voices of his buddies at the high bar called out in unison, "Speech!"

Embarrassed, he raised his hands to silence the laughter and replied, "Thanks everyone. Your applause was my reward. That and Tommy's check, of course."

Laughter and backslapping followed him all the way to the high bar where Ron handed him a drink, patted him on the back and said in words slightly slurred, "Mr. Thomas, you do good work!"

Out on the patio later on that evening, the slowly dwindling group of lingering loyalists found Neal conversing with the Sterling ladies until Tommy surprised him with a house speaker request to perform on the keyboard. When he complained, Tommy told him that for what he was paying for the painting, he owed him that favor. Powerless to argue with his cunningly persuasive friend, he took his place at the instrument and played whatever came to mind, and some that didn't. At least by performing, the need to converse with those who would bore him with questions about his past, present and future could be politely ignored, at least until he took a break. It was during one such break that he joined Dusty and the Sterling woman at their table. Following a brief conversation about the success of the party in general, all three expressed their desire to leave and stood to initiate the process. After exchanging friendly embraces, they left with Dusty following protectively behind, leaving Neal to his own devices.

Although the patio was alive with conversation, the mood seemed to have changed to one of a more subdued nature, leading Neal to consider joining his buddies for the rest of the evening. His attempt to leave, however, was interrupted by an approaching waitress carrying a fresh drink and a folded piece of paper. Handing them to him, she winked, flirtatiously, and left. Tucked inside the paper he found a five-dollar bill and a note that read, *Play Misty for me.*

Hoping to find a smiling face looking at him from a dark corner, he looked around the patio, but found no one who looked as if they had made the request. Shrugging his shoulders, he began playing. After all, he thought, five bucks is five bucks, no matter where you are.

Because the song had always been one of his favorite melodies, he played it several times, in several different styles and enjoyed himself in the process. When he finished, there was still no one who looked particularly interested in the request until a soft clapping sound from inside the restaurant captured his attention. Assuming that the singular applause came from his benefactor, he went inside to thank the person, and to end the evening by having one last drink with his friends before going home. As he stepped inside and walked past the low bar he was stopped in his tracks by a smiling face looking up at him. It was Becky Parker. Impressed by how attractively groomed and well dressed she looked, he grasped her by the hand and asked, "When did you get back in town? I thought you were going to call me."

"I did," she replied, "but I got your answering machine instead. I left a message, but you can ignore that now. How are you?"

"Very well, thank you. How did you know I was going to be here tonight?"

"The owner of the gallery down the street left a message on my machine while I was out of town. She said the man in my painting had purchased it and wanted to talk to me. When I called the gallery today to let her know I would be coming in to pick up my check, she mentioned that you were being honored this afternoon for a painting you had been commissioned to do for Bully's. She's the one who had it framed. So, I put two and two together and gambled on you still being here. Looks like I won."

For the next hour they dabbled in small talk relating to what they had been doing since last seeing one another. Betsy's dialogue, as he expected, was reserved, and never once hinted of anything remotely connected to what Dusty Lewis had revealed to him about her real name and background. Enjoying her for just who she was at that moment was all he needed to know, and it was certainly none of his business if she was the person Dusty identified as Gloria Donaldson. He, on the other hand, was quite candid about his activities and openly discussed Paula's business opportunity and her decision to relocate in support of that goal.

"You must have been crushed," Becky remarked. "I don't know that I could have handled that kind of a separation after being with a man for as long as you and Paula have lived together. Weren't you angry?"

He thought about her question long enough to realize that it was inappropriate to debate the issue, so he replied, "Getting mad at someone for trying to improve his or her life is kind of selfish, isn't it? Paula and me weren't married, and we parted good friends. How many marriages do you remember ending that way?"

"I'd have to think about that," she remarked cautiously, "but that's beside the point. The important question is where do you go from here?"

He motioned to the bartender to refill their drinks and then addressed her question:

"I'm committed to have the first draft of a book I'm writing on my publisher's desk in a couple of weeks. Plus, I have been approached recently to draw a series of poster-like illustrations for a new product developed by a local entrepreneur. Nothing immediate, but I'd say I was going to be very busy again, very soon."

"Too bad," she commented, with a hint of disappointment. "I was going to suggest something, but your time seems to be pretty well committed for the next few weeks."

For the first time during their brief relationship he became aware of something almost seductive in her voice, suggesting that what Dusty had discovered about her might have had more credibility than he had given it earlier that afternoon. Curious about what she had intended to suggest, he smiled and replied, "That all depends on what you had in mind."

Looking over at him with her eyes fixed on his, she recognized the adventurous little boy she had been attracted to when she first met him on the beach weeks ago. Ever the temptress, she said, "Tomorrow morning at six o'clock I'm leaving the Oceanside Marina for a two week vacation at my condominium on Catalina Island. If you'd care to join me, you're more than welcome, no strings attached. I have everything onboard you need to continue work on your book and keep in touch with the mainland, should you wish to do so. From what I've seen and heard, you could use a little R&R."

"That's very generous of you, Becky," he replied, "but as much as I would like to go, the Capricorn in me warns that too much is at stake to risk it all on that kind of adventure. I'll probably kick myself tomorrow for being so stupid, but that's happened before, so I'll just say thanks for inviting me."

She looked at her watch and then at Neal, smiling a little before picking up her purse. "Isn't this the part where the girl says, I think it's time to go?"

"It is for me too. Let me settle up with Tommy and I'll walk you to your car."

"I'll be waiting out front."

When he approached the waitress, she refused to accept his credit card. "Tommy's orders," she told him. "He really is happy about the painting. It's beautiful."

"Thank you," he replied, "but what about the two women I was sitting with earlier? They were my guests."

"Tommy took care of them too. Personally, I think he's kind of taken with the older one."

Removing a twenty-dollar bill from his money clip, he placed it discreetly in her blouse and remarked, "I've always wanted to do that. It's so Hollywood."

Outside, he found Becky gazing wistfully at an almost full moon when he approached. "I hope that chunk of cheese follows me to Catalina," she joked. "It makes the nights so much more romantic. I am a romantic, you know."

As they walked down the ramp to her car, he remarked, "I can't believe you don't have someone special to take with you. Surely you have a special man friend who'd jump at the offer you just made me."

"That's the problem," she sighed, somewhat reflective, "I've had too many already, but none special." Lowering the window she took his hand and held it for a moment. "In case you change your mind, my boat is tied up at the pier behind the Jolly Roger restaurant. You can't miss her. She's the big one with *The Wayward Wind* painted on her transom. Think about it. You'll have the time of your life."

Smiling, he placed his head through the window and kissed her affectionately on the lips. "Thanks again for asking," he replied, feeling awkward and embarrassed by his inability to express himself more adequately. "Have a wonderful time, and stay in touch."

She looked up at him curiously for a moment and then turned on the ignition, remarking as she backed away, "That, my friend, is a given."

The taillights on her car had no sooner disappeared around the corner than he experienced a sudden rush of anxiety that forced him to consider the possibility that he might have thrown away the opportunity of a lifetime. That he would have turned down such an invitation, considering the likelihood of it ever being offered again, taunted him all the way home.

Tired and upset with himself, he entered the kitchen and immediately mixed a strong drink, hoping it would be the straw that broke the camel's back and lull him to sleep. Such might have been the case had it not been for the blinking red button on his answering machine. Tempted to ignore it until the next morning, he vaguely remembered Becky mentioning that she had left him a message when she arrived in town earlier that day. Out of curiosity, he pushed the button and listened to its message: "Hello, Neal. This is Becky Parker calling. I had a message from the gallery in Del Mar when I arrived back in town today. The owner informed me that you had purchased my painting of you. Can we get together for a drink this afternoon? I'd like to talk to you before I leave on vacation tomorrow. Call my cell phone number when you get this message. Look forward to hearing from you."

Remembering her suggestion to ignore the message, he erased it. Convinced that he would probably never see the woman again, he retired to the living room and collapsed in his easy chair to enjoy one last moment of lonely tranquility before the weeks ahead robbed him of it. The glass was still clenched in his hand when his eyes closed and sleep took its place. It was midnight.

Sleep ended somewhat traumatically, however, when the half-filled glass of melted ice he had been holding slipped from his hand and soaked the crotch of his trousers. Wakened by the same trauma babies must experience when wetting their diapers, he sputtered a few expletives and went to his bedroom to change, unaware that his child-like accident had occurred at 4:45 that morning.

Alone and disgruntled by a sudden feeling of helplessness, his mind flashed back to the memory of Becky Parker looking curiously up at him through her car window as if to say, "You've wet your pants, old man!"

Like a medical prognosis, the sound of her voice gave rebirth to his earlier fear that he had permitted his everyday life to deny him the last chance he might ever have to experience an adventure that his aging mind and body would soon rebel against during the years to come. Looking around the companionless room that deafened him with silence, he felt angered by the false notion that he was too old and too tired to act like the spirited young man he had once been. Incensed by the thought, he rushed to the kitchen to replay Becky's message in order to get her cell phone number. Only then did he remember he had erased it.

Now that his only communication link to her was gone, he was faced with only one alternative; get to the marina before six o'clock. Realizing that the kitchen clock gave him only one hour to get there, he called an all-night cab service company that assured him they would be at his home within the half-hour or sooner.

During that hectic time he hurriedly packed a bag and withdrew money from his stash to more than cover his personal expenses. To avoid worrying his family and friends by his sudden absence, he e-mailed them all a letter that read:

Have won a free trip to Catalina. Must be on the boat early this morning. Don't worry about me. I'll be back in two weeks. Check on the house once in a while. You know where the key is. Will call later from the island.
Love you,
Neal

With everything packed, including the latest copy of his book manuscript and a few floppy discs, he locked the house and waited on the front porch for the cab to arrive.

The moon had moved since he had seen it at Bully's but was still full and beautiful. He wondered if his friend, Billy Newman was up there on a cloud somewhere looking down on him and laughing at what an old fool he had turned into. "Eat your heart out, Billy," he yelled, as the cab pulled into the driveway. "I ain't dead yet!"

His departure left the house blanketed in darkness except for the moonlight that highlighted parts of its structure through the surrounding trees. For the first time since old John Fahey had sold the house it was alone and lifeless, and would remain that way until his return.

Rather than getting off the freeway at the Camp Pendleton exit where traffic usually slowed, he suggested to the driver that he take the Coast Highway. Normally, that suggestion would have had merit. That morning, however, a slowly moving, multi-car freight train blocked the cross street that led to the marina's southern entrance, causing a ten minute delay.

Constantly monitoring his watch until the last car had passed, he prayed that Becky was not a stickler for punctuality, and encouraged the driver to do whatever was necessary to make up the time they had lost. Though the driver was eager to earn the generous tip his passenger had offered, he had no control over an eighteen-wheeler that was blocking the road in an attempt to turn into one of the restaurant parking areas, causing another delay of five valuable minutes.

With sweat beginning to gather on his forehead as they resumed their race to make up the lost time, Neal's watch indicated 5:58, with at least one more mile to go before they reached the Jolly Roger restaurant. As the cab rounded the marina's north end, his heart sank when he saw a large cabin cruiser pulling slowly away from the Jolly Roger pier. Although he could not make out the boat's name, he was convinced it was *The Wayward Wind.*

Less than a minute later, having convinced the driver to wait to see if he needed a ride back home, he stood on the empty pier frantically waving at the beautiful yacht making its turn into the outlet channel to the ocean. Frustrated and angry with himself for playing it so close, he started to head back to the taxi when a voice from a boat tied up nearby asked, "Miss your boat?"

He had been so overcome with disappointment watching Becky's boat disappear in the distance that he had failed to see a man making his boat ready for departure alongside the same pier he had just hurried down.

"Yeah, damn it!" he answered, angrily. "Some things just weren't meant to be, I guess."

Before the boatman could comment, Neal was struck with a desperate thought and remarked, excitedly, "I'll give you a hundred bucks cash if you can catch the boat that just left this pier."

"She's a powerful boat, mister," the man replied, "but she'll have to remain at low speed until she exits the harbor inlet. I can catch her, but if someone reports me for exceeding the speed limit, I could get fined, or lose my license."

"Two hundred cover it?"

"Jump aboard," the man answered. "Let's get this show on the road!"

In less than a minute, Neal paid off the taxi driver and climbed aboard the water taxi that was waiting for him with engines already idling. Casting off from the dock, they got under way, throttled to the razor's edge of maximum allowable speed. Although Becky's larger cruiser had a five to six minute head start, her size gave a speed advantage to the smaller boat once it reached the mouth of the inlet. As they raced at full throttle in her wake, Neal's benefactor turned to him and yelled, "By the way, my name's Captain Bob Willard, retired Navy!"

Neal groped for his extended hand and yelled back, "Neal Thomas, retired engineer. Thanks for the lift, I damn sure can't afford to miss this one!"

Although their smaller boat was gaining on the larger one, the race to catch her was gradually taking them closer to the fog bank that *The Wayward Wind* was heading for. It was the threat of following her into that fog that prompted Captain Bob to suggest an alternate plan. "There's a bullhorn speaker in the transom storage locker back there. Go get it and we'll see if we can end this race before they disappear in that wall of fog."

Neal retrieved it immediately and handed it to the skipper. Turning it on clumsily, he handed it back to Neal, instructing him to make his way to the bow to send whatever message he thought was appropriate. Fighting the bouncing motion of the boat, Neal fought his way to the bow and raised the speaker to his lips, shouting loud and clear, "AHOY, WAYWARD WIND. HEAVE TO! HEAVE TO! Given the hundred yards that separated the two boats the message didn't appear to have been heard, so he repeated it, adding, "IT"S ME, NEAL!"

Within seconds the bow of the yacht dropped, dramatically, and its foamy wake flattened to give the smaller boat a clear and relatively smooth pathway to her transom platform. While Captain Bob held his boat as steady as he could, Neal threw his suitcase to one of the crew who had come aft to help and then stepped over onto the platform.

While the boarding process was taking place, Becky appeared on the upper weather deck and watched with amusement as Neal struggled to retrieve his wallet so he could pay the Captain for his services. When Bob Willard saw her looking down on the comedy of it all, he laughed and yelled, "You better keep your two hundred bucks, my friend. I have a feeling you're going to need it."

Before Neal could respond, Bob reversed his props and throttled slowly away from the platform, yelling back through the bullhorn as he turned to leave, "Buy me a drink when you get back. You can pay me then!"

"You've got a deal," he shouted back, waving goodbye as the smaller boat headed back toward the marina.

Sometime later that same morning while they were slowly compassing their way through the fog, Becky asked Neal what had happened to change his mind about coming with her. Although her question was a reasonable one, he really hadn't given much thought to the real reason for being there, other than taking advantage of an opportunity to enjoy free transportation to a place he would probably never have opted to visit on his own. Something about navigating through the foreboding environment of the fog triggered his imagination and he replied, "From the time I was a little boy, I have been obsessed with romantic adventure. No matter where I went, or what I did, I had the uncanny ability to turn activities that I didn't enjoy into adventurous and sometimes dangerously romantic situations. There were times, however, when I had to suffer the repercussions of my parent's anger and disappointment for some of the choices I made. But, that was all a part of growing up. As I explained to my peers whenever they inquired about what I had received as punishment, I simply replied, whatever they thought I deserved."

During the brief interlude that followed, Becky puzzled over her mixed up feelings about the man she had lured into her own web of adventure, and reminded him that he still had not answered her question.

Giving way to her persistence, he replied:

"When I was in my teens, I was sent off to prep school because I wasn't a very good student. Although I didn't do that well the first two years I was there, I managed to attain a 3.4 average in my senior year and an outstanding athlete award that got me into an Ivy League University. Isn't it funny that, of all my memories of those wonderful years, I should remember what my prep school English teacher told me just before graduation."

"Neal, where are you going with all this?" she asked, patiently amused by his reluctance to answer her simple question.

"He called me into his office to critique a theme I had written. Despite a few grammatical errors, he gave me an A for my crude, but imaginative story, and sent me packing with a words of wisdom I shall never forget."

"And that was?"

"In essence, every day of one's life - even as a child - is a decision-making process, usually consisting of two or more options; which toy do I play with? Do I, or do I not jump off the three-meter diving board in my jockstrap? Should I, or should I not have sex with Susie Q. Your choice maps the course of your future for that day, or possibly your entire life. I'm here because I decided to walk the beach several weeks ago and met you. You, on the other hand, met me because you decided to paint on the same beach that day. Don't those coincidences suggest a higher order of things, one that defies explanation?

The smile on her face was becoming broader by the second, almost to the point of laughter, when she remarked, "I've met a lot of men in my life, my dear Mr. Thomas, but you surely take the cake. Did you study philosophy or logic by any chance?"

"Unimportant," he answered, still struggling to put some finality to her original question. "I guess what I'm trying to say is, there is no explanation. My reasons for being here are about as nebulous as this fog we're in. Only time will tell. Unfortunately for me, there's not much of that left. All I can do is make good use of it. Any suggestions?"

About that time, the bow of *The Wayward Wind* broke into the sun-bathed water surrounding Catalina Island and continued on with the maiden voyage of *Destiny's Journey*.

The End

Or is it?